JILL TRESEDER was born in Hampshire and
the sea on the Solent and in Devon, Cornwall
her husband in Devon overlooking the River

After graduating from Bristol with a degr
in social work, management development and
from the School of Management at the University of Bath along the way.

Since 2006 she has focused on writing fiction.

ALSO BY JILL TRESEDER

A Place of Safety
Becoming Fran
The Hatmaker's Secret
The Saturday Letters

MY
Sister,
MYSELF

JILL TRESEDER

SilverWood

PRAISE FOR HER NOVELS

For The Hatmaker's Secret
'There is a profound wisdom to Jill Treseder's fiction, worn lightly as befits this subtle, engaging storyteller, but always there, always thought-provoking, and always enlightening.' – Peter Stanford

'A beautifully written, intriguing and touching story of the effects of racial prejudice across generations. A compelling and satisfying read.' – Judith Allnatt

For Becoming Fran
'What seems to be a lovingly observed tale of growing up in provincial England in the 1960s turns out to be something much more, with a satisfying plot that creeps up on you unawares with an intriguing slow-burn complexity.' – Mark McCrum

To my "sis", Sara
For refugees everywhere
And in grateful memory of
Jean Thow

Published in 2018 by SilverWood Books

SilverWood Books Ltd
14 Small Street, Bristol, BS1 1DE, United Kingdom
www.silverwoodbooks.co.uk

ISBN 978-1-78132-802-6 (paperback)
ISBN 978-1-78132-803-3 (ebook)

British Library Cataloguing in Publication Data
A CIP catalogue record for this book is available from
the British Library

Page design and typesetting by SilverWood Books
Printed on responsibly sourced paper

Acknowledgements

My grateful thanks to Tom Leimdorfer, for his escape story and for introducing me to the confusing complexity of Hungarian history and politics; to Sally and Andras Kaldor, who patiently responded to my interruptions of his work, shared his experience of leaving Hungary in 1956 and lent me reference books.

Thanks are also due to Karen Hayes and to the members of my 'novel surgery' group for their constructive feedback; also to Hugh for living with these characters for so long.

The following publications have been invaluable in providing vital background information:

Cartledge, Bryan, *The Will to Survive: A History of Hungary* (London, 2011)

Lessing, Erich, *Revolution in Hungary* (UK, 2006)

Applebaum, Anne, *Iron Curtain: The Crushing of Eastern Europe* (London, 2013)

Porter, Anna, *The Storyteller: A Memoir of Secrets, Magic and Lies* (Canada, 2006)

Michenor, James A, *The Bridge at Andau* (New York, 2015)

Fischer, Tibor, *Under the Frog* (London, 2002)

The Evacuee: The Magazine of the British Evacuees Association (various 2017 issues)

If I have misunderstood or misrepresented aspects of Hungarian culture, history or politics, the fault is mine.

1

It's another stifling day. All the windows in the apartment are open: Mama's attempt to create a through draught. But not a current of air moves. Katalin longs for their old house in Buda where there was nearly always a breeze, and a garden too. Here, in the middle of Pest, there is neither. The tall buildings trap and concentrate the heat like giant radiators.

'We have a home,' Papa would say when Mama complained. 'We are all together.'

Katalin is bored. Mama has given in to Marika's whining and is reading to her, so she goes in to the bedroom to practise.

She starts with some warm-up exercises holding on to the rail at the end of the bed, although it's too high to work properly as a barre. Then she climbs up to step along the rail and across to the windowsill, turning and stepping back. There's a rattle and screech of brakes from a lorry four floors below, but she takes no notice. It's all about balance and control. She is going to be a ballerina. A dancer must practise every day. She is six years old. Along and across, turn and back, placing the soles of her feet carefully, trying only to look ahead, feeling the sweat trickling down her spine.

Her rhythm is spoilt when she notices Marika standing in the doorway. Watching. Bother. Walking on the bedrail is forbidden, especially when her little sister is about – which she nearly always is, being demanding and sticky.

'I thought Mama was reading you that story.'

Marika makes a face. 'Stupid book. I hate the princess.'

'Just 'cos she doesn't look like you.'

'I can do that.' Marika climbs onto the bed and grips the bedpost.

'No, you can't.'

'Can so.'

'You're not allowed.' Katalin jumps lightly to the floor.

Marika's legs aren't long enough to climb onto the rail so she hangs on to it upside down, clinging by her hands and ankles.

Katalin can't help giggling. 'You look like a monkey.'

'I'm a sloth, silly. Can't you tell?'

Katalin shrugs and makes for the door. There's a thud behind her.

'Help with this.' Marika is pulling at the washstand to drag it towards the bed. The legs judder on the boards.

'Shush! Mama will hear. What are you doing?'

'Getting on the rail.'

Katalin stands back, arms crossed. 'You'll never...'

'I've done it before.'

'Copycat.' Katalin feels a feather of anxiety. What if Mama comes in?

Marika is on the marble top in a second, and from there onto the flat wooden rail. Agile but graceless. She wobbles as she treads along it.

'Okay,' Katalin says as she gets to the end. She's about to say, 'Okay you did it', and put a stop to the whole thing, but her sister isn't finished. She is poised on the rail, eyeing the windowsill.

Her legs are too short. She'll have to jump and how will she stop the momentum of her fat little body? Katalin pictures her roly-poly sister flying through the window. She might land on top of a tram. She might carry on flying, out over the rooftops and miles away.

These fantasies spin through her head in the second before she realises that Marika really could fall through the window. She herself is taller and would hit the top of the frame, so it couldn't happen to her. And anyway, she has superior control. Unlike Marika.

'I'll tell. I'll call Mama.' That would put her at an advantage, and she might not get a hiding.

'I'll say I'm copying you. I'll say you dared me. Anyway, shut up. You're putting me off.'

No more Marika. Her stomach doesn't know what to do with itself at the prospect. It's griping, and jumping like the tadpoles in Grandmother Varga's pond.

Seconds pass. She could grab the arm that is seesawing above her head as Marika steadies herself. She could push her sister onto the bed. She could run and stand in front of the window and catch her.

She senses a gathering above her, a stillness. Marika takes a breath. Katalin is holding hers. The heaviness of the room presses hot on the top of her head. She tries to move. But Katalin is paralysed. She cannot move.

A whirlwind of noise shatters the silence, a tornado hurtling in from the door and across the room to land in a screaming heap against the wardrobe. The room goes spinning. Katalin buckles to the floor.

When she looks up, a yelling Marika is lying securely across Mama's lap.

Mama is glaring across at Katalin, her mouth slightly open, as if she might say something. She holds the stare and Katalin is frozen in that gaze. Then Mama gathers Marika and takes her off to the kitchen.

2

Katalin was a father's girl. Papa was always there for her, except when he was in prison. As for her nuisance sister, she'd probably hated her all along, but certainly since that day in the park when Marika was two or three years old. They cross the Margit Bridge onto the island and into the park. Mama lets her push the pram. The handle is too high. She has to hold it at the sides, which is a stretch.

Marika's harness has a stupid pink rabbit across her chest and two little silver bells. She's too big for the pram, but lots of things fit inside it that are more useful than her sister, like a picnic, a rug and a book for Mama to read out loud.

'Not far now,' says Mama.

'I've got a stone in my shoe.'

'You can take your shoes off when we get on the grass.'

The piece of grit hurts and she's about to tell Mama she has to stop *now*, when there comes a thundering noise and a draught on her cheek and this huge furry animal skids to a halt with its snout on the edge of the pram, inches away from Marika's face. There's a smell of leaves and wet doormat and Marika's eyes and mouth open wide. But the creature has taken her breath away, so she doesn't scream.

Mama jerks the pram sideways and shouts at the animal. It turns and looks straight at Katalin with its pale grey eyes, lifts its long nose and gives a strange noise, halfway between a howl and a whine.

'Shoo! Shoo! Get away wolf-dog!' Mama makes no impression, but a long whistle comes from the path above them and the dog bounds away as suddenly as it came.

'Wolf-dog just like Kati,' says her little sister. 'Kati's got wolf eyes.'

Mama makes a great fuss of Marika but hardly looks at Katalin's blister. Which proves what Katalin already knows: Marika can do no wrong and she no right.

Katalin did not consciously remember the occasion. But it remembered her, waiting somewhere in a crevice of her brain to remind her when the time came.

Meanwhile, in 1949 when Katalin was five years old, Papa was arrested. They never knew who betrayed him, or for what. Luckily, he only went to prison.

She is woken by banging on the door in the night, the sound everyone fears. It has happened to their neighbours. But this hammering is on their door, and she climbs onto the chest to peer down into the street. There it is, the most dreaded sight: a big black car parked outside the apartment entrance. Mama and Papa are in the hallway. Papa scoops Katalin into his arms and holds her close. 'Open up, Teréz,' he says to Mama. 'No point in having a broken door and no husband to repair it.'

One man restrains Papa, another starts pulling drawers out of the chest, while the other rummages through the work neatly laid out on Papa's desk – which is one end of the kitchen table. He holds up a sheaf of papers and lets the rest cascade to the floor. Then they are gone and Papa with them. On the way out, one of them puts a gloved fist through Mama's painting of the Virgin, which hangs in the shadows in the hall. Shards of glass skitter over the floor. Mama is sobbing and takes Katalin into bed with her. Katalin lies in Papa's place breathing in the smell of him while Mama cries into her hair. Marika has slept through it all.

Papa didn't come home that night. He didn't come home the next night or the next week or the next month. They weren't allowed to know where he was, let alone see him. It was hard to believe he was still alive. Even after he came home the following year, Katalin had nightmares and would wake in a sweat, convinced he'd been taken away again.

An episode with Ilona also gave Katalin nightmares. It was just before they were initiated into the Pioneers, where they were to be trained out of undisciplined ways of thinking and made to understand that Ilona's mother could be arrested for putting unacceptable thoughts into her daughter's head. But at the time Katalin was simply frightened.

The girls have been visiting a friend who lives on the Buda side of the river. On the way home they stop off at the park on the corner of Csorsz Street.

Katalin used to go on the seesaw here with Marika when they were little. Mama would chant, 'Katalin up, Marika down. Marika up, Katalin down.' But Marika's legs were too short to push off, so it was mostly Katalin up. She liked to push up really hard so that Marika would crash down, and Mama had to intervene.

It's better on the seesaw with Ilona. They are much more evenly matched. But Ilona gets carried away. She's taller and stronger, and Katalin begins to fear for her delicate ankles. She stops pushing off and shrieks at Ilona to stop.

'I have to think of my dancing.'

But Ilona laughs at her. 'You and your dancing!' she says. 'You're just a scaredy-cat.' It's autumn, and by the time they leave the park it is dark. Maybe Ilona is still in the mood to tease her. Or maybe the report really is preying on her mind. Her mother has told her that, during the Nazi occupation, squads of Arrow Cross members would round up Jews and shoot them into the river. The bodies fell into the water and were carried downstream. Some would surface and float like logs, getting caught under the bridges.

Ilona whispers, 'What if the AVO men are doing it too? It wouldn't have to be Jews.'

Katalin says, 'Nonsense', but the idea terrifies her. Ilona is right – it wouldn't have to be Jews. It could be anyone. It could be Papa.

As they cross the Chain Bridge on their way home, they peer down into the water. Ilona points and says she can make out a shape. But there's nothing to see. Ilona crosses herself. She says that the souls of the dead must rise out of the river to haunt the embankment and the bridges.

Katalin snorts. It's the sort of thing Marika or her mother would say. But the incident gives her nightmares all the same.

At ten years old, Katalin joined the Young Pioneers. She was bursting with excitement as she came home from her first meeting. She had been given an orange. She clutched it inside her bag, from time to time bringing it to her nose to inhale the zesty tang. Her friend, Ilona, had one too. Ilona was older and had been a Pioneer for a while so she knew all about oranges.

'There won't be much left once it's been divided between my brothers and sister.'

'You could eat it all, now,' said Katalin.

Ilona looked shocked. 'I couldn't do that. It's a gift for our families. You heard. Besides, they'd smell it on my hands. I couldn't be so mean.'

After Ilona turned off at her street, Katalin thought she could easily be that mean. She even went so far as to dig her thumb into the top of the fruit so that the zest squirted onto her fingers. But, as she sucked them clean, she heard the voice of the group leader. "Take it home to your family. It is a present from our good friends, the Russians." She would enter the kitchen like a hero. Marika had never brought home an orange. Maybe then Papa would stop scowling at her neckerchief.

Secretly, Katalin loved the uniform and wore the red scarf with pride. She was keen to win promotion and badges for Mama to sew on the sleeve of her white shirt. One day, she thought, I will travel abroad as a ballet dancer, representing the Hungarian Pioneers, just like the senior school boys in the basketball team, or the Hungarian football team who went to London last year and beat the English.

But when she placed her trophy on the kitchen table and said her piece about the gift, Papa looked thunderous.

'That is indeed a Soviet orange,' he said. 'A Communist orange.' He dropped his voice and Mama started clattering pan lids to mask whatever rash thing he was about to say. 'It is an eloquent symbol of what the Communists want to achieve, what they want our young people to believe. It is a symbol of seduction and manipulation.' He reached for the orange but Mama got there first.

'You're never going to throw it away!'

He shrugged.

'The poor girl brings us a treat and all you can do is pontificate. She'll be wishing she'd eaten it on the way home.'

Which was exactly what Katalin was wishing.

'This is an orange,' said Mama. 'A tropical fruit, a gift of the earth and the tree it grew on and the sun that ripened it. We will eat it and appreciate it.'

She glared at Papa and started to pare the skin away from the flesh with a sharp knife, holding it over a bowl to catch any drip of juice that might escape. She divided it carefully into four, pulling away the loose pith. Papa refused his quarter, which Mama then shared between the two girls. Katalin thought she deserved all of it, but dared not protest.

Papa spoke in a murmur. 'I will not swallow any part of a Communist orange.' He put a hand on Katalin's arm. 'Look at me, Kati. I know you have to be a Pioneer. It's unavoidable. I understand. But don't swallow what they teach you, any more than I swallow this orange. It is all lies. Take it in at a head level. Keep your heart free.'

Mama kicked him under the table. Katalin could tell from the way he drew back in his chair. They exchanged glances. Mama's eyes slid sideways towards Marika and she shook her head. Papa nodded and was silent. Mari was too young and too impetuous to risk expressing such opinions in her presence. She might betray them to her teachers without even realising she'd done it. The AVO, the secret police, would be alerted and come knocking on their door. But on this occasion there was no need to worry. Her sister was too busy slurping and sucking at her segments of orange and licking the table where the juice had fallen. Just like an animal.

At bedtime Papa gave her a hug and whispered in her ear, 'Remember what I said.'

3

Katalin would never forget the twenty-third of October 1956. She was twelve years old and it was the very day she'd been given the part of her dreams. She did not, of course, know then what an historic date this would turn out to be. She was coming home from ballet rehearsal with Ilona, excited and proud because her role as Snow Queen had been confirmed. She would be the star of the Christmas show. Today Ilona was in a strange mood. Okay, she did say, 'You're the best.' But then she added, 'The best we've got', in a way that sounded grudging. Ilona hadn't even been considered for the role, so Katalin supposed she was jealous.

'Technically perfect,' Miss Pásztor had said, and she couldn't wait to tell them at home. Technically perfect. The words hummed round her head until she was about to pirouette along the pavement when she remembered you couldn't be technically perfect in boots.

Ilona was yelling at her. 'Wake up, Kati. Listen! There's singing, there's a march, there's something going on.' She grabbed Katalin's arm and started running.

From the end of the street they could see hundreds of people streaming from the direction of the Margit Bridge. Katalin remembered something Papa had said over the weekend about some ceremony at the statue of General Bem. That would be where all those people were coming from. So it must have been important. She craned her head to pick out Papa.

'Your father's a journalist, isn't he? So he'll be up front with the Writers' Union lot.'

Ilona seemed very well informed. Papa liked to think of himself as a playwright, but he kept that quiet while he earned his living as a journalist.

'It's all about what's happening in Poland,' Ilona continued. 'Solidarity. My father says it will get us nowhere. Death and destruction, he says. Wait until I tell him about this.'

Katalin had never seen people looking so happy. The carnival mood was seductive: the tramp of feet, the surge of song and the damp tug and flap of flags overhead. Faces shone red with the cold and rain and the excitement of the occasion. There were outbursts of cheering and laughter as people waved and greeted the occupants of apartments who peered down at the parade in astonishment.

As they reached the end of their street Katalin made to turn off, but Ilona grabbed her arm.

'We're not going home yet. We can't miss this.'

Katalin thought of Mama worrying, and balanced that by remembering the boring routine of chores to be done. She shrugged and gave in. They linked arms, joining in the singing and allowing themselves to be swept along towards Parliament Square.

The word was that Nagy Imre was expected to speak. Ilona spotted some older girls from school and passed on this information, obviously hoping to impress. There were a couple from the boys' school in the group and Ilona was showing off and making eyes at one of them. He was a tall good-looking lad she recognised as Káldor Bandi, legendary centre of their basketball team.

Students clustered nearby were waving a flag with a jagged hole in the middle where the Socialist coat of arms should have been. They must be crazy. What was happening? Why had everyone except her stopped feeling afraid? She looked round for Ilona, but she was absorbed in the group of older girls and boys. Bandi was ignoring Ilona, intent on pressing forward to the Radio Building, which seemed to be the focus of the action. But even so, Katalin felt sidelined. The crowd was quieter now, in a more serious mood, concentrating on a faraway voice being relayed over loudspeakers that weren't up to the job.

She couldn't hear. She was cold and hungry and frightened by the weight of the crowd as it surged forward towards the speaker. She shoved and fought her way to the edge and threaded her way back towards home, diving into doorways to let people pass, keeping to the wall, shouldering a passage, ignoring the shouts that told her she was going the wrong way. In Andrassy Street a huge crowd was gathered at number 60. Someone shouted, 'Down with the AVO'. To shout such a thing outside the headquarters of the secret police was unthinkable. The world had gone mad. Nobody seemed to think about "safe" any more.

Mama was furious. 'Where on earth have you been? You should have been home hours ago. The whole town's seething and you're out in it! I've been worried sick.'

Mama had made dumplings and the bean stew smelled delicious. It was all Katalin could do not to cry with relief at being safe in the kitchen, but she would never admit it. Marika was smirking in the doorway, the good girl who came straight home. Katalin did her best to capture the elation of her earlier mood.

'You missed all the fun,' she said to her sister. 'It was exciting, Mama! It was like a party. They were singing the Kossuth song – you know…'

Mama just glared. 'I know. Of course I know. So, our national hero rides again, does he? Where's all that going to end? It's bad enough having your father to worry about. Now wash your hands and get that table laid.'

Ever since Papa had been in prison, Mama worried whenever he was late home. She hadn't even asked about her ballet.

As they sat down Katalin said, 'I'm definitely going to be Snow Queen.'

Marika snorted and Mama nodded.

'Miss Pásztor said I was technically perfect.'

'I suppose we must be glad of having something to celebrate.'

It wasn't the reaction Katalin had expected.

Much later, however, Papa came home with news that there was a lot to celebrate. She woke up to his call of, 'Teréz, where are you?' and laughter as he slammed the apartment door. Running from her bed, she saw him waltzing Mama around the kitchen.

'They've taken Stalin down,' he said when he saw her and came striding across the room to hug her. 'Only his boots are left and they're tall enough for a man to hide in. Go wake your sister, it's an historic day!'

She grabbed at his arm. 'Papa, I'm to dance Snow Queen!'

He nodded, hardly looking at her. 'Good. Good.'

Bother the students. Bother the rebellion. She felt cheated of her big moment.

Papa opened the wine he'd brought in and poured them all a glass. Marika was sleepy and bad-tempered and made to spit hers out, but Papa insisted she drink a toast to freedom before she handed her glass to Mama. There was a glint in his eye Katalin had never seen before.

He slammed his glass down and refilled it. 'It's what we've all been working for. Today is a landmark and we are all a part of it.'

Papa hadn't mentioned the shooting, but they found out the next day. When he eventually came home, he smelled of burning and there were dark stains on his shirt. Mama raged at him about where he had been, but he collapsed in his chair.

'János, János!' Papa was sobbing. 'János is gone!'

They all caught their breath. Mama flung her arms around him. János was Papa's great mate. They'd known each other from schooldays, worked together, shared hopes for the future.

'Died in my arms.' He bent over, cradling the ghost of János. 'I could do nothing for him.' Then the glint in his eye turned steely. 'We have to fight on. It's taken hold. The revolution is happening. The workers mean business – it's not just a bunch of students and intellectuals now. We've got a chance, a real chance, Teréz. Believe me.' He punched a fist into the palm of his other hand. 'Fight on – for Hungary and for János.'

'But you were right *there*. You could have been killed too.'

18

'But I wasn't.'

'Not that time. Okay, you've got arms, the army have come over to your side, but, oh László!' Mama grabbed his hand with both of hers. 'What can a man with a gun do against a tank? With just a flimsy barricade to protect you?'

'The tanks have been captured. We're in control. Trust me, Teréz.'

Katalin heard them whispering long into the night. It gave her the shivers. If János could be killed, then… She couldn't think that thought. By the time she got up next morning Papa had gone. His shirt was in a bowl in the kitchen and the water was thick with blood. He didn't reappear that day. By now there was shooting everywhere. They didn't go to school and only ventured out for bread.

Mama wanted them to stay in the apartment, but Marika threatened a tantrum. They held Mama's hand, hearing shots a few streets away and jumping whenever a person came round a corner. Ordinary people, not just soldiers, were carrying guns and there was no sign of the secret police.

After several days cooped up together in the apartment, Mama ventured out to work and came home grim-faced. 'Corpses on the street, covered in lime,' she said, and sat up long after Katalin and Marika had gone to bed, waiting for Papa.

Katalin tried not to think of János or of Papa as one of the corpses lying in the road and strained to hear the sound of his key in the lock. She woke to hear low voices in the kitchen and crept to the door to listen.

'The information is reliable,' Mama was saying and she heard Papa utter a curse she'd never heard him use before. 'The withdrawal is a sham. They are playing with you, playing for time while reinforcements arrive. But when they come back it won't be a game anymore.'

Papa cursed again. 'How can you say that? How dare you? That we have been playing a game?'

'*I* don't say it, László. *They* do.' She dropped her voice and Katalin strained to hear. Something about papers. 'I only have to ask. I can have them tomorrow or the day after. It's the only way. László? Don't you care about us? Is the revolution all that matters to you?'

Silence. Then Papa again, his voice heavy and choked. 'Of course I care. But to rely on this…'

'László, you know he means nothing to me. Nothing. It is just—'

He cut across her. 'As to the information, yes, I can believe what you say. There are several of our number who don't trust the withdrawal. They are lulling us into a false sense of security.' He finished with a string of expletives and scraped back his chair. Katalin ran for bed.

4

Her sister was excited to be visiting Uncle Fritz and Aunt Júlia for Uncle Fritz's birthday celebrations, but Katalin knew what it was really about. She knew they would never come back. She would never see their apartment, her ballet teacher, her friends ever again. She could understand why they didn't tell Marika – she would have gone berserk, screaming the place down and letting cats out of bags in all directions. Or she'd have blabbed it to her toys in her silly games, and you never knew who might be listening. But they could have trusted me, she thought.

She acted surprised when Papa said he was delayed by his work and that Mama and Marika were to go ahead. She already knew she was to stay and keep him company and help carry the bags. She'd started to make a habit of listening at the kitchen door and heard him persuading Mama that it would be safer, less noticeable, if they travelled separately. There was some talk of a man at the border but she couldn't hear any more because Mama's footsteps approached the door.

Katalin couldn't conceal her fury. Her dream was being snatched away. She wouldn't be dancing the Snow Queen in the 'Waltz of the Snowflakes'. Why couldn't the revolution have waited until after the Christmas show? Papa told her she must be philosophical. There would be other opportunities, he said. That was what he meant by being philosophical. He said they were probably going to London.

On the last day of October they went to see Mama and Marika off at the station. 'Like any family,' she heard Papa tell Mama. 'All Soul's Eve,' said Mama and crossed herself. Papa carried the bags and Mama held Marika's hand and kept telling her not to look at the corpses that were still lying in the street. There had been a slight thaw and the bodies were stinking, a smell that caught in the back of the throat. Katalin had to breathe quickly and swallow hard to stop herself from gagging.

On the corner of their street a dead person was swinging from the lamp post. At first Katalin wondered what it was. Then she saw fingers and felt sick. His head lolled sideways and a huge tongue was hanging out of the mouth, except it was far too big to be a tongue. Papa called her sharply as she stared at it. She was glad when they turned the next corner. Until then she had to keep peeping over her shoulder to make sure. And each time – yes, it really was a body hanging there.

The station was busy. They stood by the barrier, waving, but she doubted Mama and Marika could see them across the sea of hats. In spite of the mood of euphoria in the city since the Russian tanks had withdrawn, they obviously weren't the only people who thought it wiser to leave.

When they got home she asked, 'Why is it safer for us to travel separately, Papa?'

He looked up sharply. Then he grinned. 'My little eavesdropper.' He chewed at his bread, looking straight at her in that intense way of his. 'Because a mother might leave her husband, but she doesn't leave a daughter behind if she's planning to leave the country.'

She thought there were times when she was sure Mama would happily leave her behind, but she wouldn't want anyone to know.

'And don't let me hear you mention the subject again, is that clear?'

She nodded. 'Promise. Cross my heart and hope to die.'

'Dying is not part of the plan. We're going on a hike. A winter hike.'

They'd been on summer hikes, her and Papa, but she'd never heard of a winter one.

'For your school project about survival skills.'

'What school project? We haven't got any—'

'For your school project, Katalin,' he repeated fiercely and she understood.

But what happened in the next weeks changed everything. One morning Papa went out without polishing his shoes. Which was a bit like Katalin going out without a skirt. While he was gone, the floor in their building started vibrating like at Ilona's when a train went by. But they didn't live by the railway. When she looked out she was just in time to see a tank pass the end of their street, then another and another, juddering into the square. Where was Papa? How long would he be? Should she go and look for him? Almost certainly not. He was out on business and he never talked about business, liked it to stay private – although secret might be more accurate. She often wondered what he did, besides writing for the *Népszava,* but it was no good asking and, anyway, she wouldn't know where to start looking for him.

When he came in he was pale. All he said was, 'Come away from that window.'

They kept the apartment in darkness and hid in the back room eating bread and dripping. They packed their rucksacks with the few belongings they would take, and set them by the door. Papa said she could take one toy, but she was too old for toys so she chose her ballet shoes instead. Papa paced about and never got undressed. He had dark shadows under his eyes. Two days later he said it wasn't safe. They were to move down to the basement with the other inhabitants of their building.

She found it hard to sleep for explosions and gunfire, shouting and screaming and – when there was a lull – the constant chatter of one of their neighbours. Every so often came the rumble of falling masonry and she waited for the ceiling to cave in. In the morning, when they ventured out, sunlit shards of glass glittered on the pavement – the windows of the block opposite had all been blown out.

They'd been camping in the basement for a week when they woke to silence. No boom and rumble of tanks. No shots. No falling masonry. Papa reported a ceasefire and said it was time to go. They would leave the next morning before dawn.

They picked their way through broken glass and rubble. The air was thick with dust and the smell of death. Katalin could see into an apartment as if it were a stage set. A table teetered at the edge of the floor, close to toppling onto the pavement. Cupboards were falling sideways with the drawers hanging out. There was knitting on the arm of a chair and pictures still hanging, and in one room two people were in bed, as if asleep. There was no façade on the next block either. Room after room was open to view. Kitchens, offices, bedrooms – all exposed and deserted.

It felt rude to be intruding into those private places, to be staring at dead people. Being dead was a bit like being naked. She didn't want to look but she couldn't take her eyes away. Papa had to pull her along.

Papa said they must go by a back route where the tanks couldn't come. Several times they stopped to work out where they were, because familiar landmarks had disappeared. They heard the roar and rumble of a tank. Where was it? Would it come their way? Papa bundled Katalin ahead of him into a doorway. He crouched, pulling her down beside him.

'Be a pile of rags,' he said.

It was only later, much later, that she realised they were pretending to be corpses.

The noise of the tank was replaced by another sound. Someone was playing the piano. The notes slithered and tumbled, melting the frozen air like a waterfall. She felt Papa's shoulders drop and he breathed out. They both stood and stared up at the building opposite, searching for the open window way up there, but nothing was lit. The playing seemed to come from the stars. The music stopped. There was a pause and then it started again at the beginning of the phrase. Hesitation. A false note. The same phrase was repeated slowly several times. Then the hands set off again with more confidence and continued. When she turned to Papa his eyes were shining and a tear was running down his cheek.

'That person is practising,' he said.

Well, yes. She thought that was obvious. 'But they are good,' she said.

'Ah, but that is not the point. You only practise for the future. For a future when a person will play Chopin and people will stop to listen.' He wiped his eyes with the heel of his hand. 'A sign of hope.'

He grabbed her hand and they continued along the road, stepping over bodies as the notes of the sonata soared and faded behind them.

The train had been crowded when they saw Mama off, but when they reached the station this time there was pandemonium. Several trains left without their getting anywhere near the front of the platform. Hours passed before Papa grasped Katalin's hand more tightly and they fought their way towards the train that had just pulled in. There was no opening the doors. Instead he passed her in through a window and she wriggled between close-packed bodies to find the floor with her feet. She was thankful to be wearing trousers. Papa passed in the rucksacks, and being wiry and agile, was able to clamber after them with the help of other passengers. Conversation was guarded and nobody commented on this extraordinary exodus from the city in the direction of the Austrian border. You didn't know who might be among the crowd. She guessed they all had their good reasons for travelling – their school projects, their family parties, their sick relatives. But who would believe them now?

As they pulled away from the platform, she kept hearing the echo of the outer door of their apartment as they slammed it behind them. Such a familiar sound, which would continue to resound – into the dark vestibule and up the stairwell – without her being there to hear it.

People left the train at every town and village, but were replaced by other travellers. Papa was tense. He peered out whenever they stopped and kept checking his watch. They pulled into a tiny station and suddenly they were on the move, jumping down onto the platform.

'Head down, keep moving. Don't look at anyone.'

She peered sideways and saw the regular local passengers, the ones who were smartly dressed with only a briefcase or a shopping bag, queueing to leave by the normal exit, while a swarm of others with rucksacks, bundles and children climbed the fence and vanished into darkness. They joined these, but most of them set off uphill into the woods. Papa struck out along a path running parallel to the railway. It was a shock to be alone and breathing crisp, quiet air with the grass crackling underfoot. It was a long time before Papa spoke.

'Well done,' he said softly, turning on his heel to face her. It was as if they'd arrived somewhere, but there was nothing except the fence on one side and the tracks on the other.

'So far, so good. This path will take us to the outskirts of the town. *Then* we'll head up into the woods – much less chance of getting lost. It's a path I know. Okay, little one?' He gave her a big hug.

She squeezed him back, grinning in the dark. She was loving it. They had sheets in their rucksacks to wrap round themselves as camouflage, and she longed to pretend to be a ghost.

'Will we sleep in the woods?'

'We'll see. Stop and eat maybe. Depends how long it takes us.'

She'd have liked a proper hike with camping but she could tell Papa wanted to get through the border tonight. Which was boring. He'd already said a fire would be out of the question.

'Best foot forward now. You go in front, set the pace, then I don't have to keep turning round to make sure you're keeping up.'

'Of course I was keeping up!'

It wasn't so easy being in front and she wanted to use her torch, but Papa said they had to keep that for when they really needed it and not beside the railway. She quickly got used to picking out the track and was quite annoyed when Papa swapped over again. He had to look out for the place where they had to turn off.

Then he froze and she nearly bumped into him. At the same time a dog started barking a little way off.

'People coming this way.'

He pulled her down into the ditch and put his hand across her mouth – as if she needed to be told not to make a sound. Papa had super-hearing, but eventually she heard footsteps, as if there were several people. They weren't marching like soldiers and they weren't carrying a light, but they were coming closer. The dog had stopped barking. It must be at a farm nearer the town. At least it wasn't with them, whoever they were. The footsteps came to an uneven stop, there was a pause, and an exclamation. Someone said to hush up and there was a murmured conversation. Had they been seen? She could hear Papa's heart beating close to her ear and her rucksack was digging into her back, but she dared not move.

A beam of light swept along the grass bank. It fell on the edge of Papa's coat and she felt him stiffen. Then darkness, which seemed even darker than before. The footsteps started again and she waited for a shout, another flash of the torch, but they were softer now and steadily faded away. Papa let go of her and she found she had been holding her breath.

'Phew! False alarm, sounds like they've taken the track we're taking.'

'You mean, they're escaping too?'

'Of course. Must have come from town with a guide. Still, better safe than sorry.' He hugged her. 'You did well. Still, silent. You'd make a good spy.'

'Everyone's escaping. There won't be anyone left.'

Papa just sighed.

As she followed him into the forest Katalin felt as if she'd suddenly grown up. It was childish to be thinking of playing ghosts in sheets. She concentrated on stepping lightly, so as not to crack a twig. She was the Snow Queen riding in the forest with her Prince, surrounded by her attendant snowflakes. She was icicle-sharp, light as a bubble, dazzling with snow crystals. The pas de deux was faultless, the applause would never end, she was crowned Queen of the snowflakes. Except this would never happen.

The fantasy reignited her rage – at the Communists, yes, but at the revolutionaries too for provoking it all, at the Russians for destroying their city, driving them out. London was said to be a city of opportunity but what would it really be like? She was so cross she forgot to be weightless and bumped into a tree. Its rough bark scratched the Snow Queen's alabaster skin, and she crackled a whole load of twigs so that Papa turned with a scowl and a hushing gesture.

After that, every step was hard work as they headed uphill through the trees. The snow wasn't deep here and their footfall released the smell of leaf mould and fungus and a musky animal aroma. Not pleasant, but like perfume compared with the reek of the streets in Pest. It seemed an eternity before Papa stopped and pulled off his rucksack.

'Are we camping here?' She was surprised because the ground was steep and stony.

'Sorry, sweetheart, no camping. We need to keep on. If we keep going we can make it over the border before it gets light.' He handed her some bread and a lump of salami. 'This'll put new life in you.'

The bread was stale and dry and the salami peppery, but they shared an apple, which made it easier to swallow. And it was so good to stop and lean against a tree.

It didn't last long. Papa hoisted his bag back onto his shoulders and hugged her. 'Best foot forward. Think of a tune and try humming it inside your head. It'll help.'

But none of the tunes she knew were any good for marching, so she just counted to a hundred over and over until they emerged from the wood onto a road. Papa swore under his breath because it had begun to snow heavily. After about a kilometre they came to a house set among the trees. They skirted around behind it, made their way through bushes and came in sight of the back door.

'Wait here.' Papa put his finger to his lips and crunched away towards a window where light was showing round the curtains. She heard him tap on the glass, a double knock, repeated three times. A code, she guessed. His silhouette appeared briefly as the door opened and closed, and she was alone under the silent falling flakes.

She tipped back her head and caught them on her tongue, but got a crick in her neck before her thirst was quenched. How long was Papa going to be? What was he doing in there? She tried to brush the snow off her coat and scarf but it was coming down too fast to make any difference. Why ever had she wanted it to snow? She was shivering by the time the door of the house opened again. Papa loomed beside her and there was someone with him, a small man who shook her hand and said nothing. Over his coat he was wearing an oversize white overall, the sort Grandfather used to wear for milking the cows. She wondered if he was a farmer. He didn't look much like a farmer.

Papa whispered, 'This gentleman is a contact of mine. He knows the latest position of the border guards, the pattern of patrols. He will guide us. Just say nothing and keep up.'

The man set off along a path that took them beyond the house and ran parallel to the road. Katalin could see his grey fur hat making little darting movements from side to side like a bird on the lookout for worms. The mention of guards had iced her inside as well as out. So far, Papa had been clever – making it out to be an adventure. It wasn't an adventure. It was actually dangerous. She should have known. When had she last seen Papa smile? Her fun-loving father had been as dour as the Grim Reaper for days.

They walked and they walked. She tried counting to a hundred again but it seemed to slow her down and she had to focus to keep up, especially now the snow was deep enough to claim her foot at each step. The swirling of flakes made her giddy and she wanted to burst into tears and say, please, please can we stop this now? But she knew there was no stopping. That would be letting Papa down. It would be letting herself down. She would not be a crybaby. It was not the behaviour of a Snow Queen. She took deep breaths and let the snow blow into her mouth. It was surreal, walking through whiteness. There was no sense of moving forward, no landmarks to measure your progress. When they abruptly left the path and crossed the road she had no sense of whether they'd travelled five kilometres or fifteen, fifty even.

They climbed a gate into fields. It had stopped snowing and the expanse of white seemed endless like an enormous bed she wanted to lie down on. She certainly didn't want to walk across it. Which was what they had to do. Birdman said something curt to Papa, who got the sheets out and wrapped hers around her. He swung into his as if he did it every day and they set off. Now she saw the point of the milking parlour overall. She wondered if there was enough snow on her black hat to camouflage it, and whether she should pull the sheet over her head. Was her head a moving target or did it look like a bird? She tried to ask Papa, but he just said, 'Don't fuss and keep going.'

The snow had filled the dents and hollows in the field and twice she sank in nearly to her knees and Papa had to haul her out. There was no let-up in the pace of Birdman. Twice she let her sheet trail and fell over it. After that, Papa drew her alongside him and took her hand like he did when she was a little girl. She imagined the energy flowing down his arm into her hand, and up her arm and down into her legs. It helped. It really did.

She'd read about soldiers sleeping as they marched, except that was on long marches, like to Moscow. But she did wonder if that had happened to her, because all of a sudden they were standing alongside a hedge looking down on a river rushing along noisily at the bottom of a steep bank. Her first stupid thought was that nobody was telling the river to shut up.

Birdman pulled them out of the shelter of the hedge, indicating the glimmer of light to the left, which located the watchtower. He gestured at the river winding below and away to the right, but before he could speak there was a whooshing, popping sound like a firework going off. Birdman pushed them both violently in the back so that they fell flat on their faces in the snow with him between them, holding them both down.

'Don't move a muscle,' he said. 'And close your eyes.'

What did Birdman not want them to see? She was thinking, Papa had got it all wrong. He was going to kill them and leave them to be buried in the snow, a terrible warning to others who tried to escape. But at the same time as she was thinking this and expecting everything to go black, she was dazzled by a brilliant light reflecting off the snow beyond her nose. It was far too quick to have made it to heaven, and in any case she could still smell Birdman's onion breath to her right as he spoke.

'Bloody flares. They must have seen something move. If you hear that sound again, just freeze.'

It was the most words he'd said, and she looked sideways just in time to see his face before the eerie brightness faded. He looked so sad and she felt guilty for doubting him.

They clambered to their feet, sheets flapping soggily. Katalin staggered sideways, unable to see a thing. Of course. That's why he'd told them to close their eyes. She'd lost her night vision. Birdman was giving them instructions.

'There, on the other side, that ploughed field, is no man's land, not Austria. Just over the ridge there's a ditch. Good place for a breather. Hard work, ploughed fields. After that, there's another field, the length of a football pitch. Still not Austria. Just keep going. Okay? The water's the real challenge.'

He pointed down the slope where they could make out a kind of bridge consisting of logs lashed together. He did a funny sideways walk and Papa watched and nodded. Was this another kind of code, like the window-tapping? It was not until they got down to the logs that she realised he was demonstrating the best method of crossing without slipping off the icy surface.

By the time they reached the bridge, the sky was shading from black to charcoal at the approach of dawn. Papa grabbed her hand and they started on the precarious crossing.

'Don't look down at the water. Keep your knees loose,' he said.

She was never more thankful for her ballet training and the time she had spent stepping along her bedrail, holding herself upright, looking ahead, learning to balance.

The bedrail. The thought shivered into memory, a sliver of ice behind the eyes, slicing her body, causing feet to falter. She glanced down – swift, dark current below a frozen surface of water – turbulence crackling through the ice crust – rocketing forward – inscrutable depths – drawing her down, down... Depths hurtling up to meet plummeting body... As once her sister might have flown... But did not.

The moment lasted only a second. But her equilibrium was threatened. Papa's words repeated in her head. 'Don't look down.' Her arms flew up to compensate for the hesitation, the pull of gravity. She fixed her gaze ahead and crabwise progress soon brought her in sight of a shape, which was Papa, watching and waiting on the far bank.

She jumped clear of the logs and Papa pulled her up the bank.

He spoke into her ear. 'Now, run! This is still Hungary. Up the hill, over the top and into the ditch.'

The hill wasn't that steep but every rut threatened to grab a foot and twist an ankle. Eventually Katalin got into a rhythm of springing forward from ridge to frozen ridge and stumbled into the ditch with the breath rasping in her throat. They both gasped at the icy water filling their boots. By the time the next burst of light filled the sky, they were breathing normally.

'Right,' said Papa. 'Last lap. We have to reach the trees before the next flare goes up.'

They floundered rather than ran across the last field. Searchlights scissored the sky when they were about fifty metres from the tree line but they didn't flatten themselves this time.

'Keep going!' Papa yelled. 'They can't get us now.'

She had an image of Papa being gunned down and blood spattered across the snow. But no. He was right, and they crashed into the trees as the light faded. She was expecting another trek through endless forest but it was only a narrow strip of woodland.

Papa pointed up at the shadow of a flag they could hear slapping lazily above their heads. They could distinguish the light stripe across the middle and the dark stripes at the top and bottom, but it was still too dark to identify the colour of the crucial bottom layer. Hungarian green? Or Austrian red? Birdman had said nothing about trees. Had they veered off course? Had they come far enough? There was only one way to find out.

Without a word, Papa squatted while Katalin climbed onto his shoulders and launched herself at the flagpole. At first she thought she would slide straight back down. Her legs felt like jelly, but her arms were strong. She pulled herself up, using her knees to grip and stop her slipping back. Up and up she went like a looping caterpillar, until the flag was brushing the top of her head. She wrapped one arm around the pole and grabbed with her free hand to catch the fabric, pulling it down in front of her face. It was red. Wasn't it? Yes, it really was. On the way down she burned her hands, caught a knee on the cleat and collapsed into Papa's strong grasp.

'That's no way to come down a pole,' he said.

'But it's red, it's red!'

He grabbed her in a bear hug and they danced in a circle, whooping and suddenly full of energy. They were interrupted by the sound of an engine. There was the squeal of brakes and headlights were visible through the trees. As they trudged towards them, Katalin could still hardly believe they were now on Austrian soil. She might never set foot in Hungary again.

5

In Vienna, Katalin was relieved to find Marika and Mama basking in Aunt Júlia's central heating.

But all Marika said was, 'Have you got teddy's red jumper?'

No questions about how they'd escaped, no sign of being pleased to see them. Mama hadn't seemed that concerned either. They were both going on about the stupid teddy bear. Evidently, to keep Marika quiet, Mama had told her that Katalin would be certain to notice the jumper and bring it with her. As if.

When no red jumper appeared, Marika let rip. She howled like a wild cat. She was ten years old and should have known better. Apparently, it was Katalin's fault.

'Your poor little sister,' said Aunt Júlia, dropping her knitting in her lap and smoothing the brocade on the arm of the sofa. She leaned across to Mama, muttering. 'The moment that girl walks through the door, there's trouble.'

Katalin had looked her aunt straight in the eye. 'How was I supposed to know? I mean, nobody actually *asked* me to bring the stupid jumper.'

'Don't speak like that to your aunt. Really, you two girls. I don't know… Here we are safe in Vienna. Your aunt and uncle have moved heaven and earth on our behalf. The least you can do is be polite.'

Aunt Júlia sighed. 'Never mind, Teréz. I suppose it's her age.'

It had been a relief to be told to have a hot bath and go to bed. She'd slept for twelve hours solid.

Now Aunt Júlia was taking more interest.

'Suppose you tell us about your journey, Katalin, dear.'

At last. She ignored the patronising tone and launched into a description of the snow and the flares, about how scared they were crossing the water, about those dreadful furrows in no man's land and about climbing the flagpole and how terrifying it had been, not knowing that they weren't still in Hungary.

But the cold she described melted away in the heat of the room. The terror was blotted up by the thick carpet. Aunt Júlia was counting stitches.

Katalin tried again. 'I didn't think I had any strength left to shin up that flagpole.' She paused for dramatic effect. 'But it was red!'

'Of course, dear,' said Aunt Júlia. She patted the seat beside her and beckoned Marika who was still sulking about the jumper. 'Come and sit here, dear.'

'It really was the Austrian flag,' Katalin said, thinking they'd missed the point.

Mama nodded. She was picking her teeth and Aunt Júlia was looking out the window, but Katalin ploughed on. She explained how wonderful it was to climb aboard the waiting coach, the relief of not having to walk any more. Then there was the soup served out to them in the schoolhouse down the road.

'It was so hot and delicious. It was the best meal I ever ate.'

Aunt Júlia just said, 'I think we can do better than that, dear.'

They simply didn't realise how dangerous it had been.

'We'd been walking all night. We could have been shot.'

'Oh, I don't think so, dear. Even my crazy brother wouldn't take risks with…'

Mama interrupted, cigarette halfway to her lips. 'László always knows what he's doing.' Which was not what she said to Papa when they had rows about his work. Mama snapped her lighter and inhaled. 'I do like those new curtains, Júlia. They're growing on me.'

It was infuriating. They had no idea. Did they think she was making it all up? Mama talked of being safe in Vienna, but she and Marika were never anything but safe. Papa had explained that to her. Because, when he and Katalin had arrived at the former army camp where they were to be accommodated, Marika and Mama weren't there. Katalin had wanted to know why. Had they been arrested and sent back to Budapest? What would happen to them? Papa said they'd had papers to get them over the border, and they'd continued on the train right through to Vienna.

'Papers? How did they get papers?'

Papa had shrugged. 'Your mother plays her cards very cleverly,' he said.

What cards? she wondered.

He'd tried to make it sound like a good thing, but she could tell from the tense way he tapped out a cigarette that he didn't like it. He wouldn't look at her when he said it, and he clammed up after that and went all moody. She was left with loads of questions. How could Mama be married to Papa and yet be given safe passage? Was she right that Papa was wanted as a revolutionary? What did he do with his "associate", the Birdman? Her parents were a mystery.

Now Aunt Júlia was promising Marika that she'd knit her teddy a new jumper. It was sickening the way they spoilt her. Her sister was careful to sulk for a while longer on the edge of the Chesterfield and then she cosied up to Aunt Júlia.

'There's a good girl,' said Aunt Júlia with her I'm-a-clever-auntie smile.

Katalin left the room. In five minutes, their aunt would be feeding Marika chocolates like some lap dog. She didn't want to see it. She went in search of Papa, but he was closeted with Uncle Fritz in the study. Their heads were close together and they were talking, low and serious. When Papa spotted Katalin in the doorway he shook his head and waved her away. Uncle Fritz didn't even turn round. Usually he liked showing her his collections of silver cigarette cases and musical boxes. He remembered what he had paid for each one. He made the conversion for her from schillings to forints and their value amazed her. Uncle Fritz had a malty, peppery smell and spoke to her as if she were grown up. He said, 'Excuse me', when the telephone rang instead of just answering it as if she didn't matter. He spoke sharply on the phone, as if he was angry with the person on the other end. But then he would put down the receiver and laugh and give her a mint humbug, which she much preferred to chocolates. He and Papa must be discussing the political situation in Budapest. She wanted to listen and learn but she didn't want to risk getting on the wrong side of anyone else today.

She sat on the bottom step of the stairs. She couldn't hear what they're saying, but there was plenty to look at. This was no ordinary house. The hall was tiled in pinky-grey marble with a pattern like veins and arteries, which made it seem warmer than it was. The staircase took up two whole walls. It was the kind you might sweep down in a ballgown like they did in films, one elegant hand resting on the silky-smooth bannister. Miles up there was a painted ceiling with ladies in long gowns, knights on horses, and a sun, moon and stars. Suspended between the two floors was a chandelier with crystals hanging from it. It was like a huge sea creature with tentacles and it sparkled even when it wasn't lit. No wonder Uncle Fritz could afford to send them to England.

They were fortunate to be here, she knew that. The refugee camp was horrid, though Papa said it was well organised. The straw mattress was okay, but she couldn't get warm at night. After the euphoria of escaping and the business of settling in, the camp was boring, even though it was seething with people.

'It's called anti-climax,' Papa said. 'It brings us to earth. Time to focus. Excitement is dangerous. You get excited, next minute you are dead. No time even for fear.'

It was unlike Papa to be so negative. But when she looked up, he had tears in his eyes and she remembered János.

He shook his head. 'Life must go on – the work must go on. That's the duty we owe to the dead. The price we pay for being still alive. Strikes me, that's what life after death really means.'

Katalin nodded and tried to look as if she understood. Most of the time Papa would sit in a corner with his eyes closed, although she knew he wasn't asleep.

Thank goodness they only had to stay two days. Papa had got word to Uncle Fritz and on their third morning a huge black Cadillac drove up to the reception area. It caused a stir when a uniformed chauffeur leapt out, took their tatty rucksacks and opened the rear door. Good old Uncle Fritz. Papa was embarrassed, but she hadn't minded one bit.

Mama always said, it was who you knew, not what you knew, that counted. It was certainly true in the camp. Some families had been there for weeks with no prospect of getting out and no idea where in the world they might end up. It might be England, America or New Zealand. That must be horrible. Papa said Uncle Fritz was organising their travel documents for London and paying for everything. He could even afford for them to fly.

Katalin climbed to the level of the chandelier. All that crystal must weigh a tonne. It would kill you if it fell on you. She reached out, but couldn't get anywhere near touching it. She stretched. She could stretch and stretch and she might fall. Once again, a body threatened to fly. That only led to a guilty place, so she turned away quickly and continued upward. The stair treads were so wide she couldn't even take two at a time.

The bedroom she was sharing with Marika was full of her sister's new clothes. They were scattered about the bed and floor where she'd been trying them on and prancing about, with her fat little tummy spoiling the shape of the dresses. It wouldn't be long before Mama and Aunt Júlia took her shopping. What she wanted was a pair of blue jeans, none of this frilly stuff. But she wouldn't be allowed.

She cleared some tissue paper and a petticoat from her side of the room and burrowed in her rucksack. She started to unwind the ribbons of her ballet pumps, but her heart wasn't in it. If only she could be meeting her friends to rehearse the Snow Queen. It was all so unfair.

Even Papa was ignoring her now. If they were at home he'd be playing a game. He'd come in and show them a card trick before he'd even taken his coat off. Her favourite was the raisin game. He'd put a raisin under a cup on the table with two cups on either side. He'd say, 'Keep your eye on the raisin,' and move the cups back and forth so quickly that it was hard to tell whether the raisin went with the cup or stayed where it was. Then he'd say, 'Where's the raisin?' If she pointed to the right cup, which she often did, he'd say, 'Eagle eyes, Kati,' and give her the raisin.

But Marika would whine that it wasn't fair, so she got a raisin too, which was really, really unfair, so Katalin would insist on an extra raisin. If neither of them got it right, Papa would eat the raisin himself and they would shriek and attack him until he gave them one each. Then Mama would complain that they were eating all the raisins. 'There won't be any more when those are gone,' she'd say, and Papa would grab her and silence her by kissing her on the mouth.

That thing Mama did with her hips. Yuk. She would rush out of the room, yanking at Marika, who always stared when they got smoochy. She told her sister it was rude.

She pushed the image out of her mind and finished unrolling her ballet shoes. She'd told Papa when they were packing that she was too old for toys, but she had cheated and brought her secret mascot. It fitted inside one of the pumps, so it didn't really count.

It had to be secret because she'd found it one day in the art room at school. The seniors had obviously been in there sketching from life. Except not from life. That would have meant a model, unless they painted Miss Farkas and no one would want to do that. They'd been using wooden mannequins with jointed limbs in all sizes and in different poses. You could see from the pictures pinned up round the walls.

Right beside her desk Katalin had found this miniature wooden creature with moving arms and legs and hands and feet. She'd fingered it in the bottom of her pocket for the rest of the day.

The figure was smooth, clean, skeletal. It was featureless, but she liked the nakedness of it – entirely functional, no frills, no face, no embarrassing bits. She put it into each of the basic ballet positions and it could hold them all and even stand up. She rubbed saliva onto the mannequin's head and baptised her Pavlova.

She talked to Pavlova and polished her every day, like Aladdin with his lamp. Pavlova still didn't have a face. Katalin could tell which way round her head was from the grain of the wood; she didn't want to make her look like a doll. Pavlova was her forerunner, a talisman. Pavlova would dance on ahead and if Katalin followed in those steps she would succeed. It was the opposite of having a doll you stuck pins in to sort out your enemies.

Katalin set Pavlova to doing the splits on the dressing table while she told her what a difficult time she was having, living in luxury in Vienna.

6

The early light simplified vision, eliminating colour. The elms were an etching, the twiggy ends of their branches trimmed as if with nail scissors to form a perfect arc against a pale sky loud with rooks. Klára closed the door behind her and stood listening, breathing it in. Should she go down to the sea or up to the woods?

She whistled for Finn, who was on his usual patrol of the garden, and set off up the lane. The sea was good for thinking, but she couldn't resist the primroses.

So, László had brought his family to England. Her beloved younger brother. It was no surprise that he'd had to leave Hungary. László was always too committed, too principled to hold back when it came to freedom and justice. She knew he'd been in prison some years before – coded messages had reached Júlia, references to "the dog being banished to the woodshed" which alluded to a game they used to play as children. He must have written a provocative article or a satirical play too many. They'd both become writers but had taken such different paths. She'd retreated to Devon with her poetry. She made a living from writing articles and translating, but it was the poetry that mattered. László used journalism as a cover for his serious writing. He'd obviously been making waves in the thick of politics, putting his family at risk. His family.

Klára abruptly turned her attention to the banks and hedges, which were bursting into spring life. The primroses were early this year, their bold clumps of creamy yellow contrasting with the more acidic celandines. A few ferns were uncurling their scrolls, but most were still tightly curled like ammonites. Occasional violets were showing purple and white. She breathed in the damp-moss smell of sap rising.

A dark shape was moving along the ridge. A familiar silhouette. That would be Father Patrick. Moving more swiftly than usual. Must be late for Mass. He was the priest at the Church of the Sacred Heart in Kingsbridge – a good friend since Klára's teaching days when he'd been roped in by the Head to help with the school production of *King Lear*. They'd been drawn together by a shared passion for Shakespeare and Yeats. She dropped back to avoid an encounter. This was not the time of day for meeting people. They agreed on that, if not on the interpretation of *Lear*.

So, László's family: the girls she'd never met and his poisonous wife.

She had first met Teréz at Lake Balaton. How dare Júlia bring a friend? It was supposed to be a *family* holiday, the time when they all got together, but here was a stranger in their midst. A stranger whose swimming costume was a size too small and who massaged oil into her shapely legs while gazing across at László. Klára had been mad at her brother for taking the bait, for failing to see he was being seduced. He didn't care. He *wanted* to be seduced. For Klára, it had been a betrayal.

In retrospect, "poisonous" was a strong word to use, but it had never been the same with László after that. He'd even told her not to be a gooseberry.

Teréz was an unlikely friend for Júlia, come to think of it. Júlia was always so cool, dutiful and bossy in her role of being the eldest. Maybe she hoped some of the glamour would rub off on her. Maybe, by now, Teréz had grown more responsible and less voluptuous.

At the stile she rested and looked out across the fields waiting for Finn, who was rootling in the hedge. The trees on top of the far bank were like a row of besoms upended, sweeping the dark floor of the sky, sending dust clouds scudding. Down in the valley Patrick was approaching his mud-coloured car. The billow of his cassock disappeared inside like an umbrella being folded.

László's letter made no demands. He didn't seem to require anything of her. They'd been in the country some time already. She'd felt a stab of pain at that. Why hadn't he let her know they were coming? *Júlia and Fritz were wonderful.* Why hadn't Júlia been in touch? Had the family written her off? Klára quickly bandaged the hurt with relief that she hadn't been required to be wonderful.

He wrote of their flat and his job. Reading between the lines of his comment, "You have to start somewhere", she guessed that neither was perfect. Knowing László, he'd be working on that. London was a long way off, so she wouldn't have to see much of them. Should she invite them to Devon for a holiday? The thought of having Teréz in her house made Klára shudder. Maybe she and László could meet up separately. And what of the girls, her nieces? He'd want her to meet them. He'd expect her to behave like an aunt. An aunt. That was a disturbing thought. She'd wouldn't know where to begin.

Halfway across the field the rain started – a black cloud had loomed from nowhere and was shedding its torrential load. In seconds her hair was flattened against her head, and Finn looked up reproachfully as if she had turned on this particular tap. As they started back, Klára started to compose a reply to her brother. She would express delight that they were in the same country, inquire about the children, emphasise how busy she was, and make no mention of Teréz.

Maybe that was too pointed. A cool "Remember me to Teréz" might be as effective, but still polite. Perhaps Teréz had changed. Should she give her another chance? But there came a warning voice in her head: "Give her an inch and she'll take a mile." Life was too short to spend time with people you disliked, even if they were married to your brother.

As they turned in to the yard, Finn ran ahead to the door, eager to get back to his rug by the Aga. Sun was glinting off a series of puddles that reflected a clear blue sky. Not a cloud in sight.

7

Katalin hated her new home in Kentish Town. It was what they called a flat-above-the-shop. And the shop was in what they called a parade. She kept looking out of the window to see if *they* were going to come marching past. Like the parades in the revolution. But Papa said they didn't need a revolution here, they already had democracy. He also told her and Marika that they should stop thinking of *them* and *us* because it was important to assimilate, whatever that meant. Katalin noticed he didn't try saying anything of the sort to Mama.

The people who kept the newsagent's downstairs had moved out into a house, which was what people did in this country if they wanted to be anyone. You couldn't blame them for not wanting to live in the flat. They made out they were doing a social service – being broad-minded enough to take refugees as tenants. Katalin heard the woman telling people in the shop, 'Nice little family. Pitiful, you know...*so* sorry for those two little girls...the least we could do.'

The rooms were pokey. The living room looked over the street and was also Papa and Mama's bedroom. They slept on a thing called a put-u-up, which they had to pull out at night. Mama swore at it every morning when she folded it up. 'I'll give you put-u-up, you creaky old bastard!' Except "put-u-up" didn't translate into Hungarian. It made Katalin snigger and Mama got crosser than ever.

The kitchen was tiny and also contained the bath, covered by a lid, which was the only storage space. Everything had to be moved on bath nights, all the pots and pans, tins of beans and jars of pickles. They stacked the pans on the stove and carried the rest through to the table in the living room. All of which made Mama very bad-tempered, especially when Marika put the eggs on the seat of the armchair and then forgot and sat on them.

The tiny back bedroom had bunk beds, which were the worst invention ever. Katalin and Marika fought about who should sleep on top.

'She'll bounce about up there and keep me awake,' said Katalin.

'She'll kick me on the way up the ladder,' said Marika. 'Oh yes, you would!'

To begin with, Mama made them take turns. But Katalin found even the top one intolerable. She could touch the ceiling, which made her feel claustrophobic, like the filling in a sandwich. So Marika slept up there and Katalin pulled her mattress onto the floor and hoped her sister wouldn't trample her in the night, which she would if she weren't such a good sleeper.

Katalin still felt the ceiling was coming down on her even though it was further away. She tried to imagine she was in the apartment in Budapest with its lofty rooms and tall windows. The place had been shabby, with peeling paint, but now she saw it had style and the shutters had kept them safe from breaking glass. She didn't want to think about the glass. It would let in the horrors. Instead, she screwed her eyes tight and imagined the hot street in summer, coming home from school, the cool stairwell, a day when Mama was at home and had made lemonade. That was better. That was safe. Papa said those old apartment blocks were built to keep warm in winter and cool in summer. This flat was the reverse.

Mama said it wasn't fit for living in. 'I don't understand how this place gets to be cold and stuffy at the same time.' It made her constantly bad-tempered.

The walls were so thin you could hear the next-door people having rows, and the kids screaming when they got thumped. The horrid metal windows ran with condensation and the mould had to be scraped off the kitchen walls every week. Mama did it before she had a bath. She couldn't bear to lie there looking at it.

They weren't allowed to come into the flat through the shop. Mama raged about that. She would have been just as mad if they'd been obliged to come in that way. 'For all to see!' Katalin could just hear her saying it.

Their entrance was at the back where the dustbins were kept, using a staircase which was really a fire escape. Katalin always felt sneaky, as if she were trying to break in, except that your footsteps went clang-clang on the iron treads. Everyone knew when you were coming and going, which made it even more embarrassing.

All the flats had these staircases but nobody else used them and nobody bothered to clear up round the bins. It made them feel like second-class citizens.

'We *are* second-class citizens,' said Papa. 'We're refugees. We've been taken in and we're lucky to have this place. We have to make our way. It will get better.'

Which didn't quite go with his no-*them*-and-*us* rule. Papa never stopped being cheerful and optimistic. When Mama grumbled, he said, 'What could be more convenient? All the shops you want for buying food right here. No carrying heavy bags. No bus fares.'

It was true. As well as the newsagent's downstairs, there was a greengrocer's next door to the right (which meant smelly old cabbage leaves out the back) and a butcher's to the left, followed by a fish and chip shop which opened most evenings and all day Friday and Saturday. After that came a shop that sold liquor, which was called an off-licence, and next door to that a general store where Mama went to stock up on basics.

The food in the reception centre where they'd stayed on arriving in England had been tasteless and soggy, but Mama had promised them a treat of her special *gulasch*. It didn't work out. She complained that there was only one type of paprika available in the store and raged at the inadequacy of the pans for cooking such a dish. Worse was to come. The paprika must be stale. They all tasted the red grains. Mama was right – they had no bite. Mama had emptied the whole pot of paprika into the stew but the result was not remotely spicy.

Papa had to stop her tipping the pan into the bin. 'It's delicious,' he said.

Katalin agreed. It wasn't *gulasch* but it was better than any meal they'd eaten since leaving Vienna.

Beyond the general store, which sold stale paprika, there was an afterthought shop that didn't seem to belong with the others in the row. It opened unpredictably and everything it sold was second-hand – furniture, crockery, pots and pans, pictures, mirrors, toys, books and even hats. Whenever the sun came out the shopkeeper sat on the pavement with a bottle of beer. She was a big, bony woman with lots of dyed red hair, which she tied back with an emerald green ribbon. The surprise was that she sat there doing embroidery, all in ivory linen and very delicate, which didn't go with her big hands.

A few days after the failed *gulasch*, Marika dragged Katalin in there. She'd spotted a glass cabinet, full of ornaments and jewellery. They'd hardly got inside when a voice boomed out from the shadows at the back.

'I've not seen you two before. Mind you don't 'alf-inch nothing. I've got eyes like a hawk.'

They just looked at each other. Katalin wanted to leave but Marika stood on her foot.

'Cat got your tongues, then? What's yer names?'

'I am Katalin, and this is my sister, Marika.'

'Not from round 'ere then. Where d'you live?'

Katalin told her and she stopped scowling. 'Aah, the refugees. 'Eard about you lot. 'Ungarian, ain't it?'

Katalin nodded, surprised she knew about them.

'What a bleedin' shame. 'Aving to leave your 'ome. Everything must be a bit strange here.'

Marika burst into tears. For once Katalin didn't get mad at this drama queen behaviour. She felt her own eyes pricking. It was the first time someone hadn't told them how lucky they were to be in this dreary country. The woman had her arm round Marika, who was relishing every moment.

'I'm Wilkie, by the way. Everyone calls me that.' She whipped a crisp white square from her pocket and shook it out as if she was going to produce a rabbit. But it was just a handkerchief that she gave to Marika. ''Ere. I'll 'ave it back when your Ma's washed it.'

It was only then that Katalin noticed how oddly the woman was dressed – a purple woolly jumper under a pinstriped man's jacket and brown corduroy trousers with plimsolls and red socks. Around her neck was a floaty orange scarf with sequins sewn round the edge.

She saw Katalin looking and said, 'You're a quiet one.'

Which was odd because Katalin was the only one who'd actually spoken.

To Marika she said, 'You better now? Come back any time.'

Then she looked back at Katalin. 'Tell your Ma she might find some useful things in 'ere.' With a flash of big rings, she waved her hand round the shop. 'Stuff for setting up 'ome. I'll give 'er a discount, tell 'er. Poor buggers. None of your fault, I'm sure.'

Katalin tossed her head. 'The only thing our mother needs is some decent paprika. The stuff from the shop was stale.'

Wilkie guffawed in a most annoying way. 'She'll be wanting a bit of spice. It wasn't stale, love. That's just English paprika for you. Tell 'er, there's a store up the road. Only three bus stops away. Tell you what, I'll take 'er if she likes. They've got all foreign stuff there.'

Wilkie turned up at the flat the very next day and insisted on paying the bus fare for the three of them – 'Just this once, mind!' Mama found all the tins of paprika she wanted, plus proper Hungarian sausage and vegetables that didn't feature on the parade. To celebrate she made *lecso* and even invited Wilkie as a thank you. But Wilkie politely declined, saying she suffered with her digestion. No wonder, English food being what it was.

The only good feature of the flat was the stairwell down to the shop. It didn't go anywhere because of the locked door at the bottom. Marika kept her toys there, a doll on each stair tread. But Katalin liked to lean on the door and read. It was the only place where she didn't feel like crying or kicking her sister.

Often she went down there to think, or to do the number puzzles Papa set for her, which he called magic squares. She didn't feel real in England. The puzzles made her feel – not real – but safe. They gave her a sense of order. When he first showed her how they worked it did seem like magic, but now she knew it was logic.

'It stops the world,' Papa told her. 'Gives you focus. Keeps your head down, if that's what's required. And it often is.'

Katalin could imagine Papa doing the puzzles in shop doorways or cafés, looking casual, concentrating. She knew not to ask what he did, apart from being a journalist, but she knew it was often dangerous. But that was then, in Budapest, where most activities were dangerous, and people you thought you could trust changed or disappeared almost daily. She never felt disorientated by those conditions in Pest, but here she was disorientated all the time.

She needed to start thinking ahead. She and Marika were soon due to start at the school down the road. It looked rough, a place to be avoided. She must make a plan. That's what she was doing on one particular morning. She was up before Papa, but he didn't even glance down the stairs and went off to work without noticing her. He'd got a job in a warehouse and his shift started early.

She could hear them opening up in the shop. Always bad-tempered, they were. She wanted to bang on the door to shut them up. But she got interrupted anyway by a voice from the top of the stairs.

'You're not to go without me.'

Marika was standing there clutching her teddy bear by its neck. How did she know?

'Go where?'

'Back to Vienna. To stay with Aunt Júlia, 'cos we can't go back home. You're plotting.'

'Rubbish, of course I'm not.'

'Oh yes, you are. I can hear your brain go click, click, click.'

How could Marika possibly know? She was right of course. Ever since Uncle Fritz took them all to the ballet at the Vienna State Opera House Katalin had wanted to go back. It was magnificent, magical… Words weren't good enough. She wanted to *be* the prima ballerina being showered with single roses to thunderous applause at the front of the stage. She had to find a way… Surely Uncle Fritz would understand.

'I don't know what you're talking about.' Katalin shivered and ran upstairs to get dressed. But when she tried to get by, she was blocked by Marika's solid little body.

'If we go anywhere, we go together, right?' Marika pushed her pug nose up into Katalin's face and wouldn't let her past until she promised.

As it happened, they did go somewhere and they did go together, but it was none of Katalin's doing.

8

Katalin was watching and listening. She had been doing that a lot since she and Marika had arrived in this place, practising what Papa had taught her at home – home meaning Budapest, not London. 'When you're in a public place,' he'd told her, 'become invisible. Imagine you are a red coat with a dull lining. Fold yourself inside out, so that only the grey fabric shows. Nobody notices you, but you notice everything. Senses are on high alert, absorbing what's happening around you. Gathering information.' Katalin was doing just that, with her eyes on the floor.

They were supposed to think themselves lucky to be here at the Priory Academy for Girls – a "public" school, which in England meant private and privileged. It was certainly better than the state school in London, which they had only attended for the summer term. Apparently some benefactor was paying for them to have this opportunity. Marika didn't think they were lucky. She'd had a tantrum when Mama said they had to go. Katalin wasn't yet sure whether they were lucky or not.

They'd been told to wait on these chairs to see the housemistress. The hall smelled of polish, which Katalin liked, and she could see a carpet on the floor of the room opposite where the door stood open. Katalin was practising, 'Good morning, Miss Morrison,' in her mind.

They'd had to wait on the station platform too, when they arrived from Paddington. Nobody was there to meet them, just a great brick mausoleum crouched like a monster alongside the railway, looming over them. Was it a madhouse or a prison? Whatever it was, it was not welcoming. Then this large, homely woman had arrived in a little green car. She was full of apologies for being late and told them the monster building was the main school – where they would go for lessons. She was Miss Morrison and she'd driven them here, to Hill House.

Katalin fingered her unfamiliar ponytail. The rules said that all hair had to be "off the collar", and Matron had provided a packet of rubber bands. She looked sideways at Marika and gave her a sharp nudge because she was picking at her blackheads again. Always picking at something – her nose, her spots, a scab on her knee. Marika shoved back so hard that Katalin nearly fell off her chair.

She heard steps on the stairs beside them so she looked down at the floor and froze. A pair of brown leather button shoes, identical to her own, stopped in front of her. She reminded herself she was in England now and looked up. She was tall, this girl who stood so arrogantly before her: long red hair tied back; creamy skin; one hand on her hip.

She said something which Katalin didn't understand. Not that she spoke fast. It was her accent. That, and the way she looked down her long nose, which was enough to make Katalin forget her English and feel angry.

But she said her polite good morning. The girl's reply was not polite. As if she was arguing with her already. She asked another question, which Katalin didn't understand because of that snooty accent.

'What – are – your – names? *Comment vous appellez-vous?*'

The girl must think her stupid. 'I am called Katalin. This, my sister…'

Marika cut rudely across her, smiling at this girl as if she were the Queen of Sheba.

Katalin was saved when Miss Morrison called them into her study. 'Ah, making friends already, I see. Thank you, Amanda. Come on in girls.' Miss Morrison was about to close her door when she whipped it open again. 'And you can go round by the back stairs, Amanda Maitland-Jones!'

'Yes, Miss Morrison.'

She'd ticked the girl off quite sharply. It was not clear what she'd done wrong, but Katalin was pleased to know her name.

Patty Allen was feeling homesick and missing her golden retriever. Bracken was arthritic and Patty worried that her mother wouldn't give the old dog enough attention. Her friend Lizzie hadn't yet arrived, so Patty wandered into Amanda's dorm. How come Amanda's regulation underwear, laid out on the bed, managed to look so sophisticated?

'Well, well! Did you ever?' Amanda rushed in, giggling. 'Guess what? I've just seen some new girls in the hall! They've just gone in to see Mo, in her study.'

Amanda made herself tall and narrow by stretching up and pulling in her elbows. Then she puckered her mouth and stiffly extended a hand. 'I am called Katalin,' she mimicked in a strangled voice. Amanda collapsed onto her bed, doubled over with laughter.

'Golly, they *are* an odd-looking couple. Beauty and the Beast. That's it! That's what they shall be called. But even Beauty isn't very. Beautiful I mean. She's got a neck like a giraffe. And not the brightest. I mean, everyone speaks English, don't they?'

'Where are they from?'

'How should I know? Goodness only knows what they're doing here. It was lucky the Katalin person wasn't standing up. I think she might have curtsied and then I would have wet myself.'

Typical Amanda, imagining people might want to curtsey to her. She would show the poor new girls round and boss them about until she got bored.

'The other one, the one with the funny name, my God, she's an ugly cow – those dreadful blackheads.'

Amanda was now head-down in the bottom of her trunk, scooping out the last items.

'At last.' She dropped a pair of black plimsolls on the floor and held up a tin. 'Toffees. I was beginning to think Mummy had forgotten to pack them.' She prised off the lid. 'Want one, Patty?'

They each unwrapped a toffee and munched.

Amanda closed her trunk and hauled it into the corridor. 'Wait till I tell Ena about these two. Where's Ena? You haven't seen her have you?'

Patty shook her head. She hadn't seen Ena although she had spotted the Foleys' Daimler in the drive. She didn't mention it. She was enjoying having Amanda to herself.

'Wonder which dorm they're in. They could really be quite amusing. Do us a favour Patty? Run along and see if Ena's around, while I get my stuff ready for checking.'

In the doorway, Patty bumped right into Ena who ignored her and rushed at Amanda. They both started on about dances they'd been to and some boy called Piers. Ena gave Patty a look and started whispering, so Patty went off to her own dorm to unpack.

At supper the two new girls were seated on either side of Matron who made the classic mistake: the less they understood, the more loudly she spoke. Amanda had exaggerated, of course. They looked quite normal.

Katalin picked at her food, sitting straight and still as if she didn't want to touch her neighbour or the table. Her sister put her elbows on the table, as if protecting her plate from thieves, and ate like a pig, although, as Amanda said, that was unfair on pigs. Matron fingered the wisps of grey hair escaping from her skinny bun, and went through a crazy mime to demonstrate that elbows were not allowed. She even repeated the feeble joke about the only joints on the table being for carving. But the girl looked at her as if she was off her head and took no notice whatsoever. By the end of the meal Matron had a bright pink spot on each thin-veined cheek.

Patty hardly saw the sisters for the next two days, what with settling in and working out her rota of who she was going to walk to lessons with each day. It was a painfully long distance from Hill House to the main college if you were with someone you didn't get on with. She didn't get Amanda on her list at all, which was boring. But she got Lizzie twice, and only Brenda Levy one way on Thursdays. Patty was always scared Brenda would be in one of her terrible moods. When she set off with Lizzie on Monday they were so busy catching up that she forgot her PE kit and had to run back for it.

Which was how Patty came to see the face at the window. A little kid. Probably with one of the cleaners. The girl was biting on a finger and sooty curls stuck to her cheeks as if she'd been crying. Huge dark eyes seemed to take up all of her face. Then she jumped and half turned as Matron appeared behind her. The finger came out of her mouth and the weirdest thing happened. Her face seemed to turn inside out and it wasn't a child's face at all. It was the younger of the new girls. The one Amanda called the Beast. They'd had to stay back from lessons for a medical check because they were refugees or something.

Patty waved, but the girl made a face, screwing up her nose and sticking out her tongue. Patty laughed, rushed inside to the cloakrooms to fetch the PE kit and raced off to catch up with Lizzie and the others. Once or twice during the week she noticed the girl at mealtimes. Every time their eyes met the girl made a rude face. It got to be a joke between them.

She didn't look anything like her sister. The older one was pale as glass and flat like a playing card. She reminded Patty of the new fridge they'd got in the holidays: tall and elegant with this cool green inside. *Eau-de-nil*, her mum called it. It made ice cubes and Patty found herself wondering if Katalin made ice cubes. She looked as if she washed her hands before and after doing just about everything.

The dark one was plump and messy and had a temper.

'The new kid bites,' said Lizzie who was head of the sisters' dormitory. She showed Patty the marks on her arm. 'Honestly! Just because I woke her up! I mean, the bell had gone and she was going to be late for breakfast.'

'Doesn't her sister sort her out?'

'No, she's always tidying the top of her chest of drawers. Bit weird. Then Marika jogs it, accidentally on purpose, and Katalin gets in a terrible bate. Nobody understands what they say, but they obviously hate each other.'

Katalin was brainy. She was in Amanda's year and in the top set for most subjects, like Amanda. Everyone said the younger sister was a dimwit. But how could they tell when her English was so bad? They'd put her in the bottom set for everything, so Patty didn't see her in class although they were in the same year.

On Saturday Patty ended up at shoe-cleaning with her. The girl pointed to the name on Patty's locker and said, 'Potty.'

Patty shook her head. 'No! It's pronounced "Patty". You're Marika, aren't you?'

Patty pronounced it *Mareeka*, like she'd heard it all week from other people, mostly Lizzie and Matron.

Marika snarled and stamped her foot. 'Maarika,' she almost screamed.

Everyone turned round to watch. Patty heard Matron start, 'Now, Mareeka…'

Patty suddenly understood the problem. So she faced up to Marika, stamped her foot and yelled, 'Patty!' back at her. Then she added, 'Maarika.'

They both laughed. It was the first time she'd seen the girl smile properly. The amazing eyes came alive. Everyone started talking again and Patty noticed Katalin giving her an odd look. Hostile, as if Patty had nabbed something of hers.

Patty spread out the newspaper and showed Marika what to do. Evidently she'd never cleaned a pair of shoes in her life. She sniffed the polish and made a face like it was dog poo. Which was rich because Marika was smelly. It was like her skin sweated old onions and her breath was as bad as dear old Bracken's. Honestly, it was no wonder Marika was unpopular. Lizzie had mentioned it more than once. She couldn't get her to strip-wash properly. It was difficult to know what someone was doing behind a dressing gown, but Lizzie was sure no soap was getting to the bits that mattered, plus the water was still clear when Marika emptied her bowl into the slop bucket.

She was messing about now, putting her hands inside the lace-ups and walking them up and down and tearing the newspaper.

'You clot!' said Patty. 'You've got polish all over you. Don't let Matron see.'

Lizzie caught up with Patty as they all trooped through to the common room.

'Watch out, Patty. You don't want to get landed with her.'

'Why not?'

Lizzie shrugged. 'If you're so matey, maybe you can make her wash.'

Next day, Patty promised Marika her spare deodorant on condition she got up at the bell and washed herself. Marika fell about laughing when Patty put on her dressing gown and demonstrated – an elaborate mime of soaping a flannel and scrubbing away down there. Marika wanted her "Mum Rollette" but she wasn't giving her that.

Katalin walked in and rolled her eyes. 'My little sister, she is actor. She pretend, so you be her friend and give her things. And clean shoes.' Katalin did a fancy little twirl. 'Papa always clean shoes. She is lazy cow.'

Marika went to shove her, but Katalin sidestepped out of the door. Patty watched her snake off with that strange sinuous walk which would be graceful if it weren't so self-conscious. What a strange pair they were.

Marika sulked about that deodorant and wouldn't speak to Patty for days.

Then Patty got a letter from home. Her mother wrote that they'd had to put Bracken down. She couldn't go on reading. She didn't cry because she refused to believe it. She put the letter away and told no one.

Marika came up to her at break. Patty thought she was after her bun because it was Thursday doughnuts, and everyone knew Patty hated them. Tuesday and Wednesday were the decent buns – the ones with icing and Chelsea buns. Doughnuts were Marika's favourites – all that grease and sugar to feed the blackheads.

But now Marika said, 'You sad. What happen?'

'How do you know?' Patty didn't even know herself, not really.

'You in black cloud.' Marika circled her arms. 'I see it round you. Why?'

'Nothing,' Patty said and burst into tears.

'Cry is good. You lose friend?'

Patty told her about Bracken. 'It was only a dog.'

'Dog is friend.'

Patty nodded.

'You lose dog. I lose home. Dog is worse.'

9

It was in the spring term of 1958 that Katalin clashed with Brenda Levy. It all began after hair-washing. Patty saw the whole episode.

Brenda was a force to be reckoned with. She had what everyone called a screw loose, but at some level she knew about this loose screw, which made her sensitive about anybody apparently showing her a lack of respect. Brenda was heavy, and strong with it. She could be useful in a lacrosse match, thundering down the wing and slamming in a goal. The look of terror on the goalie's face was something to see. Often, the ball had to be dug out of the mud. Sometimes Brenda lost it completely and it took three staff and a couple of prefects to hold her down until she'd had an injection. Brenda would be sheepish afterwards and apologise. 'Had to have one of my little rests,' she would say.

Brenda had taken against Katalin. It was all about the way she stood with her head held high – looking down her nose, as Brenda put it. This evening, after hair-washing, Katalin had a towel round her head, piled up like a turban. She was holding herself especially upright in order to keep the towel in place, so the haughty look was exaggerated.

Brenda started with, 'Here comes the Queen of Sheba', which anyone might have said, but Katalin took it badly and pushed past Brenda. Next, they were on the floor and Marika piled in to pull Brenda off her sister. Brenda's nose was bleeding when Matron came in, and Marika was the one who ended up being sent to Mo.

A week later somebody asked Katalin, quite innocently, why she had left Budapest. Brenda repeated the question in the tone of voice that said she should go right back there. Patty could see where this conversation might go.

'We were refugees,' said Katalin.

'Go on, then, refugee,' Brenda said, managing to put a powerful sneer on the "ee" of "refugee". Sometimes, when Brenda gave that sneer, she could be diverted into her Elvis impression. She'd slick back her hair and clown her big frame into

"Jailhouse Rock", complete with gestures and hip-thrusting. Everyone would be nearly wetting themselves. But on this occasion, Brenda was not about to turn entertainer.

'It was the time of the student revolution, what they call the Uprising,' said Katalin.

Brenda curled her lip. 'So, you left because someone rose up? Got to their feet?'

There was a general titter. Patty saw Marika trying to catch Katalin's eye. But Kati wasn't a good judge of a situation. She didn't twig that Marika was warning her and continued to glare at Brenda.

'They stood up for themselves,' she said. 'All these students doing peaceful protest. And the Communists shot them.'

There was a gasp from a few people, but Brenda still had her sneery look.

'They shot into the crowd. Innocent people. Then many tank come and destroy our city. Buildings all broken. Dead people everywhere. Books burning in the street. Body hanging from lamp post.'

Katalin's voice cracked. Brenda was clearly taken aback, but she wasn't about to climb down.

'You don't expect us to believe that. It isn't the Middle Ages.'

There was a general murmur of relief, as if several people didn't want to believe it either. Katalin burst into tears. Amanda went to put an arm round her, but she shrugged her off and stormed out of the room. Marika was about to follow when Brenda started up again.

'Or then again, maybe the Hungarians are just savages. After all, we do know at least one of them who has a savage temper.'

Marika flew off the handle. She lunged at Brenda screaming, 'Hungarian very civilised, is cultured people!'

There was a roar of laughter. Amanda and Patty pulled them apart, but not before Marika had a black eye. Both she and Brenda were sent to bed.

Mo had the sisters in for a talk next day. Marika said she should get Brenda in to apologise. Katalin laughed. That was never going to happen.

'You have to make allowances for Brenda,' said Mo. For once she wasn't meeting their eyes. She was looking into the garden. 'She has a difficult condition. And I'm sure you realise she is Jewish.'

Of course they did. There were a lot of Jewish pupils – lucky so-and-sos who didn't have to attend prayers or go to church like everyone else.

'We have to remember, the Jews had a bad time in the war, under the Nazis.'

'So did we,' said Katalin, quick as a flash.

'But you are not Jewish,' said Mo quietly.

'Then we had the Communists. They were just as bad. That is why we are refugees. We—'

'I know, Katalin. I know. But the Communists did not have the gas chambers.'

'But, Miss—'

'The trouble is, Katalin, Marika,' and here she looked straight at each of them in turn, 'the trouble is, what happened in your country is not widely known. People *do* know about what happened in Germany. You are in a minority and—'

'The Jews are rich and powerful.'

'That is an unwise remark, Katalin. It comes across as prejudice. We do not have anti-Semitism here.'

Not with all those rich Jewish families paying school fees, thought Katalin, noticing that Mo hadn't contradicted her. She had nothing against Jews, apart from Brenda, and she was sure Mo didn't either. Mo wasn't a judging kind of person.

'It's not fair,' said Marika. 'Why they pick on us? They don't pick on Farida for being black or Wai-Pin for the slanty eye.'

Mo's eyebrows shot up. 'I suppose it's because you are new.' With more emphasis she added, 'And Farida and Wai-Pin conform. They fit in. The rules are the rules. Think about that.'

'But Miss—'

'That will be all, girls.' Mo stood up and opened the door.

'You heard what she said,' said Katalin when they were outside. 'Obey the rules. Don't ask why all the time.'

'But it's so unfair! Wait till I get that Brenda!'

'Don't you dare. Don't poke your nose in. You "mind your beeswax", as they say here. You give us a bad name, with your temper. You're as bad as she is.' Katalin turned away and stalked off.

Marika stuck her tongue out at her back and called after her. 'I only do it for you, Kati!'

Matron appeared. 'What's that naughty tongue doing? And remember, we have a rule. No Hungarian. How will you ever improve your English?' She raised her voice. 'And that goes for you too, Katalin.'

There were two aspects of school life which inclined Katalin to agree with Marika – that they were unlucky to be in this place. The first was the humiliation of lacrosse, which was taken by Miss Shipman.

'Cradle, cradle, cradle! Hold it *close!* Don't flop about. You are not an octopus.'

'Yes, Miss Shipman. No, Miss Shipman.'

'And what is it you are trying to do?' Miss Shipman was leaning forward, smiling, like a friend inviting a confidence. Cornflower-blue eyes, so disarming in a taut, tanned face. Trust me, said the starburst of wrinkles around each eye. You could almost be fooled.

'Shoot a goal, Miss Shipman.'

'And so, where would you aim the ball?'

'Into the goal, Miss Shipman.'

'And will you aim high? So that Alexandra can catch it?'

'No, Miss Shipman. Aim low, into the corner of the net.'

'Go do it, then.'

Miss Shipman retreated to the sidelines, like a benevolent spider who had decided not to eat the fly just yet. She gave a short blast on her whistle. Katalin had one more chance.

'Cradle! Keep it tight. Good. Dodge! Good. Now twist and flick! Reach up! And… Down!'

The ball rocketed out of the top of Katalin's net before she could direct the damn stick downward. It was in Alexandra's control and away upfield before Katalin had time to turn round. The whistle sounded.

Miss Shipman moved in for the kill. '*Where* did you say you were planning to aim that ball?'

Katalin had heard it all before. How she was fast, how she was agile and accurate in the gymnasium, but could not get a small ball into a huge net with a lacrosse stick. Her penalty was to swap with the goalie. Why couldn't she be like Amanda? She was swift and neat, flicking the ball with precision past her opponent and into the corner of the goal. Miss Shipman stalked off to give hell to the players on the other side of the hedge.

The hedge, though bare of leaves, was thick with brambles. Even Shipman's X-ray eyes couldn't see through that. When the attackers bore down on her, Katalin ran round to the back of the goal. Her defending teammates howled with indignation. She shrugged. That bullet of a ball could break your nose or take your teeth out. What idiot would just stand there to get black and blue?

The second disaster area was a missing activity. There was no dancing in this barbaric place. Only the sixth-formers were taught to dance – if you could call it that. Katalin had peeked through the double doors of the assembly hall. It would have been funny if it hadn't been called dancing; all those girls in clumpy shoes stumbling about to Victor Sylvester and his ballroom orchestra. They were preparing for May balls, but the tall ones had to dance the man's part, which wasn't going to help them one bit. Miss Perceval swooped about yelling, 'One-two-three, one-two-three', and picking up the hairpins which fell out of her bun. Miss Perceval taught piano and couldn't hold a tune. She was a joke, which said everything about the value placed on dancing by the Priory Academy for Girls.

When it was PE, Katalin always got to the gym first and used the wall bars as a barre. She'd get in some pliés, some battements and an arabesque to each side before the others arrived. They would snigger, 'There goes Katalin. She doesn't half fancy herself!'

Miss Yates, the gym mistress, kept Katalin back at the end of a lesson.

'Have you heard of the Royal Ballet School? Covent Garden?' She gave her a magazine. 'You might enjoy reading this.'

Miss Yates didn't know what she started. She'd given Katalin a dream. Each night in bed she clutched the mannequin under her pillow and thought about going to the Royal Ballet School.

It was a Saturday afternoon in the summer term of 1959 and they were having what was called a heatwave. Which meant it was like real summer at last. They were all back from Walks and were allowed in the garden because it was boiling in the common room.

But Miss Morrison called Katalin back inside. Mo was wearing her usual suit as if it were still winter.

'Ah, Katalin. Come. I need to have a word with you.'

Mo closed the door to her study and sat down behind the desk.

'It's a pity you two sisters don't seem to get on.'

Katalin resisted saying that she had never asked to have a sister.

'But then you are not your sister's keeper.' Mo gave a little laugh as if she'd made a joke.

Katalin waited. Usually she liked Mo. She was a safe kind of person, but today she was making her uneasy.

'You two have been here some time.' Mo sighed as if she thought they'd been there quite long enough. 'Nearly two years, in fact.'

Was she going to send them home again? To that pokey flat and the horrors of the rough school down the road?

'Sit down, Katalin, sit down. You're looking a bit pale.' Mo shuffled a pile of papers. 'Katalin, you are fifteen, old enough to go up to the main school in the autumn. To live, I mean. You have heard of School House, I'm sure.'

Only the dregs went up to School House. That's what Ena Foley said.

'Normally we would keep a girl of your calibre...'

Katalin frowned.

'Meaning, you are intelligent, responsible, sensible. In other circumstances we would keep you here for a year to stay on and run Hill House as a prefect. You would be an asset.'

That would be nice. Those girls had their own sitting room. She'd get away from Marika. The prefects used the door of that room to emphasise their privilege and power. They closed it firmly for privacy. They opened it wide enough on a winter Sunday for the glow of the gas fire to be glimpsed, and for the smell of toasted marshmallows to waft along the corridor. If someone came knocking they were kept waiting.

Yes, she would like that. It would depend who the others were, of course. But Amanda, for sure. She had calibre. She was in control. Even after games her blouse would still be neatly tucked in to the brown shorts, their box pleats swinging, mud-free, the regulation three inches above unscathed knees. No strand of red hair escaping her ponytail.

'However,' Mo was saying, 'I have observed that relations between you and your sister have not improved over time. I have come to the conclusion that you would benefit from having separate territory. So, Katalin, you will be going up to the main school, to School House.'

She'd lose Amanda. Ena would gloat. She was always saying, 'Three's a crowd.' They'd swan about being prefects without her.

'You understand it is no reflection of your behaviour.'

How was she to tell people? It would be a disgrace, humiliating. She tried to breathe and choked on the stifling air. Mo was pulling the rug from under her, sending her away to a new place, a new set of rules. And it was all Marika's fault. She felt sick.

'My dear child. You're white as a sheet. I hope you aren't upset by what I've said.'

She shook her head. 'The sun. It's my head. I think I have a migraine.'

That magic word, which got you to lie down in a darkened room.

'I'll call Matron. She'll put you in the sickroom for an hour or two.'

Mo strode to the door and called up the stairs, 'Mrs Ray! Mrs Ray, you have a young patient down here.'

10

Patty cornered Amanda one day at break at the beginning of the autumn term.

'You'll never guess what I caught Marika doing!'

Amanda shrugged.

'This morning. In Bathroom 3. She was washing her ST in the basin! Her *used* ST. Blood everywhere.'

Amanda gawped. 'But that's where we get our hair washed.'

'Exactly.'

'But why?'

'She only just started,' said Patty. 'The curse, I mean. She thought it was normal. Where they come from they couldn't always get STs. Her mother had to cut up old sheets. Imagine! Poor thing! She thought the packet of towels from Matron was for the year.'

'God, that's *so* disgusting! I hope you told her…'

'You bet. I suppose there's no one else to explain to her – now Katalin's gone up to School House.'

Amanda smirked. 'Mind you, Katalin might be too clean to bleed.'

The incident set Patty wondering why she stuck with Marika as a friend. She was still unpopular even after two years at the school, and Patty felt sorry for her. She'd even got her parents to agree to invite Marika on a weekend exeat. ('A refugee, that's interesting, dear.') They would have a picnic by the river and dinner at the Abbey Hotel. Marika had written home and a letter had come back giving permission. Marika kept saying it would be the biggest treat she'd had since her Aunt Júlia had taken her shopping in Vienna.

Mo warned Marika, 'Keep your nose clean', which meant no fighting.

Shortly before her parents' visit, Patty noticed that Brenda and Marika were sitting on either side of Matron at supper. Matron looked quite nervous, as if she might be called upon to act as referee. The red patches on her cheeks were very noticeable. Patty found she was quite anxious herself as she watched from further down the table.

It was Queen of Puddings that day. Marika's favourite. Most people's favourite. Being next to Matron, she and Brenda would get first chance at seconds. There was only a small portion left, too small to divide. Matron offered it to Brenda first. But, to Patty's amazement, Brenda refused. Matron scooped it into Marika's dish, Brenda looked across and winked. She must be up to something. The spots on Matron's cheeks deepened.

In the common room, when she and Marika bagged the sofa to watch *77 Sunset Strip*, Brenda joined them. She handed round a bag of mint humbugs and included Marika. Not many people did that.

Then Brenda leaned in and whispered, 'Those things your sister talked about – the bodies and the blood and the tanks and everything – did you see those too?'

She had a weird gleam in her eye as if she were getting a kick out of the horror. It gave Patty the shivers.

'No, I didn't see. Poor Kati, she—'

'So, she could have been making it up?'

Marika was indignant. 'No! She wouldn't do that. Anyway, why would she?'

'Get attention. Get sympathy. You two don't get a lot of that, do you?'

Patty didn't like Brenda's manner, but Marika seemed relaxed.

'I tell you, it's true. It happened,' said Marika.

'In that case, why didn't you see it?'

'Because me and Mama left before. We couldn't all—'

'Oh, "Mama" is it? So, you and "Mama" left before the violence. But why did you leave? That doesn't sound like refugees, as such.'

Brenda was talking in a normal voice now and other girls were listening. Patty watched Marika closely.

'My father was wanted. He's a journalist. He wrote for the underground paper. He'd written a play—'

'Oh, a play. Hey, girls, Marika's father wrote a play. That's dangerous. He'd be persecuted for that.'

'Yes, actually, he would. He—' Marika was getting red in the face.

Brenda laughed. 'A little pen-pushing newspaper man? Or is he famous, your father?'

Patty nudged her friend. 'Don't rise to it,' she muttered. 'Remember what Mo said.'

'No, he not famous, but...' Marika took a deep breath. Patty shot her a warning glance. She closed her mouth.

'You see, you can't contradict me, can you?' Brenda curled her lip. 'See folks? They were just cowards escaping before the trouble started. If there *was* any trouble. So you could come here and come to a posh school and take advantage.'

Marika's hand flew out and smashed into Brenda's face.

Patty leapt up to drag her away. But it was too late. Brenda was on her and they were wrestling on the floor. A deep bellow came from the doorway. It was Mo.

'*What* is going on here?'

A clear voice spoke from the back of the room. 'It wasn't Marika's fault, Miss Morrison. She was being baited. And Brenda was talking though the back of her head. Of course writers are persecuted. Of course they are dangerous. Look at McCarthyism. Look at Arthur Miller and *The Crucible*. And that's America, so-called land of the free. And, of course, the Nazis burned books.'

It was Ruth Goldsmith. Shy, clever Ruth, who came top in all the top divisions, was defending Marika. It certainly took Brenda aback. Everyone respected Ruth. She would always win an argument.

Mo look mystified. 'Be that as it may. The details will have to wait,' she said. 'What is absolutely clear, is that neither Marika nor Brenda will be going on exeat this weekend. You are thirteen, nearly fourteen now. Old enough to know better. The rules are the rules and this fighting must stop.'

Patty said there would be another time, but Marika was inconsolable. Through sobs, she tried to explain.

'I meant to keep calm. But saying that about Papa. I think of him slaving in that warehouse – he saving up for a flat with a proper bathroom. And Mama…' Marika burst into tears all over again. 'She – she hate to clean at the pub down the road. I so mad. I see red. I hate that Brenda.'

Patty was amazed. Maybe it was just as well Marika was missing the exeat. Mummy and Daddy wouldn't consider Marika a suitable friend. Mummy had never worked. And a cleaner! Her parents never visited a pub even to buy a drink. As to the bit about the bathroom – what did she mean? And what did "refugee" actually mean? Her parents knew some Russians, but he was a count so that was different. She'd get Daddy to buy Marika a box of Cadbury's Milk Tray to make up for it.

Brenda's parents turned up anyway. Mr Levy ranted at Mo in the hall and threatened to call the police if she didn't let him take his own daughter out. What was Mo to do?

It was in the summer term that Patty discovered that Marika was religious. They each had a verruca and were sent to the chiropodist to have them cut out. The chiropodist was a witch of a woman who butchered feet. It hurt to walk the mile back to Hill House, socks slipping in blood-filled shoes. When Marika stopped at a church and said she was going inside, Patty was glad of the rest.

When Marika opened the door Patty was astonished at the dazzle of light. It was clear from the way Marika reached her fingers into the holy water that she'd been there before. When? How did she know about it? As Marika crossed herself and made a deep genuflection, Patty turned away in Anglican embarrassment. So people really did do that stuff.

Marika read her thoughts. 'You don't do it in your church. You have no respect.'

No wonder Marika had been in her element during the confirmation frenzy. But everyone got religion at that time, so she hadn't stood out. They'd all gone weak at the knees for Jesus, swapping confirmation cards with white doves and blue-draped Madonnas. Amanda and Ena had argued about whose crucifix was best. Should the cross be plain or complete with the crucified body? These trappings were all very un-C of E – and quintessentially Roman Catholic – Patty now realised.

Marika disappeared into a side chapel and Patty was left gazing at white walls, white pillars, gold columns and clear glass windows streaming with sunshine. Nothing could be more different from the sombre grey interiors of every church she'd ever known. What would her Methodist grandmother say?

The music in the abbey on Sundays did affect her, she had to admit. There were times when clarinet music soared to the vaulted roof and she felt something like bliss. But the bliss was quickly extinguished when the service started: the fat surplices intoning dark songs; the self-righteous hymns; the beetle-browed sermons, preaching an exclusive heaven.

She could see Marika on her knees, head bowed, in the Lady Chapel and sat down to rest her poor foot. Marika soon joined her.

'He not here today.'

'Who?'

'There is young priest. Very handsome.' She grinned. 'I talk to him. Make my confession.'

When Patty asked if Hungary was a Roman Catholic country, Marika said, yes and no, it wasn't straightforward. The family was Roman Catholic, but they couldn't practise openly. Marika had taken her first communion at a secret ceremony in a cellar.

Patty frowned. 'But Katalin was confirmed into the Church of England.'

Marika shrugged. 'We have to be religious chameleon.'

She was clearly pleased with herself for using the word "chameleon".

October was warm that year, but the rules insisted on winter uniform in the autumn term. The girls were buttoned and belted, laced and buckled into tweed and gabardine, leather and lisle for the steep walk up to church and for Walks.

Marika wasn't yet fourteen, but she was well-developed for her age and knew how to customise her uniform. With Katalin in School House there was no sister to restrain her.

'Is sexy,' she would say pulling her tie down and undoing the top two buttons of her blouse.

Patty's pet hates were the thick stockings but Marika just laughed.

'Stockings not nice. But suspender belt is super sexy. Boy like that.'

This seemed totally irrelevant to Patty as they never set eyes on anyone of the opposite sex, let alone spoke to them. But talking was not what Marika had in mind.

'We just go down this little path,' she said on their next walk. 'Is tree for shade.' She pointed at a stunted hawthorn. Patty followed, keen to get out of the sun.

As soon as they left the others, Marika loosened her hair and shook it out.

'Hair is sexy,' she said.

Two lads appeared out of nowhere. Marika was obviously expecting them. Before Patty could take in what was happening Marika was down in the grass behind a boulder and the better-looking lad was grabbing her and kissing her.

'Come *on*, Patty! Get down! They see us.'

Patty certainly didn't want the others to see. She flumped down with her back against the thorn tree. The other boy joined her and made a grab for her hand. She pulled it away and looked across at Marika. The boy's hand was up her skirt, exposing her suspenders and she was writhing about. Horrible. Patty scrambled to her feet.

'Come on, Marika. I'm going back. You'd better come.' Her whole body burned as she waited for a response.

The boy under the tree guffawed and Patty felt the sweat running down inside her dress. She heard her name being called.

'Patty! Patty! We're going back down. Where have you got to?'

'I'm going,' she hissed at Marika. 'That's Lizzie. She'll come looking.'

She ran down the path to Lizzie.

'What's up? You okay? You look—'

'I'm fine.'

Lizzie persisted. 'Where's that Marika? She's up to something. What's going on, Patty?'

'She'll catch up. She's having a wee.'

Marika reappeared when they were half way down the hill. She was flushed and had grass in her hair. Looks flew round the group.

'What have you been doing?'

'I lie down. I fall asleep.'

'You've been with those boys I saw,' said Lizzie. 'You have, haven't you? Hasn't she, Patty? Is that where you were?'

There followed a chorus of 'What boys?' 'What did you do?' as well as 'Slag' and 'Slut'. Patty cringed. What would her parents say? She so wished Marika was not her friend.

She didn't have to worry for long.

As soon as the others had changed their shoes and left the cloakrooms, Marika pinned her against the lockers.

'Why you leave me? You no friend! I could be raped! You leave me with two boy.'

'You never asked me! I never wanted... Who were they? Why go with them at all?'

Marika ignored Patty's questions. 'I not cheap.'

'Aren't you? You go with any old boy you never met before, and you say that's not—'

'I not let him put it in. I not stupid. I never... I only do snog.'

'Oh, so that's all right, then. To snog every Tom, Dick and Harry...'

'I try to give you some fun. You too straight-buttoned. You always so studying, is boring. Sex is fun.'

'Then you can keep your fun!'

Patty summoned her fury and shoved Marika in the chest. It was very satisfying. Marika was taken by surprise and it sent her flying to the other side of the cloakroom where she sat down heavily with a yell. With a huge sense of relief, Patty stomped off to find Lizzie.

11

Katalin was in her second term in School House. She rarely saw her sister, which was an improvement. But there was still a void where dancing should have been – a vacuum she filled with the dream of going to the Royal Ballet School.

She was nearly sixteen. Was it too late to turn the dream into reality? She would approach the benefactor with a proposition. If he was prepared to spend a fortune on school fees for this place, why not spend his money sending her to ballet school and get the reward of her becoming famous? The problem was that letters – meek little thank you notes – went via Miss Hodges, the headmistress, who would not approve of her plan.

She was despairing of discovering the benefactor's address, when the answer was handed to her on a plate. Her dream must be meant to come true.

She was sent to Miss Hodges with a message from Miss Yates.

'Such a coincidence, Katalin,' said Miss Hodges, smoothing a sheet of handwritten paper on the desk in front of her. 'A coincidence that you should come to me today. I have just received a charming letter from your benefactor. She is pleased with the progress report I sent and would like to offer you the opportunity to take piano lessons.'

So the benefactor was female. But piano lessons. Pooh. Now, if that had been dancing lessons. But none were available.

Katalin tried to look pleased. 'May I know the name of the benefactor? I could write to thank—'

'You may bring the letter to me and I will forward it,' said Miss Hodges, addressing the picture beyond Katalin's left shoulder. 'As you well know, benefactors prefer to remain anonymous. It is normal procedure.'

At that moment the telephone rang and Miss Hodges turned aside to answer it. Katalin craned forward to see the letter. It was written on headed notepaper in a strong flowing hand. It was hard to read the address upside down: 8 Cavendish Garden Crescent, London. There were letters for the area, but Miss Hodges intervened.

'Katalin!' She had her hand over the mouthpiece of the telephone. 'That's enough sneaking. Off you go back to class!'

'Sorry, Miss Hodges. Yes, Miss Hodges.' Katalin was careful not to skip out the door.

She had what she needed. No name, but she now knew the benefactor was a lady. With notepaper like that she might even be a Lady.

She took her writing paper up to her secret place on the roof. It meant climbing through the window of a disused music room on the fifth floor. She set her mannequin in first position on the ledge beside her and began, "Dear Madam". She aimed for a balance of buttering up and logical argument, plus an English idiom or two with one word deliberately wrong. Enough to remind the lady that she was succeeding at being a genius in a language not her own. Not that she used the word genius. The English didn't like you to blow your own trombone.

There was a breeze up on the roof and she was reluctant to go back down. She pushed off from the chimney stack, shuffled on her bottom down to the parapet and peered over at girls crossing the quad far below. She couldn't recognise anyone. It was like the view when they came in to land at Heathrow – cars creeping along and people doing ordinary stuff, unaware of the eyes in the sky watching them.

She rested her chin on the flat top of one of the crenellations. Imagine walking along them! Would people down there even notice her? She knew she could do it. She had perfect balance. But it would be foolish. The thought took her straight back to that day when they were little. The awful day when Marika nearly fell out of the apartment window and Mama wouldn't speak to her. She thought she'd left that incident behind. It had given her nightmares for weeks. The memory still made her feel sick.

She turned away from the edge of the roof and climbed back through the window. The table stacked with yellowing sheet music had to be pushed back against the wall as it was before. No one came in here, but you couldn't be too careful. Nobody knew about her secret hideout, not even Amanda. Not even Marika. Especially not Marika. Bother Marika.

She was supposed to look after Marika. They were supposed to be in it together. Mama would be horrified if she knew about her letter.

She shouldn't do it. She shouldn't abandon her. Mama would call her selfish, but Papa would not. He'd say something like, a man must do what a man must do. She was sure that went for a girl too.

'I have a secret,' she told Marika. 'You have to swear you won't tell. If you do, I'll tell Papa you sneaked. He hates a sneak. And I'll tell him about the things you get up to.'

'What things? You mean, getting reports for talking? For running? He would laugh at you, my prissy sister.'

'He wouldn't laugh about what you do up on the hills – with boys.'

'Papa wouldn't believe you. He doesn't trust you.'

'He does so. Don't talk rubbish. Anyway, we have to go to my secret place so no one will hear. After tea.'

'You mean your place on the roof through Room 91?'

How did she know? Marika must have been stalking her, a fact that helped to harden Katalin's heart.

On hearing the news, Marika threw herself at Katalin, whining that she could have her sweet ration for the next year if she didn't abandon her.

'Get off! Don't be stupid. One, my career is more important than sweets. Two, you always break your promises. Three, I don't like those sickly English sweets, anyway. Mars bars – yuk.' She pirouetted out of her sister's grasp. 'I have my destiny to follow'.

'Destiny, *Pestiny*! What about sisters? We are supposed to look after each other. Sisters love each other, don't they?'

'It's not like you *choose* your sister.'

Marika sheered away when she said that. Working up a tear, no doubt, rubbing her eyes. Then came a little voice, 'I'll miss you, Kati.'

It was almost like she meant it.

Marika turned round. She was really crying. 'You really mean it, don't you? You're really going. Don't leave me, Kati. Let me come with you.'

'You can't. I'm not running away. Like I said, I'm being transferred. It's not as if you're going to get into ballet school.'

Marika started howling then and she was afraid someone would hear. It sounded so loud on the still air.

'Don't be such a crybaby. Come on. We'll be late for prep.'

She bundled her sister towards the window. For once Marika didn't put up a fight. Her arms were hot and sticky and there was a big patch of sweat on the back of her dress. Inside the room she turned, suddenly her usual aggressive self.

'I hate you, beastly sister. I shall tell Mama, and she will come and get me.' She stamped her foot like a little kid and rushed ahead, down the stairs, making enough racket to alert Miss Williams, the housemistress of School House, who happened to be passing.

'Where have you been, Marika?' Katalin heard Latin-Willie say. 'You know quite well you're not allowed up there. Didn't you hear the bell for prep? Run along to your classroom. And blow your nose, child.'

Katalin waited, standing back out of sight at the top of the stairs until she heard Latin-Willie shuffling away down the corridor.

12

This was supposed to be my story, too. I was fourteen now, but so far I hadn't got to tell it because my bossy sister thought it was her story. Being in this school was lonely without Kati. You wouldn't think it would make that much difference. I mean, we didn't see much of each other when we were here together, what with school routines. But I always knew that if anything really bad happened, Kati would stick up for me, even if she put the boot in herself afterwards. She was a link, too. With home and with our language. She might have been a pain, but she was a comforting pain in this place where Hungary didn't exist.

The trouble was nobody liked me. Except Patty for a while. But she only *be*friended me. To befriend is different from to be friends. She did it because she thought she ought to. But Patty was better than no friend. Since the business with the boys she wouldn't even speak to me. She was best friends with Lizzie and they avoided me.

Even Mo gave up on me. She had me transferred to School House to take Kati's place. Something to do with numbers. I didn't believe a word of it, but it suited me. We had more freedom in School House. The rules were the same but it was easier to break them. There was no Matron patrolling the dorms and no prefects leading walks. Anyway, there was a new girl in my dorm called Angie, a pathetic creature with blonde curls. She was a bit of a drip, but I decided to befriend her.

In the middle of the summer term something happened that changed everything. It involved Brenda Levy. Brenda had a ready-made new victim in a girl called Sue Rees. Sue was tiny for her age, quick and wiry with a weasel face. You could imagine her as one of Fagin's urchins in *Oliver Twist*. Sue had taken to teasing Brenda and following her. If I'd been Brenda, I'd have wanted to kick out at this little terrier yapping at my ankles.

Brenda did better than that. Sue had been up to her usual tricks at break one Wednesday. After the next lesson period, Brenda managed to be behind Sue as everyone migrated between classrooms. I was coming down from the floor above, so I got a bird's eye view of the whole incident.

When Brenda got to the third floor landing she suddenly grabbed Sue from behind and lifted her clear over the balustrade so that her legs dangled into the stairwell. I thought how glad I was to be podgy for once. Brenda would never have been able to do that to me.

Sue screamed and the entire staircase, crowded with girls, fell silent. She was squirming like a fish on a hook.

'If you wriggle, I'll drop you,' said Brenda.

Sue squawked, but hung limp.

'Now, Brenda, bring her back over.' It was the calm voice of Miss Shipman who had appeared from the staffroom, alerted no doubt by the sudden eerie silence. At least this was someone Brenda respected. But Brenda made no response.

'Just bend your arms and bring her back.' Such a calm Miss Shipman, so unlike her style on the lacrosse pitch.

'They won't bend, Miss Shipman. They're locked.'

Sue started sobbing, gasping with the effort to keep still.

'Try again, Brenda.'

'They're wearing out, my arms are wearing out.' Brenda actually sounded distraught.

'Then just step back, Brenda. So that I can reach the child.'

Miss Shipman was beside Brenda, stretching out her own arms towards Sue.

Then it happened. Brenda let Sue go. She dropped her. Sue's plummeting scream echoed through the building like a cat in the night.

'I'm sorry, Miss. My arms gave out.' Brenda gave one look at Miss Shipman's horrified face and burst into tears. I felt sick to look at her.

Miss Shipman was galloping down the stairs, roaring at everyone to stand back. Already towards the bottom of the staircase, three storeys down, girls were stampeding towards the bottom of the stairwell.

Stupidly, no one had thought to rush to the basement with a blanket, like they do in films when the child is thrown from the burning building. It was as if everyone was hypnotised. But Sue was lucky. She was light and there was a heap of laundry bags awaiting collection which softened her fall. Even so, she had concussion and broke her arm. We never saw Brenda again.

The episode finally decided me. I was scared. Not that something similar could happen to me, but that if I stayed in this place where people shunned me and expected me to lash out, I could end up like Brenda Levy. It was a horrifying thought.

If Kati could leave, so could I. It would be easy enough to get myself expelled. I'd been up before the headmistress several times for minor infringements that were considered big crimes. I knew Miss Hodges would just love to get rid of me. There was one snag: the benefactor. It seemed that, not only did this person pay for us, but she protected us too and would persuade Miss Hodges to make allowances when it came to misdemeanours that other girls would be expelled for. Like thieving, for example, or talking to a boy. So I knew I had to do something really awful, something that would threaten to taint the school if I stayed.

I knew exactly what to do.

My plan involved Angie, who wasn't very bright. She had a stupid crush on one of the prefects called Madeleine. Angie had got hold of a photo of Madeleine holding some silver cup, a lacrosse trophy I think it was. She must have cut it out of the school mag. Anyway, every Saturday afternoon, after Walks, Angie would take to her bed with a book. But inside the book was the picture of Madeleine and she'd be masturbating. She'd stop when I came in, but I could tell from how flushed and breathy she was. Plus, she never finished the book.

On this particular Saturday we were having dorm inspection. Latin-Willie and Miss Delahaye, the senior housemistress, teamed up. They went round checking cupboards and drawers for contraband and generally invading your privacy. These inspections were supposed to be a surprise but, as usual, we'd got wind of it and had hidden any forbidden items. But the news hadn't filtered through Angie's thick skull.

I made sure Angie was in my group for Walks. She was telling me about how much she missed her pony and her brother. Mostly the pony. I even started feeling sorry for her. Off she went up to the dorm as soon as we got back. Everyone else went to the common room. I leafed through a magazine for a bit before setting off upstairs. I only hoped they hadn't done the inspection while we were out.

As I approached our dorm I could hear Latin-Willie and Delia talking a few doors down the corridor. Perfect.

Angie had taken off her skirt and folded it over her chair. I did the same on my chair.

'Oh,' she said. I could hear the disappointment in her voice. 'You got a headache or something?'

I took off my knickers and left them, very obviously, on top of my skirt. 'No. I come to help you.' I pulled back her bedclothes and got in beside her. 'Move over.'

'Whatever…?'

'I show you what to do. So you can give Madeleine a good time.'

Angie gasped. 'I never… She doesn't… I wouldn't…'

'Course you would. You like this?'

I found the damp crotch of her knickers, stroking, pushing it aside. She gasped again, only in a different way and got very wet.

'You like? You do it for me too. Is easier with knicker off.'

She was very tentative with her hand and I had to encourage her and push it against me so that the fingers found their own way in.

We were away. I was even enjoying it. When Latin-Willie and Delia walked through the door there was no doubt about what the two girls in the bed were up to. I was surprised they didn't both faint with shock.

Miss Hodges was pacing. She could never look anyone in the eye, but today she couldn't even look in my direction. Usually she was very stern and clear when I saw her, meting out punishment in her steely accent. I'd never seen her flustered like this. I could see she'd like to pace straight out of the room.

That's what Latin-Willie did when she and Delia found us. Delia didn't flinch. She ordered us out of bed and looked out of the window with her nose in the air while we got dressed.

Now Miss Hodges was advising me not to become a lesbian, although she couldn't get that word past her thin lips. Instead, she said "person of that persuasion".

'You no worry,' I said (as if she would). 'I prefer boy, but—'

She cut me off. 'I am well aware… However, my greater concern is with your leading an innocent child like Angela astray. Introducing her to er, erm – practices of which she need know nothing…'

'Oh, she knew, Miss Hodges. She like girl better. I think you not choose which you—'

'That is a matter of opinion and none of your business. We are not here to discuss er, erm… Now, where was I? Yes, I have had to make a difficult decision here.' She paced away, muttering almost to herself. 'I now understand Miss Morrison's dilemma.' At that she turned and looked me in the eye. 'You do know, don't you, Miss Morrison sent you to School House because your behaviour was setting a dangerous example? Not fit to be in contact with younger girls.'

She sat down suddenly behind her desk and consulted a piece of paper as if it would tell her what decision she had reached.

'I have spoken to your benefactor. She is shocked and although previously she has always prevailed upon me to keep you here in order to teach you better ways…' She drew breath and swallowed. 'On this occasion, in view of your depraved behaviour, she has agreed that I have no alternative but to expel you from the Priory Academy for Girls.'

I smiled with relief.

'Really! That will do.'

She rearranged papers on her desk, seeming as shocked by my smile as by anything so far. 'You have not even apologised. To Miss Williams, to Miss Delahaye or to me.'

'I not sorry.'

She wrote something on the paper in front of her and underlined it savagely.

'I am sending you to the sanatorium until arrangements can be made for your journey. Angela will sleep in the sick bay. I do not want any fraternising with other girls.'

Obviously Hodges thought our "condition" was actually contagious. And that I was more infectious than poor Angie. I wanted to giggle, it was all so ludicrous.

Miss Hodges stood and gave my left ear a long, hard look. 'I fail to see what is in the least bit funny.'

'Is not like we have the measle—'

'Enough! Marika, I cannot let you go without saying this – you came here, you and your sister, as displaced persons. You were given a great privilege. At least your sister had a goal when she left, an ambition. I hope she fulfils it. But you. You, Marika, seem determined to throw away the advantage you were given. Academically, you have never put yourself out. Socially, you have made little effort. Regrettably, you have proved yourself equally unable to meet the moral standards set by the Priory Academy for Girls.'

I opened my mouth to say that we had never asked to come to her beastly school, but she held up a hand like a policeman.

'That is my last word. I have no more to say to you.' She swept past and held open the door, looking back at her desk as I walked past her.

Outside, Valerie Troop, the head girl, and Madeleine were waiting to escort me to the san. Last time, when I had tonsillitis, I was taken in Mo's car and made a great fuss of. This time I had to carry my overnight bag and walk with Valerie, with Madeleine walking behind in case I made a run for it. Why would I do that when I could take a rest in the san and get my train ticket paid for?

When I got off the bus in the parade I could see Mama and Kati waiting at the window. Neither of them waved but they didn't seem surprised to see me.

As soon as I got inside, Mama sent Kati to the bedroom and stood me in the front room.

She sat down heavily at the table. 'Your father and I are disgusted with you.' She tapped the envelope that lay there beside her glasses. 'I really don't want to have to read it to you.'

Now I realised why I was kept in the san for two days. I'd thought it was a kind of quarantine, as if I was being fumigated. But Hodges wanted to be sure that her letter arrived at home before I did.

'Why? What did they say I did?'

'You know perfectly well. You were caught in bed with another girl – doing – things.'

My story was ready. I'd had the whole train journey to work it out.

'Angie was upset. Her parents live abroad most of the time and she'd just heard that her pony had to be put down. She thinks of her pony like her only friend in the world. I sat on her bed and she pulled me in. She only wanted me to cuddle her. To comfort her. That's all we were doing.'

'That is not what Miss Hodges says.'

'Of course not. They are all old fogies. They are spinsters who like to have fantasies. You don't know how their minds work. They like to think the worst of people. You ask Kati. Why do you think she left?'

'Between the two of you I don't know what to think. Throwing away your chances. But at least she has an ambition.'

'But you know she can't dance. I used to read her school reports. Technically precise, but lacking in—'

'That will do. We are not talking about Katalin.'

I tried another tack.

'If only you could see them, Mama. You would laugh, you really would. Latin-Wi' – she hastily corrected herself – 'Miss Williams is ancient. She has whiskers and she looks very masculine. She wears tweed suits and has this really mannish haircut.'

I felt mean, because Latin-Willie was a sweet old thing who didn't have anything to do with it. If she'd been on her own I bet she'd have backed out and never said a word. But my description had got through to Mama. I could see her lips twitching. She was trying not to smile. I put Mama's glasses on the end of my nose.

'This is Miss Williams coming into the room.' I peered over the glasses, puckered up my eyebrows and flapped my hands. 'People! People! What do we seem to have here?'

Mama actually laughed. She was pleased to have me home.

13

It had come to this: Katalin, the best snowflake in Budapest, Snow Queen, relegated to the bottom division. Not even the bottom division of the Royal Ballet School. The bottom division of Costello's School of Dance in some place called Finchley. If only they had stayed in Budapest.

Katalin had been so proud when Miss Costello singled her out.

'You at the end with the blue hairband.'

She was a new girl so she supposed it was excusable that her name was not yet known. They would know it. She would show them, these lumpy British girls. And she did show them, stepping forward from the line at the barre and demonstrating an arabesque as instructed by Miss Costello.

But then the Costello woman said, 'That is how *not* to do it.'

What? Had she heard right? Was she not in a proper ballet school? Did they learn a different method in England?

'Now Annabel, you come forward and show us how it should be done.'

Annabel executed a perfect arabesque. But it was no better than hers. Annabel was obviously the favourite. She was being made the victim because she was new and a foreigner.

At the end of the class Miss Costello called Katalin's name. She had her back turned, consulting a long list.

'Ah! It *is* you,' she said as she swung round towards Katalin. 'I thought so. The standard must be very different where you come from. Which is…?'

'Budapest. Where the standards are excellent.'

'There is no need to be rude.'

What was rude about that? Miss Costello was the one being rude.

'So, what makes you think you can dance?'

'I have always been a natural dancer.'

Miss Costello's eyebrows shot up. 'Hmm. A natural dancer, you say? I suppose next you will say that nerves are making you so stiff?'

Katalin burst into tears. It was as if she'd been slapped in the face. How could this be happening to her?

'You see, Katalin, at this stage we *assume* accuracy. But accuracy is not everything. We expect more.'

Katalin sniffed.

'I'm sorry, child, but we have to keep up standards. There is a queue of girls on our waiting list. Any one of them could have your place.'

'It's not fair! I don't suppose they've been locked up in a school where they only danced the quickstep to that Victor Silver-something man.'

Miss Costello frowned. 'Victor Silvester? Oh, dear. I heard that you were privileged, that you attended an elite public school.'

'Privileged? They did not know the word "ballet". Only the gym teacher had heard of it.'

'Really?' Miss Costello sounded sceptical. 'How long were you there?'

When Katalin told her she threw up her hands in a theatrical gesture. 'You mean you have not danced in all that time? Not been doing daily practice?'

Katalin shook her head. 'Only twice a week before gymnastics.'

Again the hands went up. 'No wonder! It is as if you are starting again, aged seven. We really cannot—'

Katalin interrupted her with a sob. 'I was a refugee. What could I do? At least I got myself out of there.' The tears were flowing well now and they seemed to work.

'So you were. So you did.' Miss Costello rubbed her forehead and sighed. 'I suppose it has not been easy.'

She turned back to the papers on the table, looking through a cardboard folder, pulling out a letter, which she scanned. She sighed again, impatiently this time.

Katalin peered over her shoulder. The headed stationery was familiar. The letter must be from the benefactor.

'Ah, I see. You are sponsored. Letters will have to be written.' She rolled her eyes in Katalin's direction.

Then she turned back to Katalin. 'Meanwhile, I'll try to lick you into shape.' She raised an eyebrow and gave a twisty little smile.

When Katalin reached the changing room, Annabel was still there, pulling on her boots, although the others had left. She must have been slow deliberately because she turned on a special smile. The toad.

'Bad luck,' she said. 'Is she throwing you out?'

'Certainly not. Why would she do that?' Katalin pictured throwing Annabel out – down a deep well with a rock tied round her fat neck.

'Oh, you're foreign. I suppose that's why. Where are you from?'

'Hungary. I—'

'No wonder.' Annabel picked up her bag and swung away to the door. 'I've never heard of any Hungarian dancers.'

Ignorant cow! 'What about Kovács Nora?' Katalin shouted after her.

But the banging of the door swallowed her words. Damn. Annabel wouldn't have understood anyway. She should have said it the English way – Nora Kovach. Not that it made any difference. Katalin slumped down onto the bench and put her head in her hands. Her dream had turned into her worst nightmare. She was the outsider and she dreaded Monday when she would have to come back and attempt to dance her way into Miss Costello's favour.

The events of the weekend, however, meant that Katalin didn't return on Monday or on any other day.

On Saturday, Katalin was using the bannister in the narrow hall as a make-do barre. She was finding it hard to loosen up because the atmosphere that morning had been enough to make anyone stiff. Miss Costello's words kept echoing in her head. Stiff indeed! She would show her. Her and that smug Annabel.

Papa was out with Marika, taking her to the Tate Gallery. He'd been very insistent on setting off immediately after breakfast and had been impatient when Marika was slow getting dressed. He said the exhibition was very popular – they would have to queue to get in, but Katalin knew better. He would be "seeing a man about a dog". That was one of those strange English expressions which meant nothing. There was never a dog in sight. She didn't trust dogs. All Papa ever did on these excursions was hand over an envelope.

It was by chance that Katalin first saw him do it. She was coming from the toilet in some museum and saw Papa walking across the foyer. He stopped to talk to a man and looked at his watch. Afterwards, he didn't have his newspaper. He'd had it under his arm. She knew he did.

'Why did you give that man your paper?'

'What man?' Papa said. Then, 'Oh, some fellow asked me for the time. But I didn't give him my paper. Damn, I must have left it in the Gents.'

She tried to catch him at the newspaper trick again, but he must have got more subtle. He was always twitchy to begin with on those days out. Then he'd vanish for a bit and when he came back he'd be relaxed and like Papa again and he'd say something like, 'How do you like these old fossils?' She'd say she was bored and they'd go off to a café. He was always in search of decent coffee.

Mama didn't approve of these meetings and said he should have left that sort of thing behind in Budapest. Katalin didn't care because she enjoyed the outings. Today, however, it was Marika's turn, which was a pain because Katalin had to stay behind with Mama.

Mama had been horrid the day before when she got home from school. She hadn't been at all sympathetic about Miss Costello, implying she would never make the grade at ballet in London. Papa had supported Katalin, but then spoilt it by telling Mama that if a thing was worth doing, it was worth doing badly. She obviously wasn't meant to hear. It was devastating that her family had no more faith in her than the beastly Costello. They just didn't understand.

Papa and Marika didn't come back for lunch as expected. Katalin had hoped Papa would bring them all fish and chips from the shop in the parade, but he was probably giving Marika some kind of treat instead. In sulky silence she ate stale bread and cheese with Mama, who went on about not setting her sights too high and getting a secretarial qualification.

'And now,' she added, 'you can do something practical like washing the dishes. It's time you girls did more chores. Stop jumping about in the hall and do something useful for a change.'

Mama went into the living room to write to Aunt Júlia.

If only they could go back to Vienna. Aunt Júlia had servants and went to the ballet. She wouldn't be expected to wash up. The crockery had been piled in the sink since last night's supper. Marika could do it when she got back.

Katalin stamped into the bedroom, burrowed into her ballet bag and dragged out her Pavlova mannequin. It had been dear to her but it no longer served. In the kitchen drawer she found a potato peeler with a point for gouging out the eyes. It was the perfect weapon. She jabbed into the figure's heart area. But the wood was hard, and the flimsy metal buckled before she had made more than a dent in the smooth surface. She scraped the now-hooked tip back and forth across the torso, carving a crude cross, before tossing the peeler aside. She gripped the right leg of the model and rotated it up and back at the knee, twisting and turning so that the internal spring contorted irretrievably.

Before the amputation was complete the doorbell rang loud and long, making her jump. Mama called for her to answer it and she flung the mannequin under the bed.

A policeman and a policewoman stood there and asked to speak to her mother. Mrs Varga, they said. They knew the name.

When Mama came to the door they asked to come in, sat Mama down on the sofa and shut the door, leaving Katalin on the landing. She heard low voices, then a shriek from Mama followed by a screaming that tore through the flat and threatened never to stop. The door ripped open and Mama stood there shouting, 'László! László! Marika! Where is Marika?'

Nobody said anything to Katalin. She followed her mother and the police-woman down the iron staircase which shuddered with the heavy footsteps of the policeman coming down behind her. It had been drizzling all morning and now a pale sun reflected off the dustbin lids and made oily rainbows in the puddles. The policewoman sat in the back of the police car with them. Mama was still saying Marika's name over and over. Katalin heard the policeman talking into his radio about an accident on the Northern line. Mama started shouting again and the woman told her she'd see Marika at the hospital. So that's where they were going. Nobody mentioned Papa.

Katalin expected to go to a ward and see Marika and Papa all bandaged up, but instead they were taken to a waiting room in the Almoners' Department.

'What is almoner? Why are we here?' Mama was saying, but let herself be sat down in one of several upright chairs in a row against the wall.

The policeman disappeared and soon a squat woman wearing a navy blue suit appeared, leading Marika by the hand. No bandages, but not a Marika that Katalin recognised. It was like in *The Nutcracker Suite* when the toys come to life, but the opposite had happened. Marika had come to death.

Mama rushed to hug her.

The squat woman in the suit said she was the almoner and held out her hand, but Mama didn't notice. She said Marika had been treated for shock and she had been checked over by a doctor. She should be kept quiet but she was perfectly fine.

Anyone could see that wasn't true, thought Katalin. Marika was rag-doll limp, glued into Mama's arms as if she would fall to the floor if Mama let go.

The almoner said they could go home and Mama turned Marika towards the door. The policewoman stepped forward and said they would be taken back in the car.

'But we haven't seen Papa yet,' said Katalin.

Everyone looked at her and then at each other. The policewoman frowned, the almoner's bristly eyebrows shot up and Mama's mouth fell open. She held out a hand and Katalin was pulled into her arms alongside Marika. Her sister's normally hot little body was cold and shaking while Mama was hot and sweaty. Katalin tried to back out of this unpleasant sandwich, but Mama gripped her round the waist and spoke into the top of her head.

'We won't ever see Papa again. Papa is gone. Papa…he is…dead.'

When she heard it, Katalin knew she'd known all along, even though nobody had actually told her. All she could think to say was, 'Why?' Which could have been, 'Why didn't anyone tell me?' or 'Why or how does he come to be dead?'

Mama shook her head. She opened her mouth but no sound came out. Katalin looked round at the almoner who was muttering and shaking her head. It was the policewoman who put a hand on her arm.

'It was on the Underground,' she said. 'Your father fell. He was run over by a—'

But Marika let out a yell that drowned the last word.

Someone said, 'Time to get them home.'

They were bundled out of the room and into the lift as if they were all time bombs. Marika had already exploded and Katalin felt as if she might go off at any moment.

Wilkie was waiting for them in the newsagent's. It seemed everyone knew what had happened. She stubbed out her cigarette and took over from the police. Upstairs in the flat she settled Mama on the sofa and put the kettle on. She undressed Marika and put her to bed. Then she made tea and started on the dirty dishes.

'You'd better find some clean sheets,' she said to Katalin. 'You'll be sleeping in with your mother. Keep her company. I'll sleep on the floor with Marika. Keep an eye on her. But I'm not sleeping on any top bunk, that's for sure.'

Wilkie was moving in.

14

Aunt Klára met us off the train and drove down darkening lanes in her rackety car like a mad woman. I felt carsick and Kati said, 'Don't you dare!' But Aunt stopped for air that smelled of wet grass. There were tearing sounds and murky shapes beyond the gate that Aunt said were cows. After that I got to sit in the front, which was hard cheese on Kati.

Aunt said she'd forgotten her Hungarian, she'd lived here so long. She wasn't sophisticated like Aunt Júlia, or handsome like Papa, although she had his nose. There it was, sticking out under a shapeless hat, poking towards the steering wheel as if it was leading the way. This aunt was the middle one of the three of them, Papa's older sister, and known as "the runaway", which was probably the real reason we'd never met her, although Papa always said we couldn't afford the train fare.

The story was that, just after Aunt Júlia got married to Uncle Fritz, Klára went to stay with them in Vienna. She met a handsome prince in the shape of an English student – not a real prince of course, but she married him and went to live in England. She doesn't look like the sort of person to do anything so romantic, but it was a long time ago and her prince is long dead. At least Aunt Klára gave me something to think about, to keep out the horrible thoughts, and when we got onto a straighter road I fell asleep.

'Not long now,' said Aunt when I woke up and she saw me looking. She slowed down and started to hum in a tuneless wheeze as we turned into a bumpy track. The headlamps lit up a tunnel of tree roots with branches meeting overhead. I began to think she must live in a rabbit hole. I thumped Kati awake. We needed to be in this together.

There was a great booming noise as we got out of the car. We clung to each other, trying to see where Aunt Klára had gone, and Kati didn't even pull away from me. Then a light came on in a big stone porch and Aunt was holding my hand and leading us across a cobbled yard.

'It's only the foghorn. Up at the lighthouse. Must be foggy out at sea.'

We looked at each other and Kati made a face. Nobody had mentioned the sea.

'Come on. In you come. Meet Finn.' Aunt opened the inner door and all at once a grey shape circled round us and cannoned back to Aunt Klára, who seemed to be almost hugging it.

Kati shot back towards the car and wouldn't move until Aunt Klára took hold of the creature's wide collar.

'This is Finn. Gentlest dog in the world. No need to be afraid. He's just excited to see us and wants to meet you.'

We weren't at all keen to meet him and Kati wouldn't come into the house until he was shut away.

'I'll put him in the conservatory,' said Aunt. She came back shaking her head and muttering, 'Poor Finn.' Kati bared her teeth at Aunt's back.

The house smelled of wood smoke and cabbage and something else that must have been dog. Aunt sat us at the kitchen table, cut hunks of bread and ladled soup out of a black pot.

'You'll get used to him,' she told us. 'Everyone has dogs in England. In the country, that is. He's a wire-haired lurcher, by the way.'

So what? We ate our soup in silence after that and when we'd finished she led the way upstairs.

'Your room,' she said, holding open a door.

'Two bed,' I said, thinking no more horrid bunk beds. 'That nice.'

Aunt hugged us both then, in a clumsy kind of bundle and went off, blowing her nose.

Klára woke early, as she usually did. It took her a moment or two to remember why the house felt different. She was no longer alone. Other people were breathing in the room opposite. She stared into the darkness, bracing herself to face this fact. She was a solitary person. For more than ten years now she had lived alone with only the sea, the trees and the rooks for company. And Finn, of course. Now she had taken in her nieces, László's girls. Niece. A strange word – but not half as strange as they might turn out to be, after all they'd been through.

But László... Oh, László. She hadn't had time to take it in. Júlia on the telephone from Vienna... "You must take the girls. I'll deal with things in London." Stepping in, organising, as she always did. She'd wanted to refuse, to say she needed time. Time to think, to come to terms, to sit on a rock by the sea, to tell the birds. But, of course, she'd had to agree. It was the least she could do. Her brother's children. Her precious little brother. Don't go there. Lock it away. Deal with it later.

She'd done the same when David went. Went down in flames, his plane, they said, into the Channel. Nineteen forty-two that was, and she'd locked that away too, gritted her teeth and carried on driving her ambulance through the London Blitz. To be honest, she hadn't wanted the war to end. She was glad to see the end of the killing and devastation, of course she was. But she'd missed the camaraderie of the job, and peace brought the need to come to terms with being on her own.

Losing home and country had been bad enough. Losing David, husband and best friend, was devastating. Teréz must be facing that now. Klára struggled to feel sympathy for her. According to Júlia, Teréz had never got over leaving Hungary, never engaged with English culture. Foolish woman. Always so self-centred, so beguiling, so… What was the word?

Klára turned over and checked the time. Just a few more minutes. Sexy. That was the word.

She'd been forever grateful to David for giving her the chance to escape. László had been dismissive. Deserting, he called it. First Júlia, moving to Vienna, then her settling in England. But she'd never regretted it. Here in Britain, the war had brought terrible loss, but people pulled together. All the conflict was "out there". But in Hungary the conflict was internal, inside people, poisoning families and friendship. What with Nazi occupation and then a Communist regime, how could it be otherwise?

And now it had come to this. The inquest would say his death was an accident. She was sure of that. Just as she suspected it was no such thing.

She swung her legs out of bed and padded about, pulling on clothes. Best not to run a bath. She might wake them. It irritated her to notice that she was already adjusting her routine. All day yesterday she'd told herself they would fit in with her. Not the other way round. But the drive from the station had already shown her it was going to be difficult. She'd been so tense until they'd both fallen asleep. Only then had she been able to relax, free of their consciousness intruding on her own. How could she let go of this obsession with being private? Where was her spontaneity? At forty-eight, she was far too young to be so set in her ways.

She let Finn out and went, as she did every morning, to the conservatory to meditate. But she could not empty her mind. It was full of images of the two girls as they stepped off the train – the desperate arrogance of the elder, who would not meet her eye, and the neediness of the younger, who had reached out to touch her at every opportunity. Fear and mistrust would have been endemic in Budapest. How much had they been affected by growing up in such a climate? How much had they understood about what László got up to?

Her eye followed Finn as he moved routinely from tree to tree, sniffing tenderly, leaving his messages. She felt more affinity with her dog than with her relatives. Did that make her an unnatural woman? *They are only children*, she told herself. Aged sixteen and fourteen. Children who had lost their father and, if her bossy elder sister was to be trusted, their mother too, to mental illness. She hoped for their sake that the illness Júlia described was only temporary, a result of shock. Finn pushed open the door and joined her, his head warm and heavy on her thigh. He wasn't going to find it easy either. *They are only children*, she repeated. But that was just the problem, another species really. She was ashamed to admit to being afraid of them.

She'd never wanted children, not really. Who wanted to bring children into a world at war? Plenty of people had, of course, and those people pitied her when she didn't have a child to make life worth living afterwards. The Luftwaffe had cheated her of a life with David but at least she was free to shape her own future. Children had remained an unknown quantity. If only László had brought them all to stay for the odd weekend at least. That might have made it easier. But she'd never got round to inviting them. If only. If only.

Be that as it may, the girls were now with her for the foreseeable future. It was ridiculous to be so ill at ease. Just think of them as people, she told herself, and gave up the attempt to still her mind.

In the kitchen she filled the kettle and set it on the Aga to boil. What would they want for breakfast? She reached down the tin of coffee, wondering if they would eat porridge.

She crept into the hall and listened. The house creaked around her as pipes tapped into heat and timbers settled into the day. There it was. A different sound. The twang of bedsprings, the faint rattle of a curtain being pulled back. Should she go up and see if they were all right? What would she say? What could you say to a child whose father has been killed? The kettle started to belch steam behind her. Best leave it a while.

Now it was morning and Kati was still sleeping, neat in her bed like a saint on top of a tomb. It was the first time in a week, the first time since it happened, that I hadn't had the nightmare and woken myself up screaming. But that big dark cave was still there in my head when I remembered. The cave where the black bat lived. I thought of Mama back in London, but Aunt Júlia was there. So I didn't need to worry about Mama. I didn't want to think of how she was when we said goodbye. She looked right through me as if I wasn't there. Aunt Júlia pulled me away and mopped my face with her scented handkerchief. She said Mama would soon be better, but how soon was soon? And what medicine did you take to make you see your daughter again? Did Mama think it was my fault? Was that why she couldn't see me? Was it my fault? Could I have stopped it?

I pulled back the curtains and peered out. Not a rooftop in sight. No sirens or buses. Silence. Eerie. The view was spooky too. The valley was a bucket of smoke and it was rising in layers like strips of bandage. I could see treetops, so there had to be hills out there, but they were wiped out of shape, smothered. I leaned on the windowsill, breathing in my own smell, hot and musky, and pulling at the edge of the thought that had woken me. It was all lies they'd been telling about Papa's death, a smokescreen like that mist out there. I wanted to lift the corner and rip it off and see the raw earth underneath.

Kati hadn't understood at first. She'd started with her sainted-sister talk about me being a drama queen – until she got it. Got what had happened. Even Kati wouldn't think I'd mess with something like that.

Papa was not a person who would kill himself. He certainly wouldn't have killed himself right there in front of me. That stink kept catching at the back of my throat, the stink that had belched out of the tunnel like bad breath ahead of the train. It tasted of silted dirt and soot. I swallowed but it wouldn't go away, and nor would the picture that went with it.

We'd lingered too long in the Tate. When we got to the Underground, the rush hour was already beginning to build. I stood close to him, right at the front of the platform, nervous of the growing crowd behind us. There was a murmuring, protests. Some pushy person trying to get to the front. Everyone looked right at the sound of the train rumbling towards us. Papa shifted position next to me, putting his paper away, tucking it into the top of his overcoat. I waited for his hand to find mine, ready to push forward together onto the train. No hand, so I turned, grasping towards him.

Breath stops. Black bat flying. Black coat, skirts swinging out. Screech and roar of train. Swallows everything. No Papa.

Now, when I screwed my eyes tight shut, I still saw the giant bat shape suddenly flying. That's all I had. The only image. But I knew that somewhere inside me, in my gut, I knew more. I held the truth. My body was there. My body recorded it. One day, it would move that memory through the layers of cells and blood and spit it into the place where you remembered. Like it was only a matter of time before the sun burned through the mist out there beyond the garden.

I'd no idea what time it was, but I needed to pee. I found the bathroom we had used last night and sat there looking round, taking it in: a pile of pebbles on the end of the bath; a grey-white robe on the back of the door topped by a green bath cap spattered with white paint, as if Aunt Klára wore it for painting the ceiling rather than taking a bath. There was a splayed toothbrush in a beaker by the basin, an unfamiliar tube of toothpaste and a cake of orange soap in a saucer. None of the bathsalts and pots of cream that Mama kept on the kitchen window-sill. I missed the smell of Mama more than anything – her special mix of perfume, nicotine and fried onions. This bathroom only smelled of being clean, and the lavatory paper was the harsh shiny sort like we had at school.

When I came out onto the landing, Aunt Klára called up the stairs. Like she'd been waiting and listening. I peered into the hall. It was dark down there.

'Come and have a hot drink. Is Katalin awake? If not, let her sleep.'

Certainly, I would. It was rare for Kati to sleep in, something to take advantage of.

The kitchen was full of the scent of coffee. The dog got up from a rug by the range and came towards me. It was a shaggy creature, all skin and bone and much quieter than it had been last night.

'Just put out your hand and let him sniff. He wants to get to know you. That's it. He won't bother you if you don't bother him. Good boy, Finn.'

The dog started to lick my feet, which made me dance about on the icy stone floor.

'Oh, you haven't got any slippers! No dressing gown, either. Here, sit by the Aga.'

She disappeared. I moved cautiously towards the chair but the dog ignored me, lay back down and didn't seem to mind my feet sharing its rug. Aunt came back with a long camel coat and a pair of furry boots.

'Get inside those. Hot drink? What would you like? I'm making porridge, but it's not ready yet.'

'Coffee?'

She looked surprised, but poured from a jug set at the back of the range. I took it from her before she could spoil it with milk. I held the mug in both hands and inhaled the bitter nuttiness of it. I hadn't smelled this since Mama made it at home in Budapest. I was too young to drink it then, but I used to taste Papa's and think that one day I would like it. Everywhere in England coffee was made with orangey-brown powder and tasted disgusting. As I huddled into Aunt Klára's coat and felt the hot steam on my face I knew everything was going to be all right. It wasn't a happy feeling exactly. But I felt safe. Yes, that was it. I felt safe.

Aunt Klára was buttering toast and she passed me a slice thick with butter and honey. I was just sinking my teeth into it when there was a thundering on the stairs and Kati appeared in the doorway.

'Trust you to sneak down without telling me,' she said.

The fact that I had honey dripping down my chin made me feel guilty, even though I had no reason to.

'And good morning to you, too,' said Aunt Klára. 'I told your sister not to wake you.'

Then Kati saw Finn and froze.

'Finn, stay,' said Aunt. 'Come on, Katalin, you have to learn to be in the same room.'

'I don't like dogs.'

'That's a shame. But, as I say, you have to co-exist. It's his home as well as ours.' She pulled out a chair at the table and passed Kati a slice of toast. Hers was on a plate.

Kati edged forward and slid into her seat.

'Coffee?'

'Only if it's with hot milk.'

Aunt Klára eyed her. 'That can be arranged,' she said, and reached down a saucepan from a rack.

Kati was being worse than she usually was in the mornings. And Aunt Klára didn't like it. I couldn't remember saying please or thank you or anything myself, but she hadn't seemed to mind.

The porridge was better than I expected and she let us have honey on it, although she sprinkled salt on hers. I thought I'd try that next time.

'This is the time when Finn and I go for a walk,' said Aunt Klára after breakfast. 'You don't always have to come, but this morning you need to see where you're living.'

Kati pulled a face but Aunt took no notice. Finn was already nosing the door. Aunt told us to shut the inner door before she unlatched the outer one, which meant we all had to squash together and Kati made a fuss because she was too near to Finn.

'I told you, he's perfectly harmless.' Aunt yanked at the door with more force than necessary and a flurry of leaves scuttered in.

Kati squawked as Finn pushed past her legs. 'But it's raining,' she said.

'Not raining, just what we call "soft",' said Aunt. She handed me a pair of boots. 'These should fit you, Marika.'

Kati looked at Aunt as if she was the one who was soft. 'Then why are the cobbles all wet?'

'Ah, maybe it's turned into mizzle. That's halfway between mist and drizzle. Actually precipitating. Anyway, let's get going.' Aunt eyed Kati. 'If you stopped doing things because of rain, you'd never do anything, living here.'

Kati made a face and pulled on her coat. 'We could wait until it stops. Or go tomorrow.'

'We'll need to get you some wellies,' said Aunt. She shoved her thin feet into the boots in the porch. '"The rain it raineth every day." Anyway, what about Finn? He needs a walk.'

Finn wasn't looking that keen, Kati was muttering about staying behind and Aunt was busy ignoring her.

'I hope it doesn't – rain every day, I mean.'

'Well, it rained every day for a hundred days one winter.' Aunt's dimple showed and I wondered if she was teasing us. 'Not all day, but every day. That was a bit much, even for me. And I quite like rain.' Aunt slammed the door behind us and looked up at the sky. 'Oh, this is just a shower. Look, blue sky over there.'

I ran to keep up as she turned down the side of the house on a path that led through the garden. A big vegetable patch opened up on the right, and on the left a tree with pears on it growing against the house wall. Aunt paused to test one of the fruit.

'Nearly ready to pick. You'll be able to help. I hate going up the ladder.'

'I don't like to go up the ladder either,' said Kati.

'Then you can pick the bottom ones.'

'I'll go up the ladder,' I said.

'Good,' said Aunt, and Kati kicked me.

'That's where I work,' said Aunt as we passed a conservatory. I thought that meant it was a private place. I was getting the impression that Aunt was a private person. She didn't chat like Mama or Aunt Júlia.

We set off through the garden with Kati lagging behind, kicking at stones and generally being moody. Aunt took no notice.

The dog had disappeared into a wood at the end of the lawn and now came bounding back to see where we'd got to. Kati squealed and hid behind me, but Finn ignored her, and so did Aunt. We wound our way into trees on a path slithery with leaves that led into a big circular clearing. There was a kind of stone table at one side. Black birds like giant bats were circling and cawing overhead.

'My resident rooks,' said Aunt Klára as if they were her friends. She disappeared among the trees on the far side of the clearing.

'Let's play "words for rain",' I said when we caught up. It would take my mind off the birds and annoy my sister. I was rewarded by an exaggerated sigh from Kati, who hissed, 'Sucker-upper!'

Aunt gave me one of her looks. 'Well, if this rain got a bit harder, we'd call it steady rain, and if all the blue sky disappeared it would probably be "set in" for the rest of the day.'

'Then would we go home?'

Again, Aunt ignored Kati. 'Then there's driving rain and penetrating rain, which has some force behind it and gets through anything that isn't waterproof.'

'This rain's getting through my coat,' said Kati.

'I'm not surprised, Katalin. We'll have to get you both proper macs. Those thin things aren't much good.'

Russet leaves rustled and crunched. 'Beech nuts,' said Aunt picking one up and holding it out. 'And there, sweet chestnut. No, don't—!'

But it was too late. I'd already grabbed the bright green ball. So soft underfoot, so painful to the fingers. I shook the spiny case from my hand and jumped about, to Kati's delight.

'Wilkie used to say it was raining cats and dogs,' I said to change the subject.

'Yes, that's for really heavy rain, a downpour, when it's coming down in stair rods.'

'Stair rods?' That was a new expression. I rather liked it.

'When it's coming straight down, as opposed to driving rain, which has a wind behind it. Raining sideways means a very strong wind.'

Raining sideways made even Kati smile.

'Then there's bucketing rain, a deluge, a cloudburst and torrential rain. I might turn back if it was torrential. Finn doesn't think much of that.'

At this point we came out of the wood and Aunt clambered over a stile into a field.

'But see? It's stopped.' She held out her hands and looked up. 'We might even get some sun.'

But I wasn't looking at the sky. I stopped dead and clutched at Kati's arm as she caught up.

'Look! What's that?'

A vast wallowing surface spread out beyond the field and stretched into infinity, meeting a grey sky. Close to the edge of the field the wallow reared into green caves topped with foam. It was a bit like a horizontal fountain, but instead of falling harmlessly into a basin, this cascade looked as if it would thunder on and engulf us.

Kati shook off my hand. 'It's the sea, stupid. She said there was sea. Last night.' She was pretending to be offhand, but I'd caught her wild eyes when she first looked out across the field. She was just as scared as me.

Aunt Klára looked back just then. 'Come on, you two.' Then she checked herself. 'Oh, lordie! Of course. Have you never seen the sea? I remember the first time I saw it. I thought it was going to swallow me up. I'd only ever been to Lake Balaton in calm summer weather. You too, I suppose?'

We nodded.

'Now, I couldn't live without the sea. Or trees. If I had to choose…' She shrugged. 'But I'm very blessed. I don't have to choose.'

She came back to the stile and handed us over. 'We'll go down to the beach.'

We weren't at all keen, but Aunt didn't consult us and strode off as if visiting the beach was an urgent necessity. We stopped dead at the top of the shingle.

Aunt rounded on us. 'Breathe!' she said. 'Get some of that in your London lungs.'

She took an exaggerated breath and her blue eyes glinted at us as if the sea had lit them up. Then she took both our hands and marched us over the pebbles towards the water. Neither of us wanted to be the first to waver. But Kati suddenly gave a little yell, dug her heels in and pulled back. She shook her hand free of Aunt's and started to run back up towards the grass. Finn bounded after her. Maybe he thought it was a game, but when she turned on him and shouted, 'Go away, you beastly dog!' he dropped his tail and loped back to Aunt Klára's side. I didn't know a dog could look hurt, but he did.

15

I missed Wilkie. It was nice having her in the flat looking after Kati and me. Mama never liked Wilkie, and I thought she would send her away. But she didn't even seem to notice. Aunt Júlia treated her like she was a servant, which was embarrassing. I've always adored Aunt Júlia, so it was shocking. I had to rearrange her in my mind. Like when Mr Horváth on the floor below us in Budapest turned out to be an informer. He used to give me sweets, but after that I didn't take them.

It was a relief that Wilkie took us to Paddington. The bus was crowded so we had to sit separately and Wilkie was standing nearly all the way. I tried to give up my seat for her, but she wouldn't take it. Then she just bundled us onto the train and stood on the platform, telling us to write her a letter and that we'd be home before we knew it.

Wilkie didn't normally do double messages – like when adults say one thing and mean another. But that goodbye remark of hers was one of those. If we were going home again so soon, we wouldn't need to write, would we? A postcard would have done, saying we'd arrived safely.

I kept going over that last day with Papa. We went to the Tate Gallery, which was nice because it's on Embankment, and I always liked to see the river. It reminded me of the Duna. I was wearing my new plum coat, double-breasted with a revers collar, which made me feel grand. It didn't have a belt but fitted snug to the waist. Kati's grey one looked better because she has a more elegant shape and it hung loose. But Mama said I was curvy like her and I liked that because it was sexy. Mama wished she hadn't told me the double-breasted bit. Every time Kati called me "fatty" after that, I told her I wasn't fat, I was double-breasted. Papa explained it wasn't a ladylike turn of phrase. I didn't care about being ladylike, but I didn't want to upset Papa so I just went back to calling my sister Flatty Kati.

There was a Picasso exhibition on at the Tate and we had to shuffle along in a queue for ages to get in.

'A talented man,' said Papa. 'But a signed-up Communist.' He glanced about him as he said it, although there was no need in London. Would we ever lose the habit?

'But at least he was anti-fascist,' Papa went on. I knew what was coming next. 'Beware of "isms", Mari. They are the problem. That swing from one to the other, fasc*ism*, commun*ism* – all forms of extrem*ism*, with no sanity, no common sense, no middle ground. No live and let live. Such fear of difference, such a waste of the richness of cultures coming together. Creativity cut off. And our country the victim of it all.'

By the time Papa had finished his familiar rant we had reached the exhibition. I was so fascinated by the Picassos that I didn't mind Papa doing his usual disappearing act. There was always someone he had to meet on these trips. I just knew not to mention it to Mama. I never thought much of it. Now I think a lot about it. Was it connected? If only... No, stick with the good bit.

The sad images of Picasso's blue period and the jagged shapes of his distorted people jangled me.

'You see people like that every day,' I said to Papa when he rejoined me. 'On the tube. I feel like it myself sometimes. Bits missing, other bits put back in the wrong place.'

He sighed. 'You notice, don't you? You understand.' He hugged my shoulders to his side. 'You should write about it, Mari. You were always good at composition. You write well, you have good intuition.'

I shrugged, glowing with pride but not deserving it. 'I can't do it any more. They—'

'Of course you can. You must. You mustn't waste it.'

'But they say the grammar is all wrong. My pieces come back covered in red ink...'

'To hell with grammar. I suppose I shouldn't encourage you to write in our own language, but... To get started?'

'No! That would be going backwards.' It was tempting, but I knew my English would get worse if I went back to Hungarian.

'Then write any old how,' he said then. He was so animated that people turned to look as we made our way down the stairs. 'Be creative with English. It's a rich language. Be a poet. And if you want, we'll work on the grammar together afterwards. Describe that picture, for instance.'

'But I like the blue period best...'

'Fine! We'll buy a postcard – over there! You choose one.'

I don't know why, but I liked a picture of a sad lady ironing. Papa gave one look and said, 'Ah, *La Repasseuse*. The early period. One we didn't see, in fact. I don't think it's here. Representing the oppressed masses. It's very gloomy. Are you sure?'

I was sure, and he joined the queue to pay.

'Right. Let's take it home and you can get started. In fact, let's go straight home and we'll get fish and chips and a bottle of that Tizer you like so much. Cheer Kati up. I think she had a bad time yesterday. You have to be nice to her.'

As if I wasn't always nice. It was Kati who was horrid. Didn't he realise?

Then came the bit I try not to think about, until Wilkie was there, holding the world steady. She said to write, so I did.

Dear Wilkie

This week we did cylinders in school in geometry. We had to think of things that are that shape. I thought of Aunt Klára but our teacher said a person cannot be a cylinder. Which is silly, because Aunt Klára is cylinder-woman – no hip. She wears always long skirt and tunic like tubes that hug close to her body, but her body stays inside. My body is more adventurous, always wanting to escape. People don't like that either. Where I have curve, she is straight. Narrow shoulders, hollow chest. No titties.

She moves along the edge of places though she is not shy person. Like when she took us to see the school and meet the headmistress. In the corridor she slide along the wall against the flow. I follow, but everyone bump into me. Always she like to wear green to go with her hair – copper hair curling on her shoulder. I like to have that hair. Today, shoes are green, soft suede lace-ups, like little mossy stones.

I don't like the school as much as the one in Kentish Town. It is goody-goody school like the Priory. I don't mind that they want to learn a lot, but I do mind they don't like to have fun too. I am always making joke and the girls get cross, not just teacher. And no boy. That was main reason I like the Secondary Modern. I think it should be called Best Modern.

This morning Aunt Klára helped me do my homework before Kati woke up and interfered. Kati used to be always up early but now she sleep and sleep.

Aunt was sitting like all mornings in the conservatory with her long sad face but when she see me in the doorway she gives me that special Aunt-smile. It start with a puckering of the mouth. Then the nose catches it, and twitches. Next the sun come out in her eyes. That's if the sun can be blue. A blue like an electric shock, the colour of the flower in her garden with the glossy leaf. Periwinkle, she told me. She takes off her special hat, her writing hat, a floppy faded suede thing, but blue, not green. Her father used to wear it when he told her stories as a child. That's why it special. It take me a while to twig that her father was our grandfather. I don't remember him. She take off her hat and put her writing away and I know I will talk and she will listen.

This morning we made the story I must write. She make me work it out, what I wrote, but she helped. I am not so good at grammar as Kati. But Aunt Klára says I am better communicator. I don't know how that work. Then we make the porridge and the lovely coffee.

Now I must stop because it is Saturday and we go to market.

You told me to write and practise my English and tell me about where we have come to. I hope you understand okay.

Your Marika xx

P.S. I forget two thing. The sea – which is like a green monster that lives on the beach across a field at the bottom of the garden. The second is Finn – who looks like a monster, a grey one, that lives in the house with us and is not frightening when you get used to him. He is Aunt's dog.

My first talk with Aunt Klára happened because of Finn. I came downstairs when Aunt was still in the conservatory, like she is every morning. Finn gave a little woof. Aunt waved me in and pointed to a chair and the dog licked its paws. After a bit Aunt stopped writing in her notebook.

'You must miss him,' she said.

'I miss Mama.'

'Ah, yes.'

I couldn't say I didn't miss Papa. And I couldn't say I did miss him. Because that place was a blank wall. It was bricked up inside me. I could miss Mama because I expected to see her again. But Papa – all I could think was "if only". If only we hadn't been at the front. If only I'd made him hold my hand. I could have held tight and saved him. If only.

After a bit, Aunt said, 'I've missed him for years.'

'Because we never came to see you?'

'Well, that too. But before that.' Aunt sounded vague, staring out at the garden.

'We couldn't afford to come. But you could have come to see us. You could have stayed at Wilkie's.'

Her eyes shifted back to me when I said Wilkie's name. They took a while to focus. 'Wilkie? Ah. Yes, I could have come. It was foolish. Just because Teréz and I…'

'You don't like Mama.'

'Not true. We just never… Nothing in common. She was Júlia's friend. They were older than me – and she liked parties and I liked books. I daresay she's changed.'

'Not really. She get bored in London.'

Aunt was looking out into the trees again. 'But it was long before that I lost him. Before I went to Vienna and met David. We had a silly row.'

'What was it about?'

'In the garden, it was. We were weeding and he was talking. I laughed.' She paused and frowned. 'Can't remember why… He thought I was laughing at him. I was laughing because I felt stupid, except I didn't know that then. I couldn't cope.'

Aunt went quiet again and Finn put his head on her knee. She was rubbing the place behind his ears and I kept quiet.

'It was about politics. I lost him to bloody politics.' She looked up, suddenly fierce. There were tears in her eyes. 'I suppose you did, too.'

She stood up then, walked to the door and stood with her back to me, rubbing her sleeve across her face.

Politics. That sounded like Papa. But what was the row about? Did that mean they were on opposite sides? Did that mean Aunt was a Commie or a Nazi? Which was worse? Aunt Júlia would never have sent Kati and me here if she'd known. It would be weird because Papa said the British fought the Nazis and were always hunting down communists. English people were afraid of "reds under the beds" but Papa said it was better than having them *in* the bed. That always upset Mama, and they'd end up being edgy all day.

'I remember now.' Aunt's voice sounded as if it was coming from far away. 'I must have been indiscreet and László was telling me, "The more you care about something, the more you keep it quiet." As if I didn't know. I asked him what he cared about. He said he cared about the right to free speech. And I said, "And you keep quiet about it?" That was it, that was what started me laughing. I couldn't stop. Silly, childish laughter because I couldn't cope with my little brother being so serious.'

Aunt gave a sharp sigh as if she was cross with herself and there was a crack in her voice when she went on. 'He tried to shut me up, got hold of me by the shoulders and shook me. He was frowning, trying to explain. It made me laugh even more. Then he got mad, threw down the hoe and stalked off. I remember he stopped at the back door. "Not funny, Klára," he shouted. "Not funny." I can hear him now. "Not funny".'

I crossed over to where Aunt was standing. It didn't seem quite right to hug her, though I did want to, so I just linked my arm through hers.

'Didn't you see him again?'

'Hardly at all. Events overtook us. I had to leave – but that's another story. Expected to come back, of course. But I ended up here in England. Then came the war... Blew us all apart. What fools we were.'

We were both staring out through the glass and the pane I was looking through made the tree trunks change shape in spooky ways when I moved my head. As if they were alive.

'It's a crazy place, our country, with its crazy, violent history.' She squeezed my arm into her side. 'Pulled every which way by all those warring people. I always felt throttled by the politics. I could never understand what I was supposed to believe in and what I was supposed to keep quiet about. It's the reason I left.'

Finn whined gently and pawed at the door, and Aunt let him out.

She turned to me, suddenly brisk. 'I don't know why I'm carrying on like this. It's not what you want to hear. You lose your dear father, and I go on about politics…'

'Papa *was* politics.'

'Oh, Marika!' She hugged me then, a surprising hug. It felt very big for such a narrow person and her voice vibrated into my head. 'You *know*. You're right. He was a brave man and he lived by his principles.' Another squeeze and she let me go. 'But now, it's time for porridge, I think.' She opened the door. 'Come on, Finn. Breakfast.'

Klára reflected on this conversation after she'd dropped the girls off to catch the bus to school. It felt like a breakthrough, a real communication at last. But it was also disconcerting, confronting. She'd lived in her own world too long – with her own construction of reality.

For instance, when little Marika had spoken of "Mama" with moist eyes, it had taken Klára a moment to realise that "Mama" was Teréz. Of course she was. And evidently a very different Teréz from the one she remembered. A Teréz she was obliged to respect if only for the sake of the girls.

Klára was also shocked at how glibly she told Marika she'd left Hungary because of the politics. She'd almost come to believe it herself. Okay, she'd been glad to leave them behind. She always thought of herself as an honest person, but that was only a sliver of the truth. Nothing to do with the panic and the urgency of the time – pretending Júlia had invited her to stay in Vienna, and praying all the way on the train that her faith in Júlia and Fritz was not misplaced.

Then, just as Klára was thinking she could at least get on with little Marika, an event took place which took her back to square one with the two young madams. They'd been at school a couple of weeks and seemed to be happy enough. There had been no concerns from the Head, who was a reasonably good friend of hers. They'd even established a Saturday routine that felt quite like a real family. The girls would come to market in the morning and help carry the bags to the car, Klára would give them money for chips and the cinema and off they'd go into town. She headed home for a peaceful Saturday afternoon with Finn, having a bonfire or making bread until it was time to meet them off the bus. She thought she'd cracked this children business.

On this particular Saturday she was going down with a cold and indulged her sore throat by lighting the fire and settling down with a book. Finn was well pleased. She felt sorry for herself, haunted by regrets that she'd never made her peace with László. Now it was too late. It wasn't just about the row in the garden. It was Teréz. Teréz had stolen him. Hadn't she? Having Marika here was forcing her – reluctantly – to think about Teréz as a real person, a much-loved mother, a wife whom László cared about.

How did that fit with the Teréz she remembered? Teréz had been an exuberant personality, always exclaiming and enthusing. She was sensuous and tactile, whereas Klára and her family were a serious cerebral lot, more given to intellectual discussion than hugging. A daunting family to join. But what about that seductive behaviour? Suppose Teréz had looked across at László and it was simply mutual attraction? Suppose what Klára had witnessed was not the malicious stealing of her brother but two people falling in love? Was it possible that it was all down to her jealousy?

She woke when a log fell in the grate. She banked up the fire and had to rush to meet the bus.

As she parked in the lay-by at the end of the lane, a police car turned in from the main road. That was a rare sight, so she wondered where it was heading. Almost immediately the bus pulled up. There was Katalin, caught in the headlights as she crossed the road. She was running, which was an event in itself. It took Klára longer to notice that she was alone.

Katalin ripped open the passenger door. 'Marika! She wasn't at the bus stop! I didn't know whether to wait for her or to come back.'

Klára wasn't that surprised. She found it more remarkable that they'd both caught the bus each time so far. 'We'd better go and pick her up.'

But Katalin shook her head. 'We should ring the police.'

'Really? It's a bit soon, isn't it? She's probably at the bus stop wondering when the next bus is.'

'She knows there isn't one. Anyways, I spoke to her friend and she was worried. Marika went out of the cinema in the middle of the film. She'd been acting strange. I think she was meeting someone…'

'Well, that's not necessarily—'

'A man, Aunt Klára.'

'A man? Why would you think that?' And why this unaccustomed concern for your sister, she wondered.

'She's been in trouble before about sex. She was always going with boys in London. And she was expelled from the Priory for sex.'

She tried not to grin at the way Katalin spat the word "sex" as if it were a bug in her salad. This was getting worse by the minute. She knew about the expulsion via Júlia, who'd had it in a letter from Teréz. But that was with a girl and Klára suspected it was innocent and that the school had overreacted. Maybe they were looking for an excuse to get rid of the odd refugee who didn't fit their academic standards.

'Please, Aunt Klára, let's go home and ring the police.'

She started the engine and did a three-point turn. A headache was throbbing behind her eyes. She was glad to avoid traipsing round town with an agitated Katalin in tow. How worried she seemed. Hopefully it meant that a real bond existed between the sisters underneath the hostility. Or was she just eager to drop Marika in it with the police? Klára gave herself a mental slap for being so cynical.

Deep in these thoughts, she was totally unprepared for the scene lit up by the headlights as they turned into the farmyard. The police car she'd seen earlier was parked right in her way and the constable was banging on the door of the porch. Unusually for him, Finn was barking wildly from inside. Marika was leaping from the back of the patrol car, pursued by a policewoman who seemed about to wrestle her to the ground.

Marika wriggled away and ran into Klára's arms as she got out of the car.

'What on earth is going on?' Klára asked over the top of Marika's head.

'I had to restrain her. We thought, she's too young for handcuffs, but she's been spitting and biting like a wild thing.' The young woman sounded rattled as she straightened her hat and tried to tuck stray hair behind her ears.

'Let's all get inside and sort this out.' Klára turned to Marika. 'Thank goodness you're safe. Katalin was so worried.'

'Kati? Worried? About me?' She shot Katalin a look.

Klára showed the police into the sitting room and went to put the kettle on. Nothing happened in England without tea. In the kitchen Katalin had Marika pinned against the wall and Finn was whimpering under the table.

'Stop it, you two!' Klára took Katalin by the shoulders. Her whole frame was vibrating with rage.

Katalin jerked away. 'I'm going to bed.' She kicked the doorframe and stomped up the stairs.

Next morning in the conservatory Klára heard the real story behind Marika's shoplifting of a lipstick from Woolworths in Fore Street.

'I had to have one,' Marika said. 'At home I used to borrow Mama's. I need it to look sexy for those boy.'

"Sexy" at fourteen? Was this how Teréz had brought them up? Lending her lipstick? Klára checked herself. Stop blaming Teréz. Marika probably just helped herself to the lipstick. She took a breath. 'But you don't need lipstick to look nice. You're fine as you are.'

Marika shook her head. 'I ugly mug. They all say so, not just Kati. I have pug nose and blackheads and pimple.'

Klára had to interrupt. 'You have beautiful eyes, pretty hair! Your skin will clear...'

But Marika frowned as if she thought her aunt needed glasses. 'Anyway, I need lipstick to distract. Then they look at mouth. I have good mouth. Good mouth, good leg, good titties.'

Now Klára really was out of her depth. Poor girl. Beastly children, mean sister. Boys, sex. Under age. Ye gods! She could get pregnant. 'But Marika, you're only fourteen—'

'Nearly fifteen! My birthday in January. Only three weeks. You didn't know, perhaps?'

She didn't know. Birthdays. She hadn't given them a thought. At least now she knew what to give Marika. Would she have to rethink the Christmas present? Furry slippers with a rabbit face had seemed perfect when she bought them.

16

Katalin felt for the mannequin under her pillow. It wasn't there. She opened one eye onto the high-ceilinged room with the tall window. They had been here months but it still happened – a cruel trick of forgetting where she was and what had happened. Her mascot was gone. Papa was gone. She was marooned in the country with her sister and a strange aunt. It was not to be endured. How could she live her life without her mannequin dancing ahead of her?

Katalin crept onto the landing and watched Aunt Klára through the railings at the top of the stairs. Her hair was like flames in the dim light. Did she dye it? How odd to wear it loose at her age. She was lighting the candle in the niche in the hall where she kept the black Madonna figure and the terracotta bird woman with feathers for hair. She took the little porcelain bowl into the kitchen and Katalin could hear the tap running. She loved that dish, the silky glaze and the fish painted in the bottom.

Where was Marika? Those two probably thought she didn't know they'd been having cosy chats in the conservatory every morning. But Katalin did know. She couldn't eavesdrop without being seen so she was determined to join in. But what was her sister doing now? There was no sign of her.

Aunt Klára replaced the bowl carefully, completing the display with a clear quartz crystal from a drawer under the shelf, which Katalin had never noticed. She lifted her dreadful old hat off its hook. Now she'd go to the conservatory, thought Katalin, like she did every morning.

But this morning Aunt Klára paused.

'Today is the Winter Solstice, Katalin, the shortest day. Did you know that?'

How did Aunt Klára know she was there? She was looking up at her with a funny expression Katalin was never sure about. Annoyed? Trying not to laugh? Mocking?

'Don't look so scared. I always know when you're there. Eyes in the back of my head, you know.' The dimples showed on either side of her mouth. 'Anyway, it's an important day. There will be a ceremony. I would like you and Marika to join me. Will you do that?'

'What will we have to do?'

'Always so wary. Come down here and look at me.'

She walked slowly down the stairs into the blue gaze that seemed to drill through her.

'I am the guardian, you see. The guardian of the gateway between light and dark.'

Katalin blinked.

'We have been moving steadily into the darkness. Into the womb of the earth. Now it's time to start travelling up into the light. I will perform a ritual to pass through that gateway. I'd like you and Marika to witness it, that's all.'

Was her aunt completely mad? Dotty mad, or scary mad? Where was Marika?

'Marika's in the garden with Finn,' said Aunt Klára. She must be a thought-reader. 'They're fetching something to represent the earth. It's all about honouring the seasons, the seasons and the elements. Nature. You see, we're part of it – but we need to keep reminding ourselves, hold the connection.'

Katalin didn't see. When Marika burst in, she had leaves in her hair, just like the dog. Katalin snorted when her sister handed over a muddy stone half-covered in moss.

'Perfect,' said Aunt Klára and gave Katalin a fierce look. She placed it on the shelf and stepped back. 'Now we have all the elements – fire and water, earth and air.' She stroked the bird woman's feathers. 'And this morning we can *all* go to the conservatory.'

Katalin worried that she might be required to say something, but it wasn't like that. Aunt Klára started on about going into the darkness, but after that she got more normal.

'You – we – but especially you, are going through a dark time. A time of grieving. Connecting with the earth helps us to grieve, because the earth and the plants and animals follow a constant cycle of dying and rebirth. Us humans, too, but we like to think we're different. Death shows us we're just the same. And losing someone as close and as special as your father… Well, I don't have to say how hard that is.'

Katalin didn't like this talk of Papa. She tried to shut it out.

'László, your father, went through dark times too. But he was a survivor. For instance, as I said to Marika the other day, not many came back from the Russian front. He did. A miracle he survived.'

'Mama said he slept for a week and he didn't even wake up when she dressed his feet – which must have been agony because they were ripped to pieces.'

Aunt Klára shuddered and her lips set in a thin line.

Katalin had heard the bloody feet story so often, but she supposed Aunt Klára had not. Or maybe it wasn't the story that made her stiffen. Marika reckoned Aunt Klára didn't like Mama. Perhaps her sister was right for once.

'Why did they send him?' Katalin wanted to change the subject and the question popped out of her as if she'd always wanted to ask it. Maybe she had, but had learnt not to ask questions that might have "walls have ears" kind of answers.

Aunt Klára turned to her. 'They sent people they wanted to get rid of. He was an intellectual, a writer, he liked poetry, wrote plays…' She almost stopped then and her voice cracked when she continued. 'And all those dangerous activities. Plus, he had Jewish friends at the university. Need I say more?'

'But why…?'

'Sending people to fight the Russians didn't look like a purge. But it was. At least, that's one way of looking at it. When you think how few we were – the Hungarian army – and how many Russians there were.'

'If he hadn't come back, then Kati wouldn't have been born.'

'Nor would you, stupid.'

Aunt Klára ignored them. 'László always thrived on politics. He threw himself into resistance. Even when he was in hiding.'

'Was he hiding from the AVO?' asked Marika.

'No, stupid. It was the Nazis then, the Arrow Cross gangs who did that stuff.'

'Katalin's right. During the occupation. I get confused myself. Not being there. But letters came from Júlia – always long after the event – but, even so, they made my hair stand on end. You'd think he'd have kept a low profile, but he took risks all the time. I'd have been worried sick if I'd known.'

Katalin found herself wishing their father had been a cobbler or something ordinary and useful like that. And if Aunt Klára was so worried about him why hadn't she rushed to welcome him to England?

'Didn't he write to you?' said Marika.

'Sadly, no. Even since the war, no real news got past the censors. You had to read between the lines.'

'So how did you find out?'

'As I said, Júlia used to write. Your Uncle Fritz had ways of getting information through his business associates. And Júlia wrote in a kind of code – the one we used when we were playing games as kids.'

Marika grinned, as if it was all a game, not Papa risking his life.

Again, Aunt Klára ignored her. 'Then there was a short happy time when he could write. Maybe you remember, Katalin? He was back at his job on the paper, the *Népszava*? Júlia wrote that you were visiting in Vienna, that you could travel again.'

Katalin nodded. Yes, she remembered. Aunt Júlia made such a fuss of Marika, who was about two and got away with murder, while she was expected to have good manners and behave.

'I used to help Uncle Fritz.'

Aunt Klára looked surprised.

'With his collection.'

'Ah yes, his collection. Rich man's toys, László used to say. But he's always looked after Júlia and he's been good to you.'

'Of course he has.' It made her cross to hear Uncle Fritz talked about like that, as if he was just a moneybags. But Aunt Klára took no notice of her indignant tone.

'László wrote that life was good. I have to say, I read between the lines that it was too good to be true. And so it turned out. Far too good to last. But we have to be proud of him, your father, refusing to kow-tow and toe the Communist line—'

Marika interrupted. 'That's when he went to prison.'

'Yes. What year would that have been? How old were you?'

'She was only three. I was five. It must have been 1949. I remember.'

'So do I!'

Katalin shook her head. 'You slept through it.'

She told the story of the banging on the door in the night, of the black car parked down in the street and the ugly men who burst into the apartment.

'They took Papa's playscript. Mama cursed that he'd left it on the table. But they'd have found it anyway. That way they didn't ransack the entire apartment.'

'Your poor mother. It must have been awful.'

'I helped her. I used to look after Mari. We were always hungry. But so was everybody.'

'Where did they take him? Could you see him?'

Katalin shook her head. 'We never expected to see him again. That's what Mama said.'

'But he did come back,' said Marika. 'One day, suddenly, I came home from school and he was there again.'

Katalin nodded. 'For no apparent reason, they released him.'

Papa was too weak to hold a pen when he came home. He'd gone to bed for days, or was it weeks? They fed him broth. He would never talk about where he'd been held or what he had been through. She didn't want to talk about it either. Especially not with this mad, witchy aunt.

It was very dark that night although the skies were clear, pinpricked with stars scattered around the sliver of a new moon. Katalin thought it best to cooperate with Aunt Klára's plans. She had made it plain at lunchtime that the ritual was more important to her than Christmas. It was not a good idea to provoke a mad person when they were performing a ceremony. After all, there were often swords involved on such occasions, or potions.

What would Mama have thought if she'd known Aunt Klára was so strange?

But Mama had taken to her bed with no thought for her and Marika. Katalin had written to Mama, but her reply was just a note scribbled in pencil. It said, "You two always have each other." As if they were bosom sisters. It was folded into a letter from Wilkie, who asked her not to upset her mother.

Marika was always sucking up to Aunt Klára, which meant she'd volunteer for some dreadful role in the ritual. Maybe she'd be sacrificed. Katalin grinned to herself. It was a nice idea but she didn't think Aunt Klára was that mad. But with any luck, her sister would get some kind of comeuppance.

At what Aunt Klára called the appointed hour, they stepped out through the conservatory into the garden. She and Marika were wearing ordinary coats and gloves, but Aunt Klára was wearing a hooded cloak of dark green velvet over a long black skirt and her usual black polo neck. She became invisible in the darkness under the trees.

They gathered by the stone table in the clearing and it dawned on Katalin that it was meant to be an altar. She shuddered and tried not to think of Abraham sacrificing Isaac. But trying not to think about something meant it stuck in your mind like egg on a plate. The ritual didn't amount to much. Aunt Klára walked about a bit and talked to the sky or the trees in a batty kind of way. They could hear those big birds shifting about in the branches behind the altar, as if they were quite fed up at being disturbed by Aunt Klára's antics. Katalin wondered what other creatures might come creeping out of the woods.

Marika was asked to light a big candle, which Aunt Klára produced from inside her cloak. The wind blew it straight out. Was that a bad omen?

'Thank you, girls,' said Aunt Klára in her ordinary voice. 'Now let's go back and have cocoa.'

'I think we should go to sea. It would be exciting in dark.'

Was her sister totally crazy? It would be terrifying.

'That's a wonderful idea. Shall we? Katalin?'

She shook her head violently.

'You go back to the house, then. Here, take the torch. We'll get night eyes. We won't be long.'

Aunt Klára called the dog, which had been lurking in the shadows all this time, and they set off through the trees.

Katalin grasped the torch and shone it onto the ground in front of her, walking fast, head down until she got to the door into the conservatory. She locked it behind her, ran to the front door, shot the bolt and drew breath. Then she remembered the door at the back of the kitchen. It was only ever used for going to the dustbin and she found it was already locked. There was a fire still glowing in the sitting room, so she curled up on the hearth rug, leaning her head on the arm of Aunt Klára's chair.

Now she could think. No risk of burglars or mad axe men, no one to interrupt. And she really needed to think. She must get away. Between them, Aunt Klára and Marika were driving her insane. The shoplifting fiasco had been the last straw. It was lucky the police had let her off with a caution. Aunt Klára had done well there, what with Marika getting in such a temper and lashing out. But word had got around at school and she felt labelled by association with her sister – first as a slut and now as a thief. She needed a plan.

After leaving the Priory, she and Amanda had written to each other. Amanda was working at some art gallery in Mayfair and sharing a flat with that snobby Ena Foley. Amanda's letters had got shorter, but with Mama in this state, Amanda was her only hope. She'd written to her only last week, exaggerating everything about Aunt Klára and where she lived in an attempt to be amusing and spark Amanda's interest. Next she would suggest meeting up in the Christmas holidays. She could get the train to London to visit Mama. Marika would want to come too. But that was fine. Marika would stay at the flat with Mama. She planned to stay with Amanda. It was worth a try.

Katalin was woken by Marika shaking her by the shoulders.

'Why you lock us out the house, beastly sister?'

Aunt Klára was standing in the doorway with Finn, looking none too pleased. Then she remembered locking all the doors.

'But you got in.'

'We banged and banged, but you didn't come. And there you are by nice fire...'

'Luckily,' said Aunt Klára, 'I remembered the spare key in the outhouse – the one for the back door. But it was difficult finding it in the dark. I gave you the torch, if you remember.'

Katalin smirked at the thought of Aunt Klára and Marika groping about among the cobwebs and falling over the dustbin.

'Not funny, Kati. You don't get any cocoa.'

'Don't be silly, Marika. Of course she does. Now, Katalin, make up the fire before it goes out.'

When they came back with the hot drinks Aunt Klára said, 'So, why did you lock us out, Katalin?'

Stupid, crazy woman, thought Katalin. 'To lock out the burglars, of course. It is what normal people do when they are in the house.'

For a week the hills at the back of the house had not made an appearance and at the front the wood was only occasionally visible when the fog wore thin. Katalin hated it.

Marika told her it was better when you were outside rather than just looking at it through a window. Katalin refused to put that stupid remark to the test. She needed to be in a town, a proper town. London.

'You get fog in London too,' said Marika. 'In fact it's worse there – the smoke from the coal fires getting trapped. It's called "smog". Wilkie told me.'

'But there you get on a bus or go in a shop or a cinema where it's light and dry and no fog. Here the only places to go are the field – more fog, or the wood – fog dripping off the trees. Everywhere is fog. Thick fog. Thin fog. No lights, no cars, no buildings making a shape to put up a fight.'

'You talk silly things. It is only weather.'

'I'm surprised you don't miss the shops, Mari. You were always shopping, wasting money on stuff.'

'I've been growing up. Shopping isn't everything.'

'Growing up? Sucking up, more like. You just want Aunt Klára to think you're the bee's knee.'

'What is "bee's knee"? Why is that so special?'

Katalin shrugged. 'It's just an English idiom.'

Even Christmas wasn't as they expected. Aunt Klára wrote to Teréz, inviting her to Devon, but their mother replied that she was going to stay with Aunt Júlia in Vienna. Katalin and Marika couldn't look at each other when they heard. Katalin heard Aunt Klára muttering under her breath as she peeled potatoes. Marika sulked all through supper and burst into tears as soon as they got upstairs.

'Why couldn't we go too? To Vienna for Christmas? Why doesn't Mama want us, Kati?'

Katalin had the same questions herself. Why didn't Uncle Fritz want to see her? She said, 'Maybe Uncle Fritz couldn't afford for us all to go. Maybe his business is going through a bad patch.'

She thought that was highly unlikely but it was all she could think of to say. Marika seemed to accept it, although she carried on snivelling until she fell asleep. Uncle Fritz's failing business became the myth they both held on to.

Katalin came down to breakfast next morning to hear her sister whingeing to Aunt Klára.

'You see! Even Mama doesn't want to spend Christmas with us. Nobody loves us.'

'It's not about you or Katalin. It's about her,' said Aunt Klára. 'A measure of how sick your mother is.' She added, 'We'll make sure we have a splendid Christmas here.'

Katalin groaned inwardly. Dreary Devon was no substitute for the high life in Vienna.

Aunt suddenly turned from stirring the porridge. 'To tell the truth, I'm angry with your mother *and* Júlia. I suppose I shouldn't say it and being angry doesn't help. But it makes me spit.'

Funnily enough, Katalin found that it did help. It made it okay to be cross with Mama and Uncle Fritz, which was better than being sad.

Mama being in Vienna ruined Katalin's escape plan. She and Marika would be back at school before Mama got back. So there was no reason to go to London. She would try again at Easter.

Katalin had to admit that Aunt Klára made an effort at Christmas – a goose, mince pies and taking them carol-singing in the village. She did her best with the presents too: a pair of slippers each; warm jumpers, red for Marika, navy blue for her; a framed photo each of Papa as a young man; and giant chocolate bars, milk for Marika, plain for her. But even with stockings and a tree, it just wasn't the same without Mama's cooking and Papa and his games.

17

It was Easter 1961. Six months since Papa died. Mama clung to me when I arrived for the holidays.

'Ah, Mari! It's such a relief to speak Hungarian,' she said. 'I talk to myself these days, just to hear it.'

She didn't ask about school or Devon. Nor was she much interested in where Kati was. She just went on about language, calling it the luxury she didn't know she had in Budapest.

Everything at the flat was the same: the puddle by the dustbins; the reek of rotting cabbage from the greengrocer's; the clang of the metal stair treads; the green paint blistering with rust. Even the weather was as I remembered. The early promise of spring had given way to bleak rain.

Inside it was still as dark. Automatically, I closed the kitchen door to shut away the sour drain smell that burped from the plughole in the sink. The bunk beds were still as we had left them. Mama still swore at the lumpy put-u-up as she sank onto it, and the stain was still visible in the armchair where I once sat on the bag of eggs. Everything the same, yet not the same.

Mama was the same. Except she wasn't. She wore the same make-up, patted her hair as she used to and said the same things. But I had to keep looking closely at her, as if she might be someone doing a really good impersonation of Mama.

This Mama didn't keep the flat clean. I scrubbed out the kitchen first and then set to with the vacuum cleaner. There was a clunk as I thrust the attachment under the bunk beds. When I pulled it out, an object swathed in fluff was impaled on the end of the nozzle. I hoovered it off and found I was holding that old mannequin of Kati's. She must have nicked it from the art room at school and kept it as a talisman. Now it was severely disfigured and, as I washed it under the tap, one leg snapped off at the knee.

When I showed Mama, she shook her head with impatience. 'Oh, that girl! She came home in such a temper. When they told her off at the dancing school.

She must have done it then. It was the day before… The day before László…'

'She never danced again.' My eyes welled up as I ran my finger along the grooves in the figure's chest. 'Throw it away, shall I?'

Mama shrugged. 'She wouldn't want to be reminded.'

'Poor Kati.'

Mama grunted. 'I thought she'd come with you, stay here. Doesn't she care to see her mother?'

'I'm sure she will,' I lied. Kati informed me on the train that she'd arranged to stay with Amanda and never again wanted to set foot in Kentish Town.

The air in the flat hung heavy. There was no expectation of a key in the lock, no door swinging open to bring a draught of fresh air to replace the fug we'd been breathing. I struggled to know what to say – and to leave unsaid what I wanted to say.

For the first few days at six o'clock I found myself at the window, looking along the street for the stride of a figure in a belted mac and a trilby hat. Among the bustle and shuffle of grey caps, coloured headscarves and black umbrellas there sometimes came such a figure. My perverse heart would adjust the tilt of his hat and impose a non-existent spring in his step. Sometimes I just couldn't believe that this stranger walked on without even looking up at the window.

I would turn away with wet cheeks, Mama would look up and nod and the two of us would huddle together, talking of Papa.

'László, László. He was the life of this family. How can we go on without him?'

I felt guilty when Mama said things like that, which she frequently did. Guilty, because I had every intention of getting on with my life. Guilty, because I harboured uncharitable thoughts about Mama. She seemed to wear her grief like a badge of identity so that other people would look after her.

My own grief – my grief proper – had only just surfaced, triggered perhaps by being back here in the flat. A new pain broke over me. I realised that the trauma of the *event*, the horror of that image, the recurring nightmares that I'd been coping with during the last six months – all that had somehow got in the way of grieving for *Papa*. Aunt Klára had helped – by listening and by carrying on as normal. Finn and the sea had helped. I'd been so scared of the sea at first. But gradually I'd learnt that, if I walked along the shore when I felt bad, the waves and the wind cleared my head. It was as if, each time, the tide washed away another piece of that image, replacing the sooty smell of the Tube with the tang of salt and seaweed.

The flat was full of memories – Papa making light of its limitations, joking about the mould in the kitchen and bringing home little treats, like custard tarts and humbugs. Once, he bought Mama a scarf with horseshoes on it and she'd carefully folded it in a triangle and tied it under her chin in front of the mirror.

'Just like the Queen,' she'd said. 'At the Badminton Horse Trials. I saw a picture.' She'd worn it every time she went shopping with her handbag over her arm. 'Just like the Queen'.

I'd been so keen to spend the Easter holiday with Mama, but it was not as I'd imagined. We went to Mass together on Good Friday and ate hot cross buns and chocolate eggs. Aunt Júlia sent treats, but Mama was bitter. She would exclaim, 'The luxury they live in!', and seemed to have forgotten that she abandoned Kati and me at Christmas to enjoy that luxury.

She would rant about what used to happen in Budapest, events that could not be spoken of in those days: the friends who'd disappeared in the night; the bodies in the Duna, people who'd been shot into the river to be swept away downstream. The images she conjured were disturbing. I couldn't escape, obliged to hear Mama's daily litany of determined pain.

'He brought me here. And now look what happens. I am abandoned in a strange country.'

Anyone would think Papa pushed himself under the train. I ached to hear his voice. 'Come on, Mari,' he used to say when I sulked. He would cock his head on one side. It always made me laugh. What would he have done to raise Mama's spirits?

I spotted a bucket of spring flowers outside the greengrocer's, bought a bunch of daffodils and set them on the table in a jam jar.

All Mama said was, 'You see, we have no pretty vase to put them in. All left behind in Budapest.'

She'd forgotten that, long before we left Hungary, we'd lost all such refinements as vases. But I was not about to remind her and set her off again.

Here there was no sea to help me cope and only the tame, municipal trees in the park down the road. There was no Finn leaning against my legs, no listening ear. I longed to return to Devon, to Aunt. But I'd stick it out for the promised two weeks.

I walked along the parade on the first Thursday, as I did most days, to see if Wilkie was there in her shop. She never was. Just when I really needed her. I wanted to thank her for keeping an eye on Mama. But more than anything I wanted someone to talk to.

I peered into her shop window, but it was dark and deserted inside. I wandered on, into the park. There was a clatter of black birds in the taller trees, like the rooks in Aunt's garden. Two children, sisters maybe, were playing on the seesaw – up-down, up-down, up-down with squawks of delight. Kati and I never discovered the knack of making it fun. I hated that park in Buda with the seesaw. It was scary. Until I got the hang of what to do. Then Kati wouldn't play anymore.

I sat on one of the swings, turning it and turning it with my foot until the chains closed together at the top of my head. I let go and watched the trees and the bushes and the people speed into a giddy blur. Then I spun back and forth, letting the scene come into focus as I came to rest. I would have done it again, but the two little girls were bored with the seesaw and came running towards me.

If only I could put my life into permanent spin to avoid thinking. Being with Mama was boring, but keeping it boring was the only way to stop it being painful. She'd have woken from her nap by now and would be wondering where I was. I set off back towards the flat. As I turned into the alley beside the newsagent's a tall figure emerged. Did he look at me strangely, or did I imagine it? The look was fleeting. He strode away and crossed the road. What business could such a smartly dressed person have at the back entrance to some shop on the parade? His black Homburg was still visible, moving swiftly above the heads of the people queueing at the bus stop. A stranger who looked out of place and uneasy, giving me an uneasy feeling.

Indoors, Mama was pacing by the window, pale and sweating.

'It's nothing,' she said when I questioned her.

As I made tea I thought of the stranger disappearing into the crowd. There was something about him… The hat. That look. Almost as if he might know me. The kettle shrilled into my thoughts and I poured water onto the leaves in the pot.

'Did you have a visitor?'

Mama swung round. 'Why do you ask that? Who would be visiting me?'

'Here's your tea. Sit down. Shall I get one of your pills?'

Mama settled into the corner of the sofa and mopped her face with her handkerchief.

'That's better. I'll be fine soon. Just a funny turn. No, I already took a pill.'

That was strange in itself. Mama didn't like taking the pills.

I perched at the other end of the sofa. 'A tall gentleman in black?'

Mama clattered her cup on the saucer, spilling tea. 'What did he say to you?'

'So it was him. He came here?'

'You recognised him?'

'I only meant, it must have been the man I saw.' Why was she so jumpy? 'Why should I recognise him, Mama?'

'I didn't mean… No, I didn't mean that. Oh, I don't know what I am saying.'

'Who is he? Why did he come? What did he say to upset you so much?'

'He offered his condolences.' She sipped at the tea. 'That's good, good tea. Very soothing. Won't you have a cup?'

Condolences. What a strange word. 'Tea? No, I don't want any damn tea.' Was he a friend of Papa's? One of his contacts? In which case, he would be after something. 'He left it a long time, didn't he? Mama, look at me. Who is this man? What did he want?'

As I asked the question, Mama shot me a look from under lowered lashes. In that moment I knew. It wasn't an immediate and specific knowing. I just knew that I knew. Images hovered into consciousness, images from years ago in the Budapest apartment: a black hat on the chair in the hallway; the shadow of a dark coat on the stairs; the rustle of a sweet wrapper. The images settled at the edge of my mind like jigsaw pieces waiting for me to pick them up and slot them into place. But I could only see one corner of the puzzle. I didn't know what picture I was supposed to be making. I didn't want to know.

That night I couldn't sleep. I lay there trying to piece together the jigsaw of memories. The image of the black hat in the hall took me back to Budapest and the time when I had measles.

I'm aware of a rhythmic creaking. It is a lullaby that both wakes me and sends me back to a fevered sleep. It's as much part of my world as the grooves in the panelling or the cracks in the ceiling that make a lady's face or the smell of Mama's perfume.

'Our bed is so creaky, you only have to turn over,' Mama would say. 'And your father gets so restless.'

I wonder why Papa has to turn over so much, but Papa just laughs and strokes Mama's bottom as she stands at the stove.

Now the creaking has stopped and I'm properly awake and need to do a wee-wee. This measles is a horrid, sweaty business, even if it does mean I get to stay home, with Mama off work to look after me. My nightie is sticking to me and I'm hot and shivery all at the same time.

Sitting on the chamber pot, I think about the creaking. It must mean Mama is having a nap. I hope she isn't getting ill too, with all that tossing and turning. Because it can't be Papa being restless. He's in prison. Unless… Unless… Might he have come home while I was sleeping?

I run to Mama's door and press my eye to the crack in the panel Kati and me have looked through before. I already know I'll be disappointed because I've just passed the chair in the hall. There's a black coat neatly folded on it with a black hat on top. They are not Papa's coat and hat. Papa would have flung them down and the hat would have skidded across the floor as he rushed to find Mama and me and hug us to bits.

But, just in case, I peer through the crack. I'm faced with a bottom, a gleamingly white bottom so close that I hope it doesn't fart. It moves away and disappears into a pair of trousers. Mama's skirt comes into view and as I scuttle back to bed I hear the rattle of the handle and Mama's voice. 'You must go. The child will soon be awake.'

*

This memory insisted that I used to call this person the "Thursday" man. Why? And why did I feel guilty about it? There were still pieces missing. I fell asleep trying to work it out.

Next day I decided to tackle Mama again. I made tea and took it in after her nap.

'This man and his condolences, Mama. Why did he really come?'

She sighed. 'What does it matter, Mari? You don't need—'

'I'll find out somehow. You might as well tell me.'

A silence developed in the room. A double-decker lumbered past with a shriek of brakes as it drew up at the bus stop. A lorry vibrated the saucepans in the kitchen. The usual sounds of voices and the ring of the till continued in the shop beneath our feet. But in the room the silence thickened and spread into every corner.

I could stand it no longer. I snatched the cup and saucer from Mama's hands and banged them down on the table.

'Look at me, Mama! He's the Thursday man, isn't he?'

The child in me wanted Mama to exclaim that this was ridiculous. This would be the old Mama, who would then cuddle me up and tell me some cock-and-bull story that I could pretend to believe. Then I could banish the fear that this poison from the past was still in our lives. But this was not the old Mama, but a fragile being who needed mothering herself. It was no surprise when Mama nodded and collapsed into tears.

'So, what's going on?' I said when she had calmed down enough to speak.

Mama shook her head slowly. 'Suddenly he turns up, all over again. I wish he would go away. Everywhere he follows me. Says he always will. He just wanted to give me time – after László…'

'Has he been here before?'

'No. That is why. Just yesterday, out of the blue. Giving me time, he said.'

'How did he know Papa was killed?'

'Died, Marika. It was an accident, remember? Of course he knew. These Soviets, they keep track.'

Oh, Mama, of course they did. That's how they killed him. Who was she kidding? Not even herself. But the doctor had said, 'Don't rock the boat,' so I didn't contradict her.

'What does he want? After all this time?'

'Me. He loves me. He is obsessed with me. That was how it was all possible.'

'What do you mean? What all?'

'He helped us, Marika. You have to understand. We would not have managed without him. Your father could have been shot. That first time, when he only went to prison. We had meat to eat from time to time. But most of all he helped us get out. How else do you think we were able to sit on that train all the way to

Vienna? That we did not have to get out and walk over the border like your father and Katalin?'

I stared as the jigsaw pieces fell into place, as the picture expanded.

'You mean he will come again? He will keep coming? He wants to—?'

'Stop it. I won't. I can't. I only did it before for what we could get out of it. I was never really unfaithful to László. It was always a means to an end.' She paused, staring at the wall. 'And whatever you do, don't tell your sister.'

I shook my head.

'I used Sergei, and he knows it. He could make me pay, but…'

Sergei. Somehow, knowing his name made it worse. He had an identity, this Russian who had sex with my mother on Thursdays in order that we stayed safe, ate meat, escaped. Escaped, only to fall into his hands yet again. A red rash of confusion filled me: disgust at Mama; rage at the system that led her into it; indignation for Papa; fear for the future; and a burning hatred of this Sergei. I felt physically sick.

Mama was still talking, as if a dam had been opened. I put my hands over my ears. 'Shut up! Shut up!' But she carried on, listing the benefits Sergei brought us, justifying, justifying. I couldn't bear to hear it.

'But what about Papa?'

'I told Sergei over and over that I only ever loved László, only ever will love László. He says that doesn't matter. He only wants to care for me. He wants to set me up. A flat in a nice area. With a proper bathroom. Where he can come.'

Such a look came into Mama's eyes when she said "a nice area" and "a proper bathroom". What Mama wouldn't give for such things. She was tempted. What *would* Mama give?

'What have you said to him? Have you told him, no?'

There was fear now in her eyes. 'What will he do if I say no? He has been patient. You must understand, he is not a bad man. In fact, I would say he is a good man. He has waited. Now he wants his reward. So I play for time. I string him along. After all, it is quite clear to him that I would not want to stay here. Who would want to stay here?'

'But you wouldn't do it? Would you?' I have her by the shoulders, shaking her.

'Of *course* I would not! What do you take your mother for? A tart? I tell you, I would rather be dead!'

We hugged, we cried and I was sent out to buy fish and chips and a bottle of vodka. I tried not to notice that the crisp notes I was given to pay for this luxury must have come from Sergei.

18

Still in her coat, Klára stalked through to the kitchen and sat down heavily, head in hands, elbows in the crumbs of breakfast. 'To hell with children, damn and blast,' she said to Finn, who circled the rug and curled himself neatly in front of the Aga. A finger of sunlight slanted sideways onto an upturned saucepan in the dishrack, showing how dirty the glass was. The time of year for cleaning windows, she thought. There's something those girls can do. Something to make up for this morning's fiasco.

It had been a day in late April some ten years ago when she had first stepped into that kitchen. The estate agent had given her the key to the house, a chunky iron weight that turned stiffly. Like today, clouds were cavorting across a blue sky, and a flurry of the previous year's dry leaves had blown into the hallway with her.

She'd closed the door and stood listening, looking up the curve of the stairs and at the closed doors facing her. Was she welcome or not?

She'd chosen the nearest door on the left. It swung wide and she smiled at the daffodil light dappling the flagstones. The stone sink under the window was chipped and stained and the wooden draining boards gleamed greasily. But all she saw were the acid green leaves of the beech tree which were making the patterns on the floor. She imagined herself washing up at this sink for years to come. The Aga looked decrepit but probably worked. Light, warmth and a good tree. What more could anyone want?

What she wanted today was her house back – not to have those girls invading her space when they came home from school. They'd been unsettled ever since they'd come back from spending the Easter holidays in London – Katalin edgy, sulky and uncooperative, Marika waking them all with nightmares. Seeing Teréz had clearly not been beneficial, and there was some satisfaction in that. But, after enjoying two whole weeks of peace and solitude, Klára, too, had been irritable, which in turn made her feel guilty and more irritated. They would have to get used to each other all over again.

This morning they'd had an almighty row. She still didn't understand what it was about. Katalin started it, needling her sister in whispered Hungarian over porridge. Marika had stormed upstairs and locked herself in the bathroom. Finn was whimpering under the kitchen table and Katalin refused to speak. Klára had tried to stay calm, conversing with the bathroom door, but when Marika refused to come out she'd lost her rag as well and shouted at her to stop behaving like a spoilt two-year-old. At that, Marika had flung the poor door nearly off its hinges. For a moment Klára thought Marika was going to hit her, but she stalked past with a shocked *Et tu, Brute?* glare to crash about in the bedroom.

The upshot was that they were late and she'd had to drive them up the lane to be sure they caught the school bus. Anything to get them out of her hair.

Klára paused as she swept toast crumbs off the table into the palm of her hand. What went on between those two girls? They were that in-between age. Full of hormones. They'd had a rough ride. It was only to be expected. She brushed the crumbs into the sink and set off upstairs. Might there be a clue in their bedroom? She rarely went in there, insisting they take it in turn to clean and change the bedding.

Predictably, Katalin's side of the room was neat and bare, her bed tidily tucked in. The demarcation line – a dressing gown cord anchored under Katalin's bedside table and following the line of a floorboard – was in place. Katalin was strangely obsessive about it being dead straight. Klára had had speak to Marika about kicking at it. Marika's domain was a mess: the bed unmade, underwear on the floor and a tangle of hair clips, bracelets and make-up covering the top of the chest of drawers. Only her bedside table was clear except for a photo frame. Klára picked it up.

She found herself gazing at the man who had been her brother. There was that familiar air of confidence. He always had a bit of a swagger, but here she could see him as a family man. It showed in the way his feet were planted and the way he was holding Marika – a hand round her shoulder, tucking her firmly against his side. Marika grinning, happily snuggling her head into his waist. A very different Marika from the one Klára knew.

His hair was still thick and dark with a slight wave to it, the sort that would have turned completely white in old age. Straight heavy brows shadowed his eyes that looked directly into the camera. He was wearing his perfectly ordinary clothes with panache, and he was half-smiling.

It was just a mac, but of a good length, coming below the knee where it was blowing out in the wind. The collar was turned up, which looked kind of stylish. That, and the way his free hand was thrust into his pocket. His well-polished shoes were catching the light.

Yes, she remembered that. Always so particular about shoes. Even when he was ten years old. Where other boys would have scuffed a new pair by the end of the day, László kept stopping in his tracks to spit on his handkerchief and polish the toes.

She replaced the picture carefully. Her brother had the air of a man who was comfortable in his skin, who at any moment would stride on to the next adventure. She'd been so proud of him. If only she'd told him so.

She kept thinking of the look on Marika's face as she came out of the bathroom. She'd felt betrayed. Or was it rather that she had just realised her aunt was not to be manipulated? Klára felt a moment of shame to be entertaining Katalin's view of Marika as a drama queen. What was she but a child who had witnessed her father meeting a horrible death? A child separated from her mother? Katalin too, had lost both her parents. Although older, she was still unformed, vulnerable behind the bravado. Shouldn't they be with their mother, the three of them coping with grief together? Júlia said not. Teréz was still in a fragile state, she might have to go into hospital. She could only cope in London because the neighbour, the Wilkie woman, was happy to keep an eye on her. Fritz was looking into a private clinic in Vienna. Expensive, but no more than the cost of Júlia's visits.

Enough of brooding and wondering. She must take advantage of the empty house and work on that article. The filing date was looming. Finn padded after her into the conservatory and she propped open the door. The air was warmer outside than in the house.

It was the swallow on the telephone wire that did it. She couldn't concentrate anyway and found herself wandering along the lane, taking the uphill route away from the sea, thirsty for the green smell of primroses and the tender new beech leaves. She was led by the nose, and by Finn, through drifts of wild garlic up the bridle path to the stile. Glossy saucers of pennywort reflected pale sunlight. By the time she reached the gate, her slippers were soaked and her feet sore from the stones that had penetrated the thin soles.

Ridiculous fluffy things Marika had given her for her birthday. Sweet girl, to even think of her. It hadn't occurred to Katalin to give her aunt a present. Climbing onto the stile, she set her feet in the sun and watched them steam. She must get out of this negative attitude. Her nieces were with her for the foreseeable future. She owed it to László to do the best by them. Trying not to think about them didn't work. The answer was to think about them more. More deeply. In a different way. In the way she knew best. She must write a poem. Two poems. Those two wouldn't settle for sharing a poem.

That thought made her smile. She stripped off her jumper, and set off back, pulling a few leaves of wild garlic for a salad as she went. As she padded down the path, a heron crossed overhead on lazy wings. A good omen.

111

At home she opened windows, set her soggy slippers by the Aga and got to work, putting pen to paper and scribbling a continuous flow of random reflections as they tumbled through her mind.

If Katalin were a flower, she would be a lily. Not the sensuous sort with long chilli-red stamens that drop soot and glue, but the single horn variety popular at funerals. Oh dear. But Katalin wasn't a flower. She was a bird, yes – a heron, standing tense, beak poised. She couldn't imagine Katalin dancing. Maybe she'd tried to dance her way out of her body, but couldn't break free.

She tried stringing those ideas together but the result was so cold and vengeful that she tore it up and burned it in the grate. Revenge. Was that the key to what drove Katalin? Revenge for the loss of country and father? Loss of her dancing identity? Or was there something that ran even deeper? Or was it all rubbish?

And Marika? Her flower would be a Californian poppy, that blousy scarlet, or a musk rose, heady with perfume. As a bird she would be a starling. Strutting about, insistent, raucous. Speckled black, but, in the sun, suddenly radiant with iridescent colours like a rainbow in the night sky. Not very hidden depths. It was a reason not to worry so much about Marika. She would blossom. But with Katalin it was different. Where were the depths? Hidden or absent? Nourishing or corrosive? She might survive by staying inside that carapace. But would she grow? And what could she, Klára, do? Writing bad poems wouldn't help. Cake maybe, a peace offering. Something special. Of course, Gerbeaud cake. She'd dig out her mother's recipe for *zserbó szelet*. It would take hours to make and take her mind off the girls.

It was two days after our big row and I was really worried about coming home from school and telling Aunt Klára the news about Kati. I was glad of the walk down the lane, which gave me time to work out how to put it.

Things hadn't been going well since Easter in London. We'd all been in a bad mood, even Aunt. Kati had been a pain in the neck and I kept having nightmares and waking them up. I'd told Aunt nothing about Sergei. I didn't want his presence in Devon. But the black bat was back. I'd be washing up or looking at the board in class and it would fly in front of my eyes, blotting everything out. Was it always going to be there, shutting out the future? Aunt was good at calming me down in the night but she couldn't always be there.

Finn ran to meet me as I came through the door and I could smell that Aunt was ironing. She called from the kitchen that she'd made cake. There she was at the ironing board and the strangest thing happened. It must have been a trick of the light. That and her posture, the boniness of her, leaning over, pressing down, with her hair flopping forward. She was wearing some old grey T-shirt and the whole scene was monochrome. Just like that picture. My postcard. The Picasso

I'd seen with Papa. I completely forgot about what I had to tell her.

Then she moved, looked up and gave me her big dimpling smile. And she was Aunt Klára again. 'Gerbeaud cake! Grandmother's recipe. How about that? Where's Katalin?'

Wow, Gerbeaud cake! Mama sometimes used to sneak it home from the café. Katalin's all-time favourite. Katalin. Of course. What should I say?

'Are you okay? You look as if you've seen a ghost.'

'I did a bit. You looked just like…' I'd cry if I said any more. And if I cried I'd never get to telling her about Katalin. I took a deep breath. 'But that's not… The thing is, Kati's not here. She's gone.'

For a second I saw a surprising flicker in Aunt's blue eyes. As if they lit up and then doused themselves with a frown.

'Not here? You mean she missed the bus? Don't say—'

'She's gone to London. She's not coming back. She packed all her stuff last night and hid it up the lane. She made me promise not to tell you. In case you made a fuss.'

Aunt raised her eyebrows in an exaggerated way. I wanted to laugh but I kept a serious face.

'Made a fuss? Yes, I think I would have made a fuss. Don't look so worried. I'm not about to beat you. Has she gone to your mother? Did she let her know?'

I shook my head. 'No, she's going to stay with Amanda again. She wants to go to secretarial college.'

'Just like that? Huh! How's she going to fix that up? What does your mother say? And what do you mean, "Amanda again"?'

'She set it all up at Easter. Got Amanda and Ena to help her. Ena's doing a course herself – shorthand and typing. Mama doesn't know. Kati never came to Mama's.'

'Oh?' Aunt's eyebrows shot up.

I'd promised not to tell. Aunt was supposed to think we were both staying with Mama for the holidays.

'I see. What about her A levels? She's a bright kid.'

I shrugged. 'She said she couldn't stand it anymore.'

'What? Maths? The school? Me? What couldn't she stand?'

'The country, I think.' I tried not to look at Finn and the mess of stuff on the kitchen table. I knew it was all of that, as well as Aunt herself, which had driven Kati away. Plus she'd be only too pleased to get away from me.

'I see we're going to need this cake,' said Aunt. Very deliberately she placed the last shirt over the airing rack, and folded away the board while I hoisted the rack to the ceiling above the Aga.

'I suppose I have to explain to the school. Not to mention Teréz. I really do think she might have had the courtesy to tell me. To discuss it. What does she take me for? I would hardly have kept her here against her will.' Aunt passed me a slice of cake. 'She's perfectly entitled to leave school if that's what she wants.'

We munched until I couldn't bear the silence.

'I'm sorry. I didn't—'

'It's not your fault. Of course you couldn't have told on her. I'm mad at her, not you. And not so very mad at her, either. It's been hard for her. I know we didn't hit it off. It was always edgy. You know that.'

I nodded.

'Tea! We need tea.' Aunt leapt up to put the kettle on the hot plate. 'And how, come to think of it, is that sister of yours going to finance college?'

'She's got on to that benefactor again. Wrote her a letter. She seems to think the benefactor owes her – because the ballet school didn't work out.'

'And you? Do you think she owes *you*?'

'No. She offered the school, the Priory blooming Academy for blooming Girls. I guess she thought it was an opportunity, but it was dire. We turned it down. End of story. But Kati doesn't think like that. She carries on writing... So far she's got away with it.'

'Good luck to her. But there must come a time when enough is enough.'

Aunt looked up from making tea. 'I'll ring your mother this evening. But do we have a number for this Amanda? I'd better ring there first. I don't suppose your sister will think to let us know she arrived safely.'

She banged the pot down on the table. 'Anyway, to change the subject entirely, what I really want to know – what was going on when you walked through the door? Was it the thought of telling me about Katalin? Or was it something else? You went white as a sheet.'

'Something else. But first I have to go and find something.'

I galloped upstairs, rooted about in the mess of my chest of drawers and found the postcard inside my old prayer book. I gazed at it, remembering how excited I felt when Papa gave it to me – the revelation that Papa might be proud of something I wrote. Kati was always the clever one. My sainted sister, the dancer, the slender one, the goodie-goodie, always being praised for her school marks. While I was slow, dozy, clumsy, fat and spotty. But now... I remembered how words had started tumbling through my mind as we went down the escalators into the Underground. I'd been thinking about how I would describe that picture as I stood on the platform. Before.

I rushed back down to Aunt and thrust it into her hand. 'That was you – as I came through the door. Only for an instant.'

Aunt puckered her lips in a sad half-smile. 'Except I don't exactly represent the oppressed masses.'

'Oh! That's so like what Papa said! You see, Papa...'

And then I couldn't tell her the story for sobbing.

Eventually, Aunt hugged me and said, 'Just write it, Mari. Pick up that thread. It's part of you. Forget the masses – what's *your* angle on this woman?'

I went upstairs and wrote without thinking. I *was* that woman ironing.

My angle is angular, bony and strong, all knuckles and elbows and a cold shoulder as I press down with a force of steel on the steaming iron. I have scrubbed away the stains and now I must eliminate the creases and restore this sheet to blankness, smooth as paper.

Or shall I keep pressing through the smell of scorch until brown edges frill outward into black, until the anvil shape is imprinted on the cloth, until the table top chars and smoulders, until the flat iron drops to the floor, until flames light up the shadows at my back and catch the tress of loose hair that swings with the rhythm of my work?

But who then would launder the sheet needed to pull up over my empty hips and jutting collarbone to cover the dark sockets of my eyes?

I worked hard at the piece, correcting the grammar. For the first time I cared about getting it right. I gave it to Aunt the next day. She didn't look up for ages, although she'd finished reading it, I could tell. I began to think it was pretty bad, but when she did look up she had tears in her eyes.

'Extraordinary,' she said at last. 'You have said so much. This you must keep doing.'

Oh, if only I could. But when Papa died, he took a piece of me with him. He was the only one who thought I was a creative person. He told me I could write and when he went, it went with him. I tried to explain this to Aunt.

'But that was part of you, not part of him,' she said.

'No. *He* believed it. I didn't. He'd only just told me, so it was only just beginning in my head. It wasn't real.'

'But you've just shown me it – it *is* real.'

'But only for that one thing. Because it started when he was still there. I was only picking up the thread.' I really didn't believe I could do it again.

Aunt sighed. 'What can we do with her, Finn?' Finn opened an eye and thumped his tail. 'Look, if your father did take it with him, don't you think he'd want to give it back to you?'

'Of course he would. But he can't, can he?'

'If you talk to him. Do you ever? Of course you do. Ask him for it. It's a gift you must nurture. Really.'

Aunt hardly ever said that anyone *must* do something. It had to be important.

19

It was July 1961, just months after Yuri Gagarin had become the first man in space. Amanda had persuaded Katalin to come to the Russian Trade Fair.

'Free tickets,' she'd said. 'For Earl's Court. Daddy had them spare. He says it should be amusing. Gagarin's supposed to be there.'

Amusing? It might be better than another dreary day of learning shorthand alongside a load of rich debs who were marking time until they got married. But amusing it was not. It was hot and noisy and Katalin found it unnerving to hear Russian being spoken behind the exhibition stands. The displays were boring and seemingly endless, one area leading out of another in an endless labyrinth. Whatever had possessed her to come? She kept overhearing snatches of conversation: the British public gawping at tables and chairs and exclaiming, 'Just like us', as if they imagined people in Russia didn't sit at tables and eat dinner. On the other hand, Katalin very much doubted that the classier exhibits were generally available to ordinary Russians.

'I guess you feel quite at home,' said Amanda as they gazed at a particularly ugly arrangement of living room furniture.

'I certainly do not!'

'But you lived under communism, didn't you? Wasn't it like all this?'

Katalin flushed. There were items here that reminded her of those times, but nothing she could explain, nothing she was willing to admit to.

'We had antique furniture, family pieces.' This was true although very few had remained by the time they left Budapest. She hadn't given a thought to that last apartment for years, and she didn't want to think about it now.

Amanda scoffed her way past the stands and Katalin did her best to laugh along, although she felt more like bursting into tears. A lot of solid-looking Russian men in Soviet-style suits stood about, as well as a few elegantly dressed women, who looked as self-conscious as the men. Slogans and a statue of Lenin added to the oppressive atmosphere. How odd it was, this effort to present Soviet life as sophisticated in order to attract trade from the West. Judging by Amanda's scornful remarks, the attempt had failed. Katalin too, saw past the gloss, but for her it was all too reminiscent of the worst parts of her childhood. At the same time it wakened a longing in her, a harking back to when life was simpler. She didn't want to admit, even to herself, that the restrictions of a life under communism might suit her better than the choices available here in England. She rejected the Communist regime, of course she did. But surely she could embrace the philosophy – communism with a small c – without betraying everything Papa stood for. Or could she? It was all too confusing and confronting and she longed to escape.

The Russian cosmonaut was certainly somewhere in the building. Amanda eventually found out that he was in the fashion theatre, but it was impossible to get anywhere near. The place was swarming with press and bodyguards. When he was rumoured to be leaving, Amanda insisted on joining the crush near the entrance.

'You really fancy him, don't you, this Yuri?'

'He's damn good-looking.'

'He's a bloody Russian, Amanda. A foundry worker, for God's sake. Not quite in your league.'

'What's good enough for Lady Chatterley is good enough for me.'

'But Mellors was a gamekeeper.'

Amanda rolled her eyes. 'Same difference. Here, give me a leg-up.'

She climbed onto a chair and claimed to have seen the top of Gagarin's head.

'Well, that was all a waste of time,' said Katalin as the crowd dispersed.

'Not at all. We've seen history, Kati. Now let's find a drink. I fancy a Pimm's.'

They fought their way into the nearest bar. Amanda elbowed her way to the front of the queue leaving Katalin in possession of a few feet of windowsill. As she waited, her eye fell on a group of Russians at a nearby table. Two of them were discussing Gagarin's itinerary. They seemed to be involved with his visit to London. A third was smoking and not joining the conversation. From time to time he looked up and met her eye.

She felt uncomfortable being watched as she stood on her own and was glad when Amanda returned.

'No Pimm's. I was going to get a G&T instead, but they were pushing the vodka – of course, so I got vodka and tonic, much cheaper. Cheers!'

Katalin ignored the fact that she'd asked for lemonade and took a gulp. She was thirsty and the drink was cold and refreshing. As she listened to Amanda she was aware of the quiet Russian still watching her. His companions went to the bar in quick succession, each returning with a round of shot glasses. On the first occasion the smoker stubbed out his cigarette and downed his in one. When the three of them finally toasted their cosmonaut and the two loud ones left, he stayed behind. As soon as they had gone he lifted a finger in the direction of the bar and within seconds a waiter appeared with a bottle and refilled his glass. No waiting at the bar for him.

'You're not listening,' said Amanda. 'Who's so interesting over there?'

'Nobody. Nothing.'

The Russian looked away as Amanda turned round. He took out a silver cigarette case. Another group of people moved away from the bar area and stood between them and the Russian at his table.

Katalin sipped her drink. It was iced but it wasn't cooling her down. The new people were laughing a lot and gesticulating but still the man's eyes found their way to her. She tried to concentrate on what Amanda was saying about what she should wear to a wedding on Saturday. But she could not stop her eyes sliding in the Russian's direction, just to see if he was still there, still looking. Once she thought she detected the flicker of a smile. She must turn away.

The room was stuffy and she was beginning to feel faint. 'If only this window would open,' she said to Amanda.

'So, black shoes to match my bag? Or blue to match the dress?'

'I'd say black.' She placed her glass carefully on the windowsill. 'I'll just go and find the toilet. Won't be long.'

'Powder room,' said Amanda.

Katalin was calmed by the comparative quiet of the corridor. She felt cooler as soon as she got away from the man's gaze. She could still see his grey eyes slicing through all the animated faces, setting a sightline to her face. What was some Russian doing, watching her like that? Was she under surveillance? She had to remind herself that this was England and Earl's Court, even if it had been taken over by Soviets. Once again she wished she'd never come.

She made her way towards the exhibition area, looking for a way out to some fresh air.

'Excuse me.' The voice coincided with a hand on her shoulder. A confident hand, not rough, but not in any way tentative. The voice was resonant.

Katalin turned and started: to see those eyes at such close quarters was disconcerting. Pale hair glinted silver in the overhead striplight.

'I wanted to see you closer.' He was scooping her along the corridor beside him, a hand firm in the small of her back. He smelled of expensive soap, the sort designed to make men feel tough and invincible. Even as she had the thought, she fell for it herself. Or was it the hand on her back that made him feel powerful? That, and the eyes.

He pushed a door, which swung open onto a stairway. It was cold and dim.

'I need to do this.'

He'd turned her against the wall and, as he spoke into her face, alcohol blended with the smell of soap. Unexpectedly seductive. She took in the clean-cut jaw, wide mouth, the long line of his nose. A lean face, skin stretched over cheekbones her fingers itched to touch. The eyes gazed back, moving over her features, appraising. He lifted her chin to what light there was, falling from high windows.

His touch sent shock waves through her body.

'What is it you have to do?'

'Forgive me. I may be a little drunk, but…' He didn't finish the sentence, but slid cold fingers along the back of her neck so that her hair lifted all over her scalp and goose bumps careered down her arms.

Then he kissed her. Firm lips claimed her mouth, dry, warm, oddly comforting. She closed her eyes, rested in the moment. Then the tip of his tongue was trying to penetrate the barrier of her teeth. Her own tongue went to meet it and he was inside her mouth, his body heavy, pinning her to the wall. It took her a while to identify the thing pressing into her stomach. How could it be so hard and so hot through layers of clothes?

At that instant, all her senses, every cell in her body combined to open a clear channel between what was happening in her mouth and those parts 'down there' that she never referred to. So this was desire. This was what her sister had always been on about. Katalin would always identify this as the moment she lost her virginity.

Suddenly it was over. Abruptly his mouth disengaged, leaving her gasping, empty. He released her and stepped away.

'I forget where I am. I must go.' His voice sounded different, as if he might be under water.

'But why…? What?' Her own voice sounded strange too. Higher, thinner. She gathered herself. 'Why were you watching me?'

'You reminded me of someone I used to know.' He moved away towards the door. 'I have to prepare. For the reception. Comrade Gagarin, you understand. I have to be there.'

She couldn't let him go. 'Please don't rush away.'

She wanted him. Katalin, who had always kept a man a table's width away, wanted this stranger in her bed. 'But you can't just—'

'I must not be late.' He brushed at his cuff as if it might carry telltale traces of her. 'Forgive me.'

He lifted a slender hand and was gone.

She didn't even know his name.

20

At the end of the summer term I dutifully set off to visit Mama. The day after I arrived she told me to go out for the afternoon. It was a Thursday.

'He's not still coming? Sergei?'

Mama grunted as she blotted her lipstick on a scrap of tissue paper.

'Oh, Mama! Well, if he is, then I want to meet him. I want—'

'No, Mari! You are not to meet. I don't want you involved. You are to go out and stay out. If you won't go, I will lock you in and wait outside and send him away.'

Mama almost sounded like her old self, she was so emphatic.

'Why don't you do that anyway? Send him away?'

Mama sighed. 'We've been through all that. Let me manage this my way. It is my business, only my business.'

It was a wet afternoon, so it was easy to merge with the queue at the bus stop under cover of an umbrella. Having watched Sergei turn into the entrance, I walked up the road, crossed over by the Gaumont and approached the parade from the other direction, out of sight of the flat window. I took up position behind a stack of tea chests piled up outside the garages right opposite our staircase. The tea chests were empty so I was able to shift one or two sideways to make a viewing slit.

All I wanted was a good look at this man who was so besotted with Mama. Maybe I'd be able to tell whether he really was the good man Mama claimed him to be. After a while I closed my giveaway umbrella. He wouldn't stay too long. Mama would see to that, for fear of us meeting. Luckily the rain had stopped and the sky was brightening. A crow that had been strutting on the roof took off with a loud croak.

At the same time the door creaked open. He stood on the top step, looking up at the sky, then shook his wet umbrella and started to furl it carefully, taking his time. No hat today. His hair glinted in the pale sun and I couldn't decide whether it was blonde or silver. He wore a long grey raincoat, unbelted, and seemed unnaturally tall, standing as he was at the top of the stairs. His nose was long and straight in a long thin face. In fact everything about him was long and narrow.

He ran neatly down the steps, and I relaxed as he turned away towards the street. But, in that moment, my stomach contracted. It was the way he was holding his umbrella, as many men did, grasping it halfway down so that the sharp tip pointed forward and was well clear of the ground. Nothing unusual in that. But the sight flicked some internal switch, shining a bright light on a buried memory that had eluded me until now. On that fateful occasion I'd seen such an umbrella in my peripheral vision and the image had lain dormant until now. In this instant of revelation I knew that this was how Papa had died – pushed onto the tracks by a thrusting umbrella. And here was the man who had killed him.

21

It was him. Katalin knew it was him. She'd know that pewter-coloured hair anywhere. He was head and shoulders above the stream of people surging onto the pavement from the Underground. It was lucky she was thin. She slipped and slid between people, using her natural agility and sharp elbows to gain ground. But he broke clear of the pack and strode away, turning abruptly and disappearing down a side street. She even tried calling out, but produced a strangulated cry that caused the newspaper vendor on the corner to guffaw. She was suddenly ridiculous and checked herself in order not to run as she set off in pursuit.

The vendor called after her, ''E's never worf it, darlin'.''

Oh, yes he was. She hadn't been able to get him out of her head since the encounter at Earl's Court. Today, for the third time this week, she'd been on her way to the Soviet Embassy at Notting Hill Gate in the hope of meeting him again. And here he was. Her strategy had worked. She held her breath until she spotted him again. He was slowing down now, smoothing his hair. He checked his watch and turned into a doorway.

It was a restaurant, dark-panelled and expensive-looking. The room was L-shaped and the booths lined the inner angle of the L, positioned away from the door so that passers-by could not see in. They each consisted of two high-backed settles facing each other. The red cushions and polished mahogany gleamed in the soft light in contrast to the more brightly-lit area on the street side: private cocoons reserved for secret meetings and intimate conversations.

As Katalin stepped inside, the Russian was crossing to one of the booths on the far side of the room. He bent to greet someone already sitting there who was blocked from her sight. What to do? She couldn't interrupt. She wouldn't know what to say, especially in front of a witness. A waiter escorted her to a small table at the back of the room.

It gave her a good view. The man was folding the length of himself into the booth. She could see the top of his head inclining, leaning back, his hair gilded by the glow of a Tiffany lamp suspended over their table. A waiter arrived with a tray of drinks. A tisane, a bottle of wine. An intense conversation seemed to be taking place. Katalin sipped her coffee and waited.

Katalin was on her second coffee when the Russian stood up. Briskly, he shrugged on his jacket. She recalled the tautness of his body and shivered, cold as mercury. He seemed about to leave, alone. He raised a hand towards his hidden companion and gave a half bow. Curiously old-fashioned.

Should she follow him? She grabbed her bag, counted out some coins onto the table, and sat poised on the edge of her seat. A casual glance into the booth would satisfy her curiosity about his companion.

He turned on his heel, raised a hand to the maître d' and was out of the door. But, as Katalin started forward, lightning sliced the plate glass window so fiercely that she was surprised not to hear the splintering of glass. All the lights dipped momentarily as thunder cracked overhead.

Following him now was out of the question. Shaking, Katalin sank back onto her chair. As a child she had always run in terror for the cover of her parents' bed during thunderstorms. Whether they were in it or not, the sweet-sour smell of them had been reassuring. Now there was no such bed. She would take refuge in the powder room for a while and then order a drink, a brandy perhaps.

A second lightning flash caused her to falter as she threaded her way between tables. Katalin breathed in deeply and straightened her back.

As she approached the booth, the occupant stood, just as lightning once again forked across the room. It lit up her face with eerie clarity.

'What the hell are *you* doing here?' said Marika.

'What were *you* doing with *him*?' Katalin gripped the armrest of the settle, then loosened her fingers for fear her sister would notice their white knuckles.

'You know Sergei? There's a surprise.'

A name! At last she knew his name. 'You keep your sticky hands off him.'

'Don't tell me my sainted sister's taking an interest in a man!' Marika dropped back onto the crimson cushions.

Katalin ignored her sister's open-mouthed mime of being overcome with shock. 'That is none of your business.'

'But maybe it is, Kati. You'd better sit down. It's all right – the thunder's moving away. There's still some wine.' Marika beckoned a waiter who fetched another glass. 'I didn't fancy it on my own, but we may as well drink it.'

'You still haven't told me what you were doing with him.'

Marika poured wine into both glasses. 'And you haven't told me why you followed him. You did, didn't you? Or did you just happen to—?'

'What if I did follow him?'

'I don't think he'd like it.'

'You know who he is, don't you? Of course you do.'

'And you don't. There's interesting.' Marika raised an eyebrow and smiled across at her. 'Where did you meet him?'

'At Earl's Court, at the exhibition. He was watching me. He followed *me* that time.' Katalin felt a flicker of pride.

'I'll put you out of your misery. He's some attaché at the Soviet Embassy.'

'I don't mean that. Of course he is. But what's his *role*? Why are you—?'

'You really don't know? Who he is to *us*?'

'To us? I don't know what you're talking about.' Katalin laced her hands tightly under the table. Were they lovers? In which case they would have left together, wouldn't they? Unless he was being discreet. Maybe he was waiting for Marika somewhere.

Marika stared across the top of her wineglass. 'You really don't know, do you? Oh, blimey. Now I'm wondering – suppose he knew who you were! The bastard. Or was it just chance? Did he say why he picked you out, followed you?'

'Said I reminded him of someone.' Why did she spoil it by telling her sister that? 'But he was very... He was turned on.' She didn't mention the vodka.

Marika raised her eyebrows. 'I can see this is going to take some time. I need a pee. And something to eat. This stuff is making me squiffy.'

She left the table and walked purposefully over to the bar. Her shoes were shiny patent with peep toes, sling backs and ridiculously high heels. But Marika walked in them with confidence and a flick of her hips at each step. It was an unmistakably sexy walk. She chatted to the bartender as he put up a tray of drinks, leaning on the counter with her chin on her hand laughing up at him. Her black dress was not quite too short and not quite too tight and she was not quite overweight. In fact, Katalin recognised with a shock, she might be watching Mama. Her sister had turned into Mama, meeting men in bars.

Then Marika spun round and was once again her fifteen-year-old little sister. 'I ordered us both an omelette and chips. Okay? Won't be long.' She sashayed away towards the powder room, bag swinging on her elbow.

Katalin took a mouthful of wine and waited, listening to the distant rumble of thunder as it faded away towards the East End, trying to make sense of what her sister had said.

Marika wriggled back into her seat and raised her glass. 'Drink,' she said. 'You will need it.'

Katalin looked warily from her sister to the wine and took a sip. 'So who is he?'

'Sergei is the Thursday man.' Marika gave an edge of drama to her announcement and sat back, expectant.

Katalin was puzzled. Strangely, the phrase caused her gut to contract but her head was making no connection.

'Don't tell me…' Marika was wide-eyed. 'You did know about him? Didn't you?'

Still she said nothing. She wasn't going to want this news, whatever it was. For some reason it would make Sergei undesirable, which contradicted every nerve in her body. Her sister expected her to know about his mysterious identity. Her churning stomach evidently did know, but was keeping it a secret from her brain. These facts had sinister implications.

She shook her head fiercely, as much to say she didn't want to know, as to deny knowledge.

'Oh, Kati. I thought you must know. I thought you'd help me to remember.'

Her sister wasn't mocking her ignorance, which was even more disturbing.

'Mama had this visitor,' Marika was saying, 'in Budapest. He was her lover.'

'What? You can't know that. How do you—?

'I saw his bottom. His bare bum. Through that crack in the door.'

Katalin swallowed hard. What on earth? She couldn't bear to even think of it. How dare Mama. Heat rose to her throat.

'How? When? What crack? What are you talking about?'

'When I had measles. I woke up and I heard them. Papa was in prison, so—'

'But you were only four when you had measles.'

'So? I crept and looked through the crack, like I said. And there was his coat on the chair in the hall.'

'That doesn't prove anything. That was years ago. How can you know it was him? His backside through a crack – you little sneaky spy. It could have been anyone. You were little. You could have—'

'Shush-shush, Kati. Calm down. We're in this together. It's no good being angry with me. We have to deal with it.'

'What do you mean? Deal with it? We? *I* will deal with it. No, don't you shush me. You've got the wrong end of the stick. He and I are—'

'He's pestering Mama. It's upsetting her. The trouble is, he's obsessed with her. Has been for years.'

'But how do you know it's him? I'm sure—'

'I'm not just relying on seeing his bottom, if that's what you think! Mama's admitted it. I've seen him. There's no doubt, Kati. So, whatever is going on between the two of you… Well, for one thing it can't mean much – and for another, it has to stop. Obviously.'

'Stop?' Katalin could hear her voice rise and break. She took a breath and brought it down an octave. 'Just keep your nose out of my business, Mari. I've only just met Sergei. The last thing I want is you weighing in with stupid stories and spoiling everything.'

'Are you seriously telling me you would go ahead with this? Get involved with a man who has been your own mother's lover and would like to be again?' She paused and leaned forward. 'This is Mama we're talking about.'

Katalin felt her stomach turn. At the same moment a waiter appeared in a flourish of white napkins and laid a plate of omelette and chips in front of each of them. Marika picked up her fork in one hand and a chip in the other.

'Good chips. Come on, Kati. Eat. It will make you feel better.'

Always so greedy, her sister. But Katalin could not eat.

'Why do you never come and see Mama? Why do you never phone? We worry about you. Don't you care about her?'

Katalin shrugged. 'There is never time. I…' It wasn't true. There was usually too much time. But Mama would ask what she was doing with her life and she didn't yet have an answer. Plus, she dreaded going back to the flat.

'Anyway, how did you meet him? Was it at the flat? And why were you meeting him here?'

'Mama wouldn't let me meet him. I spotted him leaving the first time. Confronted Mama. It was awful, Kati. Then I… Well, I needed to meet him so I left a message at the embassy. He thought he'd be meeting Mama. He was annoyed.'

In spite of herself Katalin had to admire her sister's nerve. 'What did you say to him?'

'I warned him off. Told him how much it's upsetting Mama. And that if he cared for her at all, he'd leave her alone.'

'Do you think he will?'

Marika shrugged. 'Who knows?' She sipped her wine and speared a chip. 'And you and Sergei? How well do you know him? How often…?'

She couldn't tell Marika the truth. She would think it bizarre. 'He and I, we—'

'You haven't already? Kati? You haven't slept with the man?'

Katalin shook her head. 'Not slept. Not yet. Kissed.' But in her head it was more than a kiss.

'What do you mean – not yet?'

Katalin said nothing. She couldn't meet her sister's eye. She picked up her fork and prodded the omelette.

'Kati, have some self-respect. Think what Mama would think.'

'You wouldn't! You wouldn't tell Mama?'

'Wouldn't I?'

'I want him, Mari. I need it.' The words erupted from her and she felt shame to be so exposed. 'You'd understand that, at least.'

Marika nodded. 'But it doesn't have to be Sergei.'

Oh, but it does, thought Katalin.

Marika was stabbing a chip in her direction. 'Think what Papa would think. And talking of Papa—'

Katalin dropped her fork. 'I need to…' She fled to the powder room, locked herself into a cubicle and leant against the door. She couldn't even throw up.

'Get a grip,' she told herself. 'Get the facts.'

She splashed water on her face and patted it dry with pink tissues that gave off a nauseous perfume. Since when had Marika been reliable? Just because she seemed in control, concerned even, didn't mean she wasn't the same old Marika.

'So, what's this about Sergei pestering Mama?' she said when she got back to the table. She even made herself chew on a chip.

'He just turned up one day. He'd heard, apparently, about Papa and came to offer his condolences.'

'How did he know? How did he know where she lived?'

Marika shrugged. 'Mama wonders that too. But they keep tabs on everyone don't they? The Soviets. And he delayed deliberately, he said. Out of respect.'

'And how come, the "Thursday man"?'

'He always came on a Thursday. She got to know him at work, at the coffee house. He bribed her. He gave us food. He made sure we kept the apartment. He even saw to her papers when we left. She told me everything.'

Katalin felt her stomach lurch like the time Aunt Klára drove too fast over a humpback bridge and the wheels left the road. Only this was worse. There was a ring of truth in what her sister said. It explained a lot. About how they'd got out. About Papa's strange moods.

Katalin wanted to protest, to yell, 'Not fair, not fair!' Where was the justice in all this? First she was wrenched away from her beloved ballet in Budapest, then thrown into that awful school, then humiliated by that Costello woman. And now, the only time she'd met a man she would look twice at, he turned out to be her mother's lover. It was too much.

Marika was grabbing her arm. 'Kati, this is serious. I need your help – because it was Sergei who killed Papa.'

Ridiculous. Whatever next? Katalin laughed. 'What utter rubbish! Now I know you're hysterical.'

'We need to—' Marika started.

'No. I'm sorry, Mari. We don't need to do anything. You need to stop pretending you're a grown-up and dabbling in business that isn't yours. You need to stop imagining things and go back to your precious Aunt Klára and get on with being a schoolgirl.'

'But Kati, if only you'd listen…'

'No. I can't cope with any more. I need to go. I need to sleep. Get the bill, can you?'

'No need. It's on Sergei's account. The least he can do. And Kati, take a cab. You look awful.'

She couldn't afford a cab, of course. But that concern. From Marika of all people. The world seemed to have shifted on its axis.

22

It was high tide on an August morning, the air already warm. Waves folded themselves gently onto the beach, hardly shifting the pebbles. Like a pan of eggs on low simmer, thought Klára. By midday the water would have drained away and there they'd be, ready for the holidaymakers to shell and eat for lunch. She smiled at her fantasy and dropped her skirt and T-shirt in a heap.

The shingle was sharp underfoot and the water still surprisingly cold. It iced upward over her knees and thighs. She paused at the edge of the shelf, feet longing to step free of the stones, warm body holding back. A wave took the decision away and she swam out, fast and breathless. She started to plough along, parallel to Finn who was keeping an eye on her from the shallows. He'd never taken to swimming. Marika had phoned the evening before and Finn had actually sat up and cocked his head when he heard her voice.

A family arrived to set up camp, loaded with picnic bags, buckets and spades. She turned onto her back and let the water finger her skull and splash over her face. A vapour trail was blurring into white wool in the clear blue sky. The sea filled her ears cutting out the shouts of the children, enclosing her in its silence. Water – so full of sound on the outside, so quiet on the inside.

Marika hadn't sounded her usual self. Almost as if trying not to cry. When Klára questioned her she'd just said London didn't suit her any more. Klára could understand that. There was no point in worrying. She was with her mother, after all. And she'd be back in a week or so.

It had been a luxury to have the house to herself for so long. Progress on her collection of poems had been slow at first but, as she got used to the solitude, the images and rhythms had started to flow. Today she was giving herself a day off, no actual writing, but time to mull.

The heat was building as Klára walked up to the house, glad of the wet trails of hair cooling her back. How on earth would those girls be managing this heat in London? Here it was glorious, but there it would be a nightmare. As she let herself in through the conservatory, she was surprised by a banging on the front door. She opened it to Father Patrick.

'Well, Klára,' he said. 'You're looking more the wild woman than usual. What's the sea temperature like just now?'

Patrick loved to swim but was constrained by his role. He'd once told her, 'Folk tell me their darkest secrets in the privacy of the confessional, but they cannot contemplate the baring of a priestly leg on a public beach.'

Once they were settled with a pot of coffee, he came straight to the point.

'I am worried about your young niece. Without breaking confidentiality, I've been perturbed by the nature of her confessions – as well as impressed that she often comes into the church and sits with the Virgin, just staring up at her blessed face. You're a wise woman, Klára, for all you're a pagan – and, as you know, I don't believe God to be fussy about such distinctions. But I thought you should know.'

'I can't say I'm at all surprised. But what can I do? She's a complicated creature.'

'And a spiritual one. But also, shall we say, very physical. It seems to me, she may be quite a naughty girl. It could have consequences for you. I wouldn't wish that upon you. Perhaps you can be talking to her – woman to woman – so to speak. All I can do is pray.'

'She has a creative gift, too. I'm trying to nurture that.'

'Taking after yourself, then. How's the poetry going? As I've said before, poetry is much like prayer.' He stroked Finn who had come to lean against his leg. 'Not all that passes for poetry, of course. But if you find one poem, one line – you know what I mean? It stops the world.'

Klára nodded.

'I often think, people would be better off reading poetry than the Bible. But don't be telling a soul I uttered such an opinion.'

Klára laughed. 'We may not share a religion, but we share a spirituality, you and I. As for young Marika, I understand. The world stopped for *her* when her father died. And not in a good way. Mind you, it's her sister I find more worrying, she's so closed off. Didn't like Finn, didn't like me, and as far as I can tell, doesn't like Marika. But she's taken herself to London. It's over to her mother.'

'It can't have been easy, being landed with the two of them.'

'That, Patrick, is the understatement of the year. Not exactly the maternal type. I flounder along and I can do with all the help I can get. It was good of you to come. I appreciate that.'

'I always enjoy a chat with you. Your coffee is uncommonly good and when you open the door like a vision of the mermaid on the banks of the Rhine, what more can a man want?'

After Patrick had gone, Klára sat puzzling about Marika, but came to no conclusions. She harvested blackcurrants and runner beans and in the evening walked to the clearing in the fading light to talk to László and the rooks about her challenging niece. The birds were clattering in the tall elms, launching off like sooty rags, settling again with a cacophony of cries. Taking no notice. Caught up in their own important drama.

23

I was relieved to see Kati coming through the door of the restaurant. I still needed to convince her that Sergei was behind Papa's death.

'Thank goodness you got here first.' I waved her into the booth.

Kati frowned. 'Did you tell him I'd be here?'

'No. He'll expect Mama. Which is why he'll come.'

'Not that trick again.'

'And instead he will be confronted by the two of us telling him to get lost.'

'But I don't want him to get lost.'

'Of course you do, Kati. You cannot want that snake hanging round Mama. *She* doesn't—'

'Not hanging round Mama. Round me. It is me he wants.'

'Oh, my sainted sister. You have a moment of lust and you imagine you're madly in love. Forget it Kati. Now, about what I tried to tell you last time— Oh, damn. He's here. He's early.'

I stood and shook hands with Sergei. He looked from me to Kati and back to me. He looked around the restaurant and back at the empty seat as if willing Mama to materialise.

I sat down and indicated the seat next to me. He folded himself into it slowly.

'Where is Teréz?' His eyes seemed to look through me.

'Mama is at home.' I shrunk like a little girl.

'But you said you were bringing her.'

'No. I said I was bringing *some*one. This is…' I pressed back on my seat as I had against the wall as a child. The memory overwhelmed me.

I am six years old hurrying home, hurrying to tell Mama that I've won a star for reading, a gold star.

A man on the stairs, a threatening smile.

'Hallo, little girl. You must be Marika.'

Backing against the wall, pressing against the rough plaster as if I can push it outward, to make more space to get past this huge coat which reeks of something strange and unpleasant.

A rustling sound and something shiny in front of my face. A bonbon wrapped in red and gold cellophane. Mustn't take it. Don't accept gifts from strangers. But I can't take my eyes off it. And he knows my name, doesn't he? Getting past the coat, stumbling on the stair, because my eye is still on the candy. At the last possible moment snatching it, scrambling up and away, stuffing it into a pocket. An echo of thin laughter in the stairwell, fading into footsteps going down and down.

Sergei had interrupted what I was saying. 'I did not expect sly tricks. This displeases me.'

I tore myself away from the past, from the bonbon, which I hid under my pillow. I indicated Kati. 'We need to talk to you and I wanted to be sure you'd come.'

Sergei was staring at Kati, who was giving him cow's eyes and a smile I'd never seen before.

'Do I know you from somewhere?' Sergei's tone was almost rude, aggressive. It wasn't an inquiry. It was a rebuttal of the come-on she was so blatantly giving him.

But Kati wasn't seeing it. 'Of course you do,' she said. 'The Trade Fair. Earl's Court.' She even stretched her hand across the table towards him. 'You were watching me – in the bar? Remember?' Her voice began to falter as no response came.

I felt a sudden surge of pity for my poor lovelorn sister. I wanted to scoop her up and take her away. At the same time I wanted to slap his face.

'You kissed her,' I said and it came out more as an accusation than the statement I intended.

Recognition dawned in his pale eyes and was quickly extinguished. 'What if I did?' he said. 'That is not a crime. It is no reason to bring me here on a false pretence.' He looked from Kati to me. 'Who is she, anyway?'

I waited for Kati to introduce herself but she had turned chalky white and was staring at the table.

'She is my sister. This is Katalin.'

'Your *sister*?' He placed both hands, still gloved, abruptly on the table and made to stand up. I grabbed his arm to hold him down.

'We need to speak to you. We have a message from our mother. She is made ill by your attentions. She means it when she says she will not see you again. You are to stay away from her.'

He turned his gaze on me, a steely glare that made me shiver. I struggled not to look away.

'I think it is not your business, what happens between Teréz and me. You will regret it, if you interfere.' He stood and brought his heels together with a click.

'Ladies.' He loaded that last word with sarcasm and turned to go.

But Katalin was out of her seat, standing in his path. 'I will come with you. I will explain. I will—'

The pain in her voice made my throat contract.

He warded off her words with a black leather palm. 'You will not. I remember now, you have been following me. Stalking. An unpleasant habit. And you are not very good at it. You will stop, or there will be consequences.' He sidestepped her and swept out of the door.

Kati turned on me. 'Look what you've done!' she slammed back into her seat, covering her face. 'You interfering cow.' She lifted her head. 'You got him here to humiliate me. Didn't you? It's nothing to do with Mama. Mama doesn't even know, does she?'

'Of course she doesn't know. But she needs help, Kati. You must help me.'

'Help you? Are you mad? After what you've done tonight? I never—'

'But Kati, you don't understand. You didn't believe me last time. You can never see him the same way when I explain.'

Kati rolled her eyes, back on familiar ground, ready to slate everything I said.

I leaned towards her and dropped my voice. 'Kati, this man really did kill Papa.'

'Don't be ridiculous. I told you before, that's nonsense.' She glared at me, but she still sat there, waiting to hear more.

I explained about the umbrella and how my memory returned, how that last piece of the jigsaw had come back to me.

'Now, do you see? You couldn't take it in before. You were already too upset – finding out about him and Mama.'

She stared, and for a moment I thought she was convinced. Then she barked an odd hollow laugh. 'I don't believe the rubbish you talk. You see a man carrying an umbrella and you accuse him of murder? Have you any idea how many people carry umbrellas in London?'

'That's not the *point*. It brought back the *image*. That was how Papa was killed. I know it. Sergei may not have actually done it himself. But don't you see? He's the obvious person. The KGB were after Papa anyway. *And* Sergei had a personal motive. He wanted Papa out of the way. He wanted Mama.'

'So if, if, *if* your ridiculous theory is correct, then we can both expect to be prodded under a train by the end of the week. Brilliant! Or are you going to the police to tell them you have solved the mystery of our father's death – which incidentally was ruled to be an accident – by seeing a man with an umbrella? I'm sure they will be arresting him in minutes.'

'I'm not such a fool as you think, Kati. I'm right. I know I'm right, but I also know I can never prove it. That is why—'

'That is why you keep well out of it. Sergei remembered me. I saw his eyes light up. I will go to him. I know he wants *me*. Not Mama. You can stop worrying about Mama. Sergei will be with me. Solves everything.'

Was my sister deranged? Her eyes were shining in a strange way. I'd never seen her like this. 'Kati, you mustn't. You heard what he said.' I paused. What on earth had I started? Kati might really be in danger. 'Pursuing him would be the worst thing. It'll make him mad.'

'So, I should play hard to get, you think?'

I stared. She was serious. Forgetting her rage in her need for advice. The enormity of what she was suggesting made me feel physically sick. I waved at a passing waiter and ordered two double vodkas.

'You don't seriously mean you would go with a man who, one, has been our mother's lover, and two, has killed or caused the death of our father?'

Put like that, I could see Kati had to stop and think. But not for long.

'He might once have been Mama's lover, but that was way back when Papa was in prison. As to Papa's death – yes, I too am convinced he was liquidated. But I do not believe for one moment Sergei had anything to do with it. So, yes, I do seriously mean I will go with him. He is a good man. I know it.'

The same words Mama used. It didn't match the ruthlessness I had seen in his eyes tonight. I'd seen him in the raw, all courtesy and old-fashioned manners swept away.

'You're mad, Kati. The man's a killer. I fear for you.'

'Don't waste any time worrying about me, my little drama queen. And don't imagine I'm staying to drink these with you.' She waved at the vodkas which had just been set before us and pulled on her coat. 'You stick with looking after Mama. Oh, and remember to go back to school. Maybe Aunt clever Klára will knock some sense into you.'

Kati was gone. I stayed and drank both vodkas and got a taxi home because, suddenly, I imagined Sergei lurking on every corner.

I woke with my head and heart pounding. I sat up and listened. Mama snoring. The tap dripping. The rumble of a bus shuddering through the floorboards. Everything as normal. I still hadn't solved the Sergei problem. In fact it had got worse. Kati was involved. Not the calculating, sensible sister I'd known all my life, but an unpredictable, infatuated creature. I'd counted on Kati as an ally, but she'd taken up with the enemy. Worse than that, she was probably more at risk from Sergei than Mama. He was perfectly capable of getting rid of her. She'd be so vulnerable. She wouldn't see it coming.

The way he'd looked at me had zapped all my energy. As if those pale eyes radiated a lethal substance. The Thursday man. Now I remembered why Thursday – how I remembered that, and why the whole affair made me feel guilty.

*

I am back there in the steamy fug of that kitchen, the smell of cabbage and the stuff Papa put on his boots to make them waterproof. Papa is writing at the end of the table.

I run to hug Mama as she comes home from work.

'Oh, Mama, you smell just like the Thursday man!' I say.

Mama is undoing her coat, filling a pan with water and lighting the stove. 'The what? I don't know what you're talking about.' She shoots me a look over her shoulder. A look that says, stop right there.

Papa looks up from where he's writing at the end of the kitchen table. 'What's that?'

Mama gives an elaborate shrug and shakes her head. 'Margit had some perfume, if that's what you mean. We were all trying it.'

Margit is one of the waitresses in the café. She is plain and smells of cabbage. She is the last person in the world to have any perfume.

Before I can say, 'Margit?', the door bursts open and Kati comes in, out of breath and trying to talk and cough at the same time. Papa sits her down and Mama brings her a cup of water and takes her coat to hang it up. As usual, Kati is getting a fuss made of her.

But as soon as she manages to get the words out that there's a demonstration in Andrassy Street, Papa is grabbing his hat and coat and is halfway out the door before she's finished talking. Mama reminds him dinner will be ready in an hour. But as the door slams behind him she turns off the gas, which is bad news as I'm already hungry.

'I'll give myself a breather for five minutes.' Mama kicks off her shoes and sits down with her feet on Kati's lap. 'Give them a rub, sweetie, it's been a long day.'

We all know Papa won't be back for supper. He may be out half the night. He may not come back at all.

But he's there the next day helping with my maths homework. It's Sunday and Mama and Kati are out. Papa says, 'Who's the Thursday man you talked about yesterday?'

I tell him about the sweets and how I knew it was Thursday because I was always carrying the extra bag with my swimming togs. He asks me questions, like which floor was he coming from? Mostly I don't know the answers.

Papa's voice sounds cross, maybe because I took the sweets.

I say, 'Anyway, I haven't seen him for ages now.'

'Not since I came out of prison, I'll bet.'

He says it quite lightly as if it might be a joke but when I look up and see his face I know it isn't. It goes with Mama's look as she lit the stove, the look that said she'd like to put me in the pot and boil me. I should never have mentioned the Thursday man. Up until that moment he's just been a smell. Now he's turned into an ogre.

It feels like the moment when you know you're going to be sick, except the feeling is in my head. How can your brain vomit?

I coped with it back then by putting it together with what I'd seen through the crack when I'd had measles – the Thursday man wasn't real; he was the result of the fever – the fiery meanderings in my head, wanting Papa to come home from prison. None of it could be true. But now, I'm facing reality and the guilt of betraying Mama.

Kati was right about one thing. I should go back to school, go home to Aunt. I was just a kid, trying to be sophisticated, drinking vodka and imagining I could influence a man like Sergei. Term would start the following week. It was time to be ironing my school shirt in Aunt's kitchen.

24

I couldn't wait to be gone. But Mama ignored me when I tried to tell her which train I was going to catch.

'I lied to your father, Mari. I never liked that.'

Mama rocked back and forth and the sweat marks on her blouse crept beyond the sepia of the existing tidemark. The room reeked of sweat and bad breath. I didn't smell too fresh myself, but it all seemed to fit with the messy truth I was hearing.

'I've never told Katalin. I know I should have, but I never had the courage.'

'Kati? What's it to do with Kati?'

'I'm coming to that. Just wait. Sergei was an escaped prisoner of war. He escaped from a German camp, made it into Hungary. 1943, it was.'

'You've known Sergei as long as that?'

Mama nodded. 'Eighteen years, yes. He was taken in by people up in Buda, one of the posh houses. That was typical of Sergei. He always fell on his feet. Some family connection of his mother's, I believe it was.'

She blew on the tea I'd made, but it was still too hot to drink.

'I worked in that house, doing the laundry mainly. Trying to make ends meet. He was a guest, but left to his own devices. He didn't like to go out. And he kept a low profile when visitors came. When the people were out he played their piano, wandered round the place, bored. One day he heard me singing. That's how I first met him.'

Oh, yes. Mama singing. Always she used to sing – while she cooked, while she cleaned. Not now.

'It kept me going, the singing. Because I'd come to accept I'd never see László again. Soldiers never came back from the Russian front. It didn't happen.'

She dabbed her eyes with one of the balled-up tissues that littered the table.

'All those fine young men. Gone. Dead.'

'Go on, Mama.'

'Where was I? Yes. Sergei. One day… You see, he didn't force himself on me. I looked up from ironing one day. He was watching me from the door. We were alone down there. The family were all out. I put the iron away and took him by the hand to a passage where there was a great heap of linen waiting to be washed. The best damask from some big dinner. We fell on each other. He had not been with a woman for some time. And I'd been missing—'

I held up a hand. I could well imagine Sergei would be a good lover, but imagining was enough.

'We were both meeting a need. That's how I thought of it. We didn't do it often, there weren't many opportunities. But I got pregnant. I was desperate, but he just smiled and said he'd come back for me after the war. He told me to call the child Nadia.'

I felt as if I'd dropped three floors in a lift. Of course. Kati. With her pale skin and her long face. Quite unlike any of us. What an idiot I'd been not to see it.

Mama's hands were shaking and she clutched them together.

'But then, of course, everything changed. I was eight months gone when we were occupied by the Nazis. March, that was. Sergei vanished overnight. Was he rounded up? Did he escape? No idea. Kati was born three weeks later. No way could I call her Nadia. As if! In Budapest at that time, a Russian name! Impossible.' She sighed. 'There I was, alone. Wondering about two men who might be dead or alive.'

'And Papa? When he got home? And you had a baby?'

'He was a good father. He never made any difference between you.' But Mama still had the faraway look that went with Sergei. Long-suffering – but taking pleasure, preening.

'That's why you were always so vague about the time Papa was at the Russian front.' I paused. 'So, when Papa was having a terrible time…' I felt sick.

'I thought he was dead, Mari.' She shook her head with the flutter of a smile. 'I was distraught. I told him I was raped. For his sake. Raped on the way home by some drunken soldier. I'm not sure he believed me, but that wasn't the point.'

'And when Sergei turned up again? Did Papa realise it was the same guy? Did he not put two and two together? Why else would a Soviet want to help you escape, if not to help his own child?'

The question turned Mama's attention to the tea. She sipped and sipped until I thought she wouldn't answer. She must have been arranging the words.

'You forget, Mari. A small matter of history. Katalin was born in 1944. We were occupied by the Nazis. There were no Russians in Budapest in 1943. As to the prisoners of war, hardly anyone knew about them. No, László never had a clue.'

I couldn't believe that my astute father, with all his underground connections and information sources, hadn't found something out. Then again, maybe he didn't want to know.

139

'But surely, Mama—'

'You also forget what I have told you often enough – the state of him when he got home. How long it took…'

Mama could no longer cope. She dissolved into sobs and tears.

I thought about it half the night. It was one thing that Sergei was Mama's lover, another that he had probably killed Papa, but quite another that he was Kati's biological father. She had to know.

Surely this news would stop Kati pursuing him. I would have one more attempt at looking after my sister.

In the evening I gathered enough coins and went to the phone box on the corner so that Mama wouldn't overhear. Amanda answered.

'Who's asking for this Katalin?'

'It's Marika, for God's sake. What's all that about?'

'Just checking you aren't one of Daddy's spies. He doesn't want her here. He says we don't consort with the sort of people who get pushed under trains. And as he's paying the rent—'

'Just get her, Mand, before my money runs out.'

I could just imagine Amanda and Ena Foley dining out on the story of Papa's death – "I just let his daughter sleep on the floor, poor thing. Daddy would die if he knew."

After what seemed an age, Kati was in my ear. 'Whatever do you want now?'

'I want you to make a promise.' I didn't wait for her questions. 'I want you to promise not to see Sergei. Not to follow him or go anywhere with him, even if he invites you. Especially if—'

The pips interrupted and I crammed in the rest of my money.

'Especially if he invites you.'

'You are mad. Of course I will go. Who do you think you are? Why does my little sister always want to spoil things for me?'

I fought back tears. 'I'm worried for you, Kati. He killed Papa, remember. No, I know you don't believe that. But even if—'

'Just shut up, Mari.'

'There's another thing. Something I have to tell you.' How could I tell Kati this on the telephone? It was so hard to say.

'Mari, you waste—'

I swallowed hard. 'You really need to know this. Listen, Kati. Sergei is—'

Damn. The bloody pips again. No more money. And I hadn't managed to tell her the critical fact.

25

She was close to him now, close enough to reach out and touch his ramrod back. But as she stretched forward he spun round.

'I can't get rid of you.'

It wasn't a question, but she shook her head.

'You must come to my apartment.'

He strode on and she followed. Did he mean it? Did he mean now?

In the lift he turned away and she was looking at his back again, the set of his shoulders, the soft gleam of his hair. She tried to breathe normally, blotting her palms against pleated Terylene. Mari's warning drummed in her head – "I want you to promise – don't follow – don't go – even if he invites you – especially…" Ridiculous stuff. She had her own life to lead.

What would Sergei do with her? Might he have a fur rug on his bed? A bearskin or a wolf pelt maybe? Or perhaps she was there to be punished, which brought to mind leather and whips. She'd read about such practices and the idea made her blush as the lift door hummed open.

The flat was cell-like. A tiny hall with four closed doors. He set down his briefcase against the wall, pulled off his gloves and smoothed them together over the top of it. As if she wasn't there. He hung his coat on the hanger waiting on one of the pegs above the briefcase and took hers to put on the other peg. He opened the first door and pulled out a chair at the kitchen table.

She was in his flat but seemed to be in a parallel universe. He didn't speak or touch her. She felt invisible. There was no window, no cooker. Just a gas ring, a kettle and a fridge, which gave off an eerie light when he opened it. He took a bottle from the icebox compartment, set it on the table and opened a cupboard. She was mesmerised by the bottle, which frosted itself and smoked like a vessel in an alchemist's laboratory. She half expected an incantation, but he merely poured the oily liquid into shot glasses and lifted his.

'So, Nadia.'

She was about to say, 'Katalin,' when he said 'Cheers', in a plummy English accent, as if mocking. Mocking her? The English? The system? Himself? What was this about?

'Drink, drink! It is best when iced.' He downed his in one as she had seen him do in the bar at the exhibition.

She sipped and the cold fire made her feel stronger, so she went on sipping until he refilled the glasses. She wouldn't drink it this time. She must keep her wits about her. All the time he stared across at her and said nothing. Why was she here? He's fucking me with his eyes, she thought. She could feel it. That was something her nympho sister might have said. And she, Katalin, wanted more than the eyes. What was happening to her?

For the second time he downed the spirit as if it were water. 'This is a dilemma like none other.' He was staring past her now, at the wall. 'On the one hand, I would like to get to know you as a lover, to make love to you.'

He paused. Her entire being lifted at those words. But why would he not look at her when he spoke them? There was something not quite human about his eyes, a feral quality, a dangerous edge that was seductive and spoke to the ruthless streak in her own character. Wolfish. That was the word: a word that hurtled her back down the years to Budapest where she was pushing her sister in the pram. A smell of leaf mould and wet fur. The howl of an animal too close up. Shaking. Marika's babyish chanting, 'Kati's got wolf eyes! Kati's got wolf eyes!' She shuddered.

Right now Sergei wouldn't meet her gaze. She started to stand, to go towards him.

But he lifted a hand. 'It is a dilemma. Because, on the other hand…' He paused again. His wolf eyes flickered strangely but kept their fixation on the wall. 'On the other hand, I would like to get to know you as a father knows his daughter.'

She felt herself plummeting as if down some deep well inside herself and as she fell she heard the echo of Mari saying, "There's something else you need to know."

'You did know? Didn't you?'

This fact, which had been flitting like a mosquito on the edge of her awareness, was coming in to land. The sting was inescapable. *Wolf eyes.*

'Maybe you really did not.' He sighed. 'So Teréz never told you. Not even after your father died?'

His eyes met hers for a moment. They were full of sadness. She shook her head.

'For that reason, you see, if I were to take you and make love to you, then we might have to kill ourselves. That would be the honourable course of action.'

He poured and drank another shot.

'I am two people, Nadia. I am the good Soviet citizen on the outside. Inside I am Russian. I love your mother as a Russian – with passion, vigour, obsession, even. I never gave up. I never changed my mind. With my Soviet self I helped her escape from what the Soviets have done to your country. She loved me as a Hungarian – beautiful, passionate, generous, manipulative and utterly seductive. Together we made you.'

She gripped the edge of the table and heard her own voice. 'I may be sick.'

'I apologise. But it is necessary to speak of these things. I wish you to know who I am.'

He steadied her as she stood. It wasn't the embrace she had hoped for seconds earlier, but merely his fingers under her elbow. He wasn't taking her to his bed, but showing her to the bathroom.

She didn't know how long she was in there. It was a clinical, white-tiled cubicle, smelling of his kiss, the expensive soap. A toothbrush stood to attention in a rack and a white towel was folded precisely over the bath. She splashed cold water on her face and stared into the mirrored cabinet above the basin. Hollow eyes. Lank hair. What could he possibly see in her? A long razor lay between the taps. The sort the barbers used in Budapest. Papa always said he'd never trust a man enough to lie back in a chair and be set about with one of those. Papa. But not Papa.

When she emerged, Sergei was standing in the third doorway, beckoning her. The room was empty except for a piano, a stool and a window. He strode over to lower the blind and gestured.

'The best view in London.'

His eyes lightened for a moment and she peered out at a blank wall of bricks and a bottomless drop between the buildings. She shuddered as the slats of the blind shut out the sight. Was this his attempt at a joke? Perhaps. In any case he was gone, fetching a chair from the kitchen.

'Maybe this will help you to understand.' He took a book of music from inside the piano stool and showed it to her.

Rachmaninov was printed on the cover. She hadn't seen Cyrillic script in years, but she could still read it. The composer was a surprise. She'd expected him to play something folksy – Party-approved music. Rachmaninov had been banned, surely.

'I furled it in my umbrella to bring it out. Fortunately, it didn't rain. I have diplomatic immunity to the British rain.'

Again the lightening of the eyes. Another joke. This time she managed a sound halfway to a laugh and his whole face changed. It was the first time she had seen him smile.

'The piano, you see, is a Blüthner, like Rachmaninov's. My namesake.' He lifted the lid, positioned the rest and placed the music on it. 'As I understand it, he took his Blüthner with him into exile in America.'

Of course. *Sergei* Rachmaninov.

He sat down at the piano. And nothing happened. She sat stiffly, contemplating his back, straight and narrow on the stool. The moment stretched until the silence in the room came hammering on her eardrums, meeting her own heartbeat. The sound of air falling and roaring. She'd never noticed it before.

The first few notes hit the silence like raindrops on a still pool, questioning almost. There followed intense activity and quiet interludes. She sensed the swan gliding serenely while the feet paddled below in the lower register. As the drama built, it was as if he were making love to the piano. Making love to her. She realised why there was no furniture: the music needed all the space. The notes surged out to all eight corners of the room filling every last fraction of each cubic inch, like the organ used to occupy the columned spaces of the Abbey at that school on Sundays.

In the *Andante* she heard complex spells being woven, bells chiming – soft, insistent, fading. The last movement grew in confidence, now playful, now powerful. Lyrical. A song of release. All her senses, her very skin, stretched to dance with its rhythms, with the fluid sway of Sergei's back, the shrug of his shoulders, the lift of his elbows. She sat on after the last note faded, paralysed by sound.

It was minutes before he spoke. 'In London one can play such music. Sadly, not in Russia.'

He swung round on the stool. It was as if a mask had been peeled away from his face. He looked more alive, almost warm.

'That was merely the piano part. Imagine when the cello joins in. That is something. I used to play it with my sister, with Nadia. A passion that we shared.'

Nadia. That name again.

He turned again to the piano and played a few bars, then came in with his voice, deep, resonant, intoning the cello part.

He stopped abruptly, shaking his head. 'I don't do it justice…'

'Oh, but you do. It is—' Katalin couldn't express the awe that she felt. 'Where is she now? Nadia?'

He turned his head away. She could see his jaw clenching and clenching. 'I don't talk of it. Never.'

If only she could pull back her words. His skin was tightening back into the mask.

He lowered the lid of the piano and closed the booklet. 'One moment.'

As he opened the fourth door off the hall she glimpsed a single bed against the wall. The room was like a cupboard and the mattress was wrapped in a grey blanket with hospital severity. Then he was back, closing the door carefully behind him.

'Look. Nadia and myself. My twin.' He pressed a small frame into her hands as if it were a sacrament. 'When we were young and innocent.'

They were on a beach. Sergei was grinning and looked like any young lad in shorts. When she looked at the girl beside him, Katalin felt the prickle of gooseflesh crawl over her body. It could have been a photo of herself.

She felt him watching her.

'Now you see it?'

She nodded. 'Thank you. And thank you…' Tears welled up and she couldn't finish, could only gesture towards the piano.

He took back the picture and pressed it to his heart. 'Nadia killed herself. After we became less innocent.'

It was said without emotion, just as he might have said that Nadia left school or went shopping.

He bowed and disappeared to return the photo. She stared after him. "After we became less innocent." Did that mean what she thought it meant?

When he reappeared he opened the bathroom door.

'Come.'

What was this? She held back, but he came and took her hand.

'Look.' He turned them both towards the mirror. 'You see it now, don't you? Peas in the pod.'

They were side by side with his arm around her shoulder, like any father and daughter. Except that the energy fizzing between his left side and her right side would have set the Thames on fire.

'Ah, Nadia. Look at us together.' He turned and took her face in his hands. 'To have a daughter is something. For that daughter to be you. That is something else.'

For a moment her gaze rested in his without tension and she could see his pain and sadness. Then his eyes flicked to the mirror and, as she glanced that way, his mouth was on hers, and it was as it was before, that first time. She was kissing him with her whole being, inside and out. The moment telescoped to eternity and was over in seconds. A spasm went through Sergei, he groaned and let her go.

'I apologise. I should not have done that.'

She wanted to say, 'Oh, you should, you should', but found herself unable to speak. He wasn't even looking at her.

Suddenly cold, she followed his gaze to the razor on the basin.

Stiffly, he bent forward to pick it up. 'May I?'

The fear must have shown in her eyes. "If we made love, we might have to kill ourselves."

His expression softened. 'All I want is a lock of hair. To put with Nadia's?'

She nodded, trembling. He held up a tress and sliced neatly so that one side of her hair was uneven and quirky.

'Thank you. And excuse me.' He held the door open, suddenly formal again.

She escaped into the kitchen and slumped down on the chair. The vodka bottle had lost its magic. It was an ordinary bottle standing in a pool of condensation. She could hear running water, the toilet flushing, doors opening and closing. Her untouched vodka was still there, but it tasted warm and thin, like medicine. She pushed the glass away. It skidded into the puddle of water and crashed to the floor, sending chips of glass skittering across the tiles.

Sergei appeared in a clean shirt and immaculately pressed jeans. She hadn't seen him in casual clothes before.

'A new man,' he said and attempted a smile.

For a moment she was hopeful. Maybe they were to go out together.

'I'm sorry,' she said.

'I'm sorry too...'

He might have gone on, but she interrupted. 'I mean, about the glass.'

He looked down at the floor and shrugged, then stared up at her, parting his lips as if about to speak. She waited.

But he clicked his heels together in a way that didn't go with the jeans.

'I have to go. You can sleep. There is food. Take a shower. Wash your hair. The towels, the sheets are clean. I will be back.'

She nodded, speechless as he left the apartment. She found herself locked in, dazed. She walked carefully with shallow breaths, standing at the door of each room. There was no telephone. Where had he gone? Why didn't he take her? Why had he locked her in? Was the place bugged?

Opening every drawer and cupboard, she found plates and cutlery for one, five laundered shirts, two dark suits and a safe in the built-in wardrobe. The bathroom cabinet and two of the kitchen cupboards were locked. Most were empty. She swept up the glass with a dustpan and brush that appeared to be brand new. In the fridge she found eggs, bread, cheese and vodka, but wasn't hungry.

She slipped off her shoes and lay down on top of the bed, turned her head to look at the photograph, as Sergei must do every night. Nadia. She leaned on one elbow and peered into their faces. But they told her nothing she didn't already know. She lay back and stared at the ceiling. There was nothing here which helped her to understand this man who was her father. She closed her eyes but tears seeped out, filled her ears and soaked into the crisp white pillowcase. When she woke, shivering, she took off her blouse and skirt and slid under the smooth sheet and stiff blanket. She ran her tongue over dry lips, imagining Sergei was kissing her. Kissing, caressing, making love to her. The weight of him. The smell of him. His touch on her, all over her, inside her. But it didn't work. She was alone and cold with dry lips.

It was still dark when she woke. She locked herself in the bathroom, bathed and washed her hair. It was warm in there and she sat on the toilet, combing her hair until it was merely damp. The day passed in moving from room to room. She opened the lid of the piano but dared not touch the notes. She boiled the kettle and drank hot water, nibbled on a slice of dark-grained bread and wondered whether anyone was missing her.

In the early evening Sergei returned. With hardly a word to her, he poured vodka and played the same piano piece. This time she was more relaxed and the music seemed to penetrate every cell of her body. Her limbs wanted to dance.

Afterwards, he took her head in his hands, his fingers still vibrating with the energy of the music. His gaze intensified the sensations of arousal triggered by inhabiting the music and watching the sway of his back.

He stroked her hair. 'Ah, Nadia,' he said. 'Like silk.' But he led her not to the bedroom but to the kitchen.

'You have eaten nothing,' he said, breaking eggs into a bowl. 'You are pale. We will have an omelette before I go.'

He presented her with a neat golden wedge, crisp and fluffy and insisted she eat. Because he was solicitous, she found she could swallow. 'You like it?'

When she nodded, he smiled and lifted his fork. They ate together, one each side of the small table. Their eyes kept meeting.

When he had finished he stood abruptly. 'I must change.'

She heard running water and he soon reappeared in one of the dark suits.

'I go to work,' he said. 'I will return. You must not be afraid.'

Katalin gathered the plates and washed up. It was almost domestic, she thought.

The next day was the same. She tried not to imagine, but emptied her mind by flattening every question mark that surfaced and by polishing – the taps, the top of the piano, the glass in the mirror and the windows. Then she focused on puzzles from the book she kept in her handbag.

On the fourth day he was stiffer than usual. He downed two shots of vodka before he went to the piano. As he stood up, he checked his watch.

'I have called you a taxi, Katalin.'

He fetched her coat but held it to him. His jaw clenched and unclenched. 'I could not… I cannot go one way or the other,' he said. 'I thought it was simply my Russian self in conflict with my Soviet identity. But I find my Russian selves in conflict with each other.' He passed long fingers across his forehead where beads of perspiration had formed. 'I fail to be the father you deserve. I apologise, Katalin – for that and for the confusion I have caused you.'

She took the coat from him. 'I understand… I fail too – to be a daughter. I should be grateful that you are an honourable man. But I regret it. I will always regret it.' She reached up and kissed him on the lips, a chaste, dry invitation. He did not respond.

He took her downstairs and saw her into the cab. He spoke to the driver and handed over some notes. Too many. How did he know where she lived? None of that mattered. He had called her Katalin. She would never see him again.

When the car turned the corner, Sergei was still standing on the pavement like an obelisk.

26

I missed Amanda's first call. I'd gone up to town to look for a poetry book for Aunt and spent half a day getting lost in Foyles bookshop. There was nothing I could afford and I ended up buying a second-hand volume of Keats in a junk shop on the way home. Mama didn't remember to pass on the message until the evening. Before I could find an excuse to slip out to the phone box, Amanda phoned again.

'Katalin hasn't come home. I thought she might be with you but your mother went ballistic when I mentioned her name.'

I pulled the living room door to. Luckily, Mama was absorbed in a programme on her latest acquisition – a television set from Radio Rentals. 'What d'you mean, "She hasn't come home"? When…?'

'Last saw her Friday morning – she was off to work.'

'You mean she was out all night?'

'Yep. Looks like she will be again. I mean, it's late already, late for Katalin, that is. I must say, I *am* a bit worried. She has been a bit weird lately, more weird than usual, I mean.'

I shuddered as images of Sergei abducting Kati flashed through my mind. Was he getting even with us for interfering in his life?

'What sort of weird?'

'Talking to herself. Muttering under her breath. In Hungarian possibly. Except it sounded different. More like Russian, I'd say. I know she speaks Russian.'

'Yes,' I say. Kati had been following Sergei. He'd been annoyed by it. Understandably. My idiotic, stubborn, sainted sister. Maybe he'd pushed her under a train like Papa. But if that had happened we'd have heard. Amanda said it was too early to inform the police, that they wouldn't take it seriously.

Next morning I rang Amanda while Mama was still asleep. Still no Kati. I went to the place I thought of as Sergei's restaurant and asked the maître d' if she'd been in, but he shrugged and shook his head. On Monday, Amanda phoned her office, but she hadn't turned up. I told her I was going to the police. Amanda told me, 'Appearances count', and not to dress like a tart. When I didn't retaliate I realised just how worried I was.

I even told Mama Kati was missing but the news didn't seem to get through to her. She'd got dressed earlier than usual, saying she had a flat to view. But the phone had rung. Mama had got there first and picked it up. The caller hardly said anything and clearly hung up before she could reply. She stared at the receiver, listening to the dial tone until I took it from her. Then she collapsed onto the sofa, throwing her lipstick across the room.

'The flat is taken,' was all she would say.

'Was that the estate agent?' I asked. But she looked blank. And when I told her about Kati she looked through me.

I was suddenly mad at her. I took her by the shoulders. 'You've got to come with me! Come to the police. Report her missing, Mama.'

She shook her head and refused to move.

My visit to the police station was a disaster. The officer on the desk was kindly, but didn't take me seriously. He wrote a few notes and then asked where my mother was and why she wasn't doing the reporting. They would need her signature. I cursed Amanda. Her warning meant I'd worn no make-up. I looked like the schoolgirl I was. When the officer said, 'Now, little girl, I suggest you go home and fetch your mother down here,' I burst into tears, which only reinforced the impression.

Mama was asleep when I got home. She looked a little crazy with one scarlet and one pale lip. The pill packet and water glass on the table told me it would be no good trying to wake her. I swallowed my pride and phoned Amanda.

'Thanks to you I didn't wear any make-up and they thought I was a kid. You'll have to report it, Mand.'

'You *are* a kid, actually, Mari. But that is very bad news. You'd think they'd have done something. And I can't just drop everything and go. I've got a hanging session right now. The artist's arrived, he's a real catch for the gallery. I can't possibly… No. I'll go as soon as it's over.'

There was nothing I could do. I wanted to ring Aunt, just to hear her voice. But what could she do, miles away in Devon? Devon. Where abductions didn't happen. Where people didn't die. Where the sea surged and the trees stood and listened.

I'd fallen asleep in the lumpy armchair when the phone rang. It was Amanda, who was still at the gallery.

'She's home. At the flat. I phoned one last time before I went to the police. She was asleep – if you ring straightaway you'll catch her before she has time to go back to bed.'

*

I realised immediately that my sister was drunk – sheen on the forehead, eyes with that swimming-under-glass look. On the phone the day before she'd sounded fragile. She went through the "Why do I need to see you?" routine, but then, 'Okay,' she'd said. 'I need to sleep now. But if we must, tomorrow after work.' I got the impression that, for once, Kati did need to see me.

Here we were again in Sergei's restaurant. She was already there drinking vodka, which was unexpected. I ordered two coffees and fell on her, but she pushed me away.

'Where have you been? What's going *on*? Why didn't you let us know?'

'You had something to tell me. When you phoned the other day.'

She was eyeing me defiantly and her voice had a brittle edge.

'But Kati, where have you *been*?'

'I'm about to tell you. That thing you were anxious to tell me. I think you will find I already know.'

'Will I? What do you already know, my sainted sister?'

'That Sergei is my father.' She raised her glass as if to toast this fact. 'That is where I've been. Staying with my father. He invited me to his flat.'

'Kati! What did I tell you? You were—'

'I think I can look after myself. As I say, he took me to his apartment and told me he's my father.'

'Exactly!'

'Then he played me Rachmaninov. Not very dangerous.' She sat back with a smug look.

'But why didn't you tell anyone? We've been worried sick.'

'There was no phone.'

'You could have found a phone box, just one call to—'

'He – well, he locked me in – when he went out. For my own safety. And when he was there, we were busy.'

'Kati! You haven't? He imprisoned you! In order to seduce you, rape you?'

'Shut up, Mari. You little drama queen. You'd like that wouldn't you? No. It was to get to know me. To consider our position. To explain about his sister.'

'His sister?'

'Nadia. He showed me a photograph. We are very alike, Nadia and me. They—' She broke off as the waiter appeared with the coffees. 'Another of these for me.' She waved her glass in the waiter's face and pushed both the coffees across the table at me. 'Don't you try to tell me what I should drink.'

'Take it easy, Kati. At least have some tonic with it.'

She shook her head. 'Russians drink it neat. Sergei, my father, drinks it neat. I am Russian, Mari.'

'Half Russian, half crazy. Do you think, my sainted sister, that just because you've got Russian blood you won't get drunk?'

Kati ignored me and drained her glass, looking impatiently round for the replacement. I stirred sugar into my coffee. I'd thought I was in control of the Sergei situation, but everything was spiralling away from me. Just because he was Kati's father didn't mean he was no threat to her. Kati would get in the way of his plans for Mama. On the one hand, that was good, but on the other…

'Will you see him again?'

The question brought a change in my sister. Her eyes seemed to swim, or was it just the vodka?

'Of course. He has to go back to Moscow. He'll be in touch when he gets back.'

Why did I think she was lying?

'It must be difficult.'

'It's part of his job.'

'No, I meant, difficult for you. Finding you aren't who you thought you were. That Papa was not your father. That Mama didn't tell you…'

'I never knew who I was. Not since we left Budapest.'

'Wasn't that about the dancing?'

She shrugged, an offhand, don't-care gesture.

I remembered the mutilated mannequin. She'd substituted Sergei. She was hanging on to him instead. I reached out a hand but she leaned away and tossed her head.

'But Kati, you can't go fancying your own father…'

'Wrong word, Mari. Why do you always have to be so crude? It was our natural attraction. Father and daughter. A confusion of feelings.'

'But that kiss you told me about. It was a big deal. You said he had a hard-on.'

The colour suddenly rose up Kati's neck. 'I said no such thing. It was only a kiss.' She gulped at the fresh vodka. 'Excuse me.'

I watched my sister make her uncertain way towards the powder room and slid her glass to my side of the table. She was going to feel dreadful in the morning. No wonder. The first man she'd fallen for. And this had to happen. "Confusion of feelings." The understatement of the year. Poor Kati.

The maître d' appeared before me.

'Excuse me, Madame. I regret that as you ladies are alone this evening I am unable to serve you more alcohol. Without the presence of our esteemed client, you understand.' He beckoned a hovering waiter. 'May I offer these? On the house.' He bowed and withdrew.

The waiter set down glasses of orange juice, clinking with ice.

'He calls me Nadia, you know,' Kati said when she came back. 'After his sister. I might change my name. Take on my Russian identity.'

She was herself again, poised, aloof. She gulped the orange juice, seeming not to notice the absence of vodka.

'Just as long as you don't do anything silly.'

'Like top myself, you mean? Would you like that? Would it suit you? Not to—'

'Oh, Kati!' I grabbed her hand. 'You don't really think that? Of course not! You're my sister. I love you, we've—'

'Only your half-sister. I only need to be half as attached to you now.' She pulled away her hand.

That stung. I hardly knew what I was saying. 'So we don't count anymore? Papa and me? You'd rather have this father you hardly know instead of Papa who brought us both up? You'd rather have a father who gave you the wrong sort of kiss than a father who died for his principles? You realise don't you? Your so-called father killed our proper father? Just so he could get his hands on our mother?'

Kati reached across the table and stood up. I felt a sudden fierce sting in my eyes as she flung the contents of the shot glass across my face.

She staggered sideways and righted herself. 'I never, ever want to see you again.'

Carefully, she made her way to the door, which the maître d' held open for her.

I wiped my eyes, making a mess of mascara on the white napkin. I'd blown it. My mission had been all about looking after Kati. But she had evaded me.

Now I had a sister who knocked back vodka. A sister who disowned me. She'd rearranged her world around Sergei. Being Russian was suddenly okay and Papa was forgotten. For all I cared, Kati could call herself Nadia and go to hell. All I wanted was to be on that train heading for the dripping trees of Aunt Klára's garden, for the cawing of rooks and one of our chats in the conservatory with Finn lying between us. But meanwhile, what would I tell Mama?

That question became irrelevant. When I got back Wilkie met me at the door. How odd. And annoying. I wanted to slip in quietly without waking Mama and go to bed. Then I'd pack up in the morning and catch the train to Devon. As planned.

'Dr Arnold's sedated her. He's persuaded her—'

'But what happened?'

'She just started screaming and screaming. Mrs Collins downstairs – lucky they were stocktaking – anyway, as I say Mrs Collins came and fetched me.'

'But why? What happened?'

Mama had woken that morning in a cheerful mood, having slept almost round the clock. When I told her Kati was back, she smiled as if she took that for granted. 'But Mama,' I started, then bit down on my indignation. There was no point. She grasped my hand, told me I was a good girl and said she was hungry. I'd made baked beans on toast and boiled the kettle for her to have a wash, because the damned water heater had packed up again. She even said, 'There'll be another flat.' When I went out she was still ordinary Mama. And now this.

Wilkie was telling me, 'It's for the best, Mari. She's agreed to go in voluntary. For the time being.'

'Go in where? Wilkie, for God's sake! Why? What happened?'

'I did wonder about that aunt of yours in Vienna?'

Nothing was making sense. I pushed past Wilkie. Mama seemed to have shrivelled up. Dr Arnold was packing up his medical bag on the sofa. I hugged Mama, but she hardly responded.

'She's much calmer now,' said Dr Arnold.

'What happened, Mama? What happened to upset you?'

'She's maybe not hearing you very clearly. The drugs…'

'Mama? What was it? Did Sergei come?'

That name got a response. It penetrated the fog. She jerked upright and her fists scrabbled about in her lap.

'Best not to upset her,' said Dr Arnold.

'But she *is* upset. Didn't you ask her?'

'She's been unwell for a while, as you know. Sometimes the smallest thing…'

I turned my back on him and shut out his doctor-words. I stroked her hands, trying to relax them and, as one began to uncurl, I saw she was clutching a screwed-up piece of paper. She slumped back into the chair again and didn't resist when I pulled the paper carefully out of her grasp.

The damn doctor hadn't even noticed. I was about to protest, but thought better of it. I slipped it into my pocket.

'That sounds like the ambulance now,' said Wilkie from the window.

'Ambulance? What ambulance?'

'Let them in, would you, Mrs Er-um?' The doctor snapped the locks on his bag. His job was done. He turned to me. 'We're admitting her to hospital, mental hospital. With her consent. For treatment.'

'She's agreed to go,' said Wilkie. 'Like I said, it's for the best. She needs help. And you've got to go back to school.'

There was nothing I could do. They stood her up and I just hugged her and hugged her until Wilkie pulled me away. They wouldn't even let me go to the ambulance with her.

Wilkie insisted on staying the night.

'You're only a kid. It's a shame,' she kept saying.

I told her I wanted to sleep in Mama's bed and she helped me pull out the bloody put-u-up. What I really wanted was to have the table lamp and Mama's papers and the vodka in the cupboard. Before long, Wilkie was snoring from my bed.

I spread out the crumpled paper under the light. Mostly it was typed:

Dear Teréz

When you read this I will no longer be in existence.

You have driven me to take my own life.

Except that, since I met you, my life has never been my own.

Men have known since the story of Eve the danger of being tempted by a woman.

But you were a force of nature – both beautiful and destructive.

I had no power against you.

You were a tidal wave in my life. But I was merely a ripple in yours.

You used me and I took my revenge.

Between you and our daughter I have no peace.

Now there is nothing.

Your Sergei

Suicide? Sergei? No wonder Mama had gone to pieces. He was blaming her. She already blamed herself for Papa's death – because of Sergei. He'd mentioned 'our daughter'. Mama must have realised that he and Kati had met. She'd blame herself for not telling Kati the truth. Sergei had tipped her over the edge.

And Kati. What about Kati? It was too much. My sister would have to wait until morning.

There was an envelope under the armchair with a note scrawled on the back.

Regarding the flat. I know you liked it. I regret that circumstances prevent that happening. S

Bastard. That phone call she took, it must have been Sergei. No estate agent would be so abrupt.

I pulled the vodka out of the cupboard. Precious little left. I swigged it from the bottle and turned to the table, which was a mess of papers and make-up. There it was. A folded sheet tucked under the electricity bill. Estate agent's details. A first floor flat in a block in Maida Vale. Nothing grand. One bedroom. Sitting room with dining end. Newly refurbished bathroom. Fitted kitchen. Luxury to Mama.

Wilkie stayed while I made the phone call to Vienna. First I spoke to Uncle Fritz and then to Aunt Júlia who promised to be on the next available flight. Uncle Fritz sounded broken up and asked about Katalin and how she was coping. Aunt Júlia just sounded put out.

27

Katalin was surprised to see the letter on the hall table. She was leaving for work in her secretarial suit, which was unused to melodrama. Ena must have collected the post from their box the evening before. Typical Ena. Amanda would have given it to her personally.

A single page. Sparse words. "I will be dead."

She halted in Amanda's carpeted hall, inoffensive envelope in one hand, outrageous letter in the other.

How could one be sure of a death announced for a future date? A future date, which had now, evidently, moved into the past? Her suit would give the note no credence, but her heart was lurching into a dark place with ominous certainty.

A hoax? A joke? A nightmare? Or a logical act? Sergei's voice echoed in her head: "We would have to kill ourselves".

She stared at the coat stand seeing, not Amanda's new emerald green coat, nor Ena's fur jacket, but the figure of Sergei, watching her taxi depart. She'd lost him then. She knew that. But it had been a comfort that he continued to exist, somewhere in the world. Now he did not.

How could he be gone? His height, his strength, his shining hair? The gaze that penetrated to her root? He must still be playing Rachmaninov. How could that not be so? His coat and hat still striding, not floating down the Thames.

The page sashayed through currents of air to the floor. The thud, as Katalin crumpled in her sensible suit, brought Amanda running from the kitchen.

Katalin ground her face into the fabric of her pillow in her sleeping place behind the sofa. She needed to weep or rage. Anything to loosen the locked place in her gut. But it tightened and screwed itself down. Amanda had been kind. Surprisingly kind. But she could never understand. She wanted to keep Sergei to herself, away from Amanda. Away from Ena. Especially Ena.

She was woken by Amanda. 'Another missive.'

A brown envelope this time. Katalin felt something hard as she took it and slid it under her pillow.

'Oh, no you don't! I'm staying here while you open it,' said Amanda. 'Don't want a repeat of last time. It's exactly the same printing.'

Katalin sighed and slit the envelope with her finger. Sergei's fingers would have held it. He would have licked the flap and pressed it down. She resisted the urge to kiss it. Not in front of Amanda. She drew out a sheet of paper and a wad of notes held together with a rubber band.

'Ooh, money!' said Amanda.

The letter was in Russian. At least Amanda couldn't read it.

'What does it say? Can you understand it?'

'Of course. And it's my business.'

'What's the hard thing? Come on, Kati. I'm not budging until I know.'

Reluctantly she unfolded a key tightly wrapped in the corner cut from a brown paper bag.

'Safe deposit box,' said Amanda. 'Maybe he's left you thousands of roubles – or Russian gold or—'

'Shut up, Amanda. Go away.'

'I'd better take that. Don't want you opening it on your own. It might be a trap.'

Katalin clutched the key and shook her head. Amanda couldn't force her. She and Ena were going to a party that evening, a private view at the gallery where Amanda worked. Everybody who was anybody would be there. They were guaranteed not to miss it. Their double-barrelled boyfriends were due to call for them at six. She would pretend to be asleep. Until then she would hide the key in her knickers.

'But, Kati—' Amanda was interrupted by the doorbell.

Katalin read the letter properly. The key was to a locker at Paddington station where he had left an envelope "in memory of me". She was to leave the key in the lock.

There will be no body. No report of my death. Don't ask any questions. You will get nowhere. That is how it is.

Katalin slid the letter under her pillow and tucked the key into her underwear. Oh, hell – it was her sister's voice in the hall. That was all she needed.

I phoned Amanda and got Ena, who confirmed that Kati had received a letter.

'About some suicide,' Ena yawned. She told me to come and deal with my sister. 'She refuses to leave her bed, which is a bore. It's in our sitting room.'

Thankfully, it was Amanda who opened the door. She looked me up and down and her raised eyebrow told me what a sight I must look.

'What's all this about, Marika? She passed out, so I read the note. What else was I supposed to do? Not that it said much. And she won't explain.'

I shrugged. 'It's not really for me…'

Amanda nodded. 'She's in there.' She indicated the door and disappeared. I could hear her talking to Ena in the kitchen. But they fell silent as soon as I closed the door, so I knew they were earwigging.

'Kati, is it really true? About Sergei? Did you have a note from him?'

An animal snarl came from behind the sofa.

'Mama had one too. Kati, she's ill. She's in hospital. In a mental hospital.' I still found that bit hard to say, even though I'd already had to tell Aunt Júlia and Amanda.

'I suppose Mama had to face it. He loved me, not her.'

'But Kati, he was your father.'

'I think I know that. He did the honourable thing. He was an honourable man.'

A hand appeared over the edge of the sofa back and a sheet of paper floated onto the seat. Kati's note was crisp and clean.

To Katalin
When you read this I will be dead.
I will have taken my own life.
I will have done the honourable thing.
Between you and your mother I have no peace.
Now there is nothing.

'Oh, Kati. I'm so sorry…'

'Sorry? So you should be. See where it's got, your interfering? Another dead father and a mother in the loony bin.'

'I meant I'm sorry you've lost him. As soon as—'

'Don't you dare even speak of him. You understand nothing.'

She'd emerged from the sofa and was standing at the window. We were both silent as I handed her back the note. She folded it carefully into its creases.

I moved towards her, wanting to put my arm around her, but she backed off, putting the sofa between us and tucked the note into its envelope. I tried a different tack.

'Will you help me with Mama? Come and visit with me?'

She turned and glared at me, a mixture of rage and terror. 'What? You want me to come with you? To visit *Mama*?' She spat out that last word. 'If I were to see her now I would attack her, I would hit her – for not ever telling me. They would probably lock me up too. I'd rather jump off a bridge.'

'But Kati, if—'

'I thought I told you, I never want to see you again.'

'Kati, please…' I was near to tears. 'I can't do it on my own… Can't we at least to sit down and try to—?'

'No! Sit down with you? You smell! And on the way out, tell Amanda she can stop babysitting me. I'm perfectly fine.'

Amanda shook her head when I passed on the message. 'I've no intention of stopping,' she said. '"Perfectly fine", my foot!'

I was about to leave when Ena sauntered in. She was wearing a silk wrap, a garment Mama would have called a *peignoir*. She switched on the transistor radio and draped herself against the fridge.

Suddenly, Helen Shapiro, the new pop sensation, was belting out her hit, asking not to be treated like a child. Ena turned down the volume.

'What I don't get,' she said, stretching "get" into two syllables, 'is how your father manages to commit suicide twice.'

I took a deep breath, suppressing the urge to wipe the carefully puzzled expression off Ena's face.

'One, my father, László, did not commit suicide. He was murdered. Two, he was not Kati's father. Her father is called Sergei, a Russian, as I am sure you know. He has evidently committed suicide.'

'So your mother took a lover. All those years!'

'Very romantic,' said Amanda.

'Very Eastern European,' said Ena.

'Very not your bloody business,' I shouted and slammed into the hall.

Supercilious cow. As I pulled on my coat, I heard Ena say, 'You see, she's still got a temper. Couldn't resist winding her up. Where's the marmalade?'

Then Amanda: 'Poor kid. You're a monster, E. She's got enough to deal with.'

There followed two days of surreal visits to Mama, who sat on a chair, staring at the wall. From time to time she would mutter, 'They were both good men', or 'I am the *femme fatale*, the fatal woman'. Mama didn't seem to notice I was there. Unlike Helen Shapiro, I longed to be treated like a child. But Mama was not about to do that.

I would grab her hands and look into her face. 'It's Mari, Mama. Kati sends her love.' But her daughters no longer seemed to exist for Mama.

When she was discharged to Aunt Júlia's care, I sat in the hospital foyer holding her hand as we waited for the taxi to the airport. Aunt Júlia was brisk when it arrived and Mama would have been gone without a backward glance if I'd not clung to her. Her arms hung down on either side as I hugged her saggy little body. She was like a sad old balloon that had been left behind at Christmas, all joy and resistance gone out of her. In a last effort I took her face in both my hands.

'This is Mari, Mama. I love you, Mama. And I'm saying goodbye.'

Aunt Júlia sighed and made a tutting noise. No doubt she was worried I would jolt Mama into not wanting to leave. But there was no danger of that.

I kissed Mama on both cheeks. As I let go, her eyes flicked up and met mine. For a moment, they brightened into recognition before clouding over again.

Tears streamed down my cheeks as I waved the taxi goodbye. It was all my fault. If I'd done nothing about Sergei, Mama might be moving into a cosy flat in Maida Vale, looking forward to being a kept woman. But Kati. If I'd done nothing, she might be having a rip-roaring affair with her own father. Kati hated me. Mama probably hated me too.

When might I see Mama again? What chance that Aunt Júlia and Uncle Fritz and their private clinic would make her well? Could someone ever get better from what had happened to her?

28

It was the time of tired cow parsley, murky greens and tanned grass. But this was the best time of day: fields renewed by darkness and dew, air still cool. Klára had left Marika sleeping, surprising Finn with an early walk. She needed time to think about her troubled niece. What a state she'd come home in. What a load of trouble she'd had to deal with – if Marika's distraught version of events could be believed.

She'd stepped off the train in a black cocktail dress with dark rings under her eyes and smudged make-up that looked as if new had been re-applied over old. Klára experienced a moment of embarrassment – as if she were meeting a tart. But she remembered the tearful phone call from Paddington, asking her to meet the train, and her heart went out to the girl. She pulled her into a hug and was hit by the reek of greasy hair, stale sweat and cigarettes. Heaven knows when she last had a bath.

That last, and least important, question had been answered after supper when Klára had gently suggested she have a soak before bed.

'I know. The water heater in the flat packed up. Couldn't get hold of the landlord. And then, well, there was no point. With Mama gone. But I stink. I know I do. It was the last thing Kati said to me, funnily enough.' Her voice had cracked then and more tears seeped into the runnels of mascara already on her cheeks.

As Klára reached the stile, Finn sprinted past, scattering rabbits into the hedge as he headed for the woods.

Poor kid. No child should have to go through such stuff. Klára felt guilty. She should have gone to London with Marika instead of luxuriating in those few weeks of solitude to work on her collection. What did a few poems matter in the face of Teréz's lover apparently preying on the girls? But how could she have known? Júlia had said Teréz was much better and no longer on medication. What more natural than Marika staying with her mother?

Oh, that Teréz! Trust her to have a Russian lover. If Marika's theory was right, it added a whole new layer of horror to László's death. She shuddered at the thought.

Marika had been almost hysterical. 'It was incest,' she'd said. 'Kati being in love with Sergei and Sergei being Mama's lover.'

'No,' Klára told her. 'It might be nasty. But not incest. He'd have to be her father for that.'

Marika had gone quiet at that and calmed down.

The summer had worn itself out. Already Klára could see rusty leaves in the crown of the big horse chestnut further along the lane and a few blackberries were already plump and purple. It was the start of the school year. Marika must settle back in school to do her O levels. Bound to be a problem. She'd go and see Patrick. Talk it through. He always restored her sense of proportion.

What Marika had said about her sister stuck in Klára's mind, repeating over and over. 'I only ever wanted to look after her. And she only ever wanted to get rid of me.' That's what Marika believed. So sad. Klára couldn't help thinking she was right.

On her way back, she stopped to admire the bindweed galloping up the wire on the telegraph pole at the end of her garden. She tried popping one of the flowers but it flopped to the ground. Finn sniffed it, then quickened his step towards the back door.

Marika was at the kitchen table. She looked scrubbed and clean and her wet hair smelled of shampoo. Finn nosed into her lap and she fondled his ears.

Marika immediately continued the conversation of the night before.

'Do you think I should have told the police about Sergei killing Papa?'

'No – even if you'd had any kind of proof. He might have turned nasty. And you didn't have much to go on. Only the motive and the way he held his umbrella. I don't think the police would have been very interested.'

'That's what Kati said. But she didn't want to believe it was true.'

'Believing it's another thing. To me, it seems quite likely.' Klára filled the kettle and put it on to boil. 'But there are times when discretion really is the better part of valour. Now, do you want porridge or just toast?'

Marika burst into tears. Now what? Klára put an arm round her.

'Oh, Aunt, you don't know how much I've longed to hear you say something like that. Porridge, yes, *and* toast. I'm ravenous.'

Klára stirred the oats and talked of the apples that needed picking and the bonfire they might have at the weekend.

'Aunt, can we go to the sea? Will you come?'

'Of course. How about we take a picnic? We might even swim.'

*

'I'd like to live by the sea,' said Marika as they dried themselves on the rocks. 'Beecombe maybe. A little cottage, looking out to sea.'

'Pretty wild in the winter.'

Marika grinned. 'I'd like that.'

She was quiet as they ate their apples and cheese. Ominously quiet.

'Fruit cake? It's only the slab cake from the shop.'

Marika shook her head. 'Aunt?'

'What?'

'I feel so guilty I interfered. With Sergei, I mean. I messed it up for Mama. If I'd ignored it all, Mama would be set up in a nice flat and he wouldn't have killed himself and she wouldn't have lost her mind.'

Klára broke a piece of cake and passed half to Marika. 'I can understand you thinking like that. But it won't ever get you anywhere. You can say "What if?" for ever – but you will never know.'

Klára wondered whether Sergei really had committed suicide, or whether it was a neat way of vanishing. Just as long as he was out of their lives, it didn't really matter.

'You see, I couldn't bear the thought of Mama being the mistress of the man who killed Papa.'

'I'd have felt the same.'

'I don't think Mama could bear it either. But sometimes I wondered. Our flat was so horrible. She might have been tempted.'

Klára reckoned Teréz was certainly tempted. She bit into her cake and gave the rest to Finn. 'And imagine if you hadn't done anything and your mother had given in to that temptation. Then you'd have felt guilty too, because of László, because of your Papa. You were true to what you believed. You just wanted the best for everyone. It absolutely wasn't your fault, what happened. You can't control other people. It's tough that you've ended up losing them both. One day Katalin will see that. She'll come round.'

'It was because of Kati that I really had to do something. Because you see… You know what you said yesterday about incest? Well, Sergei *was* her father. Mama told me so.'

'Ah.' Klára grunted and stared down at the shingle. 'A lot of things begin to fall into place.' She paused. 'Of course you had to do something. Why on earth did Teréz never tell her?'

'Mama lied to Papa, so—'

'But after he died…'

'She hardly saw Kati.'

'She should have made a point of it – especially when the man turned up again. What a nightmare! It's outrageous she left it all to you.'

'I know. But she wasn't to know Kati would meet him. That was bizarre. And she wasn't in her right mind. She couldn't cope.'

'You are very forgiving. She's a lucky woman to have such a brave daughter who loves her so much.'

Marika snorted and shook her head.

'Your mother is in good hands. She will recover. You will be able to visit.'

'Do you think so? That Mama will get better?'

'Of course. It's the best clinic. And she's got Júlia and Fritz.'

Marika was lighter on the way back, jumping from rock to rock to peer into the pools left by the tide.

When they got home she said, 'I'll be glad to get back to school. Having lessons and homework will be such a relief. And no vodka. You know, I really don't like vodka.'

29

Katalin set out with the key as soon as Amanda and Ena left for their party. On the street, she felt cold, exposed, giddy. The bus stop round the corner in the Gloucester Road seemed a mile away. Her knees had absorbed all the shock of the day. A bus came almost immediately, but the conductor had to help her aboard. He did it with such concern that she felt suddenly tearful.

At the station, the smutty smell, the shriek and bellow of trains, the crackle and boom of overhead announcements crashed in on her. A porter pointed her to the wall of lockers. Number forty-seven. Hand shaking, she turned the key and extracted a large manila envelope. Trembling, and clutching the package close to her chest, she escaped the bedlam into the nearest cab.

Back in Stanhope Gardens, she poured some of the brandy Ena kept for her Horse's Neck cocktails. Ena would notice but Katalin didn't care. She slit the heavy paper with a kitchen knife and slid the contents onto the table: a rectangle wrapped in newspaper and a booklet of sheet music. Rachmaninov. It fell open at the *Sonata in G minor for Cello and Piano*. The piece he had played for her. The piece he used to play with his sister.

Knowing what she would find, she ripped at the newspaper to reveal the framed photograph of Sergei and his twin.

His two most prized possessions. If ever she needed proof that Sergei was dead, this was it.

In the weeks that followed, Ena suggested that Sergei was not really dead at all, that he'd staged a suicide to escape the awkward position he found himself in. It sounded plausible enough. But the evidence of the Rachmaninov and the photograph contradicted the theory.

'Ah,' said Ena. 'That's just what he'd want you to think. Bet he's out there somewhere. Moscow, maybe. Even here in London.'

It was all so transparent. She was being taunted. Ena made no secret of wanting to be rid of her. Yet Ena's words were seductive. Sergei might be out there somewhere.

So Katalin walked. She would catch the bus to Notting Hill Gate and patrol from the leafy roads and grand architecture of embassy land to the street off Camden Hill where Sergei used to live. She paced up and down the Bayswater Road, gazing across at the Soviet Embassy, and shivered outside the apartment block.

How had he killed himself? She thought of the river and remembered Ilona's story of the bodies in the Duna. Was Sergei one of those floating logs? Was his soul haunting the Thames? Did he drink a bottle of vodka, fill the pockets of his long black coat with stones and step from a bridge on a dark night?

She had no religious beliefs, but in bed at night she shuddered to think of those spirits, drifting there, waiting to be released, unable to move on. The images slipped behind her eyelids as she settled to sleep.

In her dreams, the bodies all wore belted macs and trilby hats. Oddly, the hats stayed on their heads in the bloodied water. She would wake herself screaming. Sometimes she woke Amanda, or worse, Ena. Amanda would offer cocoa, but Ena once stomped in to throw a glass of water over her before going back to bed.

At other times she would wake to some external noise, a cat fight or sirens, and lie for hours with dark thoughts rolling round her head like a thunderstorm trapped in a tunnel. To ward off images of the human log-jam she forced herself to consider the shootings in a rational way. Was there an art to it? Was there a "right" place to aim the bullet to ensure the victim would fall neatly into the water? Like the skill of the forester who could drop a tree precisely where he wanted it by cutting a notch in the trunk?

Next day, after work she would walk her beat all over again. Thankfully, she had no reason to go near the Thames. If anyone had asked why she did it she would have said she was honouring her father, holding a vigil, acting in memoriam. But what of the raised heartbeat, the shiver of expectation, the craning eyes which followed every tall, thin man?

Nobody did ask because nobody knew what she did. Being with other people became impossible. She wanted to be with *him*. She would live like a true Russian person – with discipline and culture. She would be a daughter Sergei would be proud of, change her name to Nadia, maybe. But that would be complicated. Calling herself Nadia inside her head would be enough. She wished she'd been born completely Russian. They were a people famed for ballet. She would have been in the Kirov like Nureyev, but better not to think about that. She'd make a good communist – knowing how to toe the line and not hankering after possessions.

She'd always hoped to work at the Hungarian Embassy, using her language skills. But, as Amanda pointed out, with her background, she'd never be trusted.

The same applied to the Soviet Embassy. Instead, she found a job as a typist in an international law firm, and set her long-term sights on becoming indispensable as the senior partner's personal secretary.

By the following spring, when she reached her eighteenth birthday, she had saved enough for a deposit. Ena rejoiced when Katalin moved from the luxury of Stanhope Gardens to a tiny flat off Ladbroke Grove. Three box-like rooms contained her life. One to remind her to eat. One for washing. One for sleeping. At first she bought only a bed. Amanda gave her blankets and sheets and came to help clean the place.

When Amanda had gone, Katalin surveyed the rooms and sighed with relief. Her own space. No one to disturb the symmetry of the tartan rug on the bed, or the chain coiled round the plug on the washbasin. No one to leave dirty dishes in the sink. Her next purchases were a record player and an LP of Rachmaninov's *Second Piano Concerto*. It was some time before she found a recording of the *Sonata in G minor for Cello and Piano*.

30

Going back to school was like meeting my own naughty little sister. I was determined to change. But everyone expected me to be the same old Marika. My former cronies taunted me when I wouldn't join them, calling me "chicken" or "stuck-up" or "swot". And the others – the law-abiding ones I used to write off as boring – if they found me revising in the library they'd say, 'What are you doing here? Not bunking off into town to nick stuff?' or, 'What? Not off behind the bike sheds with some boy?' No wonder Kati used to get so fed up with me. Even the teachers couldn't stop their eyebrows from shooting up when I did something perfectly normal, like handing in homework on time.

Ever since I had been caught nicking lipstick in Woolworths before Christmas, I'd changed my Saturday afternoon ritual. I'd go to the cinema with the gang and then say I had shopping to do for Aunt. I'd head to Rundles, the bakery on Fore Street. Sometimes I could only afford a currant bun, like the Monday buns at the Priory. Sometimes I went for one of the little iced cakes with crushed pineapple under the dome on top. But my favourite was a custard slice: a slab of thick sunshine yellow sandwiched between flaky pastry topped with icing like snow on a roof – a gorgeous mix of sickly, gooey crispness.

The church was just opposite, right along from Woolworths, but I could slip in with my cake without being noticed. I sat with Our Lady. It was like having tea together, me and the mother of God in her sky-blue frock. Custard slices are very messy, so I'd brush the shatter of crumbs under a kneeler. She didn't seem to mind. Afterwards, I'd sit with her for a bit and chat, but not out loud in case someone came in. Then I'd say, 'Thank you for having me', and rinse my sticky fingers in the holy water on my way out.

Sometimes I used to coincide with the gang at the bus stop and once Lizzie asked me where my shopping was. I said it was being delivered, but she didn't believe me.

'You go meeting blokes, don't you?' she said.

Luckily, my bus came before I had time to smack her face. But the story went round at school that I went shagging on Saturdays instead of shoplifting.

I was glad to say goodbye to 1961. There was no Mama, so I made no visits to London. I didn't even go to the cinema. I went into the church instead. It was a good place to think. What with Papa being dead and Mama going mad, the world wasn't a safe place any more. The little blue-painted figure of Our Lady gazed down and comforted me. Sometimes I asked questions of the old priest, like whether Papa's soul would be in purgatory. He would fold his hands and clear his throat and drone on. I didn't understand a word but his Irish accent was soothing.

Going with boys wasn't the same any more. When I first came to Devon, I found the country fellows awkward. The London lads had been fun. They had assurance. They were competitive, boastful, and they looked on sex as a game, like me. I'd tried to flirt in the same way at the Kingsbridge school. I wanted comfort, I suppose, after Papa was murdered. But the boys were shy, practised with udders but clumsy with a girl's breasts and wrong-footed because mine were so readily available. Now, after all the business with Sergei and Mama and Kati, I didn't want boys anywhere near me ever again.

I was lonely that summer. Tears still welled up every time I thought of Mama and whether I'd ever see her again – and, if I did, whether she'd know who I was. Aunt let me call Vienna, but it was expensive and Mama couldn't always come to the phone. I helped Aunt in the garden. We went swimming. She taught me to cook some basic English dishes and helped with homework. I tried not to talk about Mama. Aunt had put up with enough of me and my troubles. To compensate, I was desperate to do well in my O levels, to make her proud of me.

I guess it made me touchy. When I was commended in English for an essay I'd taken a lot of trouble with, and Lizzie Tozer hissed at me that I'd cheated, I lost it. I turned on her and gave her a mighty swipe across the face. The old Marika was back, sent to the Head and on report.

My eyes were still swollen from crying when I walked out of school. A figure was waiting by the school gates and I tensed, fearing my old gang was lurking to have their revenge on me for hitting Lizzie. But it was Jack Tucker. Jack was a boy who made no waves. He was neither clever nor thick, got along with most people and had never been one to hang around girls. He had an outdoor face set on a square, chunky body.

We'd been to the cinema a few times in the last year and he'd sought me out at the carnival and bought me a cider. The cider was a mistake. Jack had only ever held my hand and pecked me on the cheek. But the alcohol persuaded me to lead his hand into my blouse and evidently it was having the same loosening effect on him, because he grasped my breast eagerly and started to squeeze it as if he were milking his prize cow. I felt invaded – which was unfair as I'd guided his hand myself. I still cringed to remember the hurt look on Jack's face when I pulled his hand out and buttoned myself up. I'd avoided Jack after that and he'd soon stopped waiting for me after school.

'Long time no see,' he said now.

It was a stock phrase of his, and I was grateful that it somehow wiped out any awkwardness. He made no comment on my tears, but handed me his handkerchief, which smelled strongly of silage.

'You've changed this term,' he went on. 'I been watching you. How come you got in detention?'

I told him about hitting Lizzie, and felt I'd disappointed him.

'I've let everyone down,' I said.

He kicked a stone down the road. 'I'd say you only let yourself down.'

It was enough to set me off crying all over again.

'What's going on, Mari? What's up?'

It all spilled out then. All the stuff about Mama, that is. I mentioned Sergei but said nothing about him and Kati. I didn't want to put him off. He listened and was quiet. Had I said too much? Was he shocked at the thought of my mother having a lover? But no. He was just thinking things through in his deliberate, Jack kind of way.

'You ought to talk to my mum. She knows what that be like. To lose your mum. She was an evacuee.'

'What's "evacuee"?'

'When the war started, they sent the kids out of the cities to the country, so they wouldn't be killed in the bombs. She was sent here. All on her own. She was only eight or nine and she was treated bad, too. She won't talk about it much.'

'She must have been pleased to see her mum…'

'Never did. Both her parents were killed. Direct hit on the house. So I s'pose it worked for her, it did save her life. But she don't see it that way.'

'So young. Not to see her mother again…'

'She stayed here and met Dad. Sometimes she says it'd be better if she'd stayed in Bristol and been killed with them. He doesn't like it when she says that stuff.'

It's the most I'd ever heard Jack say. As my bus trundled up to the stop, Jack said, 'You'd best come to tea. I'll fix it up. Meet my mum – if you like?'

I was invited to tea the following Saturday. Aunt dropped me off at the end of the farm track. As I was crossing the yard and wondering where to go, Jack appeared from one of the barns wearing dungarees and waving a pitchfork.

'Go on in the middle door. I'll be right there when I've had a wash.'

His mother was taking scones out of the oven in the range. She set them down and shook my hand and gave me plates to carry to the table at the other end of the kitchen. Everything was homemade. Home-cured ham, homemade chutney, clotted cream from their own cows for the scones, strawberry jam.

'We don't grow any tea, though,' said Jack as his mother poured from a huge brown pot.

The talk was of jobs that needed doing over the weekend. Jack's sister was out with her young man and the only tension at the table came when Jack said they were set to get engaged. After tea, Jack and his father went out to the yard and his mother took it for granted that I would help with the washing up.

She handed me a tea towel. 'You lost your mum, Jack said?'

I told her all about Papa and Mama, and she told me how she'd come on the train to Loddiswood and been lined up against a wall to be chosen by the villagers. She still sounded angry.

'The older boys went first – farmers wanted them for labour. And the little ones went next because they looked appealing and would eat less.'

Nobody wanted her – a girl of eight years old. She was left there until one of the ladies came back and walked her all around the village until one lady agreed reluctantly to take her in.

'She gave me the strap if I dropped anything. But there was worse. 'Er husband came to read me bedtime stories. He used to put his hand down the bed and touch me and then he'd do stuff in his trousers. He told me not to tell or I'd never see my mum and dad again. When they was killed, I did tell. But the teacher didn't believe me.'

It put my problems in their place. Mama was still alive. So was Kati. I had Aunt, and no one had ever treated me like that.

I went to tea with the Tuckers about once a month. After the washing up was done Jack's mother would get out family albums and show me the pitifully small number of mementos she had of her own parents. A framed photo of them on their wedding day, a silver locket, a tortoiseshell-backed hairbrush and a briar pipe of her father's. A neighbour had salvaged them from the ruins of their house. Sometimes Jack's sister, Margaret, was there and on those occasions Mrs Tucker was always more animated. They were obviously very close.

Usually, Jack walked me down the track to catch my bus but he never attempted to hold hands. We were friends and no more, and that suited me. He was a different person on the farm – strong, competent and totally at home with the animals and the machines. Once he let me try my hand at milking, but I was useless, too afraid of the lumbering great animal to relax into any kind of rhythm. He shrugged and sent me off to collect eggs. In the spring the visits stopped. Jack said they were too busy with lambing and whatever else went on in the fields.

He muttered about coming again in the autumn, but I knew it wouldn't happen.

The autumn was the future. Jack was leaving school to work full-time with his dad. I'd be back in London finding a job and trying to get Kati to talk to me.

31

Kokoschka. That word. It caught my eye on the tube. The man opposite had just turned his newspaper inside out. I stared, impatient, as he shook the pages. Why did the word excite me? There it was again. An exhibition at the Tate. I shuddered. The Tate of all places.

But I had to go. Oskar Kokoschka. Papa's favourite painter. He'd told me once that he was born in Austria, which was the next best thing to Hungary because, once upon a time, it all used to be one big empire.

I leaned on the railing opposite the Tate Gallery for a long time. I'd left school and was staying with Wilkie to look for a job. It was over a year since Sergei had vanished, Kati had disowned me and Mama had gone to Vienna. London didn't feel right any more but there was no work in Devon in winter and I had to earn a living. Amanda expected me to move in with Kati, but that was never going to happen. She even invited us both round, but Kati stormed out the moment I arrived.

Amanda was determined to find Kati a boyfriend. She'd persuaded her to help out at her parties, both at home and at the gallery. That meant new clothes and a hair-do. I was not to worry. Someone would fall for her. Good luck to her, I thought. Amanda was surprising, not snooty any more. Loyal. Generous, even.

Wilkie had welcomed me in a reek of nicotine and patchouli. She fried sausages in a blackened pan, bending over the gas until I thought her orange hair would catch fire. As she hugged the loaf to her chest to carve slices of bread, she told me the gossip about the people on the parade, our old neighbours. Memories flooded back. I didn't want to hear. I picked the threads of green angora off my bread and butter and longed to be back in Aunt Klára's kitchen.

I had to steel myself to go in to the exhibition. It gave me the shivers to think of how happy I'd been that day, coming down those steps with Papa, looking forward to fish and chips, enjoying the good mood he was in. Before. Before. I took a deep breath and crossed the road.

Mama always said Papa had weird taste. I could see immediately why he'd admired this artist. These pictures *were* weird. Vibrant and lively, with loads of paint plastered on. But not the sort of lively that made you feel good. They seemed to be all about death, or was that my imagination? Because of being in this place again for the first time? The paintings scared me, to be honest. They made my stomach churn, but I couldn't look away. The painter was seeing through people, portraying them already dead and then painting flesh back onto the skulls. Or so it appeared to me. One portrait in particular seemed to look right through me. An old man in angry colours. Big ears, hollow eyes. He looked like a torturer. Then again, he might have been tortured. I couldn't decide. Was it hatred or terror glaring out at me?

The clenching in my tummy became so bad that I hurried in search of the toilets. This was how I had felt as a child when Papa came home and whispered to Mama – frightened, sick, not understanding. Sometimes Mama cried, sometimes she raged at Papa. There'd be the murmur of a name and they'd clutch each other. Looking back, that probably meant another friend eliminated.

I sat in the cubicle, head in hands, immersed in those kitchen scenes. Conversations like that could only happen with Mama clattering saucepan lids and making the water boil so that it bubbled and hissed. They could only happen in that room with its thick floor covering and walls that didn't adjoin other apartments. I understood what Aunt Klára meant when she said she left Hungary because the politics made her ill.

The pictures were having the same effect on me. Torturer or victim? You never knew who would fill those roles next. Who was your friend or who would inform? Who should you hate or fear? These thoughts tumbled through my head and meshed into a moment of clarity. For the first time I understood Papa. How he saw the society we lived in, why he did what he did, why he was drawn to Kokoschka. These two shared a worldview. Kokoschka's art and Papa's writing had a common aim – to stop what they saw from eating them up.

But it had eaten him up. Bloody Kokoschka! He egged Papa on, he got him killed. I knew it didn't make sense but it made me feel better. Who else could I blame? Sergei was dead. Mama was out of reach – miles away in Vienna and miles away in her mind.

I washed my hands and splashed water on my face and was surprised by a tap on the shoulder. I thought for a moment the secret police had come for me. But it was Angie, hardly changed except for her clothes. Big eyes peered out from an oversized fur coat. I hadn't seen or heard of her since the day I was expelled from the Priory Academy for Girls. It seemed like half a century ago since we'd been caught in bed together.

'I thought it was you. I followed you in here. But then, you were *so* long I thought I'd missed you. Let's have lunch?'

'I really can't stay…' The thought of food turned my stomach again. Let alone the thought of eating and listening to Angie. I wanted to stay with the thoughts triggered by the paintings. I wanted to follow that sense of understanding Papa. Bother Angie.

'But I just *have* to talk to you. It won't take long. Coffee, then? If you have to go?'

I didn't have the energy to refuse. I was surprised Angie wanted to see me, that she wasn't mad at me. Maybe she'd forgotten all that.

On the way to the café I took in the new Angie: exotic fur, expensive perfume, high heels with matching snakeskin bag. So sophisticated. Yet the impression was of a child dressed up in Mummy's clothes. She settled at a table, pulling off gloves with the flash of an outsize diamond on a manicured hand. I still saw a frail creature in navy blue gym knickers looking scared. An uneasy feeling came over me.

As she shrugged the fur off her shoulders, I wondered how much she must have paid for all that honey-coloured mink.

She was chattering on, brittle. 'I don't keep up with anyone. Do you?'

My uneasy feeling wouldn't go away. I shook my head. 'My sister does. But only with Amanda. She used to stay in her flat…'

This was all reminding me of the nasty little note Patty had sent me after I got myself expelled. She said she was "disgusted" and had known "all along" that there was something not quite nice about me. I didn't want to think about that.

'Oh yes, Katalin. The dancer.'

I was surprised Angie remembered Kati and her dancing. 'Oh, and there's Ena of course. Ena Foley. Amanda shares with her. She's got one like that.' I nodded at the jewel on Angie's ring finger.

'I got married in June. I met him almost as soon as I left school…'

'You got actually married? You married a man?'

'Well of *course* a man…'

'But I thought—'

'Oh, Marika! That was just… You know, a phase. Everyone said so. I mean, I couldn't be one of *them*. It's obscene…'

'Obscene? Oh, Angie! Why? What's wrong with it? Some people are just made that way. It's the law that's wrong.'

She gave me a horrified look. 'Well, I'm *not*! Anyway, you see, my parents were back for the summer and they wanted to see me settled. I mean, I could have gone back to Rhodesia with them, but… Well, I knew they wouldn't really want me cramping their style. And I didn't fancy the heat and the natives. They simply *threw* me at Rupert and I didn't resist. I wanted someone to look after me. He's terribly rich – so no problem really.'

A waitress set the coffee pot and cups on the table and added a plate with a domed metal lid. Angie poured and pushed a cup across the table. 'Teacake?'

I shook my head and stirred two cubes of sugar into my coffee, although normally I didn't take sugar.

'I wanted to see you because I've always felt guilty.' Angie dropped her voice to a breathy whisper as if about to confess to murder. 'I know you were trying to help me. And you got expelled and I didn't. It didn't seem fair. Especially as I was the one that started it. What with having that *stupid* crush on Madeleine.'

The shock almost made me laugh. It was so different from what I'd anticipated.

But the odd feeling I'd been aware of overtook the urge to laugh. Guilt. I'd unashamedly used Angie and never gave it a moment's thought. I'd never stopped to wonder what happened to her, staying on at school, living that incident down. For a ridiculous moment I felt as culpable as the torturer in the portrait. Before, I'd always thought of myself as the victim of the system – and of Kati. I believed it didn't matter what means I used to escape from that place.

Angie was still talking, gaining confidence, looking pretty pleased with herself. 'You see, I'd like to make it up to you. Is there *anything* I can do for you? Anything I can *give* you? That you need?'

The ridiculous thought that she could bring my father back from the dead clattered through my mind. I shook my head. 'Nothing that you could—'

'Money's no object you know.'

I could have said that life had worked out for the best. I could have settled for a thumping great flask of the scent she was wearing. Or I could have said that being expelled meant I was there to see my father killed under a train. What I did say was just as shocking. It was as if the rawness of the paintings invaded me. Here was a victim who didn't even know she was a victim – a layer of confusion that needed to be ripped away. Time to be open and honest. I would own up.

'It wasn't like that, Angie. You see, I wasn't trying to help you. I did it entirely for me, selfish me. I *wanted* to get expelled, you see.' I ignored the sharp intake of breath from Angie. 'Why do you think I chose that precise moment? When Latin-Willie and Delia were about to come in? Didn't it ever occur to you it was odd?'

Angie had set down her cup and was staring at me with her mouth open. I thought at first she was going to slap me across the face with her thin fingers and blood-red nails. But, as she glared across, her eyes filled.

'It's been a strange morning,' I said. 'I've understood a lot of things. Then you turn up to tell me something else. I used you, Angie. I must apologise. I made you a victim because I was a victim. It was a bad thing to do. I'm sorry, I really am.'

I meant it. I was almost in tears myself by the time I finished speaking. Kati would have been calling me a drama queen, but this felt different. It felt momentous. But Angie was gathering her bag and her gloves and pulling her coat up to her chin as if I might make a pass at her at any moment.

'You *filthy* little bastard! They all said you were a dirty bitch, the other girls. And they were right. To *think* I defended you!'

'But Angie, I'm saying—'

'You can shut right up. I've heard *quite* enough. All those years when I felt guilty and felt sorry for you… And all the time… You can keep your so-called apology. I never want to see you again.'

She pulled a purse from her bag and dropped a ten-shilling note onto the table. 'I asked you to join me and I'll pay, but that is that. Don't even *think* of trying to follow me.'

In a flurry of mink and Chanel she was gone.

I sat on at the table in a daze. The waitress claimed the ten bob and brought change in a saucer. Ridiculous, leaving ten shillings. Talk about showing off. Little rich girl. Patronising cow. I put all the coins into my purse except for one threepenny bit, which I left in the saucer as a tip. The money wouldn't buy me perfume but it would buy me a catalogue of the exhibition. On an impulse I wrapped one of the teacakes in my handkerchief.

I sat on a bench on the Embankment before I went home, trying to get rid of the Angie stuff, trying to get back to the insight I'd had when I looked at the pictures. I'd glimpsed another dimension beyond the daily drag of getting by, of living in Wilkie's chaotic flat. Here was a world of ideas to escape into, the world Papa had inhabited. A new future began to take shape. I wouldn't get any old job and keep ticking over. I would stay on at school. I would study and study.

32

'Now, what's this you're saying? You wanted to be forgiven? By this Angie person?'

Aunt was spooning extra coffee into the pot as if she thought we might need it. She'd been a star. No hint of dismay when I phoned and asked if I could come back. Insisted on meeting me at the station, so that I didn't have to lug my case to the bus. I told her all about meeting Angie. It was dragging me down. I couldn't get it out of my head.

'I wanted to own up. I don't know about being forgiven. But I really didn't expect to be *punished.*'

'That's always a risk, isn't it? When you own up?'

I shrugged. 'Is it? I suppose so. I just wanted to get it off my chest. I *apologised.*'

'Ah, yes. I can see that. But I can also see Angie's point of view.' Steam burst from the spout of the kettle, and she paused to pour water into the jug. 'Put yourself in her shoes. You *say* you were apologising. But think about what you were actually telling her.'

'Uh? What do you mean?' Where was this going? Why was she taking Angie's side?

'Well, from what you've told me – you were telling her, one, that you never cared a fig for her, and, two, that she was pretty stupid. She got quite a slap in the face, just after she'd offered you her friendship and *her* apology. Now do you see?'

Annoyingly, I did. 'I hadn't thought of it like that.'

Aunt stirred the coffee and rattled in the drawer to find the strainer. 'You didn't even acknowledge her feelings, or her apology, or her sense of responsibility. Or did you?'

'No. No, I didn't. I didn't even think of it.'

Aunt just looked at me, not exactly smiling but with her dimples showing. This was really uncomfortable. I looked away towards the garden but all I could see was a reflection of myself in the dark glass.

'Really, it was all about you getting it off your chest.'

'Yeah, I suppose so.'

I willed her to pour the coffee, but she was taking her time, strainer poised.

'It wasn't about apologising at all. As far as Angie knew, there was nothing to apologise for. Because of the way you set it up.'

'So I shouldn't have confessed?'

'I don't think so. Not confessed to Angie, anyway. You made someone else miserable and angry. This may seem harsh, but you did ask. I'd say it was self-indulgent.'

I squirmed in my seat and would have liked to slide under the table with Finn. 'I was trying to be honest.'

'Do you want me to shut up? Had enough? Here.' She pushed a steaming mug across the table.

I shook my head and grabbed it, wrapping my fingers round it for comfort.

'In my experience, retrospective honesty – and that's what we're talking about – is all about unburdening yourself. Usually. It's your burden, but it's uncomfortable. So you give it to the other person. Then you get peeved when they throw it back in your face.'

I sipped my coffee, but it was too hot. 'Do you think that's why the Catholics have confession? Go to a priest? Get absolution that way?'

'*You* should know about that. It's one way of looking at it.' She nodded slowly. 'That may be exactly right.'

'Maybe that's what God's for.'

Aunt shrugged. She didn't do God. 'Ask Father Patrick. All I know is that being forgiven by people we've wronged is a luxury we have no right to expect.'

Hot tears dribbled down my cheeks. I'd asked Aunt what she thought. But I'd expected support, expected her to take my side against Angie. I should have known. Aunt wasn't like that.

'I know, it's difficult. If Angie had *asked* you, that would be another matter. I mean, if she'd asked you whether you did it deliberately. Then you should not have lied. And she would have been prepared. She would probably still not have forgiven you. We have no right to forgiveness.'

Aunt said it so vehemently that I wondered what she had never been forgiven for.

'It's a tough lesson. But you're used to tough lessons. Growing up's a painful process.'

I suddenly didn't want to grow up any more. I'd come off the train so determined to have this adult talk with Aunt. Now I could see my new maturity in bits under Aunt's blue gaze.

'You're tired,' Aunt was saying. 'Have a bath. Go to bed. We'll go to the sea in the morning and you'll have the chance to think it all over. It's all about boundaries and responsibility. You might not feel good now, but you'll work it out. I know you will, because you have the capacity for insight. Not many people have.'

She stood and pulled me to my feet, holding my gaze, eyes smiling. 'But nobody can manage that when they're tired and emotional. I'm sure you're worried about what's next. We'll talk about that tomorrow, too.'

Klára stomped up the dark tunnel of the lane kicking at pebbles. Only when she reached the stile did she look up through the ash leaves that were making William Morris patterns against a grey sky. She settled onto the smooth wooden bar to gather the thoughts of a sleepless night.

So, Marika was back. She'd gone off to Wilkie's in October and only lasted three weeks. To be honest Klára wasn't surprised or upset. After a day or two revelling in getting the house back to herself, she'd missed Marika.

Every time that girl went to London there was major salvage work to do on her return. This time she had planned to stay there – find a job, get some digs and make a life for herself. But one visit to the Tate, a chance encounter with this Angie and her world had fallen apart. She'd been ridiculously harsh on her the evening before, painting a picture of an unforgiving world. She'd said nothing about trust, the context in which forgiveness is possible, which makes confession a risk worth taking.

But trust could be unreliable too. She'd trusted David all those years ago when she told him about the abortion. That had been an unburdening too, just like Marika with Angie. She had wanted to offload her secret and the guilt she felt about it. She'd thought David would share it, absolve her.

She shifted off the stile and set off after Finn, following the path along the edge of the wood. Oak and beech were a tired green, their outer fringes rusting into tan and copper tints. She nodded at the stalks of foxglove marking the tree line, stiff and brown with seeds, such a contrast to the soft pouches of their June buds, the riotous energy of those pink bells. You can't fit a foxglove into an envelope. She grinned at the memory of trying to do that. Wanting to share the exuberant flower with David. Foolscap should be big enough, she'd thought. Ridiculous! She'd been sad at the truncated offering she'd eventually sealed and posted. A fool's cap was what she deserved for even trying.

On second thoughts, it was no bad thing to teach Marika something about boundaries. She was too impulsive. Generous, yes, but she shared her rage and her misery as readily as gifts and delight. No wonder her sister avoided her. Katalin was at the other end of that emotional scale. Out of sight, in fact. Katalin seemed to have a facet missing when it came to relationships. Extraordinary that she'd fallen in love. Ironic that she'd chosen someone unattainable.

She could normally see the far headland from the top of the field, but today it was obscured by low cloud. More blurred boundaries, a smudging of sea, land and sky. The weather too was neither one thing nor another – it wasn't raining but the mist was shedding moisture as it swirled about her.

It was being "in love" that had led her to tell David about the abortion. She'd believed David's love was unconditional, her own boundaries blurred by that deceptive merging into one body, one soul. David had judged her. He had stiffened and given her a hard look that said, "I thought I knew you, but I was deceived". She'd come up against an uncompromising wall, his dedication to the principle that all life was sacred, his commitment to a career in medicine, saving lives. Jealousy hadn't come into it. After all, the events took place before they'd met. He wasn't interested in the fact that she'd been raped, violated by a distant cousin at her parent's house. She, Klára, had violated his *principle*. That was all that mattered.

She shuddered at the memory, which had been more disturbing than the rape. That was a fumbled affair at the back of the hen house where the cousin had accompanied her to collect eggs. To this day she couldn't bring herself to keep chickens. As a young woman, just out of university, she had known the family wouldn't believe her story against a respected relative. She'd fled to Júlia in Vienna. Júlia had been cool, but Fritz came to the rescue. He knew someone who knew someone. Money had been no object.

Then she'd met gentle, reliable David. He took her to England. They'd married and, when it came to talking about having a family, she had made her confession. That hard look of his still haunted her. He hadn't rejected her but a spark had gone out. Would he have understood if he'd lived to experience life's more complex dilemmas? The irony was that the war had intervened and David was soon in the air dropping bombs on German cities. How he squared that with his principle of preserving life she never knew.

A relationship that had seemed so simple had turned out to be complicated. Like a gold chain that tangles in its box overnight. You coil it neatly and yet, in the morning, it's full of knots. Would she and David still be together if he had survived? Together? Happy? Driving each other insane?

Klára called Finn and started for home. Coming from the open field it was like night when she stepped into the lane under the canopy of trees. She looked at her watch – gone seven o'clock and still not fully light on a dull day. Back in the yard, the telegraph wire was spiked with tails and wings as the house martins jostled for position, preparing to leave.

'They'll soon be gone,' she said to Finn.

As soon as they got to the beach later in the morning Marika said, 'I bet you hoped you'd get your house back to yourself. And then I come back like the bad penny.'

Klára laughed. 'True enough. But I'm glad you have. And you say you want to stay on. To do A levels? Really?'

'Yes, really. I want to go to university.'

'Well, there's a surprise.'

They were scrunching through the shingle at the water's edge, pausing to examine stones or to throw a stick for Finn.

'You know the man I used to see at school? Mr Johnson. After the shoplifting and all that stuff with boys? That's what I want to do.'

'He was a psychologist. An educational psychologist. But I thought you said he was no help whatsoever?'

'That's what I thought at the time. He got me to talk about when Papa was killed. And when I described that bat shape, flying – you know?'

Klára nodded.

'He got me to draw it. Then he got me to draw a butterfly instead and told me to imagine it flying up and away and up the escalator into the sunlight. Like it was Papa's soul or something, I guess. I thought it was rubbish at the time. But I tried it again later. And it really did help. I did two butterflies, one for Papa and one for me.'

Klára nodded, looking out to the horizon, imagining butterflies. 'Well, I guess we'd better get on to the school. See if they'll have you back.'

Marika talked on and on. There was no stopping her once she'd got going.

'You see, I realised I could spend the rest of my life on that platform in the underground station, seeing the bat shape fly, being all alone, being terrified and bereft.

'Then I realised I could stay living Mama's kind of life, waiting for her to come back. But something got unhinged in her when Papa was killed and there was no sign that anything was going to hinge it back again. Not the doctors, not the drugs and not me or Kati. All the stuff with Sergei finally broke the hinge right off.

'Next, I realised I could wait forever for my sainted sister to say something nice to me, to think of me at all, let alone think we might support each other.'

Marika faltered there. The pain was clear in her voice. All that fighting, all the insults she used to hurl at Katalin counted for nothing. This was the thing that mattered most.

She was off again.

'And I thought, there's all of life teeming and rushing up above the ground in the light. I didn't want to end up like that Kokoschka portrait.

'I wanted to answer all the questions in my head. Like, who was the portrait of, torturer or victim? Why did Angie react like she did? Why did I expect to be forgiven? Why was Mama stuck the way she was? Why did Kati always hate me? Why did Sergei commit suicide? Oh yes, Sergei. That was another thing I could have devoted my life to. Trying to prove that he killed Papa. What good would that have done?'

Her challenging niece had decided to make something of her life. That was something she could support. It was exciting. Klára turned away and threw a stick for Finn so that Marika wouldn't see the tears in her eyes.

33

'Marika, I'm worried about your sister. Really worried. I thought you said you were coming to London, that you'd do something.'

'I did. I came at Easter. I told you what happened, Amanda. I waited outside her place, but when she came home from work, she told me to go to hell.'

The Easter trip had been no fun at all. My A levels were only weeks away. I'd stayed with Wilkie where it was difficult to get any revision done, the weather had been atrocious and Wilkie had a filthy cold, which she passed on to me.

'But, Marika—'

'I told you I couldn't come again because of A levels. And now I've got a job. It's seven days a week. At a hotel in—'

'But Marika, you could—'

'No I couldn't. They would sack me. I need the money. I'm saving up to go to university. And anyway, what's the point?'

Amanda was still mad that I'd failed to get a job in London after O levels. She implied it was my fault that Kati wouldn't see me.

'I tell you, Amanda. She. Will. Not. Talk. To. Me.'

'Well, anyway. At least listen to what I have to say.'

I sighed and waited.

'Well, you know how thin I said she's been getting? She doesn't feed herself properly. I mean, she hasn't even got an oven in that flat of hers. So I took her with me when I went to my parents for the weekend. Now he's retired, Daddy's relaxed about all that business with your father. He really quite likes her.'

'Yes?' I tried to move her on. Amanda always took so long to get to the point. Had Kati said something to upset Amanda's father?

'Anyway, Mummy had just got a new freezer, one of those huge chest things. She can get a whole lamb from the farmer down the road and she wanted somewhere to store it, haunches of this and that.'

I drummed my fingers on the table, wondering where this rigmarole was leading.

'Well, Katalin was fascinated by this freezer. She lifted the lid and bent inside until Mummy told her to stop letting the cold out. You'll never guess what happened.'

'No, Mand, I won't. Just tell me.'

'Well, it was the next day. It was really warm for May. Daddy mixed the G&Ts as usual. He'd been mowing the lawn and I'd been emptying the grass box. We hadn't noticed Kati wasn't around. It was Mummy who said, "Where's Katalin?"

'I thought she was probably in her room and Mummy said, "I thought you were supposed to be keeping an eye on the girl." She never much liked her. Anyway, supper was all but ready, she said. "I'll just do some peas," she said.

'Kati wasn't in her room. As I came back downstairs there was a shriek from the kitchen.

'There was Mummy with the freezer lid flung back and trying to get your bloody sister out of there. I yelled for Daddy and it took the three of us to lift her clear. Mummy sat her by the oven with the door open where she'd just taken the joint out. I fetched her duvet, and Daddy got brandy and phoned our friend Nigel who's a doctor. He said physically she was fine, no harm done, but he spent ages with her trying to decide whether he should get her into hospital, mental hospital, that is.'

I could hear Amanda underlining the word "mental" and had a picture of Mama in that awful place in London.

'But Kati seemed perfectly sane and rational. She maintained it was all a mistake. Thought it would be cool and peaceful. It was too hot and we were too noisy. I ask you! Thought she'd just be able to get out again when she wanted to. But she couldn't lift the lid. Apparently she yelled and banged. She'd given up and was falling asleep when Mummy went to get the peas.'

'Thank God she did!'

'Quite. Mummy's not got over it yet. She was all ready to send the damn freezer back, but Daddy got a padlock for it to shut her up.'

'How is Kati now? When did you last see her?'

'Daddy said she should be seeing a psychiatrist.'

I noticed Amanda didn't answer the question. She'd been a loyal friend to Kati, but she couldn't be expected to nursemaid her. Maybe I could get Wilkie to go and see her. But then, Kati had never liked Wilkie.

Amanda was still talking.

'But the other thing, Marika. I haven't told Mummy and Daddy. I haven't told anyone. On the way back to London, she said she wanted to feel how it would be in a coffin. She imagined it would be a lovely way to die. To lie down, all cool and dark. She did say, it wasn't like that at all, she got it wrong. But dying is on her mind. That's what I'm saying.'

*

I was late for work and running from the bus stop at the bottom of town when I heard my name.

'Mari! Whoa there, Mari!'

It was a voice more used to summoning cattle from the river reaches of a hundred-acre meadow than hailing a chambermaid in Fore Street. I couldn't pretend I hadn't heard and turned to see Jack striding towards me. His face was tanned and ruddy. He grasped my hand in his calloused palm and nearly shook my arm off.

'Good to see you.'

It was good to see him too. There was a time when I secretly wanted to marry Jack. Everything always felt safe when he was there. But we had nothing in common. It would have been a disaster. His life was with animals, tractors and mud. Mine was with people and ideas. He'd filled out since I saw him last. He was a man, broad-shouldered, strong-muscled. But his eyes had lost something. They'd lost their straightforward gaze. I found that troubling.

We exchanged greetings but I dared not be late. He was in town for the morning and we arranged to meet by the quay in my lunch break.

I arrived out of breath, as usual. I seemed to run everywhere these days. Jack was eating a pasty and lobbing pieces of crust to a swan.

'Give it to me, not the bird,' I said. 'I'm ravenous and I didn't have time to do sandwiches this morning.'

We shared his pasty, bite for bite. It felt more intimate than anything we'd done together.

'What you doing, working in the King's Arms?'

'Saving up for university. I'm off to Bristol in September. That's if I get good enough grades.'

He wished me luck, but in a mechanical way before diving in with his news.

'Ma's in the hospital.' He tapped his head as he said it, so I knew it was nothing physical.

That explained the look in his eyes. I didn't know what to say.

'Since Margaret got married we haven't been able to do anything with her. It got worse and worse. She was lonely, I suppose. Though Margaret's only just across the fields. Depression. They're giving her the shock treatment. Supposed to get her going again. Like jump leads, Pa says.' He shrugged and grimaced as if dubious that jump leads would do the trick.

'We're in a mess, Pa and me. Neither of us any good at cooking or house stuff.' He paused and took a deep breath. 'Would you do something for me, Mari? Ever since I saw you this morning, I've been thinking...'

I was afraid he was going to ask me to go and clean the house and do the laundry.

186

Normally I wouldn't have minded, but I did that all week at the hotel and it was exhausting.

'Would you visit her? Pa and I, we never know what to say. She won't utter a word. But she might talk to you. She always liked you. And you understand. You know. Psychology. It's what you're going to study, isn't it?'

I nodded. 'Well, I'll go. Of course I'll go. But just because…'

'I tell you what. I'll teach you to drive. In return. Take you up the old airfield. Have to be in the Land Rover, mind. But it'll give you the basics.'

I'd wanted to learn for ages and Jack knew that.

'Brilliant,' I said. 'It's a deal.'

He would drive me to the hospital in Exeter on Sunday afternoon, the only time I had off. On the way back I would have my first driving lesson.

Mrs Tucker grabbed my arm. Her grip was unnecessarily firm, as if she was afraid I'd escape.

'I hate it here.'

I looked round the dreary day room from the cream emulsion to the green paintwork to the orange curtains, trying to spot a redeeming feature. Tall windows let in plenty of light but they were set too high to allow a view of anything but sky.

'Not here, here. Not the hospital. That's bad enough.' She made a face. 'I mean the country. I've always hated the country.'

I stared at her. 'But you've always…'

'Oh, yes. I learnt the part. Cows, pigs, hens. Homemade this, home-grown the other. Doesn't mean I enjoyed it.'

'But you did it so well.'

'Did it for Jim, the kids. Well, no, let's be honest. First off, I did it for me. To have a place to belong. A home. A family. There was nobody left in Bristol. All dead. I had to have someone. But I'm a city girl. Felt trapped. Never been to London. Exeter once a year. Kingsbridge once a week. Blimey!'

'I'd never have guessed.'

'That's the trouble. Bottled it up. Never told him. I brought it on myself. I bound him to me with apple pies and roast dinners. With helping at harvest. Milking cows – the hulking great horrors. Then I bound him with children – babies I was afraid of. And then just when Margaret grows up enough to be a friend, a companion, she ups and leaves.'

She clutched at her skirt with white knuckles.

'I found I couldn't do it any more. Not without her. All day long in the house on my own. Same jobs, day in, day out. I tried talking to Jim, but he didn't get it. First thing he understood was when I threw the dinner at him. One of our own chickens, it was. Hot fat everywhere, gravy down his shirt, roast potatoes all over the floor.

'That upset him, all right. Roast dinner. That's like burning the Bible. They got the doctor and here I am. In the madhouse. Voluntary, mind.'

'But you're unhappy, Mrs Tucker, not mad.'

She didn't seem to hear. Now she had started talking she didn't seem able to stop.

'Jack's courting now. So he'll be bringing a stranger in the house. I thought at one time it might be you. Sweet on you, he was. Mooned about after you used to come. But I could see it wouldn't work. Too like me. You'd have been restless in a week.'

So Jack had thought the same way I had. I nodded. 'I was terrified of the cows.'

'Yes. That was a test – when he set you to milking. You didn't pass.' She even managed a smile, but it faded quickly. 'Anyway, it wouldn't have been right, a foreigner in the family. No offence. But Carole's from down the valley. Her family's been in farming for generations. She knows what's what.'

She closed her eyes then and sank back into the high-backed chair. She'd worn herself out.

I gathered my bag and coat and stood up to creep away. Her eyes flew open.

'I'll be going home soon. Will you come? Come and see me? It would help. I know it would.'

I felt like asking her how it would help to have a foreigner in the house, but I took her hand and promised to come.

'We're all walking on bloody eggshells,' said Jack when he met me at the bottom of the farm track. 'She still isn't normal.'

I'd thought Mrs Tucker would forget about asking me round, but Jack had phoned a few weeks later, inviting me to Sunday lunch. His mum was home and he sounded anxious. My job had come to an end the week before, when all the tourists went home. I was off to Bristol to find digs on the Monday. A fraught Sunday lunch was the last thing I wanted but I couldn't refuse.

'What d'you call normal?' I asked Jack.

'Well, doing everything. Like she used to. She can't remember the most basic things.'

'Or doesn't want to. She's had enough, Jack. I thought I told you. She'd rather go and look round the shops in Exeter.'

He laughed. 'Don't be daft. This is Mum we're—'

'I'm serious. Get your Dad to take her out. And not just the once.'

He didn't get it, I could tell. But his father got it even less.

We all sat round the table holding our breath as Mrs Tucker took the joint out of the oven. She wouldn't have any help. She kept glancing across at me like a child who's afraid of getting something wrong, but told me fiercely to sit down.

Cabbage, gravy and a jug of mint sauce were already laid out. She brought the meat to the table for her husband to carve, looking proud and pleased. He took up the carving knife and fork and looked around, frowning.

'Where's the roast spuds, love?'

She was back by the stove untying her apron and seemed not to hear.

Jack held up a hand. 'Dad, no. It doesn't matter.'

But Mr Tucker could not conceive of roast lamb without roast potatoes.

'Elsie, where are the potatoes? The roast spuds?'

Her eyes were huge as she turned round. An expression of terror. A vital part of this test had escaped her. Her hand flew to her mouth and she turned back to the stove.

'Never mind, Ma.' Jack was beside her as she lifted the lid on a saucepan. 'Oh!' he said as he peered inside.

'There you see,' said his mother. 'I knew I cooked them.'

'But you never peeled them, Ma.'

I leapt up. The potatoes were like stones in a rock pool floating with seaweed.

'Didn't you know?' I said. 'That's Irish potatoes, that is. They're all the rage in London just now.' I took the pot to the sink and strained it off. 'All we need is a big dish and lashings of butter. Oh, and some fresh mint, Jack.'

We got through that course and even Mr Tucker didn't comment on the lumps in the custard or the lack of a pie crust on the stewed fruit for pudding.

That evening, Aunt told me firmly that Mrs Tucker was not my problem and to put her out of my mind. As we set out to the station next morning, Aunt was cursing about having to drive all the way to Totnes since the closure of Kingsbridge station.

'Bloody Beeching and his cuts,' she kept saying every time we were held up behind a tractor. But I hardly heard her. I was still haunted by the look of fear on Mrs Tucker's face.

34

It was a Sunday in January. The telephone rang while Katalin was eating her breakfast toast.

Amanda. Katalin groaned inwardly when she heard her voice. Amanda had been badgering her to apply for a job she'd heard about on the grapevine – personal secretary to the musical director at the Drury Lane theatre.

'You're bored rigid with the law and those fusty lawyers, you know you are. You've stuck it for over four years.'

It was true, but Katalin clung to the routine.

'It's more dead than alive in that office,' Amanda had continued. 'And frankly, Katalin, you've had enough of death in your life. Time to move into the twentieth century, or you'll be middle-aged at twenty-two.'

Katalin shrunk inside at the thought of more arguments that she couldn't deny. But Amanda wasn't ringing about the job.

'We're taking the sledge up to Primrose Hill,' she said. 'And you're coming. Drop everything – let's get there early before the crowds.'

Katalin couldn't resist. It rarely snowed properly in England, and yesterday's fall had been significant. It would be worth the trip. She pulled on her fur-lined boots and dug out the hooded grey duffel coat she'd bought in the market during the hard winter a few years back. It wasn't the height of fashion, but it was warm and allowed room for several jumpers. She'd get a tube to Chalk Farm.

It was just before eight o'clock and London was muted. She could hear her own footsteps crunching the snow. There were few people about and the only traffic consisted of the odd snow-clearer, gritting lorry or bus. She wondered why Amanda had asked her along, but took a deep breath of snow-cleaned air and found she didn't care. It was like inhaling energy. On the train, crusts of snow fell off her boots and melted into pools at her feet. The windows steamed up and strangers spoke to each other.

From the station she walked down Regent's Park Road, before weaving through tree-lined streets where snowmen lurched in front gardens and children emerged with shrieks of excitement. The parked cars looked oddly old-fashioned, their modern angles tucked into plump white cushions. She was greeted by a man shovelling a pathway to his gate. There it was again, that English phenomenon of breaking silence in extreme weather. It was only snow. But the English couldn't cope with it. Thank goodness she hadn't stayed in Devon. Three years ago, Aunt Klára had been cut off down that lane for weeks until the neighbouring farmer got through on a tractor.

They'd agreed to meet at the Prince Albert Road entrance to the Hill, and Amanda and Ena were already there when she arrived. Amanda was carrying a proper sledge with runners and Ena, surprisingly, a blue plastic affair like a tray with a rope attached. She was quick to hand it over to Katalin. Amanda managed to look chic in a belted gabardine raincoat, wellies and a black beret. But Ena had overdone it with a fur hat. Very *Dr Zhivago*. Amanda could have carried it off, but Ena really was no Lara. Katalin was pleased to note that she looked ridiculous.

They puffed their way to the top of the hill, the snow creaking under their boots. She and Amanda arrived first, flushed and laughing, and waited for Ena who was clearly not in her element. Katalin pushed the heavy sledge off and watched the two of them career downhill. Ena was on the back, clinging on to Amanda with one hand and hanging onto her hat with the other.

Katalin was happy to be on her own, looking out across the London skyline. She could identify St Paul's away to the east and buildings that might be the Houses of Parliament. There was no mistaking the new Post Office Tower which dominated the whole panorama. The snow exaggerated the blue of the sky, enhancing the whole scene. A bit like Tipp-Ex: covering the mistakes; transforming the ugly and the boring. In the distance, the city was shimmering in the early morning light like a mirage that might dissolve at any moment. In the foreground, ordinary roofs of terraced houses became an arresting pattern of triangles. Trees were hung with a white tracery among their stencilled branches, and the shrubs at the bottom of the hill seemed to have burst into spontaneous spring blossom.

Trailing her plastic tray-sledge, she chose a slightly steeper, longer incline, which veered away from where Amanda and Ena had landed. As the icy air rushed past, Katalin remembered tobogganing in the park in Buda as a child. It was almost as good. As she gathered speed towards the bottom of the hill, the tray hit a bump. She catapulted off and rolled over and over for the last few yards, enjoying the momentum of her body.

She ended up facedown in the snow, ice on her lips and teeth and up her nose. A voice sounded in her head: 'Don't move! Close your eyes!' She was back on that vast snow-clad hillside on the Hungarian border, lying between Papa and the strange Birdman. It was all so vivid: the spark of the searchlight on snow crystals; the rushing river; the crack of ice under the slippery bridge; the lung-breaking tramp across no man's land; the tight grip of Papa's hug when they reached Austria.

Papa. She'd been so close to him during those days of escape. She missed him. The sense of loss was suddenly like a physical pain. She'd never mourned him. Not really. She'd been too intent on getting away from Devon. And then Sergei had happened.

'Katalin! Are you okay? Can you get up? Have you broken anything?'

She opened her eyes and lifted her head, blinking in the bright sunlight.

Amanda was kneeling beside her. 'We lost you. What happened?'

She got to her feet, wiping both snow and tears from her face. 'I'm fine. I just came off, that's all.'

She climbed the slope and whizzed back down one more time. But families were beginning to arrive. Fathers mostly, looking as eager as their children.

'I'm going now,' she said when Amanda and Ena arrived at her feet.

Amanda exchanged glances with Ena. 'You sure you're okay?'

Katalin nodded. 'It gets boring. Anyway, I need to get back.'

Why was she so grudging? She'd had a fine time. She tried again. 'Thank you. Thanks for ringing me. I enjoyed it.'

'Make sure you think about that job,' Amanda called after her.

It was Papa she needed to think about. After Sergei she'd been bereft – and so mad at Mama for concealing the identity of her biological father – that she hadn't given Papa a thought. She'd even taught herself not to think of László as her father. Sergei had taken over.

What was it about Papa? What was the word? He had understood her. That was it. Only now did she realise just how remarkable that was. He'd taken her as his own child and she'd never once sensed that this was forced or insincere. Papa wasn't capable of that kind of pretence. But what had it been like for him – coming home to find Mama had a baby, the child of another man? He could have rejected her, ignored her, favoured Marika. Instead, he'd made her feel special. Again, she brushed away tears. The word she was looking for – she supposed it really had to be love.

Sergei, on the other hand, had not loved her. Or only as far as she reflected his own image back to him. He was a Narcissus. He'd only loved himself, and it had taken her a stupidly long time to work that out.

She was cold and wet from lying in the snow and her fingers were hurting as they lost their numbness. Heading back towards the station, she found a steamy café and treated herself to a hot chocolate, reflecting as she stirred and sipped, that if she'd stayed with Amanda and Ena, they could have been doing this together.

But they'd be meeting up with their smart friends in Belsize Park. She could do without that, but wasn't ready to return to her empty flat. Back on the street, she headed in the other direction, boarding a bus that was trundling cautiously into the West End.

In Trafalgar Square, the lions flanking Nelson's Column were blanketed in snow and reminded her of the lions on the Chain Bridge in Budapest. She shrugged off that thought. Turning briskly away, she dodged a group of young men having a snowball fight and set off down the Strand and from there to Covent Garden. Her steps quickened. Now she knew where she was going.

Soon she was facing the big corner site on Catherine Street. 'Theatre Royal, Drury Lane,' she read aloud off the imposing façade. What would it be like to work there?

Papa would approve. He'd like the idea of her being part of a team bringing plays – even musicals – to an audience, giving people something to think about, a new perspective. Ironic, really. It wasn't how she'd planned to come to Covent Garden. Right there, behind her, was the Royal Opera House, home to the Royal Ballet. What a mad fantasy that had been. But it was all past history now.

She'd told Amanda she didn't have the experience for the job. But Amanda had seen that as an advantage.

'They're fed up with stage-struck applicants who see it as a back way into acting. They want someone practical, sensible. Someone to manage the creative types, run the director's diary, set up systems that work. Mind you, it will be a bonus that you know your woodwind from your brass.'

Yes, she was good at systems and – as Amanda said – she'd still be using her languages: it was all very international. But it was the thought of Papa that persuaded her. It would be a way of following in his footsteps, of keeping his passion alive. Even if it was in a very small way.

When she got home she went straight to her jumper drawer and retrieved the photograph of him that Aunt Klára had given her for Christmas in Devon. She'd banished it after Sergei. She set it on her desk and sat down to write her letter of application.

35

So much depended upon my white shirt with the black velvet ribbons at the collar. So much depended upon my black skirt, knee length, not too tight, and the unnoticeable shoes. So much depended upon me staying inside these clothes. They carried the conviction that I was worthy, that I was not a fraud, but an academic person who'd studied well and earned this degree. This person would hold the scroll in her hand and have a photo taken in cap and gown. Who would see it? Aunt Klára, certainly. I could send a copy to Mama. I'd like to show it to Katalin, but she'd rip it up. I would frame it and show it to myself every morning when I woke up.

I was afraid of being late. But, by the time I was dressed, I was still much too early. I had to walk up and down in my room and sit on the edge of a chair for fear of creasing the skirt. It was cheap, with skimpy seams of thin fabric that would not last. But it didn't need to last. I only had to wear it for a day. I clipped on the neat pearl earrings Aunt had given me for my twenty-first birthday in January. Very appropriate. I checked my hair and scraped in another kirby grip to stop a wisp of curl escaping in a non-academic manner.

At last I was in my seat among my contemporaries, ready to process onto the stage. Row upon row of students filed past the vice-chancellor who bestowed their degrees graciously. It was all very well for him to be gracious and bestow, but he'd had nothing to do with it. He hadn't taught us or judged us. He hadn't starved himself of sleep or food to get into this queue. I didn't want him being gracious with me. But who was I to have an opinion? I felt lucky to be here at all.

Who was I, indeed? I was Marika. I was lonely. I had no friends because I had shut myself away and done nothing but study. I still worried about my sister but I'd had to put her out of my mind. I still missed Mama and I missed Papa. I wished they could be here to witness this milestone. But I must not think of them. I had to be composed. I had to stay inside these clothes. Aunt would be here. Somewhere at the back, Aunt would be clapping just for me. Her eyes would light up, that crazy blue, and she would be trying not to smile but her dimples would show. And I would go home with Aunt and she would give me back some of myself.

Aunt said I was eating like a sparrow. I told her she couldn't talk. She was still a thin tube person, more like spaghetti than cannelloni. She made goulash like my grandmother used to make it – as a celebration, she said. I appreciated it but it made my tummy ache. It wasn't used to such richness. I'd been living on cornflakes, tinned milk, toast and baked beans. They were cheap, and quick to make if you only had one gas ring and a washbasin for doing the dishes.

Aunt lit the fire and we took in a pot of coffee with the pretty porcelain coffee cans and a tot of brandy each. More celebration. The brandy made my tummy feel better once it had burned its way down there.

'What I want to know,' said Aunt when she had poured the coffee, 'is, has it worked?'

Had what worked? What did she mean? The brandy? The goulash?

'Do you understand what is going on in the mind of the man in the painting?'

Ah. The man in the painting. The Kokoschka. No. None of the studying had got me any closer to that. To begin with I kept thinking that next week, next term, all would be revealed. It didn't happen. For the first year, I went about with that dissatisfaction like a piece of grit in my shoe. It was only then that I grasped how much I didn't know, how many preliminaries there were, how much theory I must learn before I could begin to apply the knowledge. I emptied the grit out of my shoe and got on with it.

'Not yet,' I said now to Aunt. 'But I'll have to do teaching practice during the new course. When I start in the classroom – then maybe it will make sense.'

'I wish you didn't have to go to Warwick. You look half-starved and I won't be able to keep an eye on you at that distance.'

I had my own misgivings about Warwick. Was teacher training leading me in the right direction? I dreaded facing a class of children and trying to teach them something. But it was a requirement of the course – part of my passport to becoming an educational psychologist like Mr Johnson. Then maybe I'd be able to help other kids, as he had helped me. Unfortunately, nothing in my studies so far gave me confidence that I would reach that goal.

They took me on again at the King's Arms for the summer, which gave me no time to think. I bumped into Jack in town a couple of times, but he was a married man now and there was no sharing of pasties or confidences. Before I knew it, it was time to be packing my bags again.

A few days before I was due to leave, the milkman brought shocking news.

Mrs Tucker had taken her own life. An overdose of sleeping pills – must have been hoarding them for weeks, he said. It was while the family was at the Kingsbridge Show.

I phoned the house before I had time to think about what I would say. Jack answered and broke down when he heard my voice. He told me she'd been getting worse again, but had refused to go back to the hospital.

'She kept on saying she was a horrible person. You couldn't persuade her. We all tried. Then in the end it got on our nerves. That, and the way she was with Carole. It was like she made herself into a horrible person. We lost patience. I feel so bad about that.'

'It's not your fault, Jack.'

'We never thought anything by it – her not coming to the show. She always used to hate it. We were hoping for a 'Best in Show' – thought we had a chance with the bull. And it was a relief, really. To have the day to ourselves without her being difficult.'

'Anyone would have thought the same. It must have been a nightmare.'

'You see, she never could get past the idea that her parents sent her away because they didn't want her. I don't care what the doctors say. That was at the bottom of it all.'

'I'm sure you're right…'

'Margaret calls it a selfish act. To leave us in the lurch, feeling guilty. She says she can't ever have loved us. I know what she means. It sounds silly – I mean, I'm a grown man – but I feel abandoned. I can't even say that to Carole.'

'Oh, Jack. I'm so sorry. I can't imagine… There's nothing I can say. But you've got each other, you and Carole. I think you should say that to her. She's your wife. She'll be there for you.'

I'd no idea whether Carole would understand, but it seemed wrong for Jack to be telling me and not her. Our conversation was cut short when Jack's father called him.

I woke early next morning and the sun needling on the wall opposite teased me out of bed. I crept from the house alone, to the disappointment of Finn. He was lame and slow these days and I felt in no mood to look after him. I just wanted the wind and sea to blow my head clear of thoughts of Jack's poor mother.

It was chilly on the beach and waves scudded shorewards in angry little bursts. Clouds obscured the sun that had lured me out and I began to wish I hadn't come. I chucked a pebble or two into the water, tried and failed to make some flat ones skim and bounce and was about to turn back. But then I noticed how far the tide was out. The way round the headland was clear. I could take a little wander to Beecombe and have hot chocolate and a bacon bun at the café.

I'd never ventured round there before. Aunt always told us not to when we were kids, in case we got cut off by the tide. Not that it applied to Kati. You could never get her near the beach anyway. It felt brave to be jumping and scrabbling from rock to rock with the dark overhang of the cliff looming above me.

I stopped with aching legs to peer into a rock pool and poked at a frond of lettuce-green weed to see the tiny fish dart about. It was further than I expected. Just when I thought I'd see Beecombe round the next corner, there would be another inlet, a shaley stretch, another rock-clambering challenge. It was slow going. Easy to see how the tide might overtake a person.

What if I slipped and broke an ankle? Or got a foot caught in a crevice? I'd be stuck there watching the tide lurch closer and closer until it crept up my body, inch by icy inch, while I struggled to free my foot. How many people walked round here? How long would it be before a body was found?

A soft mist had been falling, slaking the surface of rock and stone and now it grew steadily into heavy rain, sweeping across the bay and obscuring the far headland. By the time I reached the village, the leaden sky had merged its tones of grey with the sea surging onto the shore. All those pewter-coloured pebbles blotting up the light. The clammy chill at my back told me my jacket was no longer waterproof and my trousers were sticking to my legs making it hard to walk.

Above the beach, blurred by the rain, was a terrace of cottages. The upper windows peered glumly over the graphite stripe of the sea wall, their slate roofs glazed black by the rain. I set off up the steps, willing the café to be open. At the top I stopped to draw breath. And there it was. A tiny cottage with a red front door. A slash of colour in the wash of sombre grey, glowing like a fire. A handwritten notice in black crayon was propped against a window pane: TO LET.

One day I would come to a cottage like that. It might even be that very same cottage. I'd shut myself away and write and write. Watch the sea and sleep to the sound of breaking waves. One day.

36

'Amanda sent you, didn't she?'

Katalin had noticed him earlier, leaning in the corner of the room: pleated trousers, cat's tail of a tie, stylish. For the last ten minutes he'd been on the fringe of her awareness. Why was he watching her?

He took the pipe from his mouth. 'And good evening to you, too. What sort of a welcome for a chap is that? I lift my imaginary hat to you in an outmoded gesture of gallantry and you accuse me of being some errand boy sent by our so gracious hostess.'

'But she did, didn't she?' Amanda had never given up on trying to pair her off.

'And what if she did? She said I would find you interesting. She was doing her stuff – oiling the wheels of social intercourse. Believe me, if I'd found you were fat or, worse still, caked in Max Factor and drenched in perfume, I would have continued on my way to find another mind to engage with.'

He bit the stem of his pipe between bared teeth and stared steadily at her.

She looked down into her glass, watching the unwelcome lumps of fruit jostle each other in the amber liquid. 'Why did she think I'd be interesting?'

'Your mind, dear girl, your mind…'

She could well imagine Amanda saying, 'She's no beauty, but…'

'She said you read Russian literature and never miss Rachmaninov at the Festival Hall.'

So Amanda had been fooled by all those unread volumes on her shelves, Tolstoy, Dostoevsky, Pasternak. She shook her head. 'But that's not—'

He held up a manicured hand. 'But me no buts. I also find you intriguing. The way you move. The way you stand alone, but unembarrassed. Contained. Barely sipping your drink. Like a heron at the edge of a river, watching, waiting. And here I am, swimming by, wondering if you will spear me.'

She couldn't help smiling. She'd perfected the art of being at parties over the years. Amanda was always inviting her, usually with an ulterior motive. She was to keep *a* talking, or prevent *x* sitting near *y*. Today her task had been to cut up fruit for the beastly Pimm's. 'Circulate! Circulate!' Amanda would say. But Katalin would choose a spot and imagine she was standing in the wings, ready to go on stage, waiting for her cue. If her ballet training had done nothing else, it had taught her this facility. This strange man had noticed. He'd appreciated her poise. It was ridiculously pleasing.

She knew her smile was a grudging, down-turned affair, but it evidently sent a signal she had not intended.

He smiled generously in response. 'I'm Adam.'

'Katalin.'

He stepped forward. '*Enchanté*.' He took her hand and brushed his lips across her knuckles.

All very extravagant.

Adam now pocketed his pipe. 'So where do you currently earn your crust?'

'In Covent Garden.'

He lifted one eyebrow.

'At the Drury Lane, in fact.'

'Sounds very glam.'

'Not at all. I'm in admin. Not even behind the scenes. Totally out of sight, actually.'

Why so honest? Normally she let people imagine that some of the glamour rubbed off on her. The job was certainly livelier than her previous post in the law firm, but she worked with some big egos and often felt more invisible and less appreciated than before. Initially the novelty had lifted her spirits but now, after several months, it had worn off. She felt herself sliding back down into the doldrums.

'That's a shame,' Adam was saying. 'You shouldn't be kept out of sight.'

Flatterer. She changed the subject. 'What's your line of work?'

'Me? I'm a mere estate agent. Commercial property. Very dull. Now, let me get you a proper drink. That fruit salad is obviously no more to your taste than it is to mine.'

He returned with two glasses chinking with ice. 'G&T. I hope…?'

She nodded, thankful it wasn't vodka. She still kept a bottle in her fridge, for old times' sake, but she never drank it.

'So, Russian literature. Where shall we start? *War and Peace*?'

'I've never finished it.' Katalin omitted the fact that she'd never started it and was relieved when he confessed to not having read the whole book either.

'How about Pasternak? Where do you stand on the *Zhivago* film? Not seen it? I thought everyone had.'

She had seen the film but her thoughts about it were too confused to bear discussion.

Adam was still questioning her. 'Solzhenitsyn?'

'I don't have any of his…'

'Am I seeing a pattern here? You're not pro-Soviet by any chance? That would be surprising, given your background.' He gave a slight bow. 'Forgive me. Amanda did fill me in, just a few details…'

She felt like a fraud. She *was* a fraud. She'd set herself up with all these superficial icons of Russian-ness, but she couldn't stop being Hungarian. Pro-Soviet? With what she'd seen in Budapest? Impossible. Then again, she was Sergei's daughter. It was as if her two identities cancelled her out. She didn't want this Adam coming too close, finding her out.

Amanda came offering a plate – a forest of wooden spikes impaling tinned pineapple on cubes of rubbery cheese. She winked at Katalin and moved quickly on.

'And what is *your* particular interest in Russia and its literature?'

He smiled. 'You evade me. I suppose a woman must be allowed to preserve her mystery. Me? My mother was Russian and she tried her best to immerse me in the culture. To be honest, I find it all too dark and dramatic. I was born here, I feel much more English. Give me Shakespeare or Jane Austen any day.'

Shakespeare was safer ground and Katalin even found she was enjoying the conversation. One of Amanda's better parties, she decided at the end of the evening. But she didn't expect to see Adam again.

'May I join you or do you prefer to eat alone?'

The voice at her elbow was familiar, but she couldn't place it. She preferred to eat alone – eat and read her book. Today it was ham and eggs with *The Great Gatsby*. She was hoping the vain and decadent Daisy would get her comeuppance.

The voice was now on the other side of her table, pulling out the chair. 'May I?'

Adam. The man from the party. Adam in a three-piece suit and tie, carrying a briefcase and a cup of coffee. He was like another person.

She nodded. 'Of course. What a surprise.'

She narrowly avoided the cliché of "Do you come here often?". Because this was not the sort of café Adam would frequent. Neither with a briefcase, nor in party mode. It was a place for single people – secretaries in quiet colours, lowly male clerks in worn navy blue suits – people who lived in bedsits and liked a square meal at lunchtime in order to avoid cooking in the evening.

'I was doing a valuation in Holborn and I remembered where you worked.'

He set the briefcase on the floor and slid into the seat, careful not to disturb the diner at the next table. There never was quite enough room for two at these tables.

'And, lo and behold, there you were, crossing the road just ahead of me. I hope you don't mind? Please don't let that get cold. It looks rather good.'

What on earth did he want? What could she say?

He got in first. 'Do you come here often? One of us had to say it.'

She almost giggled. 'It's very convenient. And all home-cooked. So yes, most days.'

'Then I'll know where to find you.'

'You're different today.'

'Am I? Well, I guess so. Have to put on a show for a party. Especially Amanda's parties.' He gave a funny little smile. 'And, by the way, I don't actually smoke a pipe. Just for show. So don't let that put you off.'

Why should she care whether he smoked a pipe? But she was glad, all the same.

He grinned across at her. 'If I do come here again, remind me not to have the coffee. They might be able to cook, but this is filthy.'

'My father was always very fussy about his coffee.'

'You don't have to be fussy not to like this.' He pushed the cup aside. 'Was? Your father?'

'It was hard to get any decent coffee here when we first came.'

'And is he enjoying better coffee these days?'

'He's been dead eight years. You could have a chip.' She edged her plate an inch or so in his direction.

'I'm sorry. How very generous.' He picked one of moderate size. 'And your mother?'

'Still alive.'

'In London? You live with her maybe.'

Katalin shook her head vigorously. The very thought of living with Mama made her shiver, even though Aunt Júlia said she was perfectly sane and stable these days. 'She lives in Vienna. With my aunt and uncle. What about you? Where do you live?'

'Beautiful city, Vienna. I'm sponging off my godmother in Chelsea. She lets me have a room in her apartment in return for being the man about the house. Which doesn't involve much, to be honest.'

'Chelsea. Very grand.'

'Oh, it is. But she isn't. Fortunately.' He looked at his watch. 'I need to go. But what I was actually hoping – was that you'd give me your phone number. Might we perhaps take in a concert or a play one evening? Festival Hall, Proms?'

37

How could I begin to tell Aunt? She'd been so patient, so helpful. But what did it sound like? 'I met this woman on the train and she persuaded me to give up my hard-won place in Warwick to go and work for her as a trainee in a town I've never heard of'? I might have forfeited my grant, so I could even be asking Aunt to sub me when I do the training – which happened to be two years, not just one. Oh, hell. It all made so much sense when I was talking to this Miss Henriksen.

She looked scatty. That was my first impression. Grey hair pinned up and escaping in all directions, with a yellow smoker's quiff at the front. Glasses round her neck on a gold chain. As I slid back the door of the compartment, she reached down to check the little dog at her feet.

'She's a bit edgy with strangers. It's okay, Trixie.' A rich voice, gravelly – that would be the smoking – but warm. Brown eyes, high cheekbones. She must have been a beauty in her day. In fact, she still was. And elegant in a crumpled sort of way. A knitted suit, saggy at the knees, but good quality, the sort of thing Amanda's mother would have worn.

I started to read but I kept gazing out the window. Here I was, sitting on a train haunted, once again, by Jack's mother and the despair that had led her to end it all.

'Finding it hard to concentrate?' said the warm voice.

Within minutes I'd told her everything, from Kokoschka to Mrs Tucker. It was as if I'd known her for years.

'You're on the wrong track,' she said. 'Working with kids in school is important. But it's often too late by then. You want to get at the parents, the early years. That's what matters.'

It turned out she was an area manager in the Children's Department in Hampshire and was desperate for a trainee.

'You'd be a dogsbody. But you'd learn a lot. I promise you that. County would probably sponsor you to train next year. Can you drive?'

I nodded, blessing Jack for getting me started and Aunt for taking me out on the roads and giving me plenty of practice. I'd passed the test first time.

By the time Miss Henriksen changed trains at Exeter, I was as good as employed. There would be an interview, but she waved it away as a mere formality. After she'd gone I seriously wondered whether it had ever happened, but there was the page she'd torn from her diary with a name, address and telephone number stylishly written in green-blue ink. I had been bewitched. Now I had to explain to Aunt.

Dear Aunt
You will see from the postmark that I am not where you expected.
    I'm in a place called Fareham in Hampshire and start work on Monday as a trainee in the Area Children's Department.
    I couldn't explain on the phone and I couldn't afford the train fare to come and tell you properly. I hope you don't think I'm mad. I hope I'm not mad!
    I met this crazy-looking woman on the train who is now my boss. We got talking and she said teacher training would be a waste of my time and Ed Psychs have no clout and they really need people like me as child care officers. She said it was too late once the kids were in school (but better late than never) and you need to get to them as early as possible.
    I did go to Warwick – of course I did! I stayed in the YW hostel and went to the admissions office to take myself off the course. It wasn't easy – I told them my circumstances had changed, but they didn't like it one bit.

I'd found that encounter very hard and suddenly had doubts. Suppose this Miss Henriksen was as mad as she looked and made a habit of buttonholing people on trains offering non-existent jobs? Suppose there was a job, but I failed the interview? I'd end up an utter idiot having burned my boats in Warwick. I just had to trust my gut instinct that this was all meant to happen.

I trusted Miss Henriksen – everyone calls her Esmée – right away and I know you'd like her. Please don't worry. It's a huge relief. You know I had doubts about having to do teaching and I hate schools, so what was I thinking of? I have a bedsit near the office and I'm getting a car! Esmée says I'll be able to drive it down to Devon for Christmas!
Wish me luck!
Lots of love
Mari xxx

My duties as a child care trainee were varied – escorting bolshie teenagers back to special schools after they'd run away, visiting girls in the mother and baby home, and ringing round to find emergency foster homes. I'd been only too pleased to accompany Mr Desmond when he took a teenager to a new foster placement. He was young and good-looking and I fancied flirting with him.

He laughed when I asked why he needed my help. 'It's in case she cries rape – and claims I assaulted her. In theory, you're there to make sure I don't.' He gave me a knowing wink. 'These girls. You'd be surprised.'

How naïve I was. It never occurred to me that a girl would do that. I was further disillusioned to discover that he had a wife and three children, with another on the way.

'I'm a left-footed Catholic,' he said by way of explanation.

'Left-footed?'

'Something to do with an Irish spade, I'm told. Yeah, baffling, isn't it? Let's just say it's a put-down. We don't get burned at the stake any more, but we're not popular either.'

I told him about being Catholic in Budapest under the Soviets and how Mass had to be held in secret.

'That puts things in perspective,' he said and I felt we had a bond after that.

I would go to Des, as he was known, to ask about procedures or how to fill in a form rather than approach the totally terrifying office manager.

'So, you have been inspecting the private foster homes, Marika? Good. We need to keep on top of that. And we have a huge backlog of overdue visits. It's dangerous.'

I frowned. 'Dangerous?'

'Well, we haven't vetted these women. It's all a private arrangement. We inspect, but there could be neglect. A death, even. Heads roll then, you can be sure. When it's too late. There but for the grace of God, and all that.'

I was having my regular supervision session with Esmée. Regular meant regularly put off from one week to the next, but this time I was actually sitting in her tiny office with Trixie sniffing my feet. I was still reeling with what I didn't know and struggling to understand all the procedures. I'd been given a pile of pink folders, each devoted to a foster mother who took in the children of students, mostly from Nigeria. I had been curious about these mothers who came on the train from London, and had taken the trouble to meet one of them when she visited her children one weekend.

When I told Esmée about this meeting she gave me a long hard stare. She sat back and shook another cigarette out of the box on her desk. 'Who, may I ask, suggested you do that?'

'It was my idea. I—'

She held up a hand and flicked her lighter. When she'd inhaled and blown out a plume of smoke to join the existing fug, she spoke again.

'Boundaries, Marika. Boundaries, is what I say to you. You are given a brief. You stick to it. You are a trainee. Not here to start reinventing the role. I already told you that we are hard-pressed to visit all these foster homes. Let alone discover those that aren't registered. Another minefield. But I digress. Marika, it was not proper use of your time.'

'It was my own time. It was Saturday.'

'Boundaries, I say again. I don't say, "Don't get involved", although plenty of people would. In my book, you can't be effective if you don't get involved. But I do say, draw a line between your professional and your personal life.' She tapped ash into the instant coffee lid she was currently using as an ashtray. 'If you don't do that you will not survive. Self-preservation is a lesson you must learn from the very start. Boundaries. They are there to protect you as much as your clients.'

'But I wasn't doing anything that could have been damaging.'

'Not this time. But suppose you had persuaded this mother to take her children back to London. She'll be living in a bedsit not much bigger than a bed, probably with a gas fire. Those children would be with their mother for sure, but in a less stimulating and more dangerous environment. I see the headlines – "Children die in bedsit fire", "Childcare trainee persuaded mother of two…" You see where this is going? As I say most weeks, there, but for the grace of God, go we.'

I nodded, feeling both rebellious and a total fool.

'People have to live their own lives. We're asked often enough to play God. Don't volunteer for the role.'

I managed to swallow my shrivelled pride enough to apologise.

'These are things you can learn, Marika. It's what you're here for. You're doing pretty well, given how little time anyone has to spend with you. I'd rather have someone who makes mistakes than someone who doesn't care. That's something you can't learn.'

One of my tasks as a trainee was to write up the regular meetings of the local Coordinating Committee. This brought together professionals across all disciplines – from health visitors to the police and everyone in between.

'The idea is,' Esmée explained as we drove to my first meeting, 'that by understanding how other professionals work, and by sharing information about children on the At Risk register, we're able to provide much more effective help for families – a kind of safety net.' She shrugged. 'I see it beginning to work, but we're always getting snagged on issues of confidentiality and people being defensive. You'll see. But it's getting there, it's the way forward.'

What a motley crew they were. And the language! The gallows humour shocked me at first, but I soon learnt that it was a way of letting off steam and that the more laughter there was, the more serious the case.

I enjoyed writing up those meetings. It was a good counterbalance to the face-to-face work with clients.

I also loved my little car – a primrose Mini with a waggling gear lever that took a bit of getting used to. I had a couple of teenagers on my so-called caseload and I found the car an asset in getting to know them. They chatted more freely as we sat side by side with no eye contact.

The strategy was too successful with Joyce. She began to feel like a younger sister. Once again, Esmée took me to task in supervision through the usual smog.

'You're doing Joyce no favours. Her case will be closed or you will move on. She won't see you any more. She will have lost a friend. You must draw a line between the personal and the professional.'

It was a recurrent theme. I found it endlessly frustrating, just as I thought I was getting through to someone, to be obliged to pull back for fear of stepping over that line. And step over it, I did. Again and again. I let the job encroach on my time off and the worrying details of other people's lives kept me awake and haunted my dreams. I lived in a street round the corner from the office and that didn't help either.

It was one long Victorian terrace. Each house had a tiny front garden with a tiled path to the porch, and a small bay window upstairs and down. Most were lived in by families with young children.

At dusk, you could see into those lighted living rooms before curtains were drawn. Some had warm colours lit by lamps, most were exposed under the glare of an overhead bulb with a plain conical shade, and others flickered with firelight. Children would be playing on the floor or cuddled up on a sofa with a parent reading a book, while a cat posed on a windowsill looking out into the dark street.

The walk was especially rewarding as Christmas approached – nearly every house displayed a tree covered in baubles and coloured lights. As weeks passed, windows were stuck with lumps of cotton wool and paper snowflakes, and rooms were festooned with coloured paper chains.

One day, I thought, I will live in a house like that. I will have happy children and a husband who comes home every evening at six o'clock to meat and two veg and bath time with the kids.

I watched a woman light her gas fire. I imagined the roar of the gas, the pop as the match went in and the hiss as the flames climbed inside the row of white ceramic towers – crude versions of the intricate Chinese ivory ornaments that Aunt Júlia used to keep in her cabinet hundreds of miles away in Vienna. The woman positioned a fireguard and fetched a clotheshorse, which she angled round the fire and draped with shirts, socks, a tiny baby suit. I paused, hallucinating the soapy smell of rising steam.

Would I love it? Or would I be bored? I stood there too long. The front door opened and the woman came to the gate.

'Can I help you?' She didn't sound inclined to be helpful.

I couldn't think what to say.

'What do you mean by it? Standing there? My neighbour from across the street rang me. Said there was someone snooping in my window. What do you want?'

I took a deep breath. 'I'm sorry. I was miles away. I'm so sorry to disturb you.'

She gave me a curious look, muttered something about staying miles away, and was gone, slamming the front door and drawing the bolt across. As I walked away, the rectangle of light on the front lawn was abruptly eclipsed by the curtains being drawn. I walked home on the other side after that. But, every night, I conjured that woman's living room to blot out the bleak homes I visited and to help me sleep.

By the time I drove to Devon for the Christmas break I was exhausted. Aunt was sympathetic but took the same line as Esmée.

'Oh, Mari! Your spontaneity is a delight, always has been. But you do tend to rush in where angels fear, and all that. I can see what your supervisor means – it won't do your clients any favours in the long run. Plus you're running yourself into the ground.'

Aunt had her own trouble. Finn had died of old age earlier in the month. He just didn't wake up one morning. The house felt empty without him and Aunt was bereft.

'At first I couldn't bear to go for a walk, it was so lonesome without him. I still see him running ahead up the path. Like he used to be. He didn't run anywhere in the last year.'

I wished she would get another dog, but she wouldn't hear of it. She showed me his grave, which she'd marked with a beech sapling. It was in the clearing where we'd carried out the solstice ceremony. Amazing to think that was eight whole years ago when I was only fourteen.

Even without Finn, I was restored by just being with Aunt, the trees and the sea. As Aunt kept reminding me, when I worried about going back to work, it was early days. I'd only been doing the job for three months. I would learn. I would keep at it. If I didn't, nobody would take me seriously again.

It was in the New Year of 1968 that I met Dr Hadley, a psychiatrist who came to a meeting of the Coordinating Committee to discuss a child he was treating at the Child Guidance Clinic.

'Before I come to my findings on this little boy, I want to draw to your attention to the fact that his mother is the child of an evacuee. *Her* mother was evacuated from the East End in 1939 – and she had a very hard time of it.'

Evacuee. The word went right through me and took me back to my talks with Mrs Tucker, the memory of her in that hospital and the look of terror in her eyes when she came home and tried to make sense of a world that had once been hers. Dr Hadley was continuing.

'Not only did this woman – the child's grandmother – lose both her parents, she lost *attachment* – a sense of belonging and of being worthwhile – so necessary to the development of a healthy psyche. It is my belief that she was therefore unable to pass that same sense to her daughter. The pattern is therefore being repeated with this little boy. I have always said, we will take several generations to recover from the government's disastrous evacuation programme, and this family is a case in point. I suggest…'

I had seen a few people exchanging glances across the table at Dr Hadley's first mention of "evacuee", but was too engrossed to take much notice. Now there came an outbreak of muttering and eye-rolling, but he was undeterred.

I intercepted him as he was leaving and blurted out my interest in evacuees. I hoped Esmée was not in earshot. I was probably stepping over some invisible professional boundary. But Dr Hadley's eyes lit up and he tugged excitedly at the surviving wisps of his white hair.

'We must meet up. I'll look at my diary and get in touch with Esmée – get her to okay it as part of your educational programme. Now I must run – I've a clinic in ten minutes.'

Esmée laughed uproariously when I told her about this encounter. 'Ah, Ian and his evacuees. He does have a bit of a bee in his bonnet. People tend to dismiss it, but it's quite a productive bee, in my view.'

After listening to Dr Hadley's theories and examining some case studies, I enjoyed writing a piece, weaving in my experience of Mrs Tucker and developing my own analysis. Esmée was impressed and sent it to Dr Hadley. Apart from nattering on to Aunt about it when I visited for the Easter weekend, I thought no more about it.

What with witnessing the horrors of the Vietnam War on Aunt's new television and the shooting of Martin Luther King, we were both glad of the arrival of Merlin, Aunt's new dog. He was two years old and belonged to a couple who were emigrating to Australia, which had persuaded her to take him on. They were thrilled to have found him a good home and Merlin suited Aunt, who had been reluctant to house-train a puppy. He was very similar in appearance to Finn, but bigger and bouncier – so we had plenty to occupy us.

*

It was a particularly hot day in May when I was called unexpectedly to Esmée's office. I was not due for a supervision session and I feared I had overstepped some mark. But when I tapped nervously at her half-open door, she beamed and gestured for me to sit down.

'I've just had the most interesting call from Dr Hadley,' she said. 'He was most impressed with your piece on evacuees, and he's had an idea.' She stubbed out her cigarette. 'A career idea. For you.'

'But I thought—'

'Yes, you were expecting to go on to train as a child care officer. However, you may like to consider an alternative route. Dr Hadley knows the director of the Belstock and he has an opening for a research student. Ian thinks it would suit you admirably and he is willing to give you an introduction.'

I heard the message that I was being offered something special here, but I had never heard of the Belstock, whatever that was, and I had no idea what she was talking about.

'I'm sorry. I don't really understand. I…'

Esmée grinned. 'Of course you don't. How could you? But, I tell you, this is a magnificent opportunity. Let me explain—'

To my frustration, the phone cut across her. She put a hand on the receiver. 'Let's not even try to do it here. Come to supper with me this evening. I'll pop my head round when I'm leaving. You can follow me in your car.' She waved her cigarette at me and turned away. 'Yes? Esmée Henriksen. Speaking.'

Esmée's house was a surprise – a mix of modern architecture and antique furniture and, in contrast to her office, totally uncluttered. She sent me down the garden to pick strawberries and we ate spaghetti Bolognese on her rose-scented terrace. Over coffee she unravelled Dr Hadley's idea and explained the history of the Belstock Clinic and its reputation for pioneering work on child development, reeling off names, which I had seen on book covers in the office library.

'Sleep on it. Think about it carefully,' said Esmée as I left. 'It's a big decision. Ring Ian Hadley when you've decided. You don't need me in the loop.'

I hardly noticed driving home and was so excited that I made the mistake of running to the box on the corner to phone Aunt. She was extremely grumpy – 'I thought someone had died' – and told me to ring back next day. It was only then that I noticed it was one o'clock in the morning.

Dr Hadley was delighted when I rang to take up his offer. He would arrange for me to have an interview with Professor Goldstein. When I told Esmée she grasped my hand.

'I just know this is right for you. And, to be honest, it saves me a tricky decision. You see, I'm not convinced about your future in Child Care – I couldn't put my hand on my heart and recommend you to County for sponsorship. It's all about the boundaries – you know that. You have a generous personality, a little too exuberant for the straitjacket we have to wear. Sad, but true.'

They gave me a leaving party. Only for an hour after the office closed, with warm white wine and shop-bought sausage rolls, but it meant a lot. Des hugged me and wished me luck and Esmée gave me a copy of *Child Care and the Growth of Love* by John Bowlby in which she had bookmarked several passages. She told me to keep in touch and let her know how my career progressed. I walked home with tears in my eyes, proud to think that I was about to be in possession of such a thing as a career.

38

I saw Kati before she saw me. She was only twenty-five, but in spite of a new haircut, she looked like a spinster aunt in her narrow grey suit. She was sitting exactly in the middle of the bench by the pond with her feet neatly parked, side by side.

I felt stupidly nervous. I'd never expected her to agree to meet. Usually she hung up on me whenever I phoned. That used to upset me. Aunt convinced me that it said more about Kati than about me. But that was exactly why I worried about her. Amanda had fixed her up with a boyfriend last summer, but was dubious about how that was progressing. Aunt said I didn't have to be my sister's keeper. But I did – in an entirely selfish way. Kati was the keeper, the only keeper (because Mama didn't count any more) of our shared memories, our childhood.

Not only had she agreed to meet, but she was actually here. Maybe she wanted to mark her birthday by making peace.

'Happy birthday,' I said and thrust the carefully wrapped book and the freesias into her hands to avoid the moment when I went to kiss her and she ducked aside.

She sniffed at the flowers. I'd gone to a florist instead of grabbing a cheap bunch of daffodils from the bucket at the greengrocer's. Their glowing yellows and purples were suddenly garish against her pale skin. The parcel went straight into her bag.

I'd found the book on a second-hand stall in the market when I was at my wit's end about what to give her. *Jane Eyre,* bound in dark red leather with gold tooling. I wanted so much to see her reaction, to see her finger the beautiful binding. But I said nothing. I remembered how Kati could never cope with presents, reluctant to say thank you.

I gave her news of Aunt Klára and asked about her job. I thought she'd enjoy working in a theatre, but she shrugged in a bored sort of way and said it was like any other admin post.

Then she rounded on me. 'I hear you've given up on the social work training. Huh! I never thought you'd be up to it.'

'What would you know about that? Of course I'm up to it. Do you know why? Did you know I only gave it up because I was offered the chance to do something I feel really passionate about?'

'You were only ever passionate about some boy behind the bike sheds.' She said it without conviction, as if insulting me had become a habit.

'Oh, Kati! Still in the playground? I'll ignore that remark. How do you know all this stuff about me, anyway?'

'You write to Mama. She tells Aunt Júlia. Uncle Fritz writes to me.'

'Uncle Fritz? How's he? How's Aunt Júlia? Mama hardly ever writes back, and she never answers my questions.'

'Of course she doesn't. I told you. It was all her fault and she's ashamed.'

'No, Kati. She's ill. She can't help it. She got better, now she is bad again. It comes and goes, this illness.'

'She is ill from guilt. And so she should be…'

'We need to forgive her, Kati. You need to—'

'I need nothing. Least of all to sit and hear this. You know nothing. Always Mama's favourite. Always the real daughter. Always spoilt…'

Her tone had changed. I'd never heard her so full of rage. She almost choked herself, but continued.

'When we left Budapest, there I was, with my whole future ahead of me…'

'Don't we always have our whole future ahead of us?'

'You pretend to be so clever. You were always the stupid one, but you always got away with it.'

I knew I shouldn't retaliate. She used to mock me for failing tests at school. There was a childish part of me that felt my achievements counted for nothing if Kati didn't know about them. She'd never congratulate me. But I needed her to know.

'What would my sainted sister say to me being taken on as a researcher at the Belstock Clinic?'

'I'd say it was ridiculous, and you probably only got it by flapping your eyes at the director, who plans to get you into his bed.'

I hardly had time to draw breath before she was off again.

'You always get lucky. Even escaping Hungary you were sitting pretty on the damn train with Mama. But me and Papa…' Her voice cracked and tailed away.

I sighed and summoned all my energy for a last effort. 'Kati, I know it was tough for you. It was awful, all that stuff with Sergei. But it's years ago now. You have to move on. Not destroy yourself. Let's not talk about it anymore. Let's go and have lunch. It's your birthday, after all.'

Kati brushed an imaginary speck from her skirt. 'My birthday, which you have just ruined.'

The cuticle on her index fingers was broken and raw. Kati never used to bite her nails, but this less obvious habit – of using the next-door nail to pick at the cuticle until it bled – used to drive Mama mad. Evidently Kati was still doing it. I'd always thought of Kati as unassailable. But she must be in a constant state of stress for her hands to be in such a state.

Suddenly, her insults counted for nothing. I just wanted to look after her. 'Come on,' I said. 'Let's find somewhere for lunch.'

But she looked at her watch and stood up, saying she had to go, there was no time for lunch. She tried to leave the flowers on the bench, and I had to run after her. I couldn't bear for her not to have them.

I wanted her to put them in a jar on her desk, so that people would stop to smell them. They would notice her, and know that she was a person who received flowers on her birthday, a person with a sister who gave her freesias.

But knowing my sainted sister, the flowers were more likely to end up in the bin.

39

'There's something I've noticed,' said Adam. 'A mystery. I watch you move. A delight. You move like a dancer. Yet you always turn down the idea of going to the ballet. Enlighten me?'

Katalin stirred her coffee fiercely and took a deep breath. It was no use pretending to Adam when he'd got an idea in his head.

'Yes, I was a dancer once. Before we left Hungary. It was my ambition…' No need to tell him more. 'It was a childhood thing.'

They'd just sat through a programme of modern music that was not to her taste. Adam said they should widen their horizons but they'd both agreed, it had been a horizon too far. He was watching her now in that way he had, wondering whether to probe further.

'I can see it meant a lot to you. Your dancing. What happened when you came here?'

'A lot of philistines happened. But it's of no consequence. I put all that behind me years ago.'

But had she put it behind her? The question followed her home and into bed. What had really happened? Had her dancing spirit stayed behind in the snowy forests of the Hungarian border? Maybe it was the price exacted by that weird Birdman for being their guide. Foolish fanciful stuff.

Deep down she had to admit the truth behind the scathing comments of that Costello woman. That was just before Papa was killed – so nearly ten years ago – but the memory still caused her pain. Maybe she really had been as wooden as her mannequin. She was twenty-six – high time to accept that fact and move on. But she didn't need Adam rubbing salt into the wound.

She enjoyed Adam's company, but he was always trying to get her to talk about herself. For this reason she always preferred their outings to include a play or a concert. That way, if they went for a meal or a drink afterwards, there was the performance to discuss.

Adam had other ideas. 'It's Valentine's Day on Saturday,' he said. 'And we're going out for a meal. We're going to the Bistro Vino in South Ken. I'll meet you there at eight.'

She'd heard of the place, which was all the rage with Amanda and her friends, none of whom would dream of living in South Kensington. She agonised about what to wear and whether to give Adam a present and, if so, what. She settled on the black dress she kept for office receptions and found a second-hand copy of *One Day in the Life of Ivan Denisovich*, which seemed an appropriate gift from one half-Russian to another. She'd never read any Solzhenitsyn and there was plenty of time to remedy that before Saturday.

The bistro was all dim lights, bare brick walls and red gingham tablecloths. The candles were stuck in bulbous wine bottles wrapped in raffia with wax running down the necks. When she commented on the lack of proper candlesticks, Adam said she was missing the point. He recommended the chicken chasseur and splashed out on a half-bottle of wine.

Adam had been going through family photograph albums with his godmother. It had triggered memories, and he entertained Katalin with amusing anecdotes of his childhood, when his Russian mother and old-fashioned English father did not see eye to eye. She was happy to listen and the evening was turning out well. Until Adam had to spoil it.

'Katalin, I need to sort out a few things. I mean, you don't turn me away. You seem to enjoy my company, but I'd like to be clear… Clear about where we might be going.'

'Do we need to be going anywhere?' She so valued Adam's friendship, but she really didn't want it to turn into a "relationship".

'We've been friends now for a year and a half, getting on for two. I'd like to be going somewhere. But you keep me at arm's length. You don't connect…'

Here we go again, she thought. Why did he have to do this? 'I do my best, Adam. I'm a very private person. I've told you before – all that happened – leaving my country, my father dying, my mother leaving – I suppose they make me a little wary… But I've *told* you about them…'

'Oh, I know *about* you. But you speak so coolly of those events – as if you keep them in a box, as if they happened to someone else.'

'Just because I don't blabber on about myself. Really, Adam! I find it impertinent that you analyse me in this way. You presume to know—'

'Impertinent? What a word! That is precisely what I mean. Putting me in my place – a million miles away. When I'm simply trying to speak as a friend. I don't *presume* to know. I just *want* to know. I want a relationship. Intimacy.'

Her heart sank. She supposed he wanted sex. Was she prepared to pay that price for his company?

'We can have sex if you want. I thought you did not. In fact, I thought perhaps you were gay. That you preferred just the friendship.'

'Katalin, you take my breath away. How can you talk like that – so offhand? Intimacy to me is not about sex. No, I don't want to have sex – not if you talk about it like that – on a par with cleaning your teeth. Making love, that would be different, but I don't make love to women I don't know.'

She shrugged. 'I also prefer not. Why don't you find someone more lovey-dovey?'

'Lovey-dovey!' He threw up his hands. 'Because, Katalin, I care about you. Because I can't get you out from under my skin. Ever since I first saw you, at that party, it's been like that.'

She didn't understand – neither what he saw in her, nor what he wanted from her. Eventually he shrugged and poured the last of the wine, saying she would drive him insane. He really was weird sometimes, but then he would get his good mood back and rattle on about sash windows, dado rails and wainscoting. "Wainscoting" was such a lovely word.

Adam had tried to kiss her. This fact jarred Katalin's waking awareness like a cough in a concert. He'd ruined a pleasant evening and their straightforward friendship. He wasn't even drunk.

It hadn't been a clumsy attempt. Adam was never clumsy. He'd walked her home from the tube in the rain and they were sharing an umbrella.

'Katalin,' he'd said.

His voice sounded odd, so she'd looked round at him. He'd cupped her cheek with his free hand and planted his lips on her mouth. She pulled away. He sighed. That was it.

Except it wasn't. Nice lips. Firm, dry, warm. Which was irrelevant. But all the same. Perhaps he'd hoped she'd invite him in. Out of the rain. But they didn't *do* that.

She'd only been to his place once when his godmother was away. He'd invited her to afternoon tea one Saturday with Amanda and Ena and Amanda's new boyfriend. Ena had married her double-barrelled Denzil by then, but she came alone. She clearly didn't approve of Amanda's Mervyn, a musician who was known as Merv the Swerve. He played clarinet for the London Symphony and saxophone for his own jazz trio. Quite a departure from Amanda's usual style. Katalin had left with the others to avoid being alone in the flat with Adam.

He'd only been inside her flat once. He'd arrived early to pick her up and she hadn't been ready. She'd found it uncomfortable.

He'd hovered about while she finished tidying up, telling her to leave the damn dishes, but she refused.

'What a painting you would make,' he said from the doorway. 'No, don't move. The sun's just catching your neck, the creamy curve of it. Those fine blonde hairs are like gold. Just let me…'

She'd sidestepped his outstretched hand and threw him a tea towel on the way to the bedroom to apply her usual minimal make-up. She always remembered his comment about Max Factor. But she needed mascara. It brought her face into focus. All day she wondered what he'd "just" wanted to do. What had she missed?

A Sunday, that was. They'd driven to Brighton and, unlike the wild Devon waves, the sea had been under control, with the promenade and the traffic lights and the Victorian facades hemming it in. She'd enjoyed that.

In fact she'd been hoping they might go there again for her birthday. Only last week he'd hinted at Brighton for her treat. But she hadn't seen him since the non-kiss. He'd called to say, 'Sorry for apparently breaking the rules.' It sounded petulant and implied he had nothing to apologise for, which made it an empty gesture. She hadn't been answering the phone since. Brighton would have been fun. He might have bought her a present in one of those quirky shops in The Lanes. A bangle or a scarf. Something trendy to impress the girls at work. He had an eye for things like that.

Her birthday fell on a Saturday so she forced herself to have a lie-in until the post arrived – five cards. Six if she counted the notelet of violets with Mama's shaky signature, which was enclosed with the gold-embossed greeting from Aunt Júlia and Uncle Fritz. Next was a picture of a girl in a long dress on a swing from Amanda, a lone tree in a barren landscape from Aunt Klára and a photograph of Tower Bridge at night from Adam. There was a note inside.

The note said the birthday trip was still on. If she wanted to come she should be at his place by eleven that morning. The cheek of it. As if.

The sixth card she left until last because she recognised the handwriting – a tasteless *Dear Sister* extravaganza decorated with pink ribbons from Marika. Why wouldn't the girl take no for an answer? Hadn't she made it perfectly clear she never wanted to see or hear from her sister again? She found herself looking a long time at the message inside – "To my sainted sister, with lots of love…" with even two kisses after her name. Marika's voice was in her head: "my sainted sister" – always said with such a strange mixture of mockery and affection. Marika was so persistent. Even after that awful birthday meeting last year she'd phoned one day in the summer with the crazy idea that they could have a picnic by the Serpentine. *I'll bring vodka and chocolate and we can get drunk and pretend we like each other.* Silly cow. Katalin dropped the card abruptly into the wastepaper basket and arranged the others on the chest of drawers.

It was time to set off for the private treat she'd planned – hot chocolate and a croissant in the coffee shop round the corner. It was a crisp, sunny morning, perfect for an outing. On reflection she thought it was touching that Adam had remembered his promise. He could have taken someone else, but he was loyal. She would phone him next week and thank him.

When she got to the café her favourite table was taken by a couple, still steamy from bed, gazing into each other's eyes. All the tables at the back had been pushed together for a birthday breakfast, complete with heart-shaped balloons. She squeezed in beside the counter, wishing she'd brought a book. The croissant wasn't as light as it should have been and she felt stupidly lonely, hiding in the corner.

When the family at the back started a raucous singing of *Happy Birthday* she looked at her watch. Just after ten. If she ran for the Tube now, she would just make it to Adam's by eleven.

He started on at her on the way back from Brighton, not long after they left the A23. The old conversation. 'What are you thinking? Penny for them.'

She fobbed him off, but not for long. He parked the car instead of dropping her off, insisting on coming in.

'I only want to come in to your flat, not your bed. Well, that's not true. Access to head and heart is really what I'm after.'

Resigned, she put the kettle on. Only Amanda ever came here and she was always complaining that the place was so bare. "Austere" was the word she used. She didn't want Adam casting his critical estate agent's eye over her home.

But here he was, standing in the kitchen doorway holding up the birthday card Marika had sent.

'Look what I just found. A case in point.'

Katalin exploded. 'First you insist on coming in, and now you're going through my bin before the kettle's even boiled!'

'Hey, hey! Hold those horses. I was looking at your cards – I guess that's normal? Allowed? Since you set them out? And I thought this one had fallen off – into the bin. Right?'

'I put the damn thing in the bin, okay?'

'Okay. But, Katalin, the point I'm making – I didn't even know you had a sister. You never told me. Isn't that a little odd, considering how long we've known each other?'

Katalin shrugged.

'I actually feel really hurt. It's precisely the arm's-length behaviour I was talking about.'

'So I have a sister. We don't speak. We don't get on. I am the chalk. She is the cheese. In fact, you would prefer her. She is a touchy-feely person, a real tart.'

'Hmm. I'll ignore that. But she sends you a card—'

'She won't take no for the answer. Always wanting to stick a nose in my business.'

'Maybe she cares about you.'

Katalin grabbed the card from his hand, ripped it in two and put it in the pedal bin.

'What does she do? Where does she live?'

'A do-gooding job in Hampshire. No, wrong. She didn't stick at that. Now she's doing research in some clinic. But, Adam, my sister is not your business.'

'There you go again. I rest my case. No, she is not my business. But you are. Or maybe that's just where I'm wrong.' He turned away, back into the sitting room.

She made the coffee too strong and crashed mugs onto a tray. Why did he have to spoil the day? Brighton had been fun. A perfect, warm spring day. They'd walked for miles, chucked pebbles into the neat waves and shared a seafood platter sitting outside a café that was practically on the beach. He'd spent more than she expected on a lapis lazuli pendant. It was beautiful but now she wished he hadn't been so generous. Did he think it gave him the right to intrude? Why couldn't he settle for the comfortable distance they had? When she'd used that phrase he'd gone ballistic. 'What's comfortable about distance? What's wrong with some closeness? Some warmth?' He'd almost shouted.

He was standing in front of the cards when she put the tray down.

'One from Germany, I see.' A light tone, being conciliatory.

'Austria. My aunt and uncle. My mother lives with them. Remember? Something I did tell you.'

'So you did. Ever think of going to Vienna? Going to see her?'

'I'd like to see Uncle Fritz, but – no. It is better not.'

'Another mystery. It's nothing to do with the Russian, is it?'

Her hand jerked up, shaking coffee all over the table. How did he know about Sergei?

'Amanda told me there was one. That's all she would say.'

Amanda. Of course. She knew all about Sergei. Had she really not told Adam any more?

He sat down beside her on the sofa and put a hand on her shoulder. She was turning on him to tell him to get away when an odd thing happened. She found herself suddenly weeping and shouting through her tears.

'Sergei was my mother's lover. I fell in love with Sergei. Sergei is my father. Sergei is dead. My sister believes Sergei killed her father.' She gasped and blew into the silk handkerchief he offered. 'Now are you happy?'

She told him to leave after that, and sat staring at the wall. She couldn't shake herself free of Sergei. Did she love him or hate him? He hadn't loved her, but he prevented her from getting close to anyone else. She fell asleep to Rachmaninov – "Sergei's Sonata", as she called it. In the morning she wrote Adam a letter.

Dear Adam

I am sorry we will not see each other again. You want one sort of relationship. I want another. It will not work. I will never be the person you want.

I will always be an arm's-length person. My mother was an arm's-length person. At least she was with me. Not with my sister. I've thought about it. She must have been frightened to be pregnant by someone not her husband. Maybe she carried on being scared, scared of me. Never quite trusted me, as if I might give the game away. That was not possible of course. I did not know until nine years ago. But she was not a rational person.

What I said about the Russian called Sergei was rubbish, by the way. I just made it up to shock you, to serve you right for asking me things.

Thank you for taking me to Brighton and for my present.

From Katalin.

P.S. You have been a loyal friend. I will miss that.

40

'Marika,' said a voice at my elbow, a dark brown voice. 'It's Simon. Simon Goldstein.'

'Professor Goldstein! How good of you to come.'

'Why would I not?' He clasped my hand firmly and held on to it for a nanosecond as I withdrew it.

I'd heard plenty about Professor Goldstein since my interview two years ago. He'd been widowed a few years back and there were rumours about affairs with students. It had made me curious, but I'd seen frustratingly little of him during my time at the Belstock. Having him turn up in the pub for my celebration drinks was the last thing I expected.

'Congratulations,' he continued. 'I was right about you. You excited me from the start – at your interview – your ideas, your enthusiasm. Your delight that you'd finally found what you wanted to do.'

I, too, remembered that interview. At first I thought he looked dull. The smoothed back hair, heavy-framed glasses and formal three-piece suit. The polished shoes I liked. They reminded me of Papa. I'd taken it all in as he walked towards me and my heart sank. Old school, traditional. He'd prefer male applicants. Then came the rich voice and a handshake that was like being plugged into a power socket. Energy radiated from him so that I hardly noticed he was shorter than me in my heels.

He didn't sit behind his desk with me in front of it, but showed me to a sofa in the window and offered me coffee, which I refused because I thought I might spill it or choke, I was so nervous.

He asked me why I was there and he listened. He listened like Aunt used to listen, in those early days in the conservatory. His eyes lit up as he made connections and I found myself telling him about Kokoschka and Papa just as I would talk to Aunt and Esmée. By the time I got onto my ideas, it had long turned from an interview into a conversation.

When he laughed I could see a gold filling, and I thought how appropriate that Professor Goldstein should have a gold jewel in his tooth. There was something else too. When I started comparing refugees to evacuee children, one eyebrow shot up and he was eying me with his head on one side. I suddenly felt another kind of connection, unexpected, confusing. I was aroused. I hadn't felt like that since those meetings with raggle-taggle boys up in the hills at school – gypsy lads with bare chests and muscular thighs glimpsed though torn jeans. Or the bad boys behind the bike sheds at the school in Kentish Town, flash types with flicked hair and leather jackets, everything black and sharp. It was a mystery how this well-groomed intellectual with his smooth skin and long fingers could have the same effect on me.

I was afraid I was blushing, that he might have noticed. But the conversation continued until his secretary rang through to say he was in danger of being late for his next appointment.

Was it a good or a bad sign that the interview had overrun?

As he shook me by the hand at the door, I asked, 'When will I hear?'

'Hear? Oh, my dear, there's no question. Of course you must come. I knew I could trust my old pal, Ian Hadley. He's never wrong about people. My secretary will send you a letter and take you through the formalities.'

It had been a disappointment not to be supervised by Professor Goldstein. His colleagues were enthusiastic about my research and never failed to be helpful and encouraging, but they didn't have his energy, his charisma.

But here he was now, less formally dressed in an open-neck shirt, jeans, linen jacket, but all crisply pressed, as immaculate as before. He was commenting on my dissertation as if he'd read every word.

'Your language – so fresh, so… What is the word? The opposite of dry?'

'I write simply, I suppose, Professor Goldstein, because English is not my—'

'Simon, please. No. It's not that. Just that, when you interview people…'

And we were off again. It was almost as if we had taken up that original conversation where we left off.

It seemed no time before colleagues started coming over to make their farewells, off home for the evening. I thought of my sad room in the hostel and avoided looking at Simon in case my thoughts showed. I moved away, giving careful attention to kissing, embracing and shaking hands. Not that I was leaving. I'd see them all again next week. But it was a milestone, the end of an era. Next week I'd be a regular member of staff with a proper, paid job. I'd be able to move out of the hostel and find a flat. But this prospect, which had so excited me when I woke up only that morning, would lose its potential for joy if I now turned round to find Simon had left.

*

Simon's flat was painted white throughout. I didn't understand the art on the walls, but it was vibrant and the blocks of primary colour gave life to the room. Simon settled me with a glass of ice cold Chablis. I loved the way the outside of the goblet frosted and was reflected in the glass of the low table.

I sipped the wine while he whipped up a soufflé and tossed a salad. We talked about working together and about getting my thesis published. He had contacts in academic publishing but that wasn't a route I favoured.

'I want it to be more accessible...'

He made a face. 'Not pop psychology?'

'I'm not sure what you mean by that. Not superficial, not sloppy. But not elitist. Surely it can be accessible without losing its rigour?'

He laughed. 'I see we have much discussion ahead.'

We talked about ourselves after that, a regular getting-to-know exercise. But soon we talked less and gazed more. I was hungry but I didn't get a chance to finish my soufflé.

His fork suddenly clattered onto his plate. 'I have waited for this for three years. And what do I do? I sit here chewing lettuce. I make no excuse. I invited you here to make love to you. Since I first saw you, it is all I have wanted.'

'But you've hardly seen me...'

'Deliberately, I have kept away. You may have heard stories. A man quickly gets a reputation. It's true, there have been a couple of affairs. Please believe I am not a dirty old widower.'

I was to be added to a list of affairs. But did I care? I knew I would do it anyway.

'You, Marika, are different.'

'I'm sure you say that to all...'

He laughed and the gold filling showed for a moment before he was serious again. 'You will see. I care about you as I never expected to care for someone since my wife died. I hope we can be partners in work and in life.' He clapped a hand over his mouth. 'But I am going too fast.'

He leapt to his feet and pulled me to him. I'd long kicked off my shoes and we were the same height. Our bodies fitted and mine was shivering. He wrapped his arms around me and we held each other tightly for some time without moving. No attempt to kiss me. No wandering hands. Then, with a little moan of a sigh, he disengaged and crossed to an alcove that housed a music centre. He lifted the lid of the record player, flicked a switch and positioned the stylus carefully.

'Bread,' he said. 'I'm a bit of a fan of David Gates. *Make It With You.* Because that is what I hope.'

We danced, mostly holding each other close with him singing the song into my ear, which was sexy because I knew he meant it. Before long he led me into his bedroom.

He kissed me and started to unbutton my sensible denim dress. He'd only reached the third button when he stopped, turned away abruptly and walked to the window.

My underwear. He must be shocked, think I'm a tart. The set was my present to myself for achieving the PhD. A treat after all that brain work. I'd seen it in the window of the Ann Summers shop – pure silk, scarlet, ridiculously expensive. French knickers, so cool on a hot night. I'd pawned the gold cross and chain Mama gave me. I planned to get it back when my first pay cheque arrived. No one would know what was under the demure dress.

'Simon?'

He half turned and I saw tears in his eyes. I went to him and put a hand on his shoulder. He didn't shake me off.

'Your underwear. My wife…'

He couldn't manage any more before his voice choked. I was right. Damn, damn, damn.

But he grabbed me and hugged me, burying his face in my shoulder.

After some while he said, 'I once bought her some red underwear. She wouldn't wear it. Said it would make her feel like a tart. I had to take it back, change it for white.' He moved away and stared out the window. 'Daphne could be very uptight. It was the same with work. A classical analyst, somewhat – err – rigid. She was not open to discussion of her technique.' He spun round. 'But why am I talking of Daphne? When I have you here? Marika, I apologise. Where were we?'

At first he insisted I keep the garments on. Then we couldn't get them off fast enough.

Sex with Simon was like nothing I'd experienced. It would be trite to say it showed me the meaning of making love, but how else could I describe it? He made love like he listened: not merely waiting for a chance to interrupt with his opinion, but wanting to understand, wanting to respond. He didn't just enter and take what he wanted. It was more like we entered each other. He gazed at me afterwards, caressing me, lifting my hair and letting it fall. As if he'd never seen hair before.

'You are beautiful inside and out,' he said. 'Inside your brain, inside your heart and inside your cunt.' He stroked my cheek. 'You know that word, cunt?'

I nodded. '*Lady Chatterley*. There was a copy passed around at school. It had another cover glued on. *Mansfield Park*. Because of Fanny. Fanny Price.'

He laughed at that and the gold tooth flashed. That was new too: to lie in bed with a man and laugh.

In the morning I woke to the smell of coffee and we made love again while it brewed. I told him the story of the underwear, which amused him no end. Later that morning he insisted on going with me to the pawnshop and retrieving my cross and chain.

'Sex and religion,' he said as he fastened it round my neck. 'You are full of surprises.'

'They are not so different. Both routes to the soul. Well, not any old sex, but intimacy. What we had last night.' I suddenly felt shy. 'Anyway, that's what I think.'

'Your religion must be very different from mine.'

We talked of Roman Catholicism and its rituals. He'd been to a Catholic wedding.

'All a bit theatrical,' he said.

'Ah, but that's what I like. The energy of it. The ritual, the images. It's vivid. A story to get hold of.'

I already knew his family had stopped being practising Jews two generations ago, but I hadn't heard him refer to any kind of church-going.

'Do you go to a church?'

He nodded. 'Every few weeks. When the weather's too bleak for swimming. Safe old C of E. I like my religion quiet, behind a pillar.'

That made me laugh and we talked about swimming in the ponds on Hampstead Heath, which turned out to be an obsession of his. I had no idea people did that.

'Normally I go every morning before breakfast. All year round – the trick is not to stop when the weather gets cooler.'

'What do you call too bleak?'

'East wind. Hail. Thunder storm. Breaking the ice.'

'Blimey. So I'm keeping you from it. And – before you ask, no, I really don't want to come too.'

I caught a flash of relief in his expression then. It mirrored what I'd felt when I realised he would never want to come to Mass with me.

Heads were shaken at work over our relationship. Colleagues would approach me in the kitchen. The opening remark would be along the lines of 'Mari, I don't know if I should be saying this, but…' They were concerned Simon was taking advantage of me.

'How do you know I'm not taking advantage of him?' was my usual reply, and my well-wisher would laugh nervously and change the subject.

I teased Simon that he never had people sidling up to *him* in the Gents and advising him against "that Marika" leading him astray.

He laughed and shook his head. 'You would think, in this enlightened establishment, that people would not fall for these stereotypes. But people like to gossip, to interfere. However intelligent and balanced they think they are, there's nothing like a bit of scandal. But we will show them.'

What would we show them? The phrase came back to me as I was falling asleep that night, but it was the following spring before I understood what he meant.

Simon booked a country house hotel in Cornwall during the Easter break. It was a beautiful place, the grounds a riot of flaming rhododendrons and our room luxurious – a four-poster bed and views across the Fal estuary to the sea. We had been working hard and it was wonderful to relax in the panelled library, to walk the coast path and to have delicious meals prepared for us. I was also looking forward to visiting Aunt on the way home. She and Simon would get on well.

On our last evening we were warmly greeted by Yusef, the Turkish waiter. He'd told us that he was six foot eight inches tall, his height emphasised by a spare frame and upright carriage. Close-cropped hair and a beard made him appear both stately and wise. He arrived at the table bearing our plates of food, poised above our heads.

As if reluctant to part with them easily, he enquired, 'Have you spent a pleasant time on this day?'

When we agreed that we had, he announced the presence of roast cod and fillet steak as if announcing the birth of a royal baby. Only then did he relinquish the plates with due ceremony onto the table.

'It's like speaking to God,' I said.

When Simon set aside his napkin at the end of the meal, Yusef appeared to pull out my chair.

'This man has such a sense of occasion. He makes the ordinary extraordinary. I like that,' Simon said as we left the table. 'I like it particularly because this is a special occasion. He helps to make it memorable.'

I nodded.

'Our last night. Back to work on Monday. I was wondering, have the gossips been annoying you lately at work?'

What on earth was he on about? 'Bugger them. Why bring them up? Come to think of it, they've mostly gone quiet. We're the status quo now.'

I'd followed him onto the terrace. A half-moon had emerged from the cloud cover to shimmer on the water.

'We will silence the gossips. And no, we're not any status quo.'

My stomach lurched. Not the status quo? Was he finishing it? I couldn't believe he would treat me so badly. How dare he bring me here, bring up the subject of office gossip and then use it as an excuse to drop me?

He spoke before I could answer. 'This is difficult for me.' He took a deep breath. 'Marika, will you marry me?'

Still feeling defensive, I blurted out the first thought in my head. 'I'm not marrying anybody to spite a busybody.'

'Ah, Marika. That is not why. I've been waiting to see if you got bored. We are past the mad "in love" stage. It is not long off a year now. I have been afraid to ask in case you said I was too old. An amusing lover, but too dull for a husband, for the long haul. Now, I will try one more time. Will you be my wife?'

How could I have so misjudged him? Why was I so insecure?

I flung my arms round him. 'Yes, I will. Oh, Simon! Of course. I am in a shock. So I say the wrong thing. But yes, I will marry you.'

41

Katalin arrived on the Underground platform as the rumble of an approaching train stiffened the attention of waiting commuters. If she waited at the back, she might miss this one. The next wave of travellers would hurtle her to the front to contemplate the lethal rails with the surging throng behind her. She'd be first in line to face those struggling to escape the next train and those reluctant to let her in. She sidled between tense elbows to the middle of the crowd.

She hated travelling at this time, but she must catch her boss before he went home. If only the wretched meeting hadn't run over. As she positioned herself behind a broad-shouldered donkey jacket, the air displaced by the train's arrival stirred up the alien reek of soot and the silt in the grooves of the escalator treads.

Surely she must be the last one to step on board. But several bodies pressed themselves to her back, as if by squeezing the air out of her lungs they would make room for themselves. Hateful to be physically close to people, but her mental distance was safe, intact. That was why London suited her. She found a breathing hole, securing her bag with one hand.

Between the stubbled chin of the donkey jacket and a scarlet coat, she could see a young woman staring ahead as if nobody else existed. Mouse-brown page boy haircut, navy suit, tidy knees. As the train slowed to a station, there was a general push towards the door. Donkey jacket switched places with her and a voluminous woman swept past in a puff of perfume leaving an empty seat. Katalin slid into it and found herself beside the poised young woman.

As the train tunnelled deeper she closed her eyes, pressing her back into the seat. She hated this line, the downhill race, the slant of the carriage, the sense of travelling to the centre of the earth, into the dark underworld of London, as if one might arrive in Hades. The slowing of the train brought her eyes open. Too soon for the next stop. People rustled newspapers, glanced at watches, avoided eye contact. At the far end of the carriage, a shuffling of feet, a disturbance.

There followed an unnatural hush into which spoke a single voice. Someone asking for money. There were fewer people standing now, so she had a clear view of a gaunt figure in jeans and loose grey top. Shaven skull, dark eye sockets. He moved down the carriage, glance flicking from side to side, extending a cupped hand. No one moved. He paused halfway. Looked from face to face. What should she do? Give, and start something? Not give, not stand out? Everyone was thinking the same.

'Who will be the first?' came a thin voice. 'You won't look at me, will you?'

As he moved into her peripheral vision, she stared ahead at the cables dimly visible on the wall of the tunnel. She was afraid to look at a person who had nothing.

A movement next to her – the young woman taking a purse from her bag. A sober black purse with a zip across the top. She dipped into it and dropped two coins into the palm that was instantly there. He moved on, looking neither left nor right, vanishing from view.

Breathing started again like a Mexican wave. The train jolted, edged forward, jolted and stopped again, taking her stomach with it at every lurch. Finally it moved on.

You were at the mercy, she thought, every time you stepped on a tube train. In a tube inside another a tube. Nothing in your control. Fire, flood, criminals. Totally vulnerable. But how else to travel quickly from one side of London to the other?

At her stop she was carried along with the mass of people and careered into the daylight, almost colliding with a man as she stepped into the street.

'Katalin!'

'I never want to go on the Underground, ever again! Oh!'

It was Adam. She hadn't seen him for two years. He was holding her by the shoulders as if she might escape.

'What amazing chance. I'm rarely round here. Let me buy you a drink.'

She recovered enough to say she was late, and strode on purposefully.

'You haven't changed. Always hard to get.'

'No, really. I must see my boss before he leaves.'

'I'll come with you. I'll wait.' She couldn't stop him, and, to her surprise, she was pleased to see him.

Later, in the pub, they settled in a corner.

'What was all that about earlier? You came out of the station as if pursued by the furies.'

She told him about the beggar on the train, how scared she'd been, how ashamed not to have parted with any money.

He nodded. 'It's uncomfortable, isn't it? It makes us think of things we'd rather forget. Aspects of our society.'

'Something like that. Silly to get so rattled. But it seemed we were stopped for hours. Trapped. Probably only ten minutes.'

She focused on a spot on the table, rubbing a splash of beer into the surface. When she looked up he was watching her with such a strange look. A sort of glow or smile, but gentle, not mocking. 'It was more than that, though,' she continued, searching for words. 'I know. It was like looking at death.'

'But you're here. You're safe.'

He told her he'd been abroad for a year. 'Italy mostly. Sort of grand tour, but working. Waiting in cafés, grape harvest. Whatever I could get.'

'Why?' Surely Adam was too old to behave like a student.

'Had to get away. After we split up – you know. Get you out of my head. Anyway, I'm in Putney now. Decent agency. Residential, this time. I only come up here occasionally. But maybe we could have lunch? Just good friends and all that. Of course.'

He was so edgy, staccato almost. She agreed to meet. When he left to catch his train he scribbled on the back of his business card and gave it to her. It was all so formal. Would she ever feel relaxed with him like she used to?

In bed that night, she expected the eyes of the beggar to join her other hauntings, but it was Adam's eyes she saw and fell quickly asleep. In the morning she noticed an odd sensation. She took a while to identify it. She had something to look forward to.

Things to look forward to were few and far between. She was disillusioned with her job, but it was better than being at home. She was just a fringe person, a cog in the theatre machine, slipping in by a side door and up the back stairs to get on with routine tasks, while other people preened in the limelight and threw their weight about. Even her immediate boss had no idea how dependent he was on her, or how many minor miracles she achieved each day. But Adam was different. He threw the spotlight on her, made her feel visible.

42

I wriggled into the crimson dress and turned this way and that, pouting critically into the mirror. It fitted snugly. A curvaceous dress. I smoothed the silky folds over my hips. It was very Marika. But did it suit Doctor Goldstein?

When I'd phoned Aunt Klára, she'd warned against wearing red.

'Something quieter, perhaps? More academic?' Then she snorted. 'As if I would know!'

We both laughed because Aunt wasn't exactly a fashion expert and I was no conventional academic.

I said, 'If I go dressed as the scarlet woman, they can't accuse me of false pretences.'

And we'd left it at that.

The dress made me feel good, gave me confidence. I was going to need plenty of that, going back to that place, considering the way I'd left. Barefaced nerve, some would no doubt say. The dress had that in spades. Yes, it would do. Peeling it off, I rolled it carefully into my suitcase and pulled jeans and T-shirt back on.

I'd made light of the issue to Aunt, but I understood what she was getting at. I needed *gravitas* – Simon's word – because I was dressing my new identity as academic and author. Achieving my doctorate still felt like a miracle and every time I was addressed as "Doctor" I pictured the word outlined in gold leaf. The Goldstein bit was familiar after over a year of marriage, but no less of a wonder for that.

I didn't want Dr Goldstein to be a disguise for Marika to hide behind. I wanted to inhabit the title as myself, which was why I chose that particular dress. Marika would wear her hair loose, but Doctor G was crisper. All my dark curls would need scooping up, twisting away and pinning firmly in place. There was the *gravitas*. Not a disguise, but a statement.

I heard Simon crossing the hall as I closed the suitcase, and his arms came around me as I fastened the catches.

'You look stunning in that dress. You'll knock their socks off. They'll be riveted, trying to figure you out, put you in a box. What they won't know is that you don't fit in any boxes.' He gave me a long, hard kiss.

I squirmed away. 'Not now, Simon. I must ring Amanda and see how she's got on with Operation Kati.'

'Are you sure you can cope with that as well? All on the same day? Isn't it an agenda too far?'

He had a point. It was bothering me too. I hadn't seen my sister for three years. There could be a scene.

'It's my one good chance of seeing her, mending the past. Neutral territory, with Amanda prepared to get her there. I'm worried about Kati. You know what Amanda said – about her not eating again.'

Simon nodded. 'If you're sure.'

My hand hovered over the phone. 'How about this? I'll get Amanda to make sure she sticks to Kati like glue and keeps her away – until say, three-thirty. The launch will be over by then. Yeah, that makes sense.' I dialled Amanda's number.

It was Amanda who'd had the idea. She told me she was going to the Old Girls' Reunion at *that* school. Would it be a chance to get Kati and me together? It was the last place on earth I ever wanted to set foot again, and I was pretty sure that went for Kati too. But how would I know? She'd refused to speak to me since that dreadful meeting for her birthday. Amanda said she could get Kati there, so I'd felt obliged to give it a try. Anything to get my sister back.

Simon had spotted the opportunity for my book and me as soon as I mentioned the reunion event.

'The Priory Academy for Girls,' he said. 'Hmm. Great audience. Well-educated, intelligent women with social standing and good connections. Go for it!'

He told me to write to the organiser saying I'd be honoured to address their illustrious alumnae and other such phrases.

'Be magnanimous. Say you won't charge them.'

'But I'd expect to pay *them*.'

'Sometimes, Mari, you are so naïve. That is not the point.'

It seemed to work. The organiser replied that they would appreciate a donation to the proposed new sports centre.

'Give them fifty per cent of book sales at the event,' said Simon.

'Fifty percent!' I could hardly bear the thought of all my effort going towards a poxy sports complex.

'Be generous, Mari. It'll motivate the well-heeled alumnae to buy and feel virtuous.' He grinned. 'You might even get your name on a plaque.'

'Suppose I only sell a couple of books?'

'Unlikely. But then you'll have to fork out something for the fund. And they'll dedicate one hind leg of the new vaulting horse to the illustrious Dr Goldstein.'

In the end we'd agreed I should give a fixed donation to the school and that book sales would go to the refugee charity I'd worked with so closely – the British Council for Aid to Refugees.

Simon had been brilliant: rigorous critic, painstaking editor, loyal supporter. It had taken extra research and a change of writing style to shape a book out of the original thesis. Simon also made one of my dreams come true – a dream that hugely helped the writing process. When I took him to meet Aunt, I walked Simon to Beecombe. He noted the details of that cottage, fixed me a six-month sabbatical and hired it for a winter let so that I could get stuck into the re-write.

When it came to finding a title, it was Simon who had the idea. He reminded me of that woman in Fareham.

'I always remember you saying, "I couldn't tell her I wanted her life, that I coveted her gas fire and her laundry". It made a deep impression. That picture of you on the outside, looking in. How about that for a title? *On the Outside, Looking In.*'

And that was it. Perfect.

I wished Simon was coming with me. His commitments made it impossible, but Aunt would be there for me.

'Miss your book launch?' she'd said on the phone. 'Not likely. Wild horses wouldn't keep me away. I'll be queueing up for my signed copy. Can't wait to read it.'

She'd always encouraged me to write and I knew she'd be thinking of Papa and how proud he would have been.

Klára sank into her seat, glad to come to rest. She'd been up since dawn, driving north, covering page after page of her motoring atlas and leaving the sea uncomfortably far behind, to arrive in this land-locked middle-England town. Entering the building had added to her feeling of claustrophobia. She'd been glad to find a seat by an open window looking onto an avenue of limes. The event seemed well organised, this was an impressive library, but she felt oppressed. What was the word she was looking for? Self-righteous. That was it. The whole place exuded an air of smugness. No wonder those girls had felt the need to escape.

When Klára thought back to when the two girls had arrived in Devon, so young, so scared and – in Katalin's case – so hostile, she never thought she'd grow so fond of Marika. What a roller coaster it had been. Marika was a shapeshifter, like her father. A lot like László, in fact. Grabbed by the enthusiasm of the moment.

One minute she was threatening to come to no good, shoplifting and swilling vodka. Then she'd turned herself around and made it to university. But at her graduation she'd looked shrunken inside that severe skirt and what she called a librarian's blouse. Lost her spark, too. Klára had felt sad in the midst of celebrating.

Then Marika was going to save the world by becoming an educational psychologist. Until she met someone on a train and switched to social work. How on earth did the girl manage that? Should she have put her foot down, set some boundaries? Would Marika have listened? Probably not.

Even in Vienna, alarm bells rang. Apparently Marika wrote all this to her mother and Teréz showed the letters to Júlia. It gave Júlia the opportunity to imply that she, Klára, wasn't doing her stuff as Marika's guardian. Huh! She'd actually used that word. Klára had never signed up to be anybody's guardian. Even so, she'd fulfilled any obligations that even Júlia might have dreamt up.

Marika coped with a lot when you put it all together – all that stuff with her mother and Katalin and then poor Elsie Tucker. She was really cut up about that. But it had turned out to be an inspiration. Nice that the book was dedicated to Elsie. Klára had hoped that Marika would come down to deliver a copy to Jack. But apparently she had bumped into him and his wife the last time she had visited and Carole was quite frosty, so Marika thought it best to post the book. Jack was always sweet on her. Carole must have picked up on that.

It would never have worked. Marika as a farmer's wife was unthinkable. No, she'd really found her niche with the research. Got back her oomph. Got herself a PhD and a husband, too. In that order, fortunately. And now a book. Klára liked Simon. He hadn't cramped Marika's style. Quite the reverse. She'd mellowed and blossomed. Klára wondered whether they would have children.

The one she should be worrying about was Katalin. It couldn't have been easy for her, all that business with the Russian. But she'd cut herself off from family. So what could anyone do? Klára supposed she'd put all that behind her. As far as she knew – via Amanda, who kept in touch – Katalin had ticked along in admin jobs, same flat, same routine, day in, day out, for years.

Katalin regretted coming to the reunion. The headache that had been looming all week was building ominously. If it got any worse she'd have to lie down in a darkened room. She was pleased to have remembered this out-of-the-way toilet with the wooden seat. It was her favourite as a schoolgirl. The morning sun used to shine through the tiny frosted window straight onto her shoulders. Nobody today had thought of using it. Placing a pill on her tongue, she cupped her hands to gather enough water to swallow it. Again with a second pill. Should she take three, or would two be enough? Only a few left in the packet. Better keep them for later. She splashed water on her face and scraped a comb through lank hair, enjoying the sensation of the teeth raking her scalp – a sharp counterpoint to the thunder inside her skull.

It felt strange to be in this godforsaken place, transported back in time. Her plain navy suit and flat shoes did not look that different from the uniform she'd been

234

wearing when she was last here. Every other woman was dressed to the proverbial nines, and doused in expensive perfume as if to prove how far they'd come since the days of navy blue knickers, lisle stockings and lace up shoes. Some paraded bemused-looking husbands like trophies. As the chattering crowd poured through the gym on the way to the dining hall, Katalin thought how shocked Miss Yates would have been to see all those stiletto heels on her precious floor.

Lunch was a great improvement on the old school dinners. Smoked salmon and boeuf bourguignon instead of mince and stodge. Not that she'd eaten much of it. Food had become less and less interesting, and being at the school took her appetite away. It was odd to be drinking wine in that austere room. Amanda insisted she have a glass for old time's sake, whatever that was supposed to mean. It hadn't helped the headache. Amanda had only invited her because Ena Foley, still her closest crony after all these years, was going to be abroad. But Ena's trip to New York had been cancelled, and Ena was here, making Katalin's presence superfluous.

She patted her face dry on the roller towel and stepped out into the corridor. Voices were echoing up the stairwell. There were a few hours to kill before the next event in the Great Hall and groups were dispersing in all directions. No sign of Amanda and Ena, thank goodness. She didn't want to spend the afternoon with them.

They were all so glamorous, her contemporaries. So confident, opinionated and loud. They shrieked with laughter, clutched each other in delight at some stupid memory and were obviously thrilled to be here. She'd seen them throwing sideways looks at her clothes and she knew when they said, 'You haven't changed a bit,' in her case they meant it, and it wasn't a compliment. They just didn't appreciate a classic style that matched the gravity of her role as a professional personal secretary.

Most had forgotten her. Others asked about her ballet career, which was embarrassing. Amazing that people remembered that about her. Amazing and humiliating, for it seemed to be the only thing they did remember. She felt obliged to invent an injury to account for the fact that it never happened.

Further down the corridor, the door to the library stood ajar. She would hide in there to give the headache a chance to recede. But the place was full. Some sort of event, a sideshow to the main programme, obviously. Some doctor launching a new book. She'd find a seat at the back in one of the alcoves. Anything not to be ambushed by someone else wanting to know why they hadn't seen her dancing at Covent Garden. She should never have come.

At least she could be sure Marika wouldn't be here. Not after being sent home in disgrace for getting that Angie creature into bed. Why, for heaven's sake? Everybody knew Marika was boy crazy, even then. It was over three years since they'd met – Marika had finally got the message and stopped phoning, thank God. Just because people were family… Marika and Aunt Klára were welcome to each other. As for Devon, you could keep all its mud and mist and nasty wildlife.

She settled into the far corner of an alcove near the door. The complete works of Goethe were on her right, with Hölderlin, Kafka and Kleist opposite. It reminded her of Uncle Fritz's study. He was the only member of the family she had any wish to see. But a visit to Vienna would mean putting up with Aunt Júlia and seeing Mama. She wasn't sure she could cope with that. She pulled out another chair so that she could put her feet up. Maybe she could manage a nap.

There was a murmur of expectation in the room beyond her hideout. A woman appeared in the doorway, accompanied by the president of the Alumnae Association who was organising the reunion. The woman wore a fitted scarlet dress that clung to her considerable curves, and was smiling and nodding at the president who ushered her towards the front of the room. The woman adjusted her dark glasses and smoothed her hair, which was pulled into a fierce bun. The style contrasted strangely with the dress and her red heels, but was in keeping with the briefcase and papers she carried. Katalin's stomach contracted at the sight of her. She craned around the bookshelves to watch her progress towards the podium at the other end of the library. There was something about the walk, the bottom, the way it sashayed forward. Just like Mama used to walk. Who the hell was she?

Even as Katalin had the thought, the announcement came.

'I am honoured to welcome Dr Maria Goldstein.' The president paused for applause. 'The Alumnae Association is proud to host the launch of Dr Goldstein's new book, *On the Outside, Looking In*. She has agreed to speak today to give us a unique insight into the process of her research – the background to her work with refugees, evacuees and other displaced children…implications for psychotherapy and counselling. Dr Goldstein…'

The announcer droned on and Katalin drifted away. The titles of Egmont, poor old Werther and Wilhelm Meister on his *Lehrjahre* blurred into one another on the shelf beside her.

Then came another voice. Strong. Unfaltering. Unmistakable. That nasal edge, the arrogant quality that people used to mistake for confidence, and still a strong accent. She sat bolt upright in her corner and her head jangled at the sudden movement. Her sister. She had morphed from Marika Varga into Doctor Maria Goldstein.

What was that her sister had said? That day in the park on her birthday? Something about research at the Belstock. There'd been a letter from Uncle Fritz, too, referring to Marika's psychological studies. Katalin had torn the letter up, just as she had ripped up the stiff card inviting her to the wedding of her sister to a Simon Goldstein. Yes, that had been the name. The card had a gold edge.

She'd run her fingers over the embossed lettering.

Doctor Goldstein. Katalin had never thought Marika capable of finishing her first degree, let alone a PhD. 'Doctor, my foot,' she muttered. A total fraud, no doubt. Did the school even know she was pulling the wool, that they were entertaining someone they'd actually expelled?

Her head was pounding, her throat dry. She struggled to concentrate, to focus on what on earth her sister was finding to make a speech about.

'To further introduce myself, I will begin by saying what I am not, in case of confusion. I am not a psychiatrist, although I work alongside psychiatrists. First and foremost I am a psychologist, and I am now training as a psychotherapist. Fortunately, we have moved on from the days when psychotherapy was thought by some to be prostituting psychiatry.'

The nerve of the girl. Katalin had the urge to walk out but she was shaking. Her knees might not manage it. How could that sister of hers stand up there in that dress and talk about prostitution? It had even got her a laugh. A cheap laugh. Now she was off on a different tack.

'My aim was to make my book widely accessible. There is no pseudo-science. It is not academic.'

Katalin managed not to laugh. That would figure. Trust Marika to make a strength of not aspiring to academic excellence.

'It was important to me that each participant in the study had the chance to tell their own story. It is a collection of stories, of case studies…'

Yes, her sister was always good at telling stories. Otherwise known as lies. Mama used to say, 'Mari has a lively imagination. She doesn't see the line between what's real and what's made up. You have to make allowances. She's only little.' Allowances. She'd always been expected to make allowances. Papa had been just as bad, encouraging Marika's stories.

Katalin rubbed her eyes and forced herself to focus.

'Preliminaries over, I want to talk about insurance. No, you haven't come to the wrong lecture. I see today everywhere an obsession with insurance. Just as you can take a bet on almost anything, so you can take out an insurance policy against almost anything happening. I suppose these are two sides of the same coin. The optimists, always sure that they will win against the odds, take a gamble, while the pessimists, convinced that things will go badly, take out insurance.

'Of course it's sensible to have insurance in case your house burns down. But I find it obscene – to use a strong word, and I do like strong words – to insure against the weather, for example. Maybe this is a peculiarly British habit. You are always talking about the weather. Such a scheme would not get off the ground in my native Hungary. Our seasons are too predictable. To insure against the weather implies that you have the right for the sun to shine upon you and that you should be compensated if it does not. Who knows whether you might not have a better holiday if it rained? What unexpected choices would lead to interesting experiences? Who might offer to share their umbrella with you?'

Katalin could hear the suggestive smile in that last phrase. A titter rippled among the listeners. She longed for a glass of water.

'So how we do attempt to insure against all the conditions we are afraid of? Against being poor, lonely, ill, losing freedom – the list is long. Money is a common way, religion another, marriage yet another. But they don't work, do they?

'Let me backtrack ten years. I want to show you one slide. It is a detail from a portrait painting and does not do justice to the intensity of the original, but nevertheless… It is a painting that I can truly say changed my life. It is why I became a psychologist.'

This Katalin had to see. Since when did Marika take an interest in art? A picture that had changed her life. How pretentious was that? Katalin moved her head cautiously and sat upright. The pills seem to have had some effect. The golf balls in her head had settled. She moved smoothly out of her alcove and slid into an empty seat on the end of a row.

'It's by Oskar Kokoschka, a favourite painter of my father's. Could we have the slide please? Some of you may recognise it, but the subject isn't relevant. A number of Kokoschka's portraits demonstrate the point I want to make.'

The slide showed a haunting male face in violent colours. Thick paint, huge black eyes, angry ears. Hideous. A painting like that could only change a person's life for the worse.

'It scared me, but I couldn't look away. I couldn't decide whether I was seeing fear or anger. At first I saw the anger and hatred of a torturer. Or, was I looking at the fear of the torturer's victim? This was what made me decide to become a psychologist, although I didn't know it at the time. I wanted to know what was going on inside that person's head.

'Was it terror? Or was he the terrorist? Or was it the same thing? Did Kokoschka intend this? I don't know. But for me, his art blurs the distinction between the perpetrator and the victim. It raises interesting questions for us all.'

Katalin grunted in irritation. Messy thinking. That had always been the trouble with her sister. Sticky fingers, sticky mind, no boundaries. You needed to keep things separate, clear, black and white. Otherwise you risked chaos. She peered around her, wondering if her sister's husband was in the audience. That was certainly Aunt Klára on the far side, looking as weird as ever, but her only neighbour was female.

A chair scraped back as a member of the audience stood up, not waiting to be invited to speak. An interruption. How would her sister cope? The woman leaned forward wagging a finger.

'Excuse me, excuse me, yes. You mentioned religion just now. In fact, you appeared to dismiss it. I understand you are a Roman Catholic, and I wonder why you consider religion just another ineffective insurance?'

'A very interesting question.' Marika treated the questioner to a dazzling smile of the sort Katalin had never seen her use in private. 'I avoid religion because religions are "isms" – Catholicism, Protestantism, Judaism, Buddhism. You are right. My family were Roman Catholics, but understand, I was brought up under a Communist regime – and Communism tends to trump all the other "isms". We did not practise – it was too dangerous.

'I also avoid religion because it brings war. Religions, they all say God is love – but then we have killing in the name of religion.'

She held up a hand at the loud murmurs of protest.

'Most followers of any one religion do not kill, of course they don't. But an extreme minority give religion a bad name. I make distinction between religion and spirituality and I choose spirit. For me, the life of spirit is about asking questions. Not about finding answers. I never say what I believe in. For one thing, is personal. But for another, if I say I believe in one thing, I get labelled. And the label comes with a lot of other beliefs attached – like flies to those sticky yellow papers which people hang in kitchens in summer. I do not wish to be the fly-paper.'

A wave of quiet laughter ran around the room and the woman sat down. Katalin sniffed. She had to admit, her sister had handled the question well, even if her grammar did slip when it wasn't rehearsed. A hot stab of pride flared in her chest, like a wire needling into her heart. As unpleasant as it was unexpected. It vanished in seconds.

Marika glanced down at her notes and continued.

'To return to the emotions in the painting. Naturally, we want to protect ourselves from the force of such fear, such anger. We want to protect ourselves from life itself. I meet people who want to skate on the surface of life and relationships. But the ice gives way. They find themselves in over their heads with anger and fear. They find themselves talking to me – that is, if they are lucky.'

Katalin glanced down the rows at the side of the room. She could see that one or two husbands were gazing at Marika in a way that suggested they would count themselves extremely lucky to be talking with her. Marika knew this, of course.

'When these people share their stories, when they peel away the addictions, the anger, the hysterical laughter, you find the fear and sadness of the lost child. The child who believes she is not lovable and does not know how to love.'

Katalin regretted emerging from her alcove. When would this ever end? The headache was back, gaining ground. It seemed to be spreading to the rest of her body. She really was feeling quite peculiar, feverish and shivery at the same time. Her sister went on to describe working with displaced children, and about being a refugee at the age of eleven, meeting people with similar trauma in their early life. Blah-di-blah. Katalin switched off. Exactly what trauma had Marika experienced in her early life?

'I heard stories from refugees from my own country of Hungary and also from British people who had been evacuated as children during the war to escape the bombing.

'Even if you don't lose family, the loss is complex. Country, culture, the life you were going to have – it all goes.'

Katalin certainly knew all about that. Without even knowing it, she'd left her ambition, her skill, her career behind, and she'd never got them back.

'Once a refugee, always a refugee. You may learn the language, you may be successful. You may integrate, but that loss stays with you always. How can a person lose their very identity in this way and continue to be a real person?'

For once her sister was talking sense. That was the real question.

'The psychotherapeutic process… A kind of internal insurance… Separation anxiety…attachment…transitional object… Groundbreaking study in the fifties…'

A load of jargon to follow the good sense. Katalin tuned in and out, wondering how much more she could cope with. A list of names and references followed: Bowlby, Robertson, Winnicott, R D Laing. Then Marika was concluding.

'Children continue to be catastrophically affected by war all over the world, and as was announced earlier, all the proceeds of book sales today will go to BCAR, the British Council for Aid to Refugees…'

Marika as philanthropist was a new concept. It was too much. The room blurred into darkness. Katalin lurched sideways and collapsed onto the floor.

At intervals during the next hour she was aware of people bending over her, some known, some strangers, their faces blurring near and far. One was Aunt Klára, those blue eyes drilling into her. Another was Amanda, with Ena hovering over her left shoulder, keeping her distance.

It was too difficult. The faces receded and were replaced by a young man with a stethoscope who examined her and asked questions she couldn't answer. It was easier to drift away.

The next time Katalin surfaced, Aunt Klára was holding her hand and stroking her arm. She tried to pull away. The stroking stopped but Aunt Klára kept a firm grip on her hand, holding her attention.

'Katalin, you have glandular fever. Plus, you have not been looking after yourself. I am taking you home to nurse you. Marika is coming with us. No, don't fuss. You've no need to talk to her, but I'll need her help getting you settled at home.'

Katalin groaned inwardly. Aunt Klára's house – the dripping trees, the sea, that awful dog. The sound must have escaped because Aunt Klára responded.

'Of course, if you'd rather, Marika can take you to her flat in London. I know you dislike the country. Her husband would be happy to…'

Katalin shook her head. Too vigorously. The golf balls inside ricocheted in warning. She gave in.

The journey to Devon reminded her of that first journey, except that Aunt Klára had let down part of the back seat and she was lying full length on lumpy cushions. There was the smell of wet dog, the slap of windscreen wipers and the murmur of Aunt Klára and Marika talking. Strange to be in such a confined space with her sister after not seeing her for so long, the sister who was now a different person, while she, Katalin, was still the same person.

When the car stopped moving she woke to a rush of cold air and the sound of beasts grunting and ripping at grass close by. She was asked if she wanted to pee. Perish the thought.

The engine started again. Images from the past came and went as the journey continued, on and on, travelling westward into the dark night.

43

Katalin's first week in Devon passed in a drift of dark into light, sleeping and waking, being alone and being attended to by Aunt Klára. Her aunt washed her and combed her hair, insisted she drink a lot of water and fed her clear broth and jellies that slid down her painful throat. The doctor visited, a whiskery gentleman whose nose whistled as he listened to her chest. She vaguely remembered him as a young locum who prescribed disgusting brownish liquid when she had tonsillitis at the age of fifteen.

One night she had a dream which was a variation on a familiar theme.

She is the Snow Queen, but without a tutu and naked except for her sensible shoes that make her waddle like a duck on top of the snow. Her partner is immensely tall. He lifts her with the steel arms of a crane, but drops her in the snow and vanishes. A witch-like creature, who is and is not her sister, appears and waves a wand. The sky grows dark with the wings of crows squawking down towards her.

She woke in a sweat and a panic. She was not used to having Marika appear in her dreams. Come to think of it, hadn't this illness started with her sister making a speech? That reunion. Amanda persuading her to go. What a disaster that had been. She'd had such a terrible headache.

'There go my rooks,' Aunt Klára was saying. 'It's a fine day.'

Katalin realised it was the rooks in the tall trees which had invaded her dream and woken her. 'Damn black birds,' she muttered, and Aunt Klára shut the landing window to muffle their raucous cries.

Katalin was aware of Aunt Klára going about her business downstairs, clattering pans in the kitchen and speaking on the phone. She was fed more soups and jellies, followed by poached fish and stewed fruits as her throat healed. Eventually she was well enough to take a bath and come downstairs for lunch, but the effort exhausted her.

One afternoon as she woke from a nap, Katalin sensed a different presence in the room. Marika was sitting beside the bed. She was reading a book. Katalin observed her through half-open lids – emerald green T-shirt, and jeans, one bare foot resting on the opposite thigh, scarlet toenails, slash of red lipstick. Dark hair curled round her face onto her shoulders. No blackheads any more. With a shock, she recognised that her sister was beautiful. When did that happen?

As if picking up on the tsunami of brain waves caused by that perception, Marika looked up from her book.

'So, my sainted sister, you're awake.'

'Are you staying here?'

'Well, that's progress. You actually addressed me. But you needn't worry. I'm staying in Beecombe – in my cottage.'

A cottage. Marika had a cottage. As well as a flat in London big enough to contain a husband. Her own flat was not big enough to contain a cat, let alone a husband. Not that she'd ever wanted a cat. Or a husband.

Marika rattled on. 'You've been so ill, but now you're on the mend I thought I'd give you the chance to speak to me before you're in a position to run away.'

'I am the sitting duck. But I don't have to talk to you.'

'Of course you don't.'

But, in spite of herself, she found herself asking about the cottage.

'Two up, two down, view of the sea. Seagulls for company.'

'Yuk, that's scary.'

Marika laughed. That throaty sound. 'No it's not. Anyway, what would you expect? It's practically on the beach.'

'Yours or rented?'

'Simon bought it. We rented it at first. A place for me to write. But we both like getting out of London.'

'London. I want to get back to London.' London was safe. She was sure she only thought it, but it must have popped out of her mouth as well.

'London? Safe?' Marika frowned and laughed. 'I never think so. I get to the point when I feel I'm going mad. Then I have to come here to the sea.'

'The sea is the scariest thing.' The words seemed to escape all by themselves. Marika had ambushed her and she was luring the thoughts out of her head.

'I thought Finn and Aunt were the scariest – back then – the things you were always wanting to get away from.'

'I haven't seen Finn yet.'

'Of course you haven't. Dogs don't live that long. Finn is long dead.'

Katalin smiled. It was the best news she'd heard for a long time.

'Well, that's cheered you up. There is a Finn replacement. Merlin. But before you let that get you down, there is some good news. Your boyfriend has been phoning every other day to see how you are.'

'Boyfriend?'

'Adam. He's eager to know when he can come down and take you back to London.'

'Adam's just a friend. He's not… Anyway, I haven't seen him for months. I—' She broke off, afraid to say too much. Adam hadn't followed up on their chance meeting. She'd been disappointed and cross with herself for minding.

'Well, he *was* a boyfriend, then.'

'No, we were never… That was the prob… But how did he know where I am?'

'He'd been trying to get back in touch. You weren't at your flat, and you weren't at work…'

'Huh! Work. I wonder how they're managing without me. Maybe my boss will notice me. Now I'm not there. Anyway, Adam—'

'When you weren't to be found, he did the obvious.'

'The obvious?'

'He asked Amanda. She who knows everything.'

'I hope you didn't tell Adam anything.'

'Well, of course we did. He only wanted to know how you were, whether he could do anything.'

Katalin closed her eyes. It was all too embarrassing.

'But I realise it is none of my business. About Adam, I mean. Hey, sis, don't go back to sleep on me.'

Katalin felt a hand on her arm. She opened her eyes. Marika was smiling at her.

'D'you know something? I miss you. I've actually missed you and your sainted-sister talk.'

'I should never have gone to the beastly reunion. Damn Amanda.'

Marika pulled a face. 'Not her fault. We plotted to get you there.'

'What?' Katalin felt a wave of damp heat sweep through her body. 'Why? To humiliate me? To show off?'

Marika gave an exaggerated sigh. 'I guess it might seem like that to your sadly warped mind. You were never supposed to get to my launch. I knew that would put you right off. Amanda was meant to keep tabs on you. Like you said, damn Amanda.'

Something odd happened then. They both laughed. The sound echoed strangely in Katalin's head, a coarse sound, unkind, as if they were ganging up on Amanda. But Amanda was *her* friend, and yet she had ganged up with Marika.

Katalin turned off the laugh abruptly. 'I didn't even realise it was you. What's with "Dr Maria Goldstein"? Trying to fool me? Or what?'

'Well, one, I *am* a doctor whatever you might think. Two, my name *is* Goldstein. Three, Maria is easier as a professional name. People can say it, spell it.

Why would I be hiding from you? The whole idea was to see you.'

'But why? What were you up to?'

'I hoped we'd talk again. The plan was to meet at the evening reception, sit together at dinner. Act like we're sisters. Like I said, I miss you.'

'Half-sisters.'

'Makes no difference. I still miss you.'

Katalin said nothing as this unlikely statement trickled into her consciousness. It was the second time her sister had said it. *And* she'd repeated it. No drama, no scene. Just said it. Could she really mean it?

'Kati? You still there? I thought you might come and see my pad tomorrow. If you're strong enough. Or the next day.'

Katalin shook her head. 'I hate the sea. Really, I don't want... I want to be in London.'

Marika shrugged. 'Okay. London it is. Either I could take you, or Adam would come and get you.'

What a thought. All that journey, just her and Marika. It didn't bear thinking of.

Her sister was rattling on. 'I used to think you'd want to leave London. Don't you find it's full of ghosts? How do you cope with all that? All the stuff that happened?'

How dare she? Refer to all that? What was the point?

'I've left all that behind. Past history. Move on.'

But Marika turned on her, suddenly fierce. 'Oh yes? Past history? Move on? Why do you think you're ill? How often do you think you'll have to be ill before you learn that the ghosts have to be answered to?'

Katalin rubbed her temples, afraid her head might start to ache again. 'That is just what I might expect from you. Go away. Now I know why you came. You came to taunt me and drag up old memories, spoil my peace. You think you're so clever now. A doctor, no less. But I won't let you do your so-called therapy on me. I don't want to be in any phony book. I was right all along. I don't want to see you again.'

'Oh, Kati! There you go with your sainted-sister talk. You idiot. I came because I care about you. Because I want you to get better. Not just now. But so as you don't get ill again.' Marika took a deep breath and grabbed her hand. 'You are my sister and I love you, Kati. But you look like a ghost yourself. Amanda says you're always off sick. She's worried that you don't eat. Please Kati, believe me.'

Katalin wrenched her hand free. 'Go away! Go away.'

She turned over and closed her eyes, afraid they were going to leak in front of her sister. She waited until she heard the slap of bare feet on the boards and the sound of voices in the kitchen. Then she got up and locked herself in the bathroom.

The dawn was heavy, as if a storm was brewing. Even this early in the day, the air was used up. It reminded Katalin of how she used to feel in the top bunk in that awful flat in Kentish Town. She couldn't breathe. Something terrible had happened. She could only see blackness and she was sobbing. She couldn't stop. It was coming from deep inside her. No. It was coming *through* her, erupting from the bowels of the earth. That was what it felt like. She had no control whatsoever.

After a while, Aunt Klára was there, holding a hand on her back, not saying anything. The sobbing subsided and Katalin looked up.

Aunt Klára met her gaze. 'A dream, was it?'

'I dreamt Marika was dead.'

Aunt Klára nodded.

'Are you sure she's all right?'

'A dream, Katalin. Marika is not dead.'

'Are you sure?'

'Of course I'm sure. I spoke to her only last night.'

'You could ring again.'

Aunt Klára sighed. 'She's on her way to London. She'll have left early.'

Katalin shook with more sobs. It was too late. Marika had gone. She had left it too late.

Aunt Klára rubbed her back. 'You thought you hated her, didn't you?'

'I did hate her. I do. I did. I did a good job of hating her. I worked really hard at it.'

'Why did you?'

'I hated her for being born. I hated her for always being there. Always in the way, always wanting bits of me. I hated her for what she did to Sergei. I hated her for being there when Papa was killed. She had a bit of him that I didn't have. It wore me out. And all the time I could have...' She trailed away.

Aunt Klára was silent.

'I could have been loving her.'

Katalin heard herself speaking those words. It was puzzling. As if two parts of herself were conversing above her head. One part was still convinced that Marika was dead for real, not just in the dream, and so it was safe to say the stuff about loving her.

Aunt Klára spoke into her confusion. 'You still can. It was only a dream. She's only going to London.'

Katalin shuddered. There it was again, that burning twinge. Just like she'd had during Marika's speech.

'What's up?' asked Aunt Klára.

'Just a spasm.' She rubbed her chest. 'Somewhere here. No, I'm not about to have a heart attack. It happened before. When this all started. Must be the fever.'

She rested her head against her aunt's shoulder and they both stared out of the window at the dappled leaves of the walnut tree.

Into the long silence Aunt Klára said, 'No wonder you could never dance.'

What had that got to do with anything? All so long ago. 'Not since I came to England. I left it—'

'I said never. I meant never.'

Katalin stared up at her. 'Never?'

'Never. Or, like a robot. Deep down, you know it.'

She did know it. But she kept the knowledge in some vault, the same place she'd kept her love for her sister. So maybe there was a connection. No, that was just stupid.

'Where do you get that from?'

'Mostly from you, Kati. From being with you. But also, the family grapevine. Your mother always told Júlia everything. And my sister takes satisfaction in dwelling on the negatives. Apparently László was worried you were so obsessed.'

So, Papa thought that. As time went by, she thought of him more and more as Papa, just as he used to be.

She sighed. 'Anyway, what's dancing got to do with hating Marika?'

Aunt Klára shrugged. 'I can't explain. I just know. And it's "loving Marika". Remember?'

Katalin frowned and nodded. Somewhere inside her it made sense, but it also felt alien and strange. It made her feel giddy, as if she'd become untethered.

'You could dance now. Dance yourself back to life, to health, to love even, since we're using that word. Love to dance. And I don't mean ballet.'

Katalin shrugged, shook her head. 'I don't think so. Just now I need some air.'

She looked under the chair for her shoes.

Aunt Klára shook her head. 'Go barefoot,' she said.

44

Thoughts of my sister kept me awake half the night and I felt drained in the morning. Yesterday's visit to Kati had been a gamble cooked up with Aunt. At one point I thought Kati and I were getting somewhere. At least we were speaking. But I pushed her too far. Too far, too soon. It was clear when I left that any more visits from me would make her worse rather than better. I'd given up on Kati. For the time being, at any rate. The Adam person could deal with getting her back to London. Simon wanted me home, and I needed Simon.

All the same, I was reluctant to leave the sea and the solitude. I took a last walk on the beach in the morning mist. A steamy kind of day. Felt like thunder. I pocketed one of my favourite lucky stones with a hole through it to take back for Simon. So much to tell him.

Kati messed up the launch in typically dramatic style. By the time I got to the book-signing table, half the audience had already left. My own fault, I guess, for putting my faith in Amanda. Trust her to lose track of Kati at the critical time.

I squatted on the stones and started lobbing pebbles into the quietly rippling tide, enjoying the fat plop and the droplets thrown up in exclamation.

All that stuff about the painting, the Kokoschka. Who was I kidding? It was half true. But it was the inside of Kati's head I really wanted to understand. I suppose that was always the case. Wanting my big sister to look after me, like me, love me. But she never did. Never would.

'Oh, bugger that sister of mine!' I heaved a small rock into the waves, where it thudded and rolled unsatisfactorily. I headed indoors to pack. I still felt amazed and blessed to own this place. Simon had said, 'To make up for the honeymoon,' which we'd spent visiting Budapest. It had seemed a good idea at the time – to take advantage of the amnesty announced by the Hungarian government on the tenth anniversary of the Uprising. What had I hoped to gain? A lost piece of my identity? Maybe. But it had been depressing to be reminded of how we used to live fifteen years before. I had been tense and irritable, and it wasn't much of a holiday for either of us. I wished we'd chosen Vienna instead.

I was soon on the road. Simon would restore me to myself. We would hug and eat and drink. He would make me laugh and we'd make love and I would feel like me again. But, as I bowled along between verges thick with cow parsley, I felt an inexplicable urge to turn off the main road and head down the lane to Aunt's house.

Aunt came to meet me at the top of the stairs.

'How is my impossible sister? Thought I'd pop in on my way. Give her another chance to be vile to me before I go back to London. Simon is pining.'

'Come.' Aunt led the way into her bedroom and I joined her by the window.

We stood there, watching Kati pick her way across the grass and into the clearing.

'What's going on?' I asked.

Aunt just put her finger to her lips, although there was no chance Kati could hear.

By the time the rain started we were clutching each other, and what happened next had us both in tears.

45

In the garden Katalin stepped carefully onto the lawn. She didn't trust the grass. It would slide from under her or open up and suck her in. But the turf was firm and springy and she could grip it with her toes. She walked between the trees and put a hand out to touch them as she'd seen Aunt Klára do. It steadied her. It was a phony thing to be doing. Wasn't it? But she couldn't seem to stop. She moved slowly from one trunk to the next, as if they had something to tell her.

The rain started with just a few fat drops resounding through the leaves of those giant trees. No wetness penetrated. Katalin wondered if she imagined it, but she could see the raindrops like a curtain of fine silver chains closing across the garden. She inhaled the smell of wet grass, and the tree that Aunt Klára called the guardian ash scattered drops in her hair. Before she knew it she was slowly twirling, lifting her arms and swooping from tree to tree. She hoped her aunt wasn't watching from the window, but she couldn't seem to stop. Phrases of the Rachmaninov ran through her head. She was Nadia dancing for Sergei. There was a sudden clap of thunder and the rain came down in bucketfuls, flattening her hair to her scalp. Oddly, for once, she was not afraid. Her nightie flapped icily against her legs, restricting movement. She peeled it off and gasped at the sluice of water on her skin. She spun and spun, needled by the deluge, tingling with the hiss and drum of it on the leaves and in her ears. All thoughts of Sergei and Nadia were rinsed clean away. She was dancing for herself. She no longer cared whether Aunt Klára was watching or not.

Eventually she came to rest against the ash tree, breathless, weak at the knees. After all, for weeks she had only tottered about indoors. The rooks clattered and cawed overhead, but kept their distance. As her breathing calmed, in place of her gasps, there seemed to come steady vibrations from inside the trunk, throbbing through the grain of the bark into her spine.

Then Aunt Klára was there, taking her by the hand and leading her into the conservatory where, towel held out, Marika gathered her in. Mari. Where did she spring from?

46

I stayed that night and slept in the other bed alongside Kati's, just like when we were kids.

I woke at dawn at the point when you have to admit the light is gaining on the darkness and you won't get back to sleep. She must have known I was awake.

'I blame Papa,' she said.

My heart sank. Why did she need to blame people? 'Blame him for what?'

'Everything that happened. It came to me in the night. You remember those silly games Amanda liked to play? If you were a flower, what would you be? Etcetera, etcetera. I was thinking of colours and I got stuck with Papa. Because Papa is no colour. He's the colour of darkness.'

I see the flying bat shape all over again. Yes, that was the colour of Papa's death, but Kati wasn't witness to that. It was not the colour of him. 'Papa was yellow,' I said. 'Yellow for light and fun and sparky ideas.'

'No, he's just shadow, because it was all his fault. He had to be different, to do all that underground stuff. It put us all in danger, Mari. If he hadn't done that, we wouldn't have had to escape, I wouldn't have lost my career. I wouldn't be an orphan twice over, with a dead father and a mad mother.'

I'd never heard Kati talk like this before. It was easier like this, lying apart, staring at the ceiling and watching the familiar cracks becoming visible.

'Mama is not mad. Simon says her depression was a perfectly understandable reaction to a terrible situation. She's—'

'Leave your Simon out of it. He never even met her! Mama is red.'

'Yes, I agree. Mama is red. Red for warmth and—'

'No. Red for fire that burns and destroys. Red for danger. I shall never forgive Mama.'

'You were jealous of Mama, because Sergei—'

Kati cut me off. 'That's nothing to do with it. Mama lied to me. That's what I don't forgive. She didn't tell me who I was. And look what happened – to me.

Betrayed by her and abandoned by him – my own father. Orphaned three times over, actually.'

'Okay, yes. Of course she should have told you – but would it have made any difference? You wouldn't listen. You were infatuated with that vile man.'

Silence. I was surprised she didn't defend Sergei who could do no wrong in her eyes. Even though he killed *my* father.

Aloud I said, 'Anyway, that wasn't Papa's fault. If we'd stayed in Budapest, Sergei would still have been around. There was *always* the Thursday man.'

'Oh, no. If Papa had conformed, kept his head down like other people, he wouldn't have been sent to the Russian front. He wouldn't have been away for years. Mama would never have met Sergei. Because she wouldn't have thought Papa was dead…'

'Oh, Kati! We'd have lived a half-life we none of us believed in, eating cabbage soup in that crumbling apartment, cut off from the rest of the world. Papa was not someone who could *ever* do that.'

She almost growled. 'Like I said, he was selfish.'

'Anyway, if none of that had happened, you wouldn't even have been born, so there's no point in even talking about it. If I'd had a sister, she wouldn't have been you. That is a weird thought in itself.'

'That would suit you.'

'Actually, it wouldn't. I can't even imagine it. You're the sister I've got. You're the sister I've always loved, though you're probably the most awkward sister anyone could have.'

The door slammed downstairs as Aunt set out on her morning walk. It was properly light now, and I shivered as I pulled back the curtain.

'I'll get some tea. Want a cup?'

Kati made a face. 'Just hot water.'

At that moment the sun spilled over the top of the hill, orange as a broken egg, and filled the room with golden light.

Kati didn't seem to notice. 'Take the robe,' she said.

It was the dreadful old thing Aunt kept in the bathroom. It felt like wearing string.

I set the kettle on the Aga. "Take the robe," I thought as it hissed into life. I'd shivered and Kati had noticed. She had told me to take the robe.

When I got back she was sitting up wearing a beige jumper that drained all colour from her face.

She took the mug and cradled it to her. 'I don't blame *him*.' I frowned and she added, 'Sergei. It was the kiss that did it. It was like… Like a…like a spell.'

She stared down into her mug. 'I loved him. Right from that moment. But he couldn't get who I was. Didn't recognise me. Then when he did know, he confused me with his sister, his twin.'

'But he knew—'

'Shut up, Mari. Of course he knew. But it must have been as if she came back from the dead. When she'd never stopped haunting him, anyway.'

'His sister?'

'Shut up, Mari. His twin. She killed herself.' She sipped her water. 'I like that he wanted me to know who he was. He played that piano like… It was like a possession.'

'Piano? He had a piano? He played for you?'

'I told you that – when we met up afterwards.'

'I assumed he played a record. I…'

'Rachmaninov. It was magnificent. But he played it for her, not for me. Every day he played it. He was showing himself, but it was all about him and her. He had no interest in me. No, that's not true. He wanted to be a father, but he couldn't manage it.'

'But keeping you there! Locking you in! For days. I still don't believe he didn't—'

'Shut up, Mari. That was his struggle. I don't care what you believe, but he hardly touched me.'

'Hardly?'

Silence. My picture of Sergei was filling out. I didn't want to see it. He was easier to cope with in two dimensions.

'I look exactly like her, you see. He showed me a photograph.'

Silence. I was beginning to understand.

'It was inevitable, what he did. He was in love with her, you see. I've tried to work it out. It must have been why she killed herself. I think love and death were all mixed up for him.'

I started, 'Oh Kati,' but she cut across me.

'Don't say anything. I didn't mean to talk of him. But maybe now you understand a bit more.'

The front door slammed again and we could hear Aunt talking to Merlin.

'She's the colour of mud,' said Kati.

'What, Aunt? Oh no, she's greeny-blue for trees and sky and a rainbow coming out of her head.'

Kati's eyebrows shot up. She laughed. It was a yap like a frightened dog. 'Definitely mud. She never·used to like me. She was always for you. You end up with Aunt Klára *and* Mama, and I have nobody.'

'You have me, and Amanda. And Aunt, whatever you think. She's been nursing you, for heaven's sake!'

'True. But she can't wait for me to be gone. As to Amanda – she's always got something more important to do.'

'How can you say that? She's been such a loyal friend. Never given up. Kept me updated all the time you wouldn't see me.'

Kati's eyes widened. She obviously hadn't known. 'Okay. But you don't get it. She's my friend, right? But I'm not *her* friend. Ena's *her* friend. I'm her project.' She laughed. Another little bark. 'But it does annoy the hell out of Ena. I enjoy that.'

We fell silent. I was still thinking of Sergei and suicide. Oh, yes. Suicide.

'Do you remember the business with the freezer, Kati? I never had the chance to ask. What possessed my sainted sister to climb into a bloody freezer? Amanda was beside herself, I remember.'

'That was years ago, Mari! It was a really hot weekend, boiling. They were playing stupid word games and screeching with laughter. I thought it would be blissful, quiet, in on top of the lamb and the vegetables. There was plenty of space.' She paused. 'But it wasn't peaceful. It was scary. So cold it hurt. I pushed at the lid, but it wouldn't go up. The vacuum – I couldn't shift it.'

She turned to me. 'That was it. I never meant to die, if that's what you're thinking. I'm not very good at living but I couldn't do what Sergei did.'

'Well, that's something.' I held out a hand across the rug that separated the beds, but she ignored it.

'Papa was the only one who ever really understood me. I was Papa's girl. Except I wasn't. There's irony for you.'

'Yet you blame him.'

She shrugged. 'And Uncle Fritz. *He* liked me.'

'We could go to Vienna. Visit Aunt Júlia and Uncle Fritz. Feed you up while you convalesce.'

Kati made a face. 'We'd have to see Mama.'

'That's true.' Don't push her too far, I told myself. Try again another time. 'What about Adam?'

'He's a friend. At one time he wanted more. I couldn't. He's too good, too nice. I sent him packing.'

'Why?'

'I never got over Sergei. The shock – it's still there, like ice inside me. You know that saying? People say "my heart melted" when they see a puppy and dissolve into sentimental mush. They mean they are warm-hearted people. They don't mean their hearts were frozen in the first place. When an ice-cube melts, the water is cold. If my heart melted, it would still be cold.'

I struggled not to get caught in the bleakness of that. 'I understand about Sergei. I think. But Kati, you have to move on. All these people – and you won't...'

'They are nice people. I'm not nice. I wanted you to die.'

'I'm sure you did. Lots of times...'

'No, really. I did. Only for a moment, two seconds maybe. But I did. And I didn't try to stop you.'

'Stop me? When? What are you talking about?'

'That time when we were little. You copied me, walking along the bedrail onto the windowsill. You nearly flew out the window. And Mama…'

'You were always doing that. Showing off.'

'But don't you remember? That time? It was very hot, so the window was open? Mama was furious.'

'I don't remember any special time.'

Silence.

Then, 'I wanted you to go through that window. Just for a second, I did.'

'But you were only a kid. It was only a thought. Nothing happened anyway.'

Silence.

'Kati? You're not serious? You think that makes you a bad person?'

'I thought it. And I didn't do anything. You might have—'

'But I didn't, Kati. I don't even remember it. To feel bad all that time. It's ridiculous. Don't you see how crazy it is?'

She ignored me. 'Maybe I could go back there. Back to Budapest. Now there's been the amnesty.'

'You wouldn't like it. On our honeymoon – when Simon and I…'

'I can't believe you did that. Going there. Not telling me…'

'You weren't speaking to me, remember? Didn't come to my wedding. Didn't even answer the invitation. Which reminds me. Mama came – with Aunt Júlia. They stayed with Simon's mother in Highgate. So Simon did meet—'

'Bugger Simon. It must have been a weird honeymoon. Weren't you afraid?'

'It was. And yes, I was afraid. It made me twitchy – having to register, signing for everything. It's a grey place with grey, shuffling people. I couldn't wait to leave.'

'I would fit there. I'm a grey, shuffling person, anyway.'

I fixed my gaze on the green movement of leaves beyond the window. 'You don't have to be. You—'

'Just because I pranced about on the grass in the rain, doesn't mean I'm a changed person, Mari. Don't imagine for one moment that—'

The edge in her voice broke. When I looked back, her eyes were welling with tears and her thin frame was shaking. I moved over to her bed and put my arms around her. She didn't pull away. It was strange to be holding my sister for the second time in two days, breathing in the pale smell of her, feeling her skin on my skin. As I had that thought, her right arm crept around my neck and clung on. Even stranger. My sister was halfway to embracing me. I squeezed her to me and felt a slight pressure in response.